26/4/18

28/...

8...

...Say

...sts and turns all over the place, **heart-stopping action ...suspense** and in the middle of it all the **brilliant Ben** ...e who just seems to get **deeper** and **more complex** with ...tory. Not many thrillers manage to combine **characters** ...really care about** with a **storyline that doesn't let you** ... five-star** book if there ever was one'

...tt Mariani is a **master of his craft**'

...st **can't get enough!**'

...n Hope is a loner **in the tradition of Jack Reacher** . . . A ...ker of truth like Robert Langdon** . . . and as much an ...gma to many as Jason Bourne is** . . . He is **a British hero** ...o is driven by tragedy in his past to right the wrongs in ...e present'

...dventure, thrills, conspiracy, terror, drama** and a **touch** ...f romance** . . . a **fast-paced** story with plenty of adventure ...nd twists, and is **not for the faint-hearted** in places! This ...ook is an **excellent** read'

'This series is **nothing short of brilliant**'

'The pages create images in your mind of **cinematic quality**, as hero Ben Hope meets and battles with many a bad guy! A **conspiracy novel *par excellence*.** Very much reco...

989900482503 F6

'One of the **finest, most gripping thrillers** I have read in a long time'

'Started to read this in bed at 10, **still reading at 4am**! Great storyline, **kept me guessing** all the way through. Would make a great film'

'A book of **breathtaking suspense**'

'If you have a day to spare and enjoy **action-packed books with a sexy and believable hero**, read this!'

'A **crazy twisting rollercoaster** from the word go'

'I am now **officially hooked** on these books'

'I've just finished reading this, **I've managed to miss two meals and a lot of sleep**, but I just couldn't put it down'

'**I adore this book** ... This was **new, fresh** and **exciting**. More please!'

'Pure **addictive** reading'

'If there is a film producer with any sense to **spot a winner** then Scott Mariani should be approached to create a film series that could surpass the Bourne films'

'Fast moving and great fun. **If you like Jack Reacher you will like Ben Hope**'

'I like to read **Wilbur Smith's books and find Scott Mariani's are just as good.** I hope he writes some more'

'Mariani is **a sort of cross between Dan Brown and Clive Cussler** . . . I can't wait for the next Ben Hope novel'

'A **brilliant** read'

'**Plenty of twists** and in the centre of it is Ben Hope with all guns (albeit reluctantly) blazing. Definitely **worth a read**'

'A **rip-roaring adventure** thriller'

'I'm **running out of superlatives** for this **incredible** series. It rivals anything else in the genre . . . Child, Flynn, Eisner . . . totally **enthralling**'

'**Mystery** mixed with **intrigue** backed up with incredibly **detailed** knowledge of the subject at hand. More please!'

'The story moves **fast** and is **superb**, with plenty of **twists**. I honestly don't think you will regret buying this book, so do it . . . NOW!'

'**Jack Reacher**-type modern day action mixed with some *Da Vinci Code* intrigue'

'A fast moving and enthralling story and further establishes Ben Hope as **an action hero alongside Reacher and Rapp**. Don't miss it'

'**Spellbinding**'

'With a hero that's a cross between **Jason Bourne, Robert Langdon, James Bond,** and the **terminator** with a heart!'

'I am now **completely addicted** to all the Ben Hope books'

'**Action packed** throughout from the very first chapter to the last. Twists and turns at every step . . . Would love to see the series filmed but who could play the **moody yet sexy** Ben Hope?'

'The **writing is sharp**, the characters are everything from **hateful** to **amusing**, and the scenes flow beautifully, something which is Mariani's trademark I think'

'I have not **enjoyed** an author's work **so much** for a very long time'

'Recommended reading for **the adventure fiend** but not for someone seeking a full 8 hours sleep, because it is **hard to put down**'

'**Warning . . . you will lose sleep** reading this book'

'I rate Scott Mariani up with **Chris Kuzneski, James Rollins** and **Clive Cussler**, but not for the faint-hearted'

'**Superb** doesn't really do it justice'

'Absolutely **sensational**'

'Loved it! **Couldn't put the book down.** The Ben Hope series is now an **obsession** with me and now my friends . . . can't get enough!'

'I **can't wait** for the next Ben Hope book!'

'**Slick,** serpentine, **sharp** and **very, very entertaining**' Simon Toyne, bestselling author of the Sanctus Trilogy

'Mariani's novels have consistently delivered on **fast-paced action** . . . you can't put the book down . . . **brilliant!**' *Female First*

'**Thrilling**' *USA Today*

'The helter-skelter pace **kept me hooked** like a prize catch' www.crimesquad.com

'An **exhilarating ride** that **races** along to an **exciting** conclusion' *Mysterious Reviews*

'A **fast-paced** arcane thriller that will **captivate** readers' *Fresh Fiction*

'A **breathtaking** ride' *Suspense* magazine

THE NEMESIS PROGRAM

Scott Mariani is the author of the worldwide-acclaimed action-adventure thriller series featuring ex-SAS hero Ben Hope, which has sold over a million copies in Scott's native UK alone and is also translated into over 20 languages. His books have been described as 'James Bond meets Jason Bourne, with a historical twist'. The first Ben Hope book, *THE ALCHEMIST'S SECRET*, spent six straight weeks at #1 on Amazon's Kindle chart, and all the others have been *Sunday Times* bestsellers.

Scott was born in Scotland, studied in Oxford and now lives and writes in a remote setting in rural west Wales. When not writing, he can be found bouncing about the country lanes in an ancient Land Rover, wild camping in the Brecon Beacons or engrossed in his hobbies of astronomy, photography and target shooting (no dead animals involved!).

You can find out more about Scott and his work, and sign up to his exclusive newsletter, on his official website:

www.scottmariani.com

By the same author

The Alchemist's Secret
The Mozart Conspiracy
The Doomsday Prophecy
The Heretic's Treasure
The Shadow Project
The Lost Relic
The Sacred Sword
The Armada Legacy

SCOTT MARIANI

The Nemesis Program

AVON

This novel is entirely a work of fiction.
The names, characters and incidents portrayed in it are
the work of the author's imagination. Any resemblance to
actual persons, living or dead, events or localities is
entirely coincidental.

AVON
A division of HarperCollins*Publishers*
77–85 Fulham Palace Road,
London W6 8JB

www.harpercollins.co.uk

A Paperback Original 2014

1

A catalogue record for this book is
available from the British Library

ISBN-13: 978-0-00-739846-1

Set in Minion by Palimpsest Book Production Limited,
Falkirk, Stirlingshire

Printed and bound in Great Britain by
Clays Ltd, St Ives plc

MIX
Paper from
responsible sources
FSC **FSC C007454**
www.fsc.org

'We've arranged a global civilisation in which most crucial elements profoundly depend on science and technology. We've also arranged things so that no one understands science or technology. This is a prescription for disaster. We might get away with it for a while, but sooner or later, this combustible mixture of ignorance and power is going to blow up in our faces.'

Carl Sagan, 1995

'I could set the earth's crust into such a state of vibration that it would rise and fall hundreds of feet, throwing rivers out of their beds, wrecking buildings, and practically destroying civilisation. The principle cannot fail.'

Nikola Tesla, 1898

Prologue

The Altai Mountains
Bayan-Ölgii Province
Western Mongolia

The biting wind was starting to whip flurries of snow across the barren mountainside, high up in the wilderness where not even the most rugged four-wheel-drive vehicle could reach. Soon, Chuluun knew, the winter snowfalls would be here in earnest and it might be a long time before he could venture out this far again in search of food.

The argali herd that the teenager was tracking had led him almost half a mile across bare rock from where he'd tethered his pony further down the mountain. Wolves were an ever-present concern, but the curly-horned wild sheep could sense the roving packs from a great way off, and having paused on their trek to munch contentedly on a scrubby patch of heather, they seemed calm enough to reassure Chuluun that his pony was safe.

There was one predator too smart to let himself be noticed by the argali. Chuluun had been hunting over these mountains for six years, since the age of eleven, when his father had become too infirm to ride long distances any more, and he prided himself on his ability to sneak up on

1

anything that walked or flew. His parents and seven younger brothers and sisters depended almost entirely on him for meat, and in the harsh environment of Mongolia, meat meant survival.

Staying carefully downwind of the grazing sheep and moving with stealthy ease over the rocks, Chuluun stalked up to within a hundred metres of his quarry. He settled himself down at the top of a rise in a vantage point from which his pick of the herd, a large male he estimated stood a good four feet at the shoulder, was nicely presented side-on.

Very slowly, Chuluun slid the ancient Martini-Henry into aiming position and hunkered down behind it. He opened the rifle's breech, drew one of the big, long cartridges from his bandolier and slipped it silently inside. Closing the breech, he flipped up the tangent rearsight. At this range he knew exactly how much elevation he needed to compensate for gravity's pull on the trajectory of the heavy bullet.

The argali remained still, munching away, oblivious. Chuluun honoured his prey, as he honoured the spirit of the mountains. He blinked a snowflake from his eyelashes. Gently, purposefully, he curled his finger around the trigger, controlled his breathing and felt his heart slow as his concentration focused on the all-important shot. If he missed, the herd would be off and he couldn't hope to catch up with them again today, nor this week. But Chuluun wasn't going to miss. Tonight, his family were going to eat as they hadn't eaten in a long while.

At the perfect moment, Chuluun squeezed the trigger.

And in that same moment, everything went insane.

The view through the rifle's sights disappeared in a massive blurred explosion. His first confused thought was that his gun had burst on firing. But it wasn't the gun.

Chuluun barely had time to cry out as the ground seemed to lurch away from under him and then heave him with terrifying violence into the air. He was spinning, tumbling, sliding down the mountain. His head was filled with a deafening roar. Something hit him a hard blow and he blacked out.

When Chuluun awoke, the sky seemed to have darkened. He blinked and sat up, shivering with cold and beating the snow and dirt from his clothes, then staggered to his feet. His precious rifle lay half-buried in the landslide that had carried him down from the top of the rise. Still half-stunned, he clambered back up the rocky slope and peered, afraid to look, over the edge.

He gasped at the incredible sight below.

Chuluun was standing on the edge of a vast near-perfect circle of utter devastation that stretched as far as his keen young hunter's eyes could see. Nothing remained of the patch of ground where the argali herd had been quietly grazing. The mountainside was levelled. Gigantic rocks pulverised. The pine forests completely obliterated. All gone, swept away by some unimaginable force.

His face streaked with dirt and tears and contorted into an expression of disbelief, Chuluun gazed up at the strange glow that permeated the sky, like nothing he'd ever seen before. Blades of lightning knifed through the rolling clouds. There was no thunder. Just a heavy, eerie pall of silence.

Suddenly filled with conviction that something unspeakably evil had just happened here, he scrambled away with a terrified moan and started fleeing down the slope towards where he'd left his pony.

Chapter One

Paris
Seven months later

The apartment was all in shadow. It wasn't normal for Claudine Pommier to keep her curtains tightly drawn even on a bright and sunny June afternoon.

But then, it wasn't normal for someone to be stalking her and trying to kill her, either.

Claudine was tense as she padded barefoot down the gloomy, narrow hallway. She prayed the boards wouldn't creak and give her away. A moment ago she'd been certain she could hear footsteps outside the triple-locked door. Now she heard them again. Holding her breath, she reached the door and peered through the dirty glass peephole. The aged plasterwork and wrought-iron railing of the old apartment building's upper landing looked distorted through the fish-eye lens.

Claudine felt a flood of relief as she recognised the tiny figure of her neighbour, Madame Lefort, with whom she shared the top floor. The octogenarian widow locked up her apartment and started heading for the stairs. She was carrying a shopping basket.

Claudine unlatched the security chain, slid back both

bolts and the deadlock and rushed out of the door to catch her.

'Madame Lefort? Hang on – wait!'

The old woman was fit and sprightly from decades of negotiating the five flights of winding stairs each day. She was also as deaf as a tree, and Claudine had to repeat her name three more times before she caught her attention.

'Bonjour, Mademoiselle Pommier,' the old woman said with a yellowed smile.

'Madame Lefort, are you going out?' Claudine said loudly.

'To do my shopping. Is something wrong, dear? You don't look well.'

Claudine hadn't slept for two nights. 'Migraine,' she lied. 'Bad one. Would you post a couple of letters for me?'

Madame Lefort looked at her tenderly. 'Of course. You poor dear. Shall I get you some aspirin too?'

'It's okay, thanks. Hold on a moment.' Claudine rushed back into the apartment. The two letters were lying on the table in the salon, sealed and ready but for the stamps. Their contents were identical; their addressees half a world apart. She snatched them up and rushed back to the door to give them to Madame Lefort. 'This one's for Canada,' she explained. 'This one for Sweden.'

'Where?' the old woman asked, screwing up her face.

'Just show the person at the counter,' Claudine said as patiently as she could. 'They'll know. Tell them the letters have to go registered international mail, express delivery. Have you got that?'

'Say again?'

'Registered international mail,' Claudine repeated more firmly. 'It's terribly, terribly important.'

The old woman inspected each letter in turn an inch from

her nose. 'Canada? Sweden?' she repeated, as though they were addressed to Jupiter and Saturn.

'That's right.' Claudine held out a handful of euros. 'This should cover the postage. Keep the change. You won't forget, will you?'

As the old woman headed off down the stairs, Claudine hurried back to her apartment and locked herself in. All she could do now was pray that Madame Lefort wouldn't forget, or manage to lose the letters halfway to the post office. There was no other way to get word out to the only people she could trust. Two allies she knew would come to her aid.

If it wasn't too late already.

Claudine ventured to the window. She reached out nervously and pulled the edge of the curtain back a crack. The afternoon sunlight streamed in, making her blink. Five floors below, the traffic was filtering along the narrow street. But that wasn't what Claudine was watching.

She swallowed. The car was still there, in the same parking space at the kerbside right beneath her windows where it had been sitting since yesterday. She was completely certain it was the same black Audi with dark-tinted glass that had followed her from Fabien's family country home two days ago.

And, before that, the same car that had tried to run her down in the street and only narrowly missed her. It still made her tremble to think of it.

She quickly drew the curtain shut again, hoping that the men inside the car hadn't spotted her at the window. She was pretty sure there were three of them. Her instinct told her they were sitting inside it, just waiting.

On her return from Fabien's place, after the scare and the realisation she was being followed, she hadn't intended to remain here in the apartment any longer than it took to pack a few things into a bag and get the hell out. But the car had appeared before she'd been able to escape – and now she was trapped.

Were these the men that Daniel had warned her about? If that was the case, they knew everything. Every detail of her research. And if so, they must know what she'd learned about their terrible plans. If they caught her, they wouldn't let her live. Couldn't let her live. Not after what she'd uncovered.

Under siege in her own apartment. How long could she hold out? She had enough tinned provisions to last about a week if she rationed her meals. And enough brandy left to stop her terror from driving her crazy.

Claudine spent the next half hour pacing anxiously up and down the darkened room, fretting over whether the old lady had sent her letters. 'I can't stand this,' she said out loud. 'I need a drink.'

Walking into the tiny kitchen, she grabbed a tumbler and the brandy bottle and sloshed out a stiff measure. She downed it in a couple of gulps and poured another. It wasn't long before the alcohol had combined with her fatigue to make her head swirl. She wandered back through into the salon, lay on the couch and closed her eyes. Almost instantly, she began to drift.

When Claudine awoke with a start and opened her eyes, the room was completely dark. She must have slept for hours. Something had woken her. A sound. Her heart began to race.

That was when the bright flash from outside lit up the narrow gap between the curtains, followed a moment later by another rumble of thunder. She relaxed. It was just a storm. The howling wind was lashing the rain against the windows.

She got up from the couch and groped for the switch of the table lamp nearby. The light came on with a flicker. The ancient wiring of the apartment building threatened to black the place out every time there was a storm. The clock on the mantelpiece read 10.25. Too late to go and ask Madame Lefort if she'd posted the letters, as the old woman was always in bed by half past nine. It would have to wait until morning.

Claudine stepped back over to the window and peered out of the crack in the curtains. With a gasp she saw that the car was gone.

Gone! Just an empty pool of light, glistening with rainwater, under the streetlamp where it had been parked.

She blinked. Had she just imagined the whole thing? Was nobody following her after all? Had the near-miss in the street two days ago just been a coincidence, some careless asshole not looking where he was going?

The rush of relief she felt was soon overtaken by a feeling of self-blame. If this whole thing had been just her paranoia getting the better of her, then she should never have sent those letters. She'd made a fool of herself.

Suddenly she was hoping that the old woman hadn't posted them after all.

The storm continued outside. Claudine knew she wouldn't get any more sleep that night. She wandered into her little bedroom, flipped on the side light and picked up her violin. One of the upsides to sharing the top floor with a deaf old woman was that she could play whenever she liked. Madame Lefort wouldn't even have heard the thunder.

Thankful that she had something to occupy her mind, Claudine cradled the instrument under her chin, touched the bow to the strings and went into the opening bar of the Bach sonata she'd been trying to master for the last couple of months.

Another bright flash outside and at that moment the lights went out. She cursed and went on playing by the red glow from the neon sign of the hotel across the street.

Then she paused, frowning. There'd been a noise. *Before* the roll of thunder. Like a thump. It seemed to have come from above. There was nothing above her apartment but the roof. Maybe the wind had knocked something down, she thought, or sent a piece of debris bouncing over the tiles. She went on playing.

But she hadn't produced more than a few notes before her bow groaned to a dissonant halt on the strings. She'd heard the noise again.

There was someone inside the apartment.

A cold sweat broke out over her brow. Her knees began to shake. She needed to arm herself with something. Thinking of the knife block on the kitchen worktop, she tossed her violin and bow down on the bed and hurried towards the doorway – then skidded to a halt on the bare boards as another violent lightning flash lit up the room and she saw the figure standing in the doorway, blocking her exit.

Too terrified to speak, Claudine retreated into the bedroom.

The intruder stepped into the room after her. She could see him outlined in the red glow from the hotel sign. He was tall, very tall. Shoulders like an ox. Black boots, black trousers, black jacket and gloves. His hair was silver, cropped to a stubble. He had a hard, angular face. Pale eyes narrowed to slits. Around his waist was some kind of utility belt, like builders and carpenters wore.

For one crazy, irrational moment, Claudine thought he was a workman come to carry out the much-needed repairs to the bathroom. But that idea vanished as he drew the claw hammer from his utility belt and came towards her.

She snatched the violin from the bed. Lashing wildly out with it, she caught him across the brow with such force that the instrument broke apart. The splintering wood raked his flesh, drawing blood that looked as dark as treacle in the red light. He barely seemed to have felt the blow. He swung the hammer and knocked the shattered violin from her hand. She cowered away from him. 'Please—'

He struck out again with the hammer. Claudine's vision exploded, white and blinding pain flashing through her head. She fell onto the bed, dazed.

The big man stood over her, clutching the hammer in his muscular fist. Strands of bloody hair dangled from the steel claw. Unhurriedly, calmly, he wiped the tool clean on the bedcover and then slipped it back into his utility belt. From another long pouch he drew out a cylindrical tube with some kind of plunger and transparent plastic nozzle attached.

He bent over her. Through the fog of pain, she saw him smile. His eyes and teeth were red in the hotel neon.

The man spoke in English. 'Now it's time for that pretty mouth of yours to be plugged up.'

A hoarse cry of terror burst from Claudine's lips as she realised what he was holding. She tried desperately to wriggle away from him but he reached out with a quick and powerful hand, grabbed her hair and pinned her thrashing head to the bed, ignoring the wild blows she flailed out at his face and arms.

With his other hand he jammed the nozzle of the tube into her screaming mouth. She cried out and bit down on the hard plastic and tried to spit it out, gagging as it was forced deep inside.

The man pressed the plunger. Instantly, something foul-tasting, warm and soft filled her mouth. It was coming out under pressure and there was nothing Claudine could do to stop it flowing down her throat. She tried to cough it out, but all of a sudden no air would come. There was an awful sensation of pressure building up inside her as the substance swelled and expanded, filling every cavity of her throat and nasal passages.

She couldn't breathe, couldn't scream, couldn't open or shut her jaws a millimetre. She stopped trying to lash out at him, and in a crazed, agonised panic she clamped her hands to her mouth and felt the hardening foam bulging out from between her lips like some grotesque tongue.

The man dropped the empty canister on the bed and used both hands to hold her bucking, convulsing body down. After a minute or so, as her brain was becoming starved of oxygen, her movements began to slacken. The man let her go and stood up.

The darkness was rising fast as Claudine's vision faded. For a few seconds longer she could still dimly register the man's shape standing over her in the red-lit room, watching her impassively with his head slightly cocked to one side.

Soon she could see nothing at all.

The man waited a few more moments before he checked her pulse. Once he was satisfied that she was dead, he left the bedroom. He unlocked the apartment door and left it ajar as he made his silent way towards the stairs.

Chapter Two

'I wish we didn't have to do this,' Jude said.

It was a hazy, warm late Saturday morning in the peaceful village of Little Denton in rural Oxfordshire. Fat bumblebees were humming around the flowerbeds, birds were chirruping happily overhead. Once in a while, a car hissed by the gates of the former vicarage.

A sharp-eyed observer might have spotted the signs that the old house nestling among the trees behind the high stone wall was no longer lived in: the unclipped ivy spreading over the windowpanes; the rather unkempt state of the lawn that stretched far down towards the river; the remnants of last winter's fallen leaves still lying about the grounds; and it wouldn't have taken much asking around to discover that the local community was still recovering from the shocking deaths, just six months earlier, of the vicar and his wife in a car crash. Simeon and Michaela Arundel had been much loved and were sadly missed by everyone who'd known them.

The vicarage had been in the Arundel family for generations and now it had passed to twenty-year-old Jude. From time to time the young man drove up from Portsmouth, where he was still half-heartedly studying Marine Biology while considering his future options now that his life had changed so dramatically, to get on with the painful, drawn-out task of sorting out Simeon and Michaela's possessions and take care of the place as best he could.

Today the task at hand had taken Jude right down to the bottom of the long garden, where he was gazing sadly up at an ancient beech tree. He wasn't alone. The same astute observer might also have noticed the physical similarity between him and the older blond-haired man, about twice Jude's age, who was standing next to him: a little taller at just under six feet, a little more muscular though still lithe and athletic-looking, and a good deal more battle-scarred.

That man was called Ben Hope. He'd been and done many things in his time, most of them involving danger and secrecy. Danger he could handle – God knew he'd handled enough of it both during his time with the SAS and since – but one secret even he hadn't known about for many years, and which had hit him like a high-velocity rifle round, was the stunning revelation that Jude was his own son. He was the product of a short-lived romance back in the distant days when Ben, Michaela and Simeon had all been students together in nearby Oxford and Ben had been set on a career in the Church.

The discovery of who his real father was had come as just as big a shock to Jude. It had taken them both months to even begin to get used to the idea.

'I seriously wish we didn't have to do this,' Jude said again, looking up at the old beech tree. 'Is it such a problem? Couldn't we just leave it?'

Ben pointed up at the thick, leafless dead branch that overhung the glass roof of the nearby summer house. 'We could just leave it,' he said. 'But come the next high wind, that branch is going to break off and crash straight through that roof. You don't want anyone to be underneath it when it happens. Or to have to fork out for the glazier's bill even if no one is.'

At that moment Scruffy, a wiry-haired terrier of uncertain breed who'd once belonged to the Arundels and now had been more or less adopted by Ben and his fiancée Brooke, burst out of the bushes in pursuit of a darting squirrel. The dog raced across the unmown lawn, ploughed destructively through some roses and disappeared at full pelt into the shrubs on the far side.

Jude rolled his eyes in exasperation at the dog's antics, then turned back to the tree and shrugged. 'Then it looks like we don't have much choice.'

Ben had found all he needed for the job in Simeon's woodshed behind the house. He grabbed the coil of rope, propped the ladder against the tree and shinnied up twenty feet to the level of the branch. Hanging precariously off the side of the ladder as Jude stabilised the bottom, he looped the rope around the branch's gnarly tip. Once he was confident that it was securely attached to the sound limb above it, he climbed back down and picked up the chainsaw. 'Now for the fun part,' he muttered.

'Aren't you supposed to wear protective clothing to handle one of those things?' Jude asked, frowning.

'Yup,' Ben said. He primed the carb, applied just enough choke.

'So aren't you going to wear any?'

'Nope.'

'You're a mad bastard, you know that?'

'So people keep telling me.' Ben yanked the start cord. The noisy snorting buzz of the two-stroke engine shattered the serenity of the morning.

It took some time to remove the large branch in sections, each one carefully secured by the rope so that it didn't plunge through the glass roof and defeat the purpose of the whole delicate operation. Eventually, all that remained of the offending branch was a pile of pieces on the ground and a big raw circle on the side of the tree.

'I hate to see it mutilated like that,' Jude said when Ben had come down and killed the chainsaw engine. 'This was Dad's favourite tree. Told me about how he used to climb right up it when he was a kid . . .' Jude suddenly went quiet.

Ben could see the discomfort in his expression, more than just sadness. He laid a hand on Jude's shoulder. 'It's okay, you can call him Dad. We've talked about this. That's how you knew him, all your life.'

'Except that he wasn't,' Jude said glumly.

'Maybe, but he was still a better father to you than I would've been,' Ben replied. Even though he was being completely sincere, his words seemed surreal to him. The truth was still hard to accept after six months. It weighed heavily on his mind that he hadn't yet drummed up the courage to reveal to Brooke the real identity of the young man she thought was just the son of a close friend. He wanted to tell her, but the 'right time' he kept waiting for just never seemed to materialise.

'Anyway, it's a shame,' Jude said, changing the subject and gazing wistfully up at the tree, shielding his eyes from the bright sun.

'If it's any consolation to your green sensibilities, once it's seasoned that'll make for pretty good firewood,' Ben said with a smile. 'Carbon neutral fuel, negligible environmental impact. Let's gather it up and stick it in the woodshed.'

Once that warm work was taken care of, it was midday and they were both ready for one of the beers that Jude had chilling to wash down a ham sandwich or two. In the airy cool of the kitchen they slouched on chairs at the long pine table, munched and sipped from their bottles. Ben was quiet, as he often was these days, deep in thought. Jude wasn't the only one whose situation had changed in a big way over the last few months. Sometimes, when Ben thought about the radical steps he'd taken towards a completely new direction in life, it made his heart thump.

'Are you nervous about it?' Jude asked suddenly, as if he'd been able to read Ben's thoughts.

Ben took out his pack of Gauloises cigarettes and Zippo lighter, and lit up as he considered the question. 'Nervous about which bit? Getting married in three days' time? Or giving up my whole career and business and going back to college yet again, to study along with a bunch of kids half my age?'

'Hey, I'm half your age, and we get on okay,' Jude laughed. 'Anyway, I wasn't talking about you taking up your Theology course again after all this time, wanting to become a vicar and all that. No problems there. You'd be great in the Church.'

'Your mother once told me the same thing,' Ben said, with a trace of doubt showing in his voice.

'I meant the wedding,' Jude said. 'That's the part that'd scare the shit out of me.'

Ben had to admit he felt pretty much the same way. Marrying his beautiful soulmate Brooke Marcel was the most exciting and wonderful thing that had happened to him in a very long time – and there'd been a time, not so long ago, when he hadn't been sure whether she'd ever speak to him again, or whether he'd even see her again. But the wedding plans weren't exactly what he'd had in mind when he'd proposed to her in a remote Peruvian rainforest village back in February.

'If it was up to me and Brooke,' he sighed, watching a

curl of blue Gauloise smoke curl and drift in the sunlight from the window, 'we'd have the quietest wedding ever. No messing around, no fuss: get in there, sign the papers, and get out again.'

Jude chuckled. 'And then Phoebe came along.'

'Yeah, and then Phoebe came along,' Ben said. Brooke's elder sister was married to a blustering overpaid idiot of a City banker called Marshall Kite, whom she'd persuaded in her interfering way to foot the bill for turning what should have been a small, private ceremony into an overblown great extravaganza. Christ Church Cathedral in Oxford was booked for the lavish wedding itself, the reception was due to take place in the county's most flamboyantly expensive country hotel, and the last time Ben had dared to check the swelling list of guests and assorted bridesmaids and other apparently indispensible personnel, it had seemed to him that half the world's population would be in attendance. Jeff Dekker, who'd been second-in-command at the Le Val Tactical Training Centre in Normandy before Ben had passed the business over to him, was going to be best man. Ben fully expected the ex-SBS commando to laugh his pants off when he saw the ludicrous scale of the affair.

In fact, the only part of the whole silly circus Ben was looking forward to with any pleasure was that he'd have a rare chance to see his sister Ruth, who was flying in later today from Switzerland in plenty of time for the full-dress wedding rehearsal that Phoebe had arranged 'just to make sure'. The rehearsal was scheduled for 2 p.m. tomorrow, exactly forty-eight hours before the big show. Ben was as steeled for it as he could be.

'Ben?' Jude said.

'What?' Ben smiled absently.

'I appreciate your coming over to help me out.'

'Least I can do. I know the last few months have been tough.' Ben looked at his watch. 'Brooke said she might be coming over sometime after lunch,' he said. She'd rushed off to London first thing that morning to hand over the keys of her old Richmond flat to her landlord and arrange for the last of her things to be delivered to the rented house in Oxford's Jericho district where she and Ben would be living while he finished his studies.

Right now, the house was in complete disorder. Ben had never realised that Brooke had so much stuff. On top of that were all the wedding gifts that had already started arriving: such as the one from Winnie. She'd been a faithful house-keeper to the Hope family for many years. After Ben's parents had died, she'd moved with him to the remote coastal house in Ireland and tried to mother him as best she could, usually to little avail. When Ben had started up the Le Val Tactical Training Centre in Normandy, rather than move with him to France Winnie had chosen to return to her home county of Lancashire and live with her elder cousin Elspeth. Winnie obviously believed that Ben had reached the age of forty without a knife, fork or plate to his name: the kitchen in Jericho was now filled with a sprawling great dinner service that could cover a banquet table.

Then there were the piled-up cases of wine and whisky from Ben's old SAS comrade, Boonzie McCulloch, who now lived in Italy with his fiery Neapolitan wife, Mirella. The gift from Commander Darcey Kane of the National Crime Agency had come with a card bearing the message 'Bastard! Love, D'. When Ben had opened the oblong box he'd found a deluxe .308 rifle cleaning kit inside. Darcey was thoughtful like that. Except that Ben didn't happen to possess a rifle. Not any more. At this juncture in his life he didn't expect to have to see one, most of all hear one, ever again.

'It'll be good to catch up with Brooke,' Jude said. 'I like her a lot.'

'I'm glad the two of you get on so well.'

'Oh – I just remembered. I've got something for you.'

'There was no need for you to get us a present,' Ben protested, hoping it would be nothing too large, and that Jude hadn't spent too much of his limited funds on it.

'I didn't. It's not, I mean, it's . . . what the hell.' Jude drained his beer and got up. 'Come and I'll show you.'

Ben stubbed out his cigarette and followed Jude upstairs to the large, airy bedroom that had once belonged to Simeon and Michaela. He felt a chill as he walked in. He still remembered the awful night they'd died, in that accident which had been anything but.

'There,' Jude said, pointing at a row of clothing neatly laid out on the bed.

Ben looked. 'These were Simeon's.'

Jude nodded. 'His vicar uniform. Or whatever you're meant to call it.'

Ben sadly ran his fingers over the clothes. The black clerical shirt, fitted with its Roman collar, lay folded on top of a pair of sharply-creased matching trousers. Next to it was the long black cassock, then the white linen surplice that Simeon would have put on to conduct morning and evening services.

'He was about your size,' Jude said. 'I reckon they'd fit you. When you get ordained one day, I'd like you to wear them. He'd have wanted it too.'

Ben wasn't comfortable with the idea. But as he was on the verge of saying no, he saw the look on Jude's face and bit his tongue. 'Thank you, Jude. It's a very kind thought.'

'Then you'll wear them?'

'I'll wear them. I promise.'

There was a silence. Then Jude said, 'So are you going to try them on, or what?'

'Now?'

Jude grinned. 'While you're doing that, I'm going to go put the chainsaw and stuff away.'

Left alone in his old friends' bedroom, Ben spent a few moments gazing sadly at the clothes. He thought about the man Simeon Arundel had been. Thought about himself, and how much he had to live up to. Through the open window he could hear Jude knocking about in the woodshed and the dog barking excitedly at something.

'Fuck it,' Ben murmured to himself. Reluctantly, hesitantly, he pulled off his jeans and put on the black trousers, then stripped off his T-shirt and buttoned up the black clerical one. Jude had been right about the fit. Even the shiny patent leather shoes could have been made for him.

Ben stared at his reflection in the full-length mirror by the wardrobe. An Anglican vicar's garb was one uniform he'd never seen himself wearing before, and to his self-conscious eye he cut an unlikely figure in it.

Reverend Benedict Hope. Could it ever really happen? He'd never turned away from a challenge in his life, but this might just be one of the hardest he'd ever faced. Maybe even harder than the hellish endurance test of qualifying for entry into 22 SAS.

Feeling self-conscious, he was about to start changing back into his own clothes when he heard the front doorbell chime in the hallway downstairs, then again, and again. Who could that be? Brooke, so soon? She wouldn't ring the bell over and over like that, so insistently.

Ben swore under his breath. He put his head out of the window and called, 'Jude! Are you going to get that?' But

Jude was now too busy throwing sticks in the garden for Scruffy to take any notice.

Ben was about to snap, 'For fuck's sake,' then caught a glimpse of the swearing vicar in the mirror and shut his mouth. He strode out of the bedroom, thundered down the stairs and across the entrance hall. The doorbell was still ringing relentlessly. 'All right, I'm coming – I'm coming!' he yelled.

Ben wrenched open the door.

There was a woman standing on the doorstep. She was slender, about the same age as Brooke. Her hair was longer than it had been when Ben had last seen her, and it had gone back to its natural dark red. She was wearing it loose, ringlets tumbling down over her shoulders.

She looked at Ben in amazement. 'Holy crap,' she said. '*Ben?*'

Ben blinked in disbelief. It *was* her.

It was Roberta Ryder.

Chapter Three

The stunned silence seemed to go on forever as they both stood there staring at one another. He was gaping at her; she was gaping at what he was wearing.

'Are you—?' she said at last. 'You haven't become a—?'

'Eh? No, I was just trying them on,' he muttered, glancing down at himself.

'Oh, right. That explains it.'

Another few seconds passed, neither of them knowing what to say. 'Well, aren't you going to invite me in?' she asked.

Ben led her through into the living-room, stunned and lost for words. Roberta Ryder, PhD, effortlessly attractive and beguiling, brilliantly intelligent, frequently cantankerous, the most opinionated and headstrong woman he'd ever known: the American scientist had once meant a great deal to him and she was someone he'd always known he would never forget.

The last time they'd been together had been on a bittersweet snowy day in Canada, a long time ago. He'd never expected to see her again. And certainly not like this.

'What are you . . . doing here?' was all he could say.

'Looking for you,' she replied. 'What else would I be doing here?'

Ben noticed how agitated she seemed. Her face was pale

and tight. She kept peering nervously through the window at the gravelled driveway and the road beyond. Ben followed her eye and saw the empty blue Vauxhall parked outside the gates.

'I called your old place in France,' she said. 'Someone called Jeff told me where I could find you. Said if you weren't at the address in Oxford you might be at the vicarage in Little Denton.'

'You found me,' he said. 'But why?'

Roberta turned away from the window to face him. 'I wouldn't have come here, Ben. But I didn't know what else to do. Who else to turn to. Something's going on. I think I'm in danger. Hell, I *know* I am. It's serious.'

She tensed as the living room door suddenly swung open. Jude walked in, took one look at her, stopped in his tracks and broke into a beaming smile. 'Oh. Hi.'

'This is Jude,' Ben told her. 'He's my . . . never mind.' Turning to Jude, he said, 'How about making a cup of coffee, Jude?'

Roberta shook her head. 'I don't want any coffee.'

'Then go make one for yourself,' Ben said, giving Jude a stern look.

'I don't really w—' Jude began, then got the point and turned to leave the room. 'Nice to meet you, whoever you are,' he called back over his shoulder.

'What do you mean, danger?' Ben asked her when they were closed in the room alone. 'What kind of danger?'

'The kind where I'm being followed,' she said seriously.

He blinked. 'Followed by who?'

'All I know is that these people are after me, Ben. That's why I'm here. I'm scared.'

Ben let out a long sigh. This wouldn't be the first time Roberta, an incurable maverick with an apparently irresistible penchant for researching into areas of science that were liable to draw all kinds of the wrong attention, had got herself into trouble. And it had been big trouble that had brought her and Ben together in Paris that memorable autumn – a scrape that both of them had been lucky to escape from with their lives.

'Please don't tell me it's alchemy again,' he said.

'It's not alchemy.'

'Or some other hocus-pocus. Go on, then. What's it this time?'

Her eyes flashed defensively. 'Hocus-pocus?'

'Whatever. It got you into a bit of a mess, if you care to remember.'

'Yeah, well, this time it's different. This isn't even about me.'

'Then what the bloody hell *is* it about?' he demanded.

Her defensive look was undiminished. 'Wouldn't folks of your, uh, *persuasion* consider it blasphemous to say that word when you're togged up in that outfit?' she fired at him.

'Never mind the outfit,' he said irritably. 'It's just . . .'

'Fancy dress?'

'A long story, Roberta. I don't think you've come all this way to hear it.'

Somewhere in the house, the landline phone was ringing. Ben faintly heard Jude pick up and talk to someone.

Roberta nodded, swallowed and then began to talk all in a rush. 'All right. Listen. It's about my friend. Her name's . . . her name *was* Claudine, Claudine Pommier. In Paris. She was killed. Murdered. The cops say it was the maniac they're calling *le bricoleur*.'

'The "handyman"?' Ben said, trying to make sense of her flurry of words.

'A serial killer,' Roberta explained agitatedly. 'He's claimed four victims in different parts of Paris. The cops say Claudine was his fifth. He's a sick piece of shit who creeps into women's homes and murders them.'

'Slow down. Why do they call him the "handyman"?' Ben asked.

'Because of the way he kills them,' she replied with a grimace. 'You want me to draw you a picture? Power tools. Nail guns. Hammers and chisels.'

'I get the idea,' Ben said, repelled. 'Go on.'

'Claudine was found with . . . Jesus, it's too awful. With her lungs full of expanding foam, the kind builders use to fill wall cavities and things. She suffocated.'

Ben had seen a good number of people die in a good many unpleasant ways, but this was almost too gruesome to imagine, even for him. He felt disgusted.

'It happened three days ago,' Roberta said. 'I only found out this morning. I'd just flown in from Ottawa to see her.' She paused to wipe away the tears of grief and rage that had clouded her eyes.

'I'm very sorry. All I can say is that they're sure to catch this guy. If there was anything I could do . . .'

Roberta shook her head vehemently. 'You're not understanding me. Let me finish. There's more to it, a lot more. I—'

At that moment the living room door swung open again and Jude stepped in, interrupting Roberta's flow. 'Ben?' he said. 'Brooke just called. Says a lorry shed its load on the motorway. Be here as soon as she can.'

'Fine,' Ben said, not taking his eyes off Roberta.

'So, you here for the wedding?' Jude asked her cheerily, appearing not to have noticed the tense mood in the room.

'Wedding?' she said, arching an eyebrow.

'Listen,' Ben said quickly. 'Why don't we go for a drive?

There's a quiet park on the other side of the village. We can talk in peace there,' he added, throwing an icy look at Jude, whose face dropped.

Outside, Roberta looked around her. 'Can we go in your car? My ass aches from driving.'

'I don't have one,' Ben said. 'I came on the bus.'

'What about that there?' she said, pointing at the rusted heap that Jude somehow managed to get about in.

'We'll be lucky if we get it out of the gate,' he said.

'So you dress like a priest and you travel around by bus,' she snorted. 'That doesn't sound like the Ben Hope I used to know.'

'Vicar,' he corrected her. 'And you're right. I'm not the same man you used to know.'

Chapter Four

Ben and Roberta left her blue Vauxhall and followed the footpath that skirted the edge of the sunlit park. They'd spoken little during the short drive through the village. Ben could feel the tension emanating from her. Whatever was scaring her, it seemed genuine, but he didn't know what to say. He waited for her to speak first.

Perhaps because of the unseasonal heat, or perhaps because the new generation of British kids preferred to sit stuffing their mouths at the computer rather than play outdoors any longer, the park was almost deserted. In the distance, a petite young mother was lifting her son of four or five onto one of the swings. An elderly, fragile-looking couple were making their slow way arm-in-arm along the footpath towards Ben and Roberta. As they passed, they both smiled at Ben and greeted him with a reverential 'Good day to you, Vicar'. Taken aback for an instant, Ben managed to mumble a reply that seemed to please the old folks before they hobbled on.

'Sure fooled them,' Roberta said drily. After a pause she added, 'So if you're not an ordained minister—'

'I'm not.'

'—isn't it against their rules to wear that outfit? Kind of like impersonating an officer or something?'

'It was only meant to be . . . oh, never mind. Just don't look at me.'

'That's hard to do. You have no idea how weird it is for me to see you dressed like that.'

'That makes two of us,' Ben replied. 'But it's a sight we may all have to get used to.'

'You're not kidding, are you?'

'This is the future I'm set on now, Roberta. It always was, I think. Just took me a long time getting there.'

'I had no idea there was this side to you.'

'There are a few things you don't know about me.'

'Pretty major life change,' she said. 'Especially for you, of all people.'

'I just want a life of peace,' he said. 'I made a vow to Brooke that that's how things would be from now on. Settle down, try to do something better with my life. No more crazy stuff.'

'You doing it for yourself, or for her?' Roberta asked a little too sharply, then immediately made an apologetic gesture. 'I take that back. None of my business, I guess.'

Ben didn't reply. The footpath ran alongside an old stone wall, through the trees on the other side of which could be seen the heavy machinery and distant half-erected buildings where a construction company were putting up the new housing estate after the villagers' protracted protests against expansion had been overruled by the local council. The workmen seemed to be packing up early for the day, vehicles rumbling out of the site's mesh gates.

'Let's sit,' Ben said a few yards further on, motioning towards a green park bench under the shade of the trees.

Roberta nodded. She sat on the bench beside him and gazed across the park in the direction of the kiddies' round-about and swings in the distance. They could hear the child's gurgling laughter as his mother began to swing him gently back and forth.

Ben said, 'Start from the beginning.'

'Claudine and I went back a long way. When I was teaching in Paris years ago, she used to lecture at the Sorbonne. We met through some mutual acquaintance I don't even remember now. We hit it off, became friends, stayed that way ever since. After I went to live in Canada she used to call me every so often, birthdays, Christmas, and emailed me now and then to keep me updated about her work projects. Some of them were real fascinating. I hadn't heard from her in a little while, just assumed she must be busy at work or something. Then yesterday, I get this letter from her by registered mail.' Roberta glanced anxiously at Ben. 'I thought it was strange that she'd write me that way, instead of the usual email. When I opened it I saw it was more like a note, real short, and you could see it was written in a hurry. She said she was in deep trouble, that she was certain she was being followed and that something bad was going to happen to her. Said not to contact her by email or phone because they'd know. They were watching every move she made.'

'Who was?' Ben asked.

'If she knew, she didn't say.'

'Have you got the letter with you? Can I see it?'

She shook her head. 'The Paris cops have it now.'

'Did it say any more than that?'

'She asked me to go to Paris to help her. To hurry before . . . before it was too late.' Roberta gave a bitter laugh.

'No indication what it was about?'

'No, she said she'd explain everything once I got there. Said I was one of just two people in the world she could turn to.'

'Why not the police?'

'Something else was going on, Ben. Something that meant she couldn't go to the police. The last line she wrote was this rushed scrawl that just said "If something happens". That was it. Underneath were a bunch of figures. She didn't even sign her name.'

'Figures?' he asked.

Roberta dug a crumpled sheet from her handbag and handed it to him. 'I copied them out before I passed the letter on to the cops. Still have no idea what they mean, though.'

Ben looked at the paper and studied the three lines of what appeared to be some kind of cipher.

$$4920N1570E$$
$$6982$$
$$2715651291$$

Codes weren't his favourite things. He stared at the sheet for a few moments, completely baffled, until the two letters in the top line suddenly flew out at him and he realised what they were. They stood for North and East.

'I don't know about the rest,' he said, 'but the top line's definitely a set of GPS co-ordinates, scrambled together. If you teased it apart it'd pinpoint a geographical location.'

'You're sure? What location?'

'I'm sure. But that's something we can come back to afterwards. Keep talking.'

'What could I do?' Roberta continued. 'She was my friend. I cancelled everything. Managed to get on a late flight to Paris. I was so worried, all I could do on the plane was sit there trying to understand what those goddamn numbers meant, but it was no use. I got into Paris just after seven this morning and took a cab straight to Claudine's apartment in Montmartre. She lived alone on the top floor of this crumbly old building in Rue des Trois Frères. When I arrived, there was a police car and a van parked outside but I didn't think anything of it at first. Then as I was heading up the stairs, these cops and forensics people were coming down, with the concierge who looks after the building. I asked if everything was okay. They asked me who I was coming to see. I said "Claudine Pommier". They told me what happened.'

Roberta paused for a moment to compose her emotions. 'It was her neighbour, Madame Lefort, who found her the morning after she was killed. The door was open, and there she was on the bed. Old lady had to be hospitalised for shock. It's so . . . so *horrible*.'

'It's bad,' Ben said. 'I'm sorry.'

Roberta sniffed, dabbed away a tear and went on. 'It happened on the same day as the postmark on the letter. She must have posted it just a few hours before she died.'

'Did she have family?' Ben asked.

'She lived alone. Lost touch with her relatives a long time back. Parents were a couple of religious assholes who disapproved of her career in science . . . oh, shit, Ben. I didn't mean—'

'It's okay.' He smiled.

'The only person in her life was a bum of an ex-boyfriend, Fabien. But he was never around even when they were together. The cops couldn't trace him, had to get a work colleague to identify the body in the morgue. Thank Christ I didn't have to do it. You can imagine . . .' Roberta shook her head, as if trying to clear the horrific picture from her mind. 'Meanwhile, they were still combing through her apartment for evidence, DNA. Nothing was stolen, apparently. The cops asked me all these questions, who I was, what I was doing there. I gave them the letter she'd sent me, but they didn't seem interested that Claudine had known beforehand she was in danger. All they could talk about was this *bricoleur*. Then I talked to the concierge, Madame Bunuel. Gave her my card and said to call me right away if there were any developments. That was when I noticed him the second time.'

Ben narrowed his eyes. 'Noticed who?'

'About thirty, tall, dark hair. I thought he was a plain-clothes detective at first. He was hanging around in the background while I was talking to the other cops. Then while I was talking to the concierge, there he was again. Looking at me kind of strangely. But I didn't think much about it at the time. I left there soon afterwards and just started walking. I was so badly shaken up about what happened to Claudine, I barely knew where I was, let alone where I was going. Before I know it I'm heading into a metro station. Abbesses, I think. Then I noticed the guy from the apartment building again, following me down the escalator, through the tunnels, hanging back like he didn't think I'd spotted him and didn't want me to. I kept walking. Tried to lose myself in the crowd. By the time I got to the platform I couldn't see him anymore. I was thinking I must have imagined it. But then as the train pulled into the station, there he was again, just a few steps away. *Staring* at me. It totally freaked me out, Ben.'

'He didn't do anything?'

'Not then,' she said. 'He never came any closer, didn't speak to me. I got on the train and he boarded the same carriage. I didn't look at him directly but I could see his reflection in the window. Just standing there at a distance, still watching me in this real creepy way. He had his arm up to hang onto the safety strap, and his jacket was hanging open. He had a gun in there, a black handgun, like a Glock or something. I didn't imagine it.'

Ben felt like pointing out that French plain-clothes detectives routinely carried concealed sidearms in shoulder holsters on, or even sometimes off, duty – but he kept quiet and let her go on talking.

'I was terrified the carriage would empty and I'd be left alone with him. I waited a couple of stops, then at Saint-Georges I got off. He did the same. Then just as the doors were about to close I pushed through the crowd and jumped back on again – like the trick they do in movies? Worked. I left the sonofabitch standing there on the platform.'

'And then?'

'Then nothing. I stayed on the line all the way to Concorde and then ran like hell back up to the street and hailed the next cab I saw.'

Ben was silent for a moment. 'You mean that's all that happened?'

Roberta stared at him. 'What did you want to hear? That he abducted me at gunpoint? Tried to punt me onto the electrified rail in front of all the crowds?'

'I thought perhaps—'

'Ben, you weren't *there*,' she said imploringly. 'It was obvious what was happening. I was so scared. That's when I had the idea of calling you.' She paused, blushed a little. 'I . . . I've looked you up a few times. Maybe more than a few times. So I knew you were in France. At least, I thought you were. When I called, this Jeff person told me you'd moved to England. Gave me an address in Oxford but said you'd been spending a lot of time at this village called Little Denton. Anyway, I didn't know what else to do except jump on the next Eurostar. Arrived in London a couple of hours ago, rented that car and drove like crazy all the way to

Oxford. Took me forever to find your place, then you weren't home, so I found this place on the map and came out here hoping I'd find you. Ben, please. I'm exhausted and I'm terrified. You've got to help me.'

Ben was silent for a minute as he tried to put the breathless rush of details together in his mind. 'I'm confused about this man who followed you from your friend's apartment,' he said. 'You told me before you thought he was a detective. Now it sounds like you're trying to imply he's the murderer.'

'Maybe he is,' she said. Her expression was intense.

'Roberta, think about it,' he protested. 'The serial killer? You really believe this "handyman" would linger about the scene of his own crime pretending to be a plain-clothes detective, hoping to knock off his victim's friends as they came to visit? He might be a maniac, but nobody's that crazy.'

She shook her head. 'Uh-uh. That would be a little far-fetched, even for me. That's why I'm totally certain that this serial killer thing is a blind alley. It wasn't the "handyman" who killed Claudine. Don't you see? It's just been set up to *appear* that way. Some bullshit story to lead the cops off the track while . . . Oh, Ben, don't look at me like that. Like I'm some kind of paranoid conspiracy loon.'

'I don't think that about you.'

'You mean, you don't want to think it. But you're thinking it.'

'I don't know what to think,' he said. 'If it wasn't this sicko who killed her, then who did?'

'How can I know that? Nobody does, that's the whole idea. They do this kind of thing all the time, when they want to rub someone out who gets in their way.'

'*They* do it all the time?'

'Yes, *they*,' she snapped.

'All right,' he said. 'Leave that to one side. Next question: who came after you on the metro with the apparent intention of doing you harm?'

'I don't know that either.'

'Roberta, if you don't know these things, isn't it simpler just to accept what the police say?'

'Since when did you ever take a cop's word for a single damn thing, Ben Hope?' she demanded hotly. 'You trust them even less than I do. Besides, the letter proves it's not that simple.'

'The letter we don't have any more,' Ben said. 'And even if we did, it proves nothing.'

'Hold on. She *knew* she was in danger. That's the whole point.'

'If this murderer hasn't been caught yet, maybe it's because he's careful,' Ben said. 'Psychopaths are often extremely cunning and devious. Sick, but smart. They've been known to plan their attacks, weeks, months in advance.'

'So?'

'So he might have been watching your friend for some time before he struck. But maybe he wasn't so careful that she didn't spot him and somehow sensed that something wasn't right about him. That could easily explain how she knew in advance that something was about to happen. She panicked.'

'Oh, so you've got this whole thing figured out,' Roberta snapped. 'Then *you* tell me who the guy was on the train.'

He shrugged. 'Maybe your first impression was the right one. He could have been a detective. You know the way their minds work. He might have wanted to ask you more questions. About the letter, perhaps. Or else maybe the whole thing is just . . .' Ben checked himself from saying more. He'd already said too much, and could see the fire in her eyes.

'Just what?' she said fiercely.

'All I'm saying, Roberta, is that maybe you need to think again. That maybe, for once in their lives, the police are right about this terrible thing that's happened to your friend.'

'And the rest I just cooked up in my imagination. That what you're saying, Ben?'

'You told me yourself you felt dazed, disorientated, after you left Claudine's place. It would be understandable. People can suffer from all kinds of confusion at a time of great emotional stress.'

'You're so sure about this, aren't you? In one way you haven't changed at all, Ben Hope. You're still just as much of a pigheaded bastard as when I first met you.'

'Thanks,' he muttered. 'Remember, *you* came to *me*. You're not giving me much of a chance here.'

'What about the numbers?' she demanded. 'The GPS location and whatever else is there? You got a theory for those too? I have. If something happened to her, she intended for me to figure it out. There's more to this, and I'm going to find out what.'

Ben leaned forward with his elbows on his knees, gazing at the ground between his feet and trying to understand. He knew Roberta well enough to know there was absolutely no point in trying to convince her to go home and wait for the police to do their job. And he couldn't ignore the voice in his head reminding him of all the times he'd seen the cops botch everything up.

'All right, then explain it to me,' he said. 'Someone murdered your friend, and now they're coming after you, and it has something to do with this letter and a coded message. Who are they? What's it about?'

Roberta paused to brush away a strand of dark red hair that had fallen into her eyes. Her brow was creased with strain. 'Fact is, Ben, I think I know. Something tells me this all has to do with Claudine's research.'

While they were deeply involved in their conversation, a hundred yards away at the other end of the park, a sleek black Audi saloon purred to a halt next to Roberta's rental car. Its front doors opened and two men silently got out. Neither of them looked out of the ordinary. The one who'd been driving was in his early-to-mid thirties with nondescript brown hair and sunglasses, the other about ten years older, more heavily built, with a receding stubble of grey and eyes narrowed to slits against the early afternoon glare. They were casually dressed in jeans and lightweight jackets.

Neither spoke. As they both gazed impassively at the blue Vauxhall the older man was receiving instructions via a mobile phone. He listened until his instructions were complete, then gave a short nod to his colleague.

The driver opened the boot. He took out the black holdall from inside. It sagged heavily in his hand.

The two men scanned the near-empty park. Within a few seconds they'd located their target on the green wooden bench in the distance and taken note of the unknown male accompanying her. The men exchanged glances when they saw how the target's companion was dressed.

It was no ordinary camera that was built into the mobile phone the older of the two men was carrying. He quickly, discreetly, used it to snap the figures on the bench, then redialled a number. 'She's not alone,' he said when the voice replied on the line. 'She's talking to a priest.'

Pause. 'Yeah, that's what I said. I'm sending the image now. Got it?'

'I've got it,' said the gruff voice on the other end. 'I see them. Okay, it's her last confession. His too. Make it quick and quiet.'

The call was over. The two men divided the contents of the holdall. Then moved unnoticed around the edge of the park to their position.

Chapter Five

The word *research*, from the lips of Roberta Ryder, held certain negative past associations for Ben. After all, it had been some bizarre experimental research of her own that had first not only brought them together but drawn the attention of ruthless people who'd very nearly succeeded in killing them both.

'You told me Claudine was a lecturer,' he said. 'Lecturer in what?'

'Physics,' Roberta replied.

'It doesn't sound very dangerous.'

'But then, what do you know about physics?'

He said nothing. Aside from weapons ballistics, the complexities of calculating long-range rifle bullet trajectories, the cold mathematics of war and destruction that he wanted to forget he'd ever learned, he didn't know much.

'That's what I thought,' she said. 'Then I don't suppose you've ever heard of a guy called Tesla? He was the subject of Claudine's research, ever since I first knew her.'

'Of course I've heard of him,' he said defensively. 'First to experiment with electricity, back in the nineteenth century. Made dead frogs' legs dance about by passing current through them. I don't see what—'

'That was Galvani, Ben,' Roberta interrupted impatiently.

'I'm talking about the great Serbian scientist Nikola Tesla, born 1856. Actually I'm not surprised you didn't know about him,' she added after a beat. 'I mean, everyone's heard of the Marconis and Faradays and Edisons of this world, but Tesla's the pioneer genius who somehow wound up forgotten. Which is pretty incredible, considering he came up with the principles behind wireless communication, remote control, radar, sonar, robotics, neon and fluorescent light, and foresaw the internet and cell phones as early as 1908. Not to mention his work on—'

'I get the picture,' Ben interrupted, knowing she was liable to launch into a whole science lecture if he didn't break her stream.

'I don't know that you do get it,' she said. She paused a moment. Gazed across the park, where the young mother was still pushing her son to and fro on the swing. The child was howling in delight as the swing's arc carried him higher and higher.

'Look at that,' Roberta said, pointing. 'That kid's mother can't weigh more than a hundred and five pounds soaking wet. She's even smaller than I am. But see how little force it takes, at just the right moment, to make the swing go up high in the air.' She looked round at Ben. '*That's* what Claudine's research was about.'

'About shoving a kid back and forth on a swing?'

She tutted. 'Don't be so obtuse, Hope. It's about the principle of resonance, the idea that tiny forces, precisely enough timed and placed, can accumulate to create massive energies.'

'You're going to have to be more specific.'

'Okay, let me put it another way. The Earth's vibrations have a periodicity of about an hour forty-nine minutes. In other words, if I were to hit something solid against the ground right now, it would send a wave of contraction through the whole planet that would return to the same point one hour forty-nine minutes later in the form of expansion. Follow me?'

'Oh, absolutely,' he said.

Missing his sarcasm, she went on: 'So you see, the Earth, like everything else, is in a constant state of vibration, ever expanding and contracting. Now imagine that at the exact moment when it begins to contract, I detonate a ton of high explosive in the exact same spot. That would accelerate the contraction, so that one hour forty-nine minutes later there would come back a wave of expansion that was equally accelerated. Now, if as that expansion wave began to ebb I set off another ton of explosive, and I kept repeating that pattern again and again . . . eventually, what do you suppose would happen?'

Ben looked blank.

'It's obvious, if you think about it. Given time, Tesla calculated that he could build up enough of an energy wave to split the Earth.'

'Split the Earth,' Ben repeated in a flat tone.

She nodded matter-of-factly, as if splitting the Earth were all part and parcel of a scientist's everyday routine. 'That's the idea. See? Small input, big effect. Pretty much all of Tesla's work was based on those principles, and that's what Claudine was interested in. She was talking about it when I first met her, and she was still talking about it the last time we had a conversation on the phone, which was about five months ago.'

'I still don't understand where this is leading, Roberta.'

'Let me explain a little more, okay? In the late nineteenth century Tesla invented a small hand-held device called the electro-mechanical oscillator. Based on the same kind of principles, he used it to show that even a subtle vibration, at just the right frequency, could unleash a whole lot of power. I mean enormous, and almost instantaneously. Enough to, say, bring down a building. A house, even a skyscraper.'

'Sounds more like a bomb to me.'

'No explosives involved,' she replied, shaking her head. 'No noise or smoke, nothing chemical, just some basic mechanical moving parts powered by steam.'

'*Steam?* What kind of bollocks contraption is that?'

'A very simple one. Basically a miniature piston engine, with a small on-board boiler heated by internal combustion. In those days, steam was the only power source that could produce enough energy to operate the mechanicals. The whole thing was supposed to have been about six, seven inches long. You could carry it in your pocket.'

'And use it to bring down a building.'

She nodded. 'Sure.'

'But it can't split the Earth.'

'Oh no, you'd need a bigger version to do that kind of damage.'

'I would have hoped you'd do me more credit than to expect me to believe such utter bloody nonsense,' he said. 'I mean, come on.'

'It really existed, Ben,' Roberta insisted. 'According to Tesla's findings its theoretical potential was limitless.'

Ben was losing patience. 'Theoretical, as in, it's never actually been done or proved. This is what your friend was into? And you think this is why someone killed her? To do with some pie-in-the-sky notion that you can vibrate a building to pieces with some daft Heath Robinson device?' He waved his hand dismissively. 'Listen, I spent years in the army learning how to blow stuff up. *Nobody* can do it as efficiently as we did. Millions are spent developing high-tech explosives and training people like me how to use them without getting themselves blasted to smithereens. And a lot of people have been killed or maimed in the process of gathering that expertise. Don't you think that if there were an easier way, Special Forces units would've latched onto it by now? Vibrations and steam,' he added with contempt. 'Splitting the Earth. Next thing you'll be telling me about science fiction death rays.'

She blinked. 'You knew about the Tesla death ray?'

Ben could see she was being earnest. 'Now this is really getting crazy.'

'Check out the evidence,' she protested. 'This is historic fact.'

Now Ben had run out of patience entirely. 'Yeah, and "historic" is the key word here. It's hardly the stuff that conspiracies are made of.'

'You got one right here,' she said fiercely. 'You just can't see it.'

'What's there to see?' he said.

'My friend's body lying in the morgue, for a start.'

Ben couldn't argue with that. 'Okay. I'm sorry.'

'You're sorry, but you think I'm full of shit.'

He threw up his hands in frustration. 'I don't know, Roberta. You come to me saying you're in trouble, then you start talking about all *this* stuff, which, frankly, sounds to me like a load of . . . what do you Americans call it? Hooey. Just like all that alchemical stuff you were fixated on before.'

'It is not hooey,' she said firmly.

'I can see you sincerely believe that. But what am I supposed to make of it? What can I do?'

She leaned close to him and replied, 'Help me.'

'What makes you think I even could?'

'You're Ben Hope. What more is there to say?' She paused, looking entreatingly into his face. 'You helped me once. It wasn't so long ago. Won't you help me again?'

He didn't reply.

There was a long silence. The young mother had taken her child away from the swings and was holding his hand as they made their way along the tree-shaded footpath into the distance. The park was empty now, apart from just the two of them sitting on the bench.

'I shouldn't have come here,' Roberta said bitterly. 'I'm wasting my time.'

'I'm getting married in three days, Roberta,' Ben said.

'Yeah. Married. Thanks for reminding me.' She shook her head sadly. 'Jesus, I remember it all so well, everything that happened between us. It seems like yesterday. Then that day you came to Canada to find me . . . I thought . . .'

'Do we have to go over this?' he said. 'I came to make sure you were all right. And to say goodbye.'

'I really cared for you. You know that, don't you? We had something together.'

'It wouldn't have worked, Roberta. A guy like me – I don't know. I was restless then. I just wasn't ready to settle in one place.'

'Or with one woman,' she said. 'But apparently, you are now.'

'I told you. I'm different now.'

'Or maybe you just found the right woman now.' She let out a long sigh, then tried to smile. 'That's fine, Ben. I'm happy for you. I mean it. I can see now that I shouldn't have troubled you. You've made a new life for yourself. Who the hell am I to turn up like this out of no place and disturb it?'

'You know who you are to me,' he said.

'Was,' she snorted. 'I guess that's ancient history too,

huh?' She started plucking at her handbag for her car keys. 'Let's go. I'll drive you back to your domestic bliss. Then I'll be gone, and I swear I'll never bother you again.'

'Hey.' He reached out a hand.

She flinched away from his touch. 'Don't worry about me. I don't need your help anyway.' Her eyes had filled with tears again. She wiped them angrily away. '*Shit*, where'd I put the goddamned keys?'

Ben's throat felt tight and he was confused with so many emotions. 'You look tired, Roberta. Why don't you stay a night or two at the vicarage? Jude would welcome having a house guest.'

She let out a mirthless laugh. 'I suppose you'd want me to come to the wedding, too? Act as maid of honour or something? No thanks.' Finding the keys, she stood up from the bench abruptly.

Ben opened his mouth to say something, but the words were still on his lips when the splinters flew with a sharp *crack* from the backrest of the bench and something smacked hard off the wall behind them.

For a short fraction of a second that seemed like a full minute, he stared at the small bullet hole that had appeared right where Roberta had been sitting just a moment earlier and only a few inches away from him.

Half a second was all the time he had to react before a volley of silenced gunfire erupted from across the park.

Chapter Six

In the same instant that splinters and pieces of tree bark exploded all around them, Ben jack-knifed violently over the back of the bench, grabbing Roberta's arm and hauling her roughly down to the ground with him.

The gunfire paused for a heartbeat as whoever was shooting at them adjusted their aim. Then another volley of bullets churned up the ground and spat dirt around the base of the bench. A round screamed off the cast-iron leg Ben was pressed hard up against and he felt the hot copper-jacketed lead pass through his hair, millimetres from his skull.

Roberta was curled up in a ball on the ground, crying out in terror. Ben scrambled over to her to cover her body with his. With his face pressed down in the dirt he caught a momentary glimpse of movement among the bushes across the park. Even as he tried desperately to shield Roberta, some detached reptilian part of his mind was busy calculating the enemy's position and strength.

Range: eighty yards. More than one shooter. Nine-millimetre subsonic ammunition, fully-automatic weapons fitted with sound moderators. This wasn't local kids larking about with airguns. Conclusion: time to get the hell away from here before they both got shot to pieces.

In seconds, the bench was riddled with holes and offering

less and less cover with every passing moment as bullets ripped through the weather-beaten wood and drilled into the ground, ploughed into the trees and threw up spatters of earth left and right. A howling ricochet off something hard and a shower of brick dust suddenly reminded Ben of the low wall behind the bench. In a momentary lull in the shooting as both gunmen reloaded their expended magazines, he sprang up, dragged Roberta bodily to her feet and half-threw, half-pulled her over the wall.

It was a four-foot drop down to the sloping grassy bank on the other side. The two of them hit the soft earth and went tumbling down the slope to the flat ground of the field adjoining the parkland.

Ben was first on his feet. 'Are you hit?' he asked urgently as Roberta stood uncertainly. 'Are you bleeding?' The shooting had stopped, and for the moment they were out of range of the gunmen. That wouldn't be the case for long.

'I don't think so,' Roberta answered. Her voice sounded faraway and dazed. Ben quickly inspected her for blood. He'd seen men mortally wounded who hadn't even known about it for several minutes after getting shot. But Roberta's only injury seemed to be the small cut to her brow where a flying splinter had broken the skin. 'You're okay. Stay there,' he said, clambered back up the grassy bank and peeped over the wall.

He'd been right about a pair of shooters. He could see them now. The two men had emerged from the cover of the bushes. One was younger, taller, dark-haired, the other older and squatter. They looked fit and strong, and were running across the deserted park towards them with an air of absolute purpose. They were making no attempt to conceal the weapons in their hands. Few men in a vicar's garb would have been able to make the identification, but

Ben instantly knew the stubby black outlines of the Beretta MX4 Storm submachine gun. He'd had half a dozen of their civilian semi-automatic cousins locked up in the armoury at Le Val. The military version was a pure weapon of war. Totally illegal in most countries of the world. Extremely hard to obtain. The choice of professionals.

Who were these men? Ben didn't have much time to consider the answer, or to yell at Roberta 'What the hell have you got yourself mixed up in?'. The shooters were halfway across the park already, running fast. Ben slithered back down the bank and rejoined Roberta.

She still appeared stunned from the suddenness and violence of the attack. 'They're coming,' he said. 'Let's move.'

'Where to?' she gasped, looking around her wide-eyed. Once they left the shelter of the wall, there'd be nothing around them but open field. The nearest cover was the half-built housing estate a hundred and fifty or more yards away, shimmering like a mirage in the heat haze.

Ben had already decided that was the only place they could run to. He could only pray that the gate he could see in the eight-foot wire mesh fence surrounding the building site wasn't locked. He took her hand tightly in his, and they set off at a sprint towards the distant buildings. The grass was long and lush, and tugged at their ankles as they ran. Roberta stumbled over a rut and went down on one knee. As Ben helped her back to her feet he saw the two men clamber over the wall, spot them across the field and give chase. 'Move!' he rasped, yanking her arm.

The chatter of sound-suppressed machine-gun fire sounded from behind. Dirt and shredded grass flew up in Ben and Roberta's wake.

One thing Ben knew for sure – the gunmen weren't interested in catching them alive. They were shooting to kill.

He let go of Roberta's hand and shouted 'Zigzag!' She glanced at him in stunned terror for an instant, then understood and began to imitate him as he tore through the long grass in a crazily erratic weave, like a hare trying to evade a chasing lurcher. A desperate strategy. It made them a harder target to hit at this range, but it also gave them further to run than their pursuers.

The wire fence was coming up fast. Signs on posts read DANGER: KEEP OUT and HARD HAT ZONE. Beyond the wire were bare-block buildings, construction skips, cement mixers, enormous mounds of sand, portacabins for the building crews. Ben's jaw clenched tighter as he saw the heavy chain and padlock looped around the mesh gates. He glanced behind him. In a few seconds the shooters would be close enough to take them down easily.

'Climb!' he yelled at Roberta. Without hesitation she hooked her fingers into the wire meshwork and started clambering up the fence. As she reached the top she swung her leg over, scrabbled frantically halfway down and then let go and hit the ground with a soft grunt. Ben was right behind her. He felt dreadfully exposed with his back to the shooters, hanging from the fence like a target on a board.

He heard the muffled bark of shots. A bullet struck sparks off the steel fencepost inches from his right hand as he climbed. He launched himself over the top of the wire and hit the ground the way he'd learned in parachute training, rolling to absorb the impact and leaping straight back to his feet in an instant run.

The buildings were clustered close together, some almost completed and clad in scaffolding, others still in the early stages of construction with bare-block walls just a few feet high. Roberta was already making for the nearest, a shell of a house with no roof and empty holes for doors and windows. She was limping.

More shots. A puff of dust off the wall to Roberta's left as she staggered inside the building, clutching her leg. Ben was ready to feel a bullet in his back as he sprinted after her, but it didn't come. He skidded through the doorway.

Roberta was pressed up against the wall, breathing hard, looking at him in alarm. 'I told you,' she gasped. '*Now* do you believe me? So much for the Paris cops and their bullshit. Serial killer my ass.'

'What's wrong with your leg?' he asked, noticing the way she was holding it.

'Twisted my ankle jumping from the fence. It's fine, I can move it,' she added with a wince of pain.

Ben quickly crouched down and tugged the left leg of her jeans up a few inches. He could see nothing bad, no swelling, no discolouration. 'You'll live. If you don't get shot.'

'Hell of a thing to say at a time like this,' she replied anxiously. 'What do we *do*, Ben?'

His mind was sharp, working fast and smoothly. Trained responses under stress were so deeply conditioned in him that even with adrenaline levels running through his veins that would reduce most men to a panicking jelly, everything appeared in slow motion. He stepped lightly across to the nearest window and peered cautiously out through the glassless hole.

The shooters had reached the fence. As Ben watched, they each aimed their weapons at the padlock on the gate and let off a flurry of gunfire that sounded like a lump hammer clanging against an anvil at impossible speed. The wrecked padlock dropped away, the chain parted and jangled loose. The men kicked the gates open with a metallic clatter and strode into the building site.

'They're coming,' Ben said quietly.

'Oh, my God. Who *are* they?'

'We can talk about that later,' Ben said. 'For now it's time to move on. Can you stand?'

She nodded. He took her hand. Put a finger to his lips and then pointed it through the house at the back door. 'That way,' he whispered.

Roberta hobbled after him as he exited the building. They skirted a low adjoining wall and crossed a patch of rubble-strewn ground to the house next door, which had its roof A-frames, beams and battens already mounted under a plastic covering that crackled in the soft breeze and darkened the skeletal rooms in shadow.

Ben thrust Roberta into a dim corner with a look that said, 'Stay there', and let go of her hand. He trotted to the window. Twenty yards away, the two shooters were stalking through the site with their weapons shouldered and ready, glancing left and right for any movement, any trace of their quarry. Their faces were steely and predatory. The older one signalled to his colleague and they split up out of sight among the buildings and construction machinery.

Ben glanced quickly around him, taking in the layout of their cover. Front door, back door, patio window, garage, other points of entry. Too many possibilities and not enough hiding places. The unfinished home reminded him with sharp discomfort of the dedicated 'killing house' that he and his SAS squads had used for live-fire room assault, hostage extraction and anti-terrorist combat drills at the regimental base in Hereford, back in the day. Nothing could escape the killing house without getting drilled full of bullets and buck-shot by the Special Forces tactical teams.

If these two guys were even half that proficient at their job, this wasn't a good place to be. Not a good place at all.

Chapter Seven

'Ben!' came a hoarse whisper. Roberta was peering at him worriedly from the shadows. 'What are we gonna do?' she hissed.

'Stay put, for now,' Ben replied softly. 'You keep out of sight and keep quiet.'

'I still know karate,' she whispered. 'I can fight.'

Now that the initial shock of the attack had passed, her expression was alert and focused. Ben remembered well enough that Roberta Ryder had always been a lot less squeamish about violence than the average female science academic. During their escapades together in Paris she'd used her Shotokan black belt skills to lethally defend herself against a knife attacker, wrecked cars, been drenched in blood and gore during a gunfight on the banks of the River Seine and later shot a man in the thigh with an automatic pistol. On that occasion she'd saved Ben's life, not for the first time.

But here, today, they were going to need more than karate moves to evade the two men who were coming after them.

Ben retreated quickly out of sight as a figure edged past the window. It was the younger of the two men. He paused for an instant to squint into the murky building, scanning left and right with the detached, professional air of a rat catcher hunting for vermin. The muzzle of his Beretta was pointing right at Ben, but he couldn't see him standing there perfectly immobile in the shadows.

Ben didn't breathe. After what seemed like an agonizingly long time, the man moved on. Ben could hear his steps padding around the side of the house.

The man's footsteps were treading closer to the door. Ben glanced towards Roberta and saw the flash of her frightened eyes in the dark corner.

Something else was standing half-hidden in the shadows. One of the building crew had left a long-handled shovel propped against a wall. Ben moved silently across to where the shovel was leaning. Careful not to let its blade scrape on the concrete floor, he picked it up. The long wooden shaft was crusty with dried cement. He took a strong two-handed grip on it.

The figure of the man appeared in the doorway, silhouetted against the bright sunlight outside. With his weapon to his shoulder he took a careful step inside, then paused, head slightly cocked to one side as though listening intently for the tiniest movement, blinking to adjust his eyes to the low light.

Nothing stirred inside the building. The only sound was the gentle crackle of the wind on the plastic sheeting stretched over the bare roof beams.

The man took another stealthy step into the house. Then another.

Then the shovel blade swung humming through the air faster than the man could react.

If Ben had hit him with the blade edge-on it would have separated the top of his skull above the eyes, like taking the crown off a boiled egg with a knife. Instead, the flat of the blade caught him just over the bridge of the nose with a resonating clang and laid him on his back. The MX4 spun out of his grip and fell to the ground.

Ben stood over him with the shovel poised in his hands like an axe. The man's face was a mess of blood. He was moaning incoherently, disorientated and only about half conscious until two swift, harsh kicks to the head knocked him out entirely.

'Still got the soft touch,' Roberta muttered from the shadows.

'He can take it,' Ben said, snatching up the fallen weapon. The submachine gun was bulky with the big sound suppressor screwed to the end of the barrel. There were still twelve or thirteen rounds in the pistol grip magazine and one in the chamber. Ben set it aside and quickly checked the unconscious man's pockets. He had no ID, no wallet, no phone, not even loose change. Nothing on him but a car ignition key on a leather fob and, clipped inside a belt pouch, two spare steel thirty-round magazines for the MX4. There wasn't time to wait for the guy to come round to interrogate him – and Ben's first priority at this moment was to get Roberta to safety.

He grabbed the two spare mags and the keys and thrust them deep into the left pocket of his borrowed trousers. Picking up the submachine gun, he stepped over the comatose body and checked from the doorway that the coast was clear. He signalled to Roberta. 'Let's move,' he whispered.

Ben wasn't one of those guys who loved weaponry for its own sake. He'd handled just about every variety of small arms ever made, witnessed with his own eyes the butcher's-shop carnage they could be used to inflict on the human frame, and at times had wished he'd never see another. Yet there was no denying the deep sense of comfort in going from being totally unarmed and vulnerable to cradling something in your hands that helped even the odds against a dangerous opponent. The Beretta felt like an old friend who'd come to the rescue.

With his finger on the trigger, Ben took a winding path between buildings and pieces of construction plant machinery in the rough direction of the site gates. With any luck, they could be through them and heading back over the field towards the park before the second shooter realised what was up.

Every few steps he glanced behind him to check that Roberta was still following close behind. She was still limping slightly on her twisted ankle, but keeping pace. They cut across a ploughed-up dirt patch that would eventually become a row of neat little back gardens, and then cut through another narrow alley between two scaffold-covered houses. Approaching the corner of the house on the left, the unchained gates came into view just twenty yards across a piece of open ground. Ben slowly, carefully peered around the edge of the wall. To the left he could see only empty buildings and a half-built wall. To the right, nothing moved among the stacks of concrete blocks. The coast seemed to be clear.

'Let's go,' he said to Roberta.

He'd taken half a step out into the open when masonry chips exploded from the wall inches away. A hard impact to the left thigh almost knocked his leg out from under him.

Chapter Eight

Ben staggered backwards under cover of the wall and almost fell over, his whole body jangling with shock as he expected to see the first fountain of blood spurting from a ruptured femoral artery.

Roberta cried out. Ben dropped his weapon and clasped his hands to his leg. It felt numb from hip to knee. He saw the bullet hole through the black fabric of his trousers.

His trembling fingers connected through the material with the Beretta magazines in his pocket. He pulled them out, saw the huge dent and the strike mark in one of them where the bullet had hit it dead on and crushed the pressed steel box almost flat. Nothing had passed through. The magazine had absorbed the full force of the impact. Ben felt something burning hot against his flesh, dug deeper into his pocket and found the jagged, squashed lead and copper disc that was all that remained of the 9mm bullet.

His heart began to beat again as a mixture of relief and ferocity welled up inside him. He tossed the ruined mag away and snatched up his fallen gun.

'I thought you were hit,' Roberta gasped.

'I've always been lucky with bullets,' Ben said. He stepped quickly back to the corner and darted a cautious look round it. The shooter was out there, and he wasn't far away, maybe twenty or thirty yards, hidden behind cover with his sights trained at his mark and just waiting for Ben to step out again. Where was he? Behind that low wall? Those cement bags, or that stack of bricks?

Ben poked the barrel of the submachine gun around the corner of the house and let off a sustained blast of return fire at his unseen enemy. The row of cement bags burst apart. The tape holding together the stack of bricks parted, and it toppled over in a cascade onto and behind the section of low wall. There was a yell. The shooter scrambled out from behind the wall and started scurrying towards the houses behind him. Ben chased him with a stream of bullets, but then his magazine was suddenly empty. The man darted out of sight.

Ben swore and rammed in his last mag. He scanned the buildings where the man had disappeared. There was no sign of him.

Silence.

Ben's mind worked fast. Having been caught out once, there was no way he was about to try again to cross the open ground to the gates. But he was just as reluctant to retrace their steps in the direction they'd come, and find out the hard way that the shooter had doubled back on himself to head them off.

Ben had a decision to make. And the wrong choice could kill them in a second.

He chose a third option. If in doubt, head for higher ground. 'That way,' he said to Roberta, pointing up at the scaffolding attached to the house. Most of the feeling had returned to his left leg now, and with it the ache from the bullet impact. Ignoring the pain, he guided Roberta to the vertical ladder that led up to the scaffold and stood guard as she clambered up to the first level, then climbed up to join her on the rickety planking. A second ladder led to the next level up, where the builders had been fitting the A-frames for the roof.

Ben led the way as they skirted around towards the back of the house. The scaffold was enclosed with a wire mesh safety barrier. Through it Ben could see where the builders had poured the footings for the neighbouring house. Judging by the slick, shiny surface of the wet concrete, like grey porridge that had been scraped smooth with the back of a knife, it had been their last job of the day.

'Did I ever tell you how I feel about heights?' Roberta said, clutching the railing and not looking down.

Ben said nothing. He surveyed the ground below. Thirty feet up, there was a much better view of the building site, but still no sign of their opponent. He moved silently along the planking, his eyes picking out every possible hiding place among the houses and garages and construction equipment. Nothing.

Roberta's sudden gasp made him wheel round in alarm.

The man hadn't doubled back to flank them. He'd done exactly the same thing Ben had done, move to higher ground and work his way around the back of the house to creep up on them from behind. He had one arm around Roberta's throat, his squat, muscular body pressed up against hers to use her as a shield and the fat tube of his MX4's silencer pressed hard into the side of her neck below the ear.

Ben froze with his gun half-raised.

'Drop it,' the man said in a flat voice.

'Shoot him, Ben!' Roberta yelled. The man clamped a hand over her mouth and ground his long submachine gun barrel harder into her flesh. She wriggled wildly in his grasp, but it was tight. His expression said clearly, 'I'm not messing about.'

Ben already knew that. He held his Beretta out at arm's length, pointing down at the planking. He let it slip from his fingers.

'Kick it over the edge,' the man said.

Ben nudged the weapon with his toe. It tipped through the gap between the planks and the safety rail and disappeared. He heard it glance off the scaffolding poles, then clatter to the ground thirty feet below.

'Nice one, father,' the man said with a crooked grin.

Ben could see the gun's fire selector switched to single shot. Could see the man's finger tightening on the trigger, and the angle of the muzzle that would direct the bullet under her ear and upward through her brain.

'You pull that trigger, you die,' he said.

The man's grizzled features broke into a grin. 'Better say a prayer.'

His grin evaporated into a look of surprise as Roberta gave a sudden heave that ripped her free of his grasp. With practised speed she raked the heel of her shoe down his shin and onto his foot in a hard stamping kick and simultaneously twisted his gun arm away from her in a painful lock that made him cry out.

The gun went off. The bullet went wide of her body and ricocheted with a howl off the wall behind the scaffold. As Roberta was about to knee him in the groin, still grasping his gun-arm, he head-butted her savagely and she sprawled down to the planking, almost falling through the gap below the safety barrier. With bared teeth the man thrust the gun down at her to shoot point-blank into her face.

But by then Ben had raced along the scaffolding and was on him. He drove the man's arm violently against the safety barrier, knocking the gun out of his hand. Before it had splashed into the wet concrete thirty feet below, Ben delivered a vicious elbow strike to the man's throat, then another. The man reeled, but he was tough, and within seconds the two of them were grappling violently against the railing. Roberta was trying to scramble to her feet, but the blow to her face had dazed her.

A powerful fist caught Ben in the ribs. A flash of pain ripped through him, then the greying stubble of the man's crown was coming hard and fast at his face.

Ben dodged the head-butt and used its momentum to steer the guy's skull full-force into a scaffold pole with a resonant clang and an impact that made the whole structure judder under their feet. Ben grabbed the man's beefy head by both ears and smashed it off the pipe again, leaving a smear of blood on the metal, then with all his strength piled a knee into the muscular paunch of his stomach.

The man staggered backwards into the safety railing. The wire mesh buckled. A joint gave way and a whole section of the barrier swung loose from the scaffolding. Ben punched him in the mouth and felt teeth cut into his knuckles.

Streaming blood, arms flailing for balance, the man wobbled on the edge of the planks for an instant and then fell backwards with a cry. But as he went, his grasping hands gripped hold of both of Ben's sleeves.

Ben felt himself being pulled over the edge. The wet concrete seemed to rush up towards him. Then a violent jarring pain all the way up his right arm to his shoulder as his fist closed on a scaffold pipe, arresting his fall. His legs kicked in empty space as he dangled precariously from one hand, reaching desperately with the other for a grip on something solid. He heard Roberta scream out his name.

The squat man turned a somersault and belly-flopped into the wet concrete. The smooth, gleaming surface erupted in a sludgy grey explosion. For a moment he lay there, stirring weakly as if on a soft bed; then the glutinous morass began to draw him down, legs first. He began screaming and thrashing in panic, reaching for the edge but finding nothing to hold onto as he quickly sank. The concrete sucked at his chest, then at his chin. Then his upturned face disappeared under the surface and his scream died as his mouth filled with concrete. The last thing to go down was the agonised claw of his hand.

'Ben!' Roberta screamed again. She scrabbled to the edge of the planking and looked down in horror. Seeing him dangling there by one arm, she reached hers out for him to grab, but it was too far to reach. 'Ben!'

For an instant, Ben thought his grip on the slippery steel pipe was going to fail. His fingers were at breaking point. He dug deep into his last reserves of strength and groped wildly around with his other hand.

Suddenly he had a grip on a hanging section of the safety railing. With a grunt of pain and effort he hauled himself higher until he was able to kick a leg up to the scaffold and hook a knee over the edge of the planking. Roberta seized his arm and helped him, dragging him away from the edge. They were both breathing hard.

'Are you all right?' he asked, sitting up. Her left cheek and jaw were inflamed from where the man had butted her, and his gun muzzle had left an angry red circle on her neck.

'Sure,' she said, gingerly touching her face and inspecting her fingertips for blood. 'It's just like old times.'

'Don't joke about it. Whoever you've managed to piss off this time, they're not kidding around.'

'That's what I have you for,' she said with a bitter smile. 'Reverend.'

Ben ignored the jibe and got to his feet. His left leg was stiffening up from the bullet impact and there was a lancing pain in his right side from the punch he'd taken in the ribs.

'Don't think we'll be seeing him again,' Roberta muttered, peering down over the edge. There was no trace of sympathy in her eyes as she watched the surface of the wet concrete smooth itself out, with hardly a ripple left to show for the man's body under it.

'Not for a few centuries,' Ben said. 'But maybe his friend can tell us what the hell's going on here.'

Chapter Nine

Ben and Roberta made their way down from the scaffold. The gun he'd tipped over the edge was scuffed from its impact against the ground, but weapons of war could take the odd knock or two. He dusted it off and kept it ready, just in case, as they headed back towards the building where they'd left the younger man lying unconscious.

When they reached the spot, Ben saw with a sinking heart that the worry that had been growing inside him was proved right: the house was empty. All that remained of the gunman was a thin trail of blood where he'd picked himself up and managed to escape. Where he was now was anybody's guess.

'It's my fault he got away,' Ben muttered in self-reproach as they left the construction site behind and hurried back across the field towards the park. 'I didn't hit him hard enough.'

'Hey, any harder, you'd have killed him,' Roberta said, then added glumly, 'Either way, we'd still be back to square one. So what happens next?'

'You got what you came for,' Ben said. 'Me. And I want to know more about all this physics research stuff.'

'I told you just about all I know.'

'Then we'll have to figure it out the hard way,' he said. 'Bit by bit, one piece at a time. How's the ankle?'

'Hardly hurts anymore.'

'Good, because we've got some travelling to do.'

Reaching the edge of the park, they climbed back over the wall, passed the bullet-riddled bench and walked along the footpath towards the car park. Ben had the MX4 wrapped up in an old cement bag he'd picked up from the building site. The last thing he needed now was 'MACHINE GUN PHONEY VICAR IN POLICE CHASE'. He already had more to deal with than he even wanted to contemplate.

As they approached the car park, Ben saw the black Audi S6 performance saloon sitting empty next to Roberta's rental Vauxhall. He reached in his trouser pocket and, gingerly against his bruised thigh, drew out the Audi ignition key he'd taken from the shooter he'd knocked out. He pressed the key's remote button and wasn't surprised when its central locking system clunked open with a bleep and a flash of indicators. The gunmen were as well equipped for travel as for killing.

'Better get your stuff out of there,' he said, pointing at the back window of the rental, to where Roberta's small travel bag was sitting on the rear seat. 'We have to ditch your Vauxhall.'

She frowned. 'You figure that's how they tracked me all the way out here?'

'Did you stop for fuel on the way? Pay by credit card?' he asked her.

'I was running on fumes by the time I reached Oxfordshire. Had to stop at the filling station just before the village. Didn't have any UK currency on me. How was I supposed to know they could follow my movements?'

Ben didn't reply. The implications were as deeply worrying as they were far-reaching. They were sinking in for Roberta too. 'What you're saying, it'd mean—'

He nodded, and finished the sentence for her. 'That whoever these new friends of yours are, they're considerably more organised and deeper inside the system than the charming bunch who were trying to kill you before. You certainly pick them.'

'I didn't pick anyone. I've done nothing wrong.'

'Someone seems to think otherwise.'

'But who? Who?'

'They,' he said. 'You said it yourself, *they* don't want anyone to know who they are. All I know is, this is going to make last time look like a cakewalk.'

'You always did have that reassuring way about you,' she muttered as she unlocked the Vauxhall to get her travel bag.

'Leave the key in it,' he told her.

Reluctantly, she tossed the key on the front seat and slammed the door. 'The rental company will totally blacklist me, not that it matters right now.'

'Join the club,' Ben said. He'd long ago stopped keeping count of the number of hire cars that had been crashed, burned or shot to pieces while in his charge. Theologians shouldn't have these problems. 'Now, give me your phone, please.'

'My phone?' she said guardedly. 'What do you want it for?'

'Just give it here,' he said, holding out a hand. She hesitated, then slipped a BlackBerry out of her pocket and passed it over. Without a word, he dropped it on the concrete at his feet, dashed it to pieces with the heel of his shoe and kicked the plastic fragments into the bushes.

'You sonofabitch, that's the second time you've done that to me. Now I've got no phone!'

'And now there's one way fewer of tracking your movements,' he said.

'Bullshit. Nobody can track a cellphone without an official warrant.'

'Ho, ho. You say *I'm* talking bullshit?' He walked up to the Audi and yanked open the driver's door. He wasn't expecting to find any clues inside the vehicle as to the gunmen's identities or who they worked for, but the car itself would do to get out of here before whoever they were sent in reinforcements to finish the job. He tossed the wrapped-up gun on the back seat. 'Let's move.'

It was almost two o'clock when Ben turned the powerful car in through the vicarage gates and rasped to a halt on the gravel. Roberta had gone very quiet. 'You all right?' he said, laying a hand on her arm. Her muscles felt hard and tense. She gave a quick nod. Pointed at the dusty Suzuki four-wheel drive that was parked in front of the vicarage. 'Someone's here.'

Ben had already noticed it. The Grand Vitara's rear hatch was open a foot and tied down with a strap. A huge rolled-up Persian rug was protruding a yard from the gap.

Brooke's car. Normally the sight of it, and the anticipation of seeing her again, would have made him break into a smile. Now it was different. Now he had to try to figure out what he was going to say to her, and it wasn't going to be easy for either of them. He swallowed, gripped the steering wheel for a moment, then murmured 'Fuck it' and swung open the Audi's driver's door.

'You want me to stay out?' Roberta asked, seeing the troubled look on his face.

'I'm not leaving you on your own.'

They crossed the yard to the front door and Ben let them inside. The sound of intense jazz fusion and cheerful conversation were wafting down the hallway from the half-open kitchen doorway, together with the smell of fresh coffee. The track playing was 'Miles Runs the Voodoo Down', Jude's favourite from the *Bitches Brew* album Ben had introduced him to. The voices were Jude's and Brooke's. Ben couldn't make out what they were talking about.

'I'll hang back here,' Roberta whispered in the hallway, nudging him.

Ben took a deep breath, walked to the kitchen door and stepped silently through it. Neither of the room's occupants sensed him come in.

Brooke was standing with her back to the door and her auburn hair lit up by the sunshine from the window. She was wearing faded jeans and a light cotton top and holding a mug of coffee in her hand.

'I didn't have the heart to tell Amal that a rug that size is never going to fit in the house in Jericho,' she was saying. 'It's large enough for a palace. So sweet of him to get it for us, though.'

'Those things cost a bomb,' Jude said. 'I thought Amal was this struggling writer whose plays nobody wants to see.'

'He is,' Brooke laughed. 'Where all the money comes from is anyone's—'

She broke off mid-sentence as Ben walked further into the room, and turned towards him with a beaming smile.

'Ben! I was just telling Jude about the amazing rug that Amal's bought for us . . .' She suddenly interrupted herself. 'Why are you dressed like that?'

Ben walked over to the CD player on the kitchen surface and turned off the music, plunging the room into sudden silence. 'Brooke,' he said. 'We need to talk.'

She set her mug down on the table and took a step towards

him, alarmed by the gravity of his expression. 'What? Ben — what's up? You're scaring me.'

'Things may have to be put off for a while,' he told her.

'Things?' She groaned. 'Oh, no. Don't tell me there's a problem with your course.'

'I'm not talking about the course,' he said.

'Then what?' Her eyes suddenly widened. 'The wedding rehearsal? The booking's fallen through?'

'Nothing's fallen through,' Ben said. 'But we have to call it off. And . . .'

'*What?!*' Jude exploded.

Brooke looked as if she'd been punched. 'And?' was all she could blurt out.

Ben said nothing. Hoped that the look in his eyes would tell her what he couldn't bring himself to come out with.

Her face paled. 'Surely you don't mean . . . you don't mean the wedding too?' she said in a low, trembling voice. 'Call off the wedding?'

'I'm sorry,' Ben said. 'I have to leave. I can't say when I'll be back.'

'What are you on about?' Jude burst out. 'Are you taking the piss?'

'Back from where?' Brooke asked. She sounded stunned, breathless.

'I don't know yet, not exactly,' he said. 'I just know I can't stay here.'

'But *why?*' she pleaded.

Jude had stepped closer to stand at Brooke's elbow, staring at Ben in dismay with his arms folded.

'Jude, would you excuse us for a moment?' Ben said.

'Excuse you?' Jude answered.

'I'd like to be alone with her,' Ben said. 'So get out.'

Brooke held up a hand. 'No. I want Jude to hear this too.'

'Fuck, yeah,' Jude said. 'I'm staying right here. This is my house, remember.'

'Fine,' Ben said, trying to stay calm. 'Let's all talk.'

'What's this about, Ben?' Brooke asked coldly.

'I don't even know what it's about,' Ben said. 'All I know is that something's cropped up and I have to leave right away. There's no choice.'

Brooke had her hands on her hips and her face was flushed. 'No choice!' she yelled. 'Ben! Have you gone mad? You *made* a choice! You chose to marry me – now you're saying you want to run off again without a word of explanation? What am I going to say to everyone? "Oh, Ben just decided to go off for a few days?".'

Ben was about to answer when he heard a light, hesitant tap on the kitchen door behind him.

'Who else is here?' Brooke said, looking past his shoulder with a frown. Her face went dark as Roberta walked into the kitchen. 'Ah. Now I think I know what "cropped up",' she seethed at Ben, pointing at Roberta. 'Her. Am I right?'

'You must be Brooke,' Roberta said, approaching her with an uncertain smile. 'I'm Roberta Ryder. Listen, I don't want to be the cause of any dispute between—'

'I know who you are,' Brooke interrupted. 'Ben doesn't like to talk about you. Now I'm wondering why.'

'Roberta needs my help,' Ben said.

'And where the hell did she come from all of a sudden?' Brooke demanded.'

'Canada,' Roberta said. 'By way of Paris. I—'

Brooke rounded on her. 'Do you mind shutting up for a moment while I speak to my fiancé?' Then, turning back to face Ben: 'And so you're just walking out on me?'

'It's not as if I want to.'

'But you're going to all the same.'

'Ben,' Roberta said, touching his shoulder. 'It's okay. I understand. You don't have to do this.'

'I'm involved now,' Ben said, keeping his eyes on Brooke. 'I can't just back out.'

Jude was shaking his head in consternation, staring at Ben as if to say 'what is the matter with you?'.

'Maybe I was dreaming,' Brooke said, tight-lipped, 'Or maybe I was delirious from fever. But I remember very clearly how, that day in the middle of the jungle when you asked me to marry you, you swore to me that there'd be no more of this running off on these insane adventures and scaring the shit out of me all the time, not knowing if you're going to come back in one piece.' Her tone began to rise. 'Didn't you make that promise to me, Ben? All about how you were going to change your ways? Telling me all you wanted was to be at home with me?'

'You didn't dream it,' he replied. 'You weren't delirious either. I did say those things. And I meant every word.'

'You mean you meant them then. But you don't mean them now.'

'Try to understand,' he reasoned. 'Roberta's in danger. Look at me. Look at her. She needs my help.'

'Well, I'm sorry if Roberta's in trouble,' Brooke burst out. 'We all have our problems. Why does this have to become mine? Why does it have to be you? Is there no other man in the world who can help her?' She turned furiously to Roberta. 'What are you doing, you stupid bloody bitch?' she yelled in a voice close to breaking. 'Why can't you stay out of our lives?'

Roberta looked down at the floor and didn't reply.

'It's not her fault,' Ben said. 'She's got mixed up in this thing, and now I'm mixed up in it too. Brooke, please listen to me.' He looked to Jude for support. 'Come on, back me up here. Talk to her.'

Jude scowled at him. 'Hey, *Dad*, it's your problem.'

Chapter Ten

There was a long, palpable silence in the room. Brooke and Roberta both stared at Jude, then at Ben.

'Oh, shit,' Jude murmured, turning a few shades paler as he realised what he'd let slip.

'What – did – you – just – say?' Brooke asked him slowly.

'Nothing,' Jude stammered.

Ben's blood had frozen into ice crystals. He'd forgotten to breathe.

'Yes, you did, Jude,' Brooke insisted. 'You said "Dad".'

Jude looked as if he wanted to run to the window and jump out. 'It's just, you know. A figure of speech. Like "daddyo". The way he's dressed. Er, or something.' At that point Jude decided to clamp his mouth shut.

Brooke turned to Ben. 'Why did he call you that? Why?'

The ice in Ben's veins turned into molten lava and he felt his face flush. He took a deep breath and said, 'He's my son, Brooke.'

'I thought there was something,' Roberta murmured, glancing wryly back and forth at the two men.

Brooke seemed to sag as if the air had been sucked out of her. She moved across to a stool by the breakfast bar and sat down heavily on it. She couldn't speak.

'Sorry, guys. It just slipped out,' Jude mumbled. 'We only

found out about it at Christmas,' he added for Brooke's benefit, as if that would help.

It took a few moments before Brooke had got her breath back. 'Would you mind leaving us alone now, please?' she said softly, looking up at Roberta. 'Jude? Ben and I need to talk alone.'

'That's what I wanted in the first place,' Ben muttered, shooting an angry look at Jude. Ashen-faced, the young man left the room without a word. Roberta glanced nervously at Ben, then followed Jude out of the door and closed it softly behind her.

Then Ben and Brooke were alone in the silence of the kitchen. She sank deep into agitated thought, wringing her hands. Her long, slim fingers were shaking.

'Were you ever going to tell me?' she asked him at last, just above a whisper.

'I was trying to find the right moment,' Ben said. 'It never seemed to come. This wasn't it either.'

'Don't you trust me? Have you no idea how hurtful this is? To be told something like that, in front of a stranger? You must have had a million opportunities—'

'I didn't know how you'd take it,' Ben said. 'I'm still trying to come to terms with it myself. I should have told you. I was wrong to hold it back for so long. What can I say? I'm deeply sorry.'

'Oh, Ben,' she said, looking at him through teary eyes. She seemed about to burst out weeping again, but then she wiped the tears away and her face tightened. He could see a million thoughts racing through her mind. When she spoke again, the cold, simmering rage had returned to her voice. 'Let me get this right. First there's this old girlfriend of yours who suddenly turns up virtually on the eve of our wedding and seems to have the power to mesmerise you away, just like that . . .'

Ben wanted to protest, but he kept grimly quiet.

'Now I find out that you had a grown-up son you never told me about,' she went on. 'Tell me, Ben. What other secrets do I get to find out about the man I was about to marry?'

'That's all there is, I promise.'

'Huh,' she snorted. 'There we go. Another promise waiting to be broken. Are you even going to tell me where you're going, or is that a secret too?'

'I haven't had time to think about that.'

'Enough time to decide to break off the wedding, though! Didn't take much to make your mind up about *that*, did it? I'm sure that part was easy for you.'

'I'm not breaking off anything, goddamn it,' he said, feeling frustration and anger welling up inside him. He didn't want to shout. All he wanted was to hold her. He took a step closer to her, reaching out his arms. 'Brooke—'

'Don't you come near me. Don't touch me.'

He pulled back. His arms dropped helplessly by his sides. 'You have to understand,' he urged her. 'You have to let me deal with this in my own way. Trust me, Roberta *is* in danger. Someone's trying to kill her. They almost managed.'

'And so you're going to go off and get yourself killed along with her?' Brooke burst out. 'I'm sorry if that sounds harsh. But I don't even know this woman.'

'You want me to go and tell her she's on her own?' Ben hissed, stabbing a pointing finger towards the closed door. 'You want me to just leave her to the wolves after she came to me for help? I can't do that, Brooke. I couldn't live with myself.' He paused, trying desperately to calm himself. 'Listen. I'll come back to you. You know I will. Soon, before you know it. Then we'll just pick up where we left off, and things will go back to the way they—'

'Until the next time you go off again,' she interrupted. 'And then the next time after that, and the next, until one day you won't come back, because you'll be lying dead somewhere.' Tears were streaming down her face. 'You've cheated me, Ben. You've lied to me.'

'No. I never lied to you.'

'You're lying to yourself too,' she sobbed angrily. 'This whole thing, you going back to your Theology, all the future plans you talked about, this whole new life that you say you want so much and want me to share with you. It's nothing but bullshit. *This* is who you are, this running off and getting into trouble. Risk, danger. You draw it to you like a magnet; you thrive on it. Can't you see? You love it, deep down. More than you could ever love me. Or your newfound son, for that matter.'

'You're wrong about me,' he said.

'Then show me I'm wrong. Prove it to me by dropping this whole awful idea, and staying here with me like you promised.'

He shook his head firmly. 'I can't. I'm sorry, but that's final.'

Brooke took a moment to digest his words. She swallowed, then nodded. 'Fine,' she whispered. 'Go. Go and help your friend. Do whatever you think you have to do. But when it's done, don't bother coming back. Because I won't be here waiting for you.'

He stared at her. 'What?'

The tears were gone now, and she was looking at him earnestly and levelly. 'I can't live like this,' she said. 'You walk away now, it's over between us. Your choice, Ben.'

Chapter Eleven

Roberta had to clutch the passenger door handle as Ben skidded the Audi ferociously out of the vicarage gates and rammed the accelerator to the floor, speeding away through the village. His face was drawn, and his narrowed blue eyes had taken on that steely look she recalled from years ago. He'd changed back into his own clothes, black jeans and T-shirt and the scuffed, well-travelled brown leather jacket that Roberta remembered too. Watching him, it seemed to her that the old Ben Hope she knew so well hadn't been buried too deeply underneath the new one. The old one felt more real to her, but she sensed he was a man Ben would sooner leave behind. *It's just who you are*, she thought. *You can't repress it, and you know it.*

He yanked his crumpled Gauloises pack from his pocket, flipped out a cigarette, and without taking his eyes off the road, bathed its tip in the flame of his Zippo lighter. The acrid smoke reached Roberta's nose and she gave a little cough. Ben shot her an impatient sideways glance, hit the window button and the glass wound down to fill the car with a roar of warm wind, blasting the smoke away.

'You didn't have to do this,' she began.

He held up a hand. 'Please, Roberta. Don't say anything.'

'How can I not say anything? I just watched your life fall apart. I'm not completely insensitive, you know.'

Ben made no reply and drove faster. They quickly left Little Denton behind them, racing along the country roads. After a few minutes Roberta was about to ask where they were going, when a sign flashed by saying 'EYNSHAM' and Ben slowed the car to enter a small town. The streets were narrow and lined with Cotswold stone houses, traditional pubs and little shops. Ben pulled into a small square next to a church, parked the Audi between a van and a stone wall and killed the engine.

'We're going to church?' she asked.

'No,' he said, 'we're getting a bus.' He pointed at the stop across the street, where a line of people were waiting and gazing expectantly up the road at the approaching double-decker. Ben got out of the car, snatched his cement bag bundle from the back seat, waited for Roberta to retrieve her travel holdall and then bleeped the locks before tossing the car key into the nearest drain. As they crossed the street to join the bus queue, he glanced back to make sure the Audi was well tucked away out of sight.

Boarding the bus, Ben led Roberta to the back, from where he could glance now and then out of the dusty rear window in case anyone was following them. Nobody was, and with a loaded machine gun bundled up at his side and his head in his hands he soon settled into a heavy, pensive silence that lasted for the whole twenty-minute trip through the winding country roads into Oxford.

Gazing around her at the bustling city for the second time that day, Roberta didn't try to make conversation. From the noisy, smoky Gloucester Green station they took a second bus, hot and crowded, out to Jericho in the west of the city. A short walk from the stop in Walton Street, then Ben halted outside a modestly-sized Victorian terraced house with a little garden. He swung open the creaky front gate, took a set of keys from his pocket and showed Roberta into the house. 'You'll have to excuse the mess, but we hadn't finished unpacking.'

'Nice,' she said, gazing around her at the clutter that filled the entrance hall. A dining table stood propped up against the wall, swaddled in bubble wrap with the legs removed. Most of the boxes were still sealed with parcel tape, others were open to reveal stacks of books on theology, philosophy and history. Roberta picked one out. 'Hmm. *Augustine: The City of God against the Pagans.* A little light bedtime reading for you?

Ben pointed down the long, narrow hall. 'Kitchen's that way if you want to get yourself a drink. I'll be back in a minute.'

Leaving her to her own devices, he ran up the stairs to the bedroom with his bundle under his arm. His pace faltered as he approached the door. Walking into the room, it was as if a dead weight had settled on his shoulders. Everything around him made him think of Brooke – the fine art prints that had hung on her walls in Richmond, her clothes and shoes neatly arrayed inside her wardrobe, the cushions on the bed, the green foliage of her beloved pot plants spilling down the wall from the windowsill, the soft smell of her perfume already imbued into the fabric of the place. He wanted to picture her smile, but all he could see in his mind was the teary look of hurt and anger that had been on her face when he'd turned and walked away.

When would he see her again? Emotions flashed up inside him: sorrow, guilt, anger, resentment against what had happened, against Roberta Ryder for bringing it on him.

No. It wasn't fair to blame her. He just had to see this

through. Everything would be all right, he told himself uncertainly.

He chucked the bundled-up Beretta machine carbine onto the bed. Nearby stood a small antique bookcase that Brooke had been gradually filling from a half-unpacked box. His eye drawn to the row of titles on the shelf, Ben spotted a familiar leather-bound spine among her assorted paperbacks and psychology textbooks. He wistfully paused to take it off the shelf. It was the volume of Milton's works given to him by Jude's mother shortly before she and Simeon had been murdered. Inside it had been the fateful letter telling Ben the secret of Jude's real paternity.

As Ben turned the book over in his hands, it fell open and he found himself staring at the first page of *Paradise Lost*.

Paradise Lost. He thought about that for a moment, then snapped the book shut and quickly replaced it on the shelf. He walked across to his own wardrobe, wrenched open the door and found his old green canvas army bag where he'd carelessly stuffed it into the back underneath a load of stuff, thinking he'd never need it again. You got that wrong, he thought as he dug it out and tossed it on the bed. The first thing to go inside was the gun, which was compact enough to fit without bits poking incriminatingly out of the green canvas. He began rummaging through drawers and boxes for items of spare clothing.

When he'd done packing, he strapped up the bag, slung it over his shoulder and said a quick, silent goodbye to the room. When he'd be back was anybody's guess.

Downstairs, he found Roberta wandering around the semi-furnished rooms and looking agitated. 'You want something to eat?' he asked her. 'There isn't much in the house. We've been living on takeaways and eating out until we got settled.' The last word stabbed him as he said it.

She shook her head with a frown. 'I'm not hungry.'

'Me neither,' he said.

'I've been thinking. We're heading back to Paris, right? Makes sense.'

'That's where this thing started,' he said. 'I aim to get there as quickly as possible.'

'But how's that going to work?' she went on anxiously. 'If these sons of bitches can pinpoint my exact location in some backwoods Oxfordshire village, just like that out of all the places I could've turned up, it means they've got access to Christ knows what kind of information. They've got to be hooked into every database out there. Which means that the moment I step over the Channel into France, they'll know right where to find me. There's no way I can travel unnoticed, is there?' She eyed the green bag hanging heavily from his shoulder. 'And if you've got what I think you've got in there, it's not something you can exactly sneak by the customs officials.'

'There are ways we can get across undetected.'

Roberta looked sceptical. 'If you're thinking of swimming the Channel, think again. I can't swim. Or maybe you were planning on stealing a rowboat?'

'Not exactly,' he replied, deep in thought. He glanced at his Omega diver's watch. Its skeletonised hands read 3.17. 'Might just about do it,' he murmured, more to himself than to Roberta.

'Might just about do what?'

Ben didn't reply. Leaving Roberta looking mystified, he took out his phone and quickly punched in a number that was extremely familiar to him.

Jeff Dekker picked up after two rings. 'Le Val Tactical Training Centre.'

'It's me.'

'Thought you'd still be rehearsing for your rehearsal about now,' Jeff replied. Ben could hear the smile in his tone of voice.

'That's one reason I'm calling,' Ben said. 'Don't bother coming over to England tomorrow.'

'Why's that, mate? You found a better best man to walk you up the aisle?' The smile was still there. Jeff thought Ben was kidding.

'I'm serious,' Ben said. 'It's off, Jeff. The whole thing's off. Long story.'

Jeff seemed about to burst out into the reaction of amazement, stupefaction, outright disbelief or a combination of all three that Ben had been expecting – but something in Ben's voice made him stop. 'You want to talk about it, mate?' he asked quietly.

'No, I don't.' Ben said. He hadn't called to pour his heart out. The second and more important reason for the call was to ask a question. 'Listen, Jeff, the old landing strip near Valognes. Driven out that way in the last couple of weeks or so?' The year before, they'd toyed with buying the disused airfield to convert into a civilian rifle range but then dropped the project as the location was too far from Le Val.

'I passed there last Tuesday,' Jeff replied, sounding bemused.

'So you'd have noticed if anyone had dug it all up or parked a load of artic trailers on it.'

'Far as I could see, it's just the way it was. What the fuck d'you want to know for?'

'One more thing,' Ben said. 'If I needed the Alpina for a couple of days, could you get Raoul or Paul to leave it there for me?' Raoul de la Vega and Paul Bonnard were the two ex-military trainers who worked as assistant tutors at Le Val. The Alpina was a high-performance BMW 7 Series used as a demonstrator for the bodyguard defensive driving courses taught at the facility, called VIP Evasion / Reaction, VIPER for short.

'Shouldn't be a problem. But what—?'

'Thanks, Jeff. I'll be in touch.' Before his friend could say anything more, he ended the call.

'Who're you phoning now?' Roberta asked as Ben immediately started stabbing in another number.

'My sister,' he replied.

She stared at him. '*You* have a sister?'

'That's another long story,' Ben said. It always seemed so strange to him that Ruth was only a call away. For so many years, she'd seemed to have been lost forever. From child kidnap victim to adopted daughter of a billionaire tycoon – whose business empire she now ran like she'd been doing it all her life – Ruth had walked a strange path, almost as strange as her elder sibling's.

'Well, hello, big brother,' her voice chirped on the line.

'Where are you?' Ben asked.

'Nice,' she said acerbically. 'The customary greeting. No "Hi, Ruth, how are things? How's your life?" All I get is "Where are you?". As it happens, I'm on my way over to you right now. We'll be touching down at London Oxford Airport in just under . . . let's see, say thirty minutes.' Her tone changed suddenly as excitement bubbled through. 'You know, Ben, I can't tell you how much I'm looking forward to this. Seeing you and Brooke getting hitched at last—'

'What plane are you coming on?' Ben cut in, interrupting her. As CEO of Steiner Industries, the mega-corporation Ruth had inherited from her adoptive father, the Swiss billionaire Maximilian Steiner, she had the pick of one of the biggest corporate fleets of aircraft in Europe.

'Wow, you are in a chatty mood, bro. Since you ask, I'm

using my favourite little runaround, the new Steiner Industries ST-1 turboprop. We do lead the way in promoting eco-friendly aviation, as I may have told you before.'

'No more than ten or twenty times,' he said. 'What's the LDR for that aircraft?'

'Landing distance required?' she replied, sounding perplexed by the question. 'Uh, minimum eighteen hundred and forty feet.' Even as a young child, Ruth had always been sharp when it came to numbers, and few things escaped her. 'But why do you want to know?'

'Range?'

'Over seventeen hundred nautical miles all fuelled up, which we were when we left Zurich. Ben, if you don't mind my saying so, you're sounding just a little bit weird. Something's wrong.'

'I don't have a lot of time to explain, Ruth, so I'll make this quick. The wedding's off. And I need to borrow your plane.'

Chapter Twelve

Forty-three minutes later, Ben and Roberta were walking across the tarmac at Oxford London airport in Kidlington towards a sleek twin-engined light aircraft that sat by a private hangar. The afternoon sun sparkled off the small aircraft's pearly-white fuselage.

'Not bad, is she?' said a familiar voice, and Ben turned to see his sister emerging from the hangar. She was casually dressed and her hair, the same exact shade of blond as his own, was tied back under a baseball cap. Not quite the image of the corporate CEO. She was known for attending high-level conferences in faded jeans and combat boots. Business bosses from New York to Tokyo just had to get used to it.

Ruth patted the plane's gleaming flank with pride. 'Prototype design. Under eleven metres from nose to tail, thirteen from wingtip to wingtip, more than twenty per cent more fuel-efficient than anything in her class, with emissions to match and almost totally made of recycled materials.'

'Still trying to save the world,' Ben said, embracing her.

'Beats trying to blow it up,' she replied, hugging him tightly. In her former radical wild-child days she might have been here to firebomb the aircraft instead of as its corporate owner.

'I'm sorry you wasted a trip,' Ben said. 'But it's good to see you. You're looking well, Ruth.'

She took a step away from him, tightly clutching both his hands and eyeing him with concern. 'Wish I could say the same about you, bro. You look awful. You've got to tell me what happened between you and Brooke. Did you two fight?'

'This is Roberta,' Ben said, evading the question, and to avoid raising more of them he added, 'She's a friend of mine from long ago. Now, listen, I hate to press you, but we really need to get underway.'

Ruth greeted Roberta with a brief, slightly perplexed smile, then turned back to Ben with a jerk of her head that said, 'Can we have a word in private?'. Leading him a few steps away, she paused under the roar of a departing light passenger jet and then asked Ben straight out: 'Are you walking out on Brooke for *her*? Is that what's going on? Because if it is, I'm not sure how comfortable I am about getting drawn into it like this. Brooke's a friend to me.'

'It's not what you think,' Ben said, making an effort to hide the pain he was feeling. 'Like I told you, she's just a friend. She's in a bit of trouble, and she needs my help.'

'And what about Brooke?'

'Brooke and I will work things out,' Ben said evenly, sounding far more confident than he really was. 'Ruth, are you going to let me use the plane or not?'

Ruth paused for a moment, then sighed and waved an arm at the aircraft. 'Whatever. She's all yours. Don't you have any more luggage than that?'

'Just what you see,' he said, hoping she wouldn't start asking questions about what was in his bag.

Waiting at the hangar entrance was a young guy with unkempt hair, a smattering of a beard and a ring in his ear – the kind of eco-hippy type that Steiner Industries employed these days under Ruth's direction. 'That handsome fellow there is Dylan,' she explained. 'He's one of the best pilots we have.'

Ben looked at her. 'Your pilot's name is Dylan.'

She shrugged. 'Sure. And he plays the guitar, too.'

'He needs a shave.'

'Believe me, you're in good hands. He'll take you wherever you want to go. You've got enough gas to take you halfway around Europe and back again.'

'We're not going that far,' Ben said. By his estimate their journey distance was just under 140 nautical miles, a mere hop and a skip for the high-tech turboprop. 'And you can hang on to Dylan. I won't be needing him.'

'Then who's going to fly the—?' Ruth blanched. 'No, no. Please don't tell me what I think you're going to say. I like this plane, Ben. Not to mention it's worth the same as a Lamborghini Reventon.'

'If I smash it up, you can get your accounts department to invoice me,' Ben said, stepping towards the plane. 'I really appreciate this, Ruth.'

'I must be crazy.'

'It runs in the family,' Ben said.

A few moments later, he was seated behind the cockpit controls, running an eye across the panels of dials and read-outs and the extensive array of high-tech computer wizardry as Roberta explored the rear section with its plush eco-friendly non-leather seating for four or five passengers to travel in style. 'Pretty neat,' she commented, opening a door and peering at a little bathroom. 'We've got food and drinks on board, too. I'll admit, I hadn't expected travelling with you would be this luxurious.'

'Don't get too used to it,' he said.

Outside, Ruth and her companions had retreated to the hangar. A couple of runway attendants in reflective vests and ear-defenders had appeared to shepherd the aircraft as it prepared for take-off. Ben fired up the engines and the twin propellers began to spin with a whine that quickly grew to a roar, muffled inside the well-insulated cabin.

'I didn't know you could fly one of these things,' Roberta said from the rear, strapping herself into a seat by one of the oval porthole windows.

'Well, I'd be lying if I said I'd ever actually flown one of *these* before,' he replied, waiting for the props to get up to speed. This state-of-the-art plane was a different animal by far from the last aircraft he'd piloted – a prehistoric Supermarine Sea Otter loaded with drums of avgas that he'd deliberately crashed onto the deck of a sailing yacht like a flying incendiary bomb, blowing the aircraft, the vessel and its contingent of thugs to kingdom come. He didn't think Roberta would appreciate those details.

'You *what?*'

'But the basic principle's the same for all these kinds of things,' he said. 'Trust me, it's like riding a bicycle.'

'Maybe I should've taken my chances with the bad guys,' Roberta muttered to herself.

The Steiner ST-1 taxied away under the anxious gaze of its owner, picked up speed and left the runway smartly to climb into the hazy afternoon sky. Content that he wasn't going to drop them down somewhere in the English countryside or into the Channel, Ben levelled the aircraft at 285 knots and a cruise altitude of 24,000 feet, settled back in the pilot's seat and set his course for Normandy.

After just twenty-five uneventful minutes in the air, Ben checked his bearings, reduced altitude and caught sight of the northernmost tip of the Lower Normandy coast far below. The aircraft overflew the Pointe de Barfleur and the towering Gatteville lighthouse, just a tiny grey needle sticking up from the rocks surrounded by calm blue sea.

Remaining steady on his course for another few minutes as they passed over Saint-Vaast and then the spreading outskirts of Valognes, the nearest town of any size to the Le Val facility, Ben gradually let the plane drop down lower on the approach to his target, the small disused airfield in the countryside a few kilometres outside Carentan. As the small tongue of concrete surrounded by green fields grew larger and details came into view, he was relieved to see that Jeff Dekker had been right about the place not having changed since the last time he'd seen it.

He checked his instruments, made his final adjustments. Flaps; undercarriage; speed; altitude: everything was in order, or as close to it as need be. The Steiner ST-1 swooped in low over the rickety barbed-wire fence, the disused buildings and the graffiti-covered hangar where local kids loitered to smoke dope, and touched down with a yelp of tyres. Ben instantly eased off the throttle and the plane decelerated on the bumpy strip, rolling to a standstill forty yards short of the sunburned grass beyond. The engine whine died away and the prop came to a halt. Ben pulled off his headset, quickly reset his Omega to French time, then pressed the control to activate the hydraulics for the aircraft's side hatch.

'Well, I must say, that came in pretty handy,' Roberta commented as she stepped down to the cracked concrete. 'Remind me to put one of these gizmos on my Christmas list.'

Ben used a remote button to close the hatch and set the locks and alarms on the aircraft. The late afternoon was warmer than England. The soft breeze smelled of cut grass and was filled with the chirping of crickets. He looked around and quickly saw that Jeff, trustworthy as ever, had delivered on his promise. The dark blue Alpina B7 was sitting on the stubbly yellowed grass a little way from the landing strip.

'That our ride?' Roberta asked, walking over, and Ben nodded. 'No key in it,' she observed, peering through the driver's window.

'Who needs keys?' Ben stepped up to the door and said the word, 'Open'. His voice was one of the four programmed into the car's sophisticated voice recognition locking system. The locks opened with a clunk and Ben popped the boot lid. Underneath the floor of the boot was a special armoured compartment that VIP close protection personnel could use, where necessary, to carry concealed weapons and other sensitive equipment through border checkpoints. Ben quickly removed the Beretta Storm from his bag and stowed it snugly inside the hidden space, then piled their bags on top.

He climbed behind the wheel. It had been a little while since he'd last driven the Alpina, but the familiar whiff of Gauloises was still faintly detectable inside. There was even one of his old John Coltrane CDs nestling in the map compartment. The Le Val high-speed evasion car felt uncomfortably like home.

Ben said, 'Start'. The Alpina's tuned engine instantly burbled into life.

Roberta raised an eyebrow. 'Very cool.'

'Special privilege,' Ben replied. 'Le Val personnel only.'

'Even though you don't work there anymore?' Roberta said. She thought about it for a moment, then added, 'Figures.'

He looked at her. 'What figures?'

'That your friend Jeff didn't delete your voice signature from the menu. He must've reckoned you'd be back before too long.'

Without a reply, Ben put the Alpina into gear and pulled sharply away. Sensing that she'd said the wrong thing, Roberta quickly changed the subject. 'How far to Paris from here?' she asked.

'A little under two hundred miles,' he said.

'Three hours?'

'In this thing, more like two and a half,' he said, and put his foot down.

'That figures too,' Roberta murmured but Ben was too focused to hear.

Chapter Thirteen

The drive to Paris was even quicker than Ben had estimated, and by evening they were filtering through the western approach into the city. He'd been deep in his own thoughts nearly all the way, and was still silent as he negotiated the hectic evening traffic into the centre. As he took a right off Boulevard des Batignolles, heading southwest down Rue de Clichy, Roberta turned to him and said, 'Montmartre is the other direction, to the north.'

'I know where Montmartre is,' he replied. 'We'll take a trip up that way later tonight.'

'So where are we going?'

'Somewhere these friends of yours can't find us,' he said. 'You've been there before.'

'I wish you'd quit calling them that,' she said irritably. 'Then you still have that old place, huh?'

She was talking about the small, simple apartment she and Ben had used as their refuge for two nights the last time they'd been here together. The 'safehouse', as he'd called it, had been a gift from a wealthy client whose child Ben had once rescued from kidnappers. There was no paper trail of ownership linking him to it. It was completely secure and so hard to find, tucked away deep in the architectural honeycomb of central Paris, that virtually nobody even knew it existed.

'Never quite got around to selling it,' Ben said. 'Maybe I was hanging on to some crazy notion that it'd come in handy again one day.'

'Fancy that,' she said.

Ben headed up Boulevard Haussmann, hung another right onto Boulevard des Italiens, and soon afterwards the Alpina swung sharply off the road and dropped down a steep ramp into the dark echoing cavern of the underground car park that was the only way into his hidden apartment.

They grabbed their stuff, left the car in the shadows and Ben led Roberta through the parking lot to the concrete passage and up the familiar murky back stairway. Someone had sprayed graffiti on the armoured door since he'd last been here, but there was no way even the most dedicated burglar could have broken through the plate steel or the reinforced wall.

The safehouse was dark, the blinds drawn over what few small windows it had. Roberta looked around her and sniffed the air as he led her inside. 'Smells kind of . . . uh, closed up,' she said.

'It has been, for a while,' he replied, switching on lights. The luxuries of home were few: a plain desk, an armchair, a no-frills kitchen and bedroom. No decorations, bare floors, no TV. Once upon a time, the safehouse had played a big part in Ben's Europe-wide freelance operations as a kidnap and ransom specialist, as he'd moved constantly from one scrape to another and lived pretty much the same kind of stripped-down, comfortless existence he'd grown accustomed to with the SAS. Now it only stood as a painful reminder of old times he'd thought he'd left far, far behind.

'Hasn't changed a whole lot since I was last here,' she commented. 'Same old neo-Spartan shit pit. But, like you said, it's safe. At least, it better be.'

He glanced at her. He knew she was thinking the same thing he was, feeling the same weird feeling that the two of them should be back here. Even though their stay together had only been for two days and nights, it had been an eventful time that brought back a lot of memories. Tender moments, like his confiscating her phone, making her sleep on the hard floor, and having to shampoo the blood and brains of a dead man out of her hair after she'd been covered in gore during a gunfight on the banks of the Seine. It was shared experiences like that which had cemented their budding relationship.

'You want a drink?' he asked her.

'I could use a shower first,' she said.

'You know where it is,' he said, motioning down the narrow hall towards the bathroom. 'There should be some clean towels.'

'Nothing I should know about? No rats or roaches?'

'Take the gun in with you, if it makes you feel any safer.'

'I'll risk it.'

While Roberta was in the bathroom and he could hear the water pittering and splashing, Ben went into the bedroom, shut the door, sat on the edge of the bed and took out his phone. He turned it on and ran a web search using just the name 'Tesla'. Within moments he was swamped in a welter of scientific and technical hoo-hah that seemed as grandiose as it did improbable.

He switched from text search results to images, and a few seconds later he found himself staring at the face of the man himself. A pinched, lean, chalky-white face with something of Edgar Allan Poe about him, something perhaps a little bit mad. The hair was oiled and parted in the fashion of the 1920s, the little brush moustache trim and neat. The eyes were sharp and foxy and seemed to bore right out of the screen and into Ben's.

'If this is really all about you,' Ben muttered, 'you've got a lot to answer for, pal.'

He gazed at the image a moment longer, knowing he was only procrastinating. This wasn't what he'd taken his phone out for.

He swallowed and quickly keyed in Brooke's number. As he waited for her to reply, he anxiously tried to think of how to express what he wanted to say. *I didn't mean for any of this to happen. Can't we just stop? Can't we just go back to the way things were?* Or just *I love you. I need you. Let me come home, as soon as this is over.*

But there was no simple formula. No backspace key, no erase button. The damage that had been done couldn't be healed with just a few facile words.

Brooke didn't even reply. He aborted the call, strangely relieved but dreading when he'd have to try again.

The pain in his body reminded him of the other damage that needed healing, too. Standing up, he painfully unpeeled his jeans far enough down to inspect the large red weal across his left thigh where the Beretta magazine had absorbed the force of the bullet strike earlier that day. Its oblong shape was almost perfectly imprinted on his skin. He touched it and winced. In a day or two it would blossom into a spectacular bruise and a rainbow of colours.

His right side was pretty tender, too, where he'd taken that particularly solid blow from the man now encased several feet deep in concrete. *I'm getting too old for this bollocks*, he thought as he peeled off his T-shirt to examine his ribs. Another florid, multicolour bruise was on its way there, too, but at least nothing was cracked internally that he could feel.

The bedroom door suddenly opened and he turned to see Roberta standing there.

Chapter Fourteen

She was wrapped in a towel that covered her from chest to mid-thigh and her hair was wet. 'Sorry,' she blurted. 'I was looking for a hairbrush. Forgot to pack mine.'

'I don't have one,' Ben said. It was impossible not to notice the gleam of her well-toned flesh, or the way her hair lay across her bare shoulder.

Her eyes flicked downwards for an instant. 'You've got scars that weren't there before,' she said.

'I suppose I do,' he said, glancing down. His torso read like a map of his exploits over twenty years.

'Jesus. I thought you said you were lucky with bullets.'

'That one wasn't a bullet,' he said. 'It was a knife. Those ones are bullets.'

'Oh.'

'The drugstore on the corner will have a hairbrush we can buy,' he said.

'I guess,' she replied. 'Anyway, shower's free if you want it.' After an awkward silence, she slipped away and shut the door.

Ben spent three minutes under the shower, letting the hot water blast away his thoughts as best they could. He emerged from the bathroom in fresh clothes and, feeling suddenly ravenous, headed into the safehouse's tiny kitchen to prepare some dinner. The worktops were lined with dust, and when he opened the fridge door he discovered that a bottle of milk had solidified into something way beyond cheese. He closed it quickly, opened a cupboard and grabbed two of the stacked tins inside, a pack of ground Lavazza coffee and a bottle of cheap red table wine that he'd forgotten he'd had left over from the old days, and was relieved to find. He hunted a can opener and corkscrew out of a drawer.

'I see you're still working your way through the same old store of canned cassoulet,' Roberta observed as she wandered through into the kitchen, slumped on one of the two plain chairs by the small table and watched him empty the contents of the tins into a saucepan over the gas stove. Her hair was towelled dry and frizzy.

'Lasts as long as tinned corned beef and tastes a lot better,' he said, stirring the saucepan.

'Oh sure, lumpy beans and overcooked sausage stewed in goose lard would be anyone's idea of a treat, come the apocalypse. But as long as I can wash it down with some of that wine, I don't give a rat's ass.'

He uncorked the bottle, poured out two brimming glasses and handed her one of them. She gulped half of it down and gasped. 'Goddamn, I needed that.'

Once the cassoulet was steaming hot, Ben ladled it unceremoniously onto a couple of plates and they sat down to eat it with more wine. 'Ah, yes,' she said, forking up some beans, 'there's survival food, then there's gourmet survival food.'

'Coming from an American,' he muttered. 'Get it down you. We're going to be busy later.' He ate in silence for a while, then looked up, aware that she was watching him. 'What?'

'I hate to say it, but this kind of environment suits you a whole lot better than the vicarage did,' she said.

'That's probably just as well, isn't it?' he replied tersely.

'Sorry. It was just an observation. Maybe it didn't come out quite right.'

'So tell me,' he said, keen to change the subject, 'How's life been for you? Apart from getting entangled in God knows what kind of trouble neither of us needed?'

'Life?'

'It's been a long time,' Ben said. 'We haven't been in touch. You must have had some kind of life.'

'Are you asking about guys?'

He shrugged. 'Not specifically.'

'Sure, I had a life. I put my old one behind me, I worked hard at my job, I did some travelling around Canada and the northern states. Then there was Dan. You remember him, I guess? Dan Wright? You saw him, when you came over that one time.'

'He was your colleague at the university in Ottawa,' Ben said. 'You and he were giving a lecture on "effects of weak electromagnetic fields on cell respiration". I didn't know what the hell that meant then, either.'

She raised an eyebrow, forkful of food poised in mid-air. 'My, what a remarkable memory you have, Ben Hope. So you must also recall with perfect clarity what you told me afterwards?'

'I told you I thought a bloke like that could be good for you,' Ben said. 'He seemed like a decent sort. Steady. Dependable. The opposite of me. And I could tell he liked you.'

'Yeah,' she said sourly. 'A few weeks after I last saw you, Dan asked me on a date. I said no. I hadn't . . .' Roberta almost spoke the words that were on the tip of her tongue, 'hadn't got over what happened between you and me', but she managed to cover it up. 'I hadn't any interest in relationships at that point. But months passed, he kept asking, and eventually I said yes and we started dating. It lasted about a year. We talked about moving in together.' She gave a little snort and knocked back the last of her wine. 'Well, you and I both made the same mistake, Ben. The great, decent, dependable Dr Wright turned out to be Dr Wrong. Dead wrong. One evening I went back to the lab to pick up some notes, and I found the sonofabitch giving an extra-curricular one-to-one Biology class to Xandra Mills, one of his more alluring final-year students. Right there on the desk.'

'Oh,' Ben said. 'What did they do, fire him?'

'You're kidding. That would have drawn *far* too much scandal for the university. He got a speedy transfer to Halifax, Nova Scotia. Or else I don't know how I could have gone on working with the jerk.'

Ben poured the last of the bottle into their empty glasses. 'I'm sorry to hear about all that.'

'Are you?' she asked, cocking her head to one side.

'So hasn't there been anyone else?' he asked.

'You seem very inquisitive about my love life.'

'I've always liked to think that you were happy, that's all.'

She smiled with one corner of her mouth. 'There wasn't anybody after Dan. But I wasn't unhappy. Being alone doesn't have to be a sad thing.'

Ben said nothing, and went back to toying disinterestedly with the last of his food.

'So what about you?'

'What about me?'

'When did you meet her?'

'Brooke?'

'Who else? Was it love at first sight, or what?'

He paused. 'I've known Brooke a long time,' he said quietly and with great reluctance. This wasn't something he wanted to discuss, least of all with Roberta.

'Ah, an old flame.' Roberta couldn't quite hide the acidity in her tone.

'It's not like that. She was a friend, that's all. I knew her back in regiment days. Then she came to work for me at Le Val.'

'She was in the army?'

He shook his head. 'She lectures on hostage psychology.'

'A head shrinker,' Roberta said, and was about to add acerbically, 'She sure shrunk yours,' but held it back.

'You'd like her if you knew her,' Ben said, catching the tone.

'I'm sure we'd get on like a house on fire.'

'I've had enough to eat,' he said abruptly after a long silence, pushing away his plate and looking at his watch. The evening was pressing on and he was suddenly feeling restless. 'I want to look at those figures from Claudine's letter. See if we can make any sense of all this.' He stood up, grabbed their plates and dumped them in the sink.

'I could use some of that coffee, if you were planning on making any,' she said. 'The wine's hitting me a little.'

'It'll have to be black. The milk's gone a bit—'

'I can imagine,' she said. 'Black's just fine. No sugar.'

The old espresso pot bubbled and burbled on the stove, then Ben filled two small cups with a thick, scalding brew that was potent enough to blast away any effects of the wine on their tired minds. He took out his Gauloises and Zippo. 'You mind?'

'If I said I did, would it make a difference?'

'Not really.'

'Those aren't good for you.'

'There are worse things in the world,' Ben said. He lit up, drew the smoke in deeply and felt the quiet, comforting little hit of nicotine take the worst of the edge off his ragged emotions. The two of them sat hunched over the table with the sheet of paper lying between their coffees so they could study those three cryptic lines of code which Roberta had carefully copied from the original.

'You still think that top line is a GPS location?' she asked, tapping it with her finger.

'Let me show you,' he said. He laid the smoking cigarette in the ashtray and slid it to one side. Using a stubby pencil and a fresh sheet of paper from the desk drawer, he copied out the line, '4920N1570E', as it had appeared in Claudine Pommier's letter. He wrote it out again underneath, this time converted into a clearer form:

$$49^{\circ}\ 2'\ 0''\ N\ 1^{\circ}\ 57'\ 0''\ E$$

'Okay,' Roberta said, nodding thoughtfully. 'Looks like you have something there. But this navigational stuff is more your kind of science than mine. I'm at a loss. What does it tell us?'

'Let's find out,' he said, reaching for his phone. He activated the GPS application, punched in the coordinates and the screen instantly flashed up with a little green map of the location.

'Out in the countryside,' he said, showing her. 'Forty kilometres northwest of Paris. The nearest towns are Condécourt and Tessancourt-sur-Aubette. Nothing much within three kilometres except farmland and forest, so we're looking at a fairly remote spot.'

'There's nothing there. It's got to be right, though,'

Roberta said, frowning at the onscreen map. 'Claudine definitely meant for me to see this.'

'Any idea why she'd point you in that direction?'

'None. Unless . . . wait a minute. Yes, it could be. Can we get more detail on that?'

Ben switched from the default map view to a satellite image, then zoomed in as close as he could get. The screen pixellated out into a blur, sharpened up again, and he saw that it was centred on what looked from the aerial view like a large country estate, at its heart a huge sprawling property that could have been a manor house, even a château.

'That's it,' Roberta said, grabbing the phone from him, her eyes fixed to the screen.

'That's what?'

'Fabien's place. She described it to me once.'

Ben stubbed out his cigarette and reached for another. 'The ex-boyfriend? You told me he was a bum.'

'Sure. A very, very rich bum. I guess he's what you call dissolute aristocracy. Only child of Gaston and Nicolette De Bourg, and something of a disappointment to his family, to put it mildly. Claudine said they had all kinds of plans for him, but he was half burned out on booze and pills before the age of thirty and pretty much incapable of holding down any kind of responsible job.'

'Sounds a strange match for a respectable physics professor.'

'I never understood what she saw in him,' Roberta said, shaking her head. 'Never met him, either. But while they were together, she insisted he was a real charmer. A little too much of a charmer, as it turned out, if you know what I mean. Join the club.'

'So our philandering Prince Charming was living on Mummy and Daddy's estate?'

'It was all his, if you can believe it. The parents quit the place and went off to live in South Africa years ago, for the climate and lower taxes. Claudine told me that Fabien lived at the old family home pretty much alone – when he wasn't running blotto around the Riviera with his drinking and gambling cronies, that is.'

Ben gazed pensively at the satellite image. 'The question is why Claudine wanted to show you this, now.'

'I can only think of a single reason. It's a message. If something happened to her, and she believed something might, she needed me to go there.'

'Why? To talk to Fabien?'

'I doubt she'd have involved him in this,' Roberta replied. 'They split up quite a while ago, and I'd be pretty surprised if she'd have let him back in her life anytime soon. No, I think Claudine sent this message because there's something else there for me to find. That is, for *us* to find. Something she hid there, something important. I mean, it's a big place. She could easily have . . . What's the matter? You're pulling a face.'

'I don't much like the idea of walking into this place without any clue what we're looking for. Sounds like a wild goose chase waiting to happen.'

'Then you tell me why the location is in the letter.'

'We don't even know what the rest of the figures mean,' he said. 'I can't make any sense of them either.'

'We'll figure it out as we go. This is something, isn't it? And it's all we have right now.'

He considered. 'Fine. We'll head over to Montmartre and check her place over. From there we drive out to the château. But first, I'm going to brew up another pot of black coffee. Something tells me it's going to be a long night.'

Chapter Fifteen

Whoever was holding the party on the second floor of the apartment building in Rue des Trois Frères obviously wasn't put off by the recent murder that had taken place above. It was a warm, sultry night, and light and music and laughter spilled out of the open balcony windows to mingle with the carefree noise of the crowded café-bar down below.

At the building's entrance, Roberta stared as Ben punched the buttons on the door buzzer system one after another. 'What are you doing?'

'Crashing a party,' he said. Moments later, there was a click and Ben pushed open the little inset door, stepping through into the echoey stone passage that led into the central courtyard. To one side was the concierge's apartment, to the other a set of stairs.

Up and up the bare spiralling steps. The second floor was alive with the clamour of the party, couples drinking and smoking and necking on the stairs and on the landing. Ben and Roberta threaded their way past and climbed upwards, leaving the noisy chatter and music behind them. By the time they reached the top floor, it was quiet and dark.

The L-shaped landing was dimly lit by a pair of iron-barred windows. One overlooked the streets and rooftops of Montmartre and the Sacré Coeur basilica in the distance, glowing like a golden idol from the highest point of the city. The other smaller window less picturesquely opened up onto a side alley and pulsated with the red neon sign of a neighbouring hotel.

There were just two black-painted doors on the top floor, one at each end of the landing. Roberta silently pointed out Claudine's, nearest the neon-lit window. There was no sign of life from behind the other door. Ben imagined that the old woman who had been Claudine's neighbour, and the one who had found her body, was either fast asleep in her bed or else staying with friends or family in the aftermath of the traumatic incident. But still, he didn't want to risk drawing attention.

He unslung his bag, took out his mini-Maglite and discreetly shone it at Claudine's door. The entrance was barricaded with bilingual police tape, as if the citizens of Paris needed to be told in both French and English not to cross the line into a crime scene.

'Maybe this wasn't such a useful idea after all,' Roberta said in a low voice. 'No way we can get in there without a key, and we can't exactly ask the concierge to open the place up for us.'

'But someone did get in there,' Ben said. He reached past the tape and nudged the old door. There was no sign of forced entry. The wood felt thick and solid, and if the many Parisian apartments he'd seen were anything to go by, the inside of the door was festooned from top to bottom with heavy iron deadlocks and bolts – the kind of low-tech security that was almost impossible to crack without using violent force. It still perplexed him that Claudine's killer could have got inside without a crowbar or sledgehammer, especially when his victim was already frightened about her safety and must have had every lock and bolt tightly shut.

'I've been thinking,' Roberta said. 'Maybe he was someone she knew. Or maybe he was pretending to be someone, like a cop. He could have tricked her into opening the door to him.'

Ben stepped across to peer out of the smaller window. The alley pulsed blood-red from the neon hotel sign. He craned his neck upwards, scanned this way and that, then withdrew from the window and thought for a moment or two.

'I don't think she opened the door to anyone,' he said. Before Roberta could reply, he added, 'Wait here,' and turned towards the head of the stairs.

'What? Where are you going?'

'I'll be back in a minute,' he said.

Knowing there was little point in pressing him for an explanation, Roberta reluctantly stayed where she was. She listened to his footsteps padding down the stairs, wondering where he was going all of a sudden, and at the same time thinking how lightly and silently he could move.

After a minute or two she suddenly felt very alone, and as more minutes went by she was beginning to feel resentful towards Ben for leaving her. She didn't understand what his game was, slipping away like that with barely a word. It was typical of him, his whole damn 'I work alone' routine, the infuriating way he had of not telling her what he was thinking. He hadn't changed a bit.

Roberta paced up and down outside Claudine's door and tried to contain her restlessness, but it was no use. Within moments, thoughts of the brutal stalker began to invade her mind. She didn't believe for an instant that he was the psychopathic maniac the police claimed, but the idea of a cold-blooded paid assassin was no less terrifying.

She couldn't stop imagining him standing right here on

this very spot, just days ago, preparing to enter Claudine's apartment and snuff her out as if she were nothing. What kind of monster would do such a thing? Why would anyone slaughter poor Claudine? What harm had she ever done to a living soul? It made Roberta shake with rage and want to cry, all at once.

Another question crept into her mind. Her ingrained scientific instinct screamed out *'Irrational!'*, but her flesh couldn't help but crawl at the idea. *What if the killer came back?*

But there it was, gnawing at her as she waited there in the darkness. What if he was still watching the place, keeping an eye out for anyone who came snooping after clues? Or what if he decided to revisit the scene of his crime, looking for something he might have missed the first time around? And here she was, all alone . . .

She glanced nervously into the long, eerie shadows on the landing and froze, her stomach knotted in fear, suddenly convinced she'd seen a movement there.

Nothing more than her foolish imagination. She breathed. Just then, the unexpected whoop of a car alarm in the street far below made her jump. 'Jesus, Ryder, get it together,' she muttered irritably to herself. The car alarm stopped. She clasped her arms around her and went on pacing, shivering despite the warmth of the night. 'Where the hell are you, Ben?' she said out loud, and hated herself for the worry she could hear in her voice.

The door of Claudine's apartment suddenly swung open with a rattle of the latch chain.

Roberta spun round with a gasp.

A figure stood silhouetted in the doorway.

A man's figure, his face in shadow, looking right at her.

Chapter Sixteen

Roberta backed away. 'Wh-who's that?' she stammered, her voice coming out as a strained croak of fear.

'It's me,' the figure in the doorway said with a touch of irritation. 'Who did you think it was?'

'*Ben?*'

Ben ripped down a few strands of police tape and beckoned. 'Stop making so much noise and come inside.'

'How the hell did you get in here?' she asked, bewildered, as she entered the apartment. Once the door was locked behind them, Ben turned on the lights.

'Same way the killer did.' He pointed upwards. 'Through the roof. There's a skylight panel over the bathroom with its fasteners missing. Glove marks in the dirt on the frame. Either he undid the screws, or someone else did it before him. Whichever it is, the police haven't twigged it. It was a tidy job.'

'But how did you—?'

'The hotel across the alley,' Ben explained. 'It's got an external fire escape, same as this building. From the top floor it's only a five or six foot jump across. Nobody would see you in the dark. At least, nobody saw me.'

She looked at him. 'You're telling me you just leaped

between two buildings, at night, with nothing between you and concrete except a long drop?'

'What about it?' he said blankly.

'You really are nuts, you know that?'

He shrugged as he walked into the apartment's modestly-sized living room. 'So people keep telling me,' he muttered.

'What if you broke your stupid neck?'

'Thanks for caring.'

'Seriously. Where would I be then?'

'Don't fuss. You sound exactly like Winnie. I got you in here, didn't I?'

'Who the hell's Winnie?' she asked, frowning, but he didn't reply as he went over to the window and eased back an edge of the drawn curtain to peer down to the street. He saw no police, and nothing else to worry about, but it wouldn't be wise to hang around here too long. He turned away from the window and ran a practised eye over the details of the crime scene. The place wasn't a great deal larger than his safehouse across town, and it looked exactly like what it was: the cluttered workspace of a busy science academic who had probably spent far too much of her time poring over books and papers. The shelves were crammed tight with hundreds of volumes, box files and folders full to bursting point.

'You said nothing was stolen?' he asked.

Roberta nodded unhappily. 'That's what the cops figured, that he just killed her and left. If that's true, then it must mean her Tesla material was never here.'

'Or that we're up a blind alley with this whole thing,' Ben said silently to himself.

'All the same, now that we're here I have to check.' Roberta hauled down an armful of thick files, laid them on the sofa and started riffling quickly through the papers they contained. 'This is awful,' she sighed as she scanned and discarded one sheet after another. 'I feel like I'm digging up someone's grave.'

Ben's gaze landed on Claudine's cluttered desk. 'Her computer's gone.'

'The cops told me they'd taken it away.' Roberta looked up from the file she was going through. 'Why would they do that?'

'To go through her emails and other files that might throw up a lead to the murderer,' Ben said. It wasn't an unintelligent procedure. Killers often stalked their victims online for weeks, even months, before closing in on them, using the handy information-gathering platform of social media sites to form a profile of their routines and lifestyles in order to plan their attack more efficiently, while posing as 'friends' to harvest yet more useful details from their soon-to-be prey. Bless the internet, manna from heaven to freaks and villains the world over.

In this case, though, Ben had a feeling the cops would hit on no such leads.

He slid open the desk's only drawer and rummaged around inside, finding all the usual things, pens, paper clips, some odd change, bills, receipts, and some personal papers including Claudine Pommier's driving licence, birth certificate and passport. He flicked through it. 'Quite a traveller, your friend.'

'You're kidding, right? She always said she hated flying.'

'Can't have hated it that much,' Ben said. 'There are more visa stamps on her passport than on mine. She's been all over the place in the last couple of years.'

Roberta frowned. 'Was she going off to scientific conferences, maybe? But I'm sure she'd have told me about that.' Still frowning, she began searching the next folder off the shelf, the first having yielded nothing of interest.

Ben left her to it and went to explore the other rooms in the apartment, starting with the kitchen and then the bedroom. He checked more drawers, cupboards. Clothes were hanging on hangers. Small, delicate shoes lined up in the bottom of a wardrobe. Everything seemed perfectly normal, as though the place's tenant might walk in any minute. The forensic examiners had left very little trace of their passing. And the killer had covered his own tracks equally well. Nobody now would have guessed a horrific murder had recently taken place in the bedroom.

Ben returned to the living room to find Roberta standing in a sea of papers and empty files. Her face was set tight as she struggled to contain her emotions. 'There's nothing here,' she said. 'Not a single mention of her work on Tesla. I didn't think there would be, and I don't think she had anything on the computer the cops took away, either. She knew these people were onto her. She was way too smart to leave anything for anyone to find.' Roberta shook her head. 'The worst thing is, it's almost as if whoever killed her knew that. I don't think they even tried searching the place.'

'Let's put everything back as it was and get out of here,' Ben said. 'We've seen all there is to see.'

'And learned nothing. Shit.'

'Not quite nothing,' he said.

As they stepped out into the dim hallway minutes later, Ben pulled the door quietly shut and heard the latch click home, then rearranged the police tape across the doorway. Sensing that Roberta was upset, he gently touched her shoulder. She pressed into his touch as if she really needed the human contact, then looked up at him with a sad smile. He could see the tears in her eyes reflected in the red light from the landing window. He didn't know what to say to her.

They were making their way back towards the stairs when there was the crash of a door bursting open. Before they could react, they were blinded by a bright torch shining in their faces.

'Who are you?' screeched a shrill voice in French. 'Don't you move, or I'll shoot.'

Ben slowly raised his hands. Even more slowly, he used one of them to flick on the old toggle light switch on the wall behind him, so that he could see their attacker.

It was the old woman, Claudine's neighbour. Her spindly frame was wrapped in a dressing gown, and she wore slippers and curlers. The steel torch she was shining at them was thicker than her arm. The small black pistol in her other hand was the kind of effective little personal tear-gas defence weapon that offered peace of mind to elderly, vulnerable French ladies in their homes while British ones were required to let themselves be robbed and beaten to death before the justice system did anything about it.

'Who are you?' she repeated in her warbly high pitch. 'Stay right where you are, or I'll spray this in your eyes and call the gendarmes.'

One part of Ben was filled with admiration and sympathy for the old woman. The other part of him didn't much relish getting a faceful of tear gas, even if it was just the dilute stuff allowed for the civilian market. Several options flashed through his mind for ways of getting the weapon out of her hand that didn't involve snapping osteoporosis-riddled bones or causing permanent tissue damage. He was on the verge of making a move when Roberta quickly stepped in.

'Madame Lefort? It's all right, we were friends of Claudine's,' she said in French. Having lived and worked in Paris for years prior to her move to Canada, she spoke the language perfectly.

At the mention of her own name and that of Claudine, the old woman hesitated but kept the pistol levelled at them.

'I flew here from Canada,' Roberta said. 'She sent me a letter.'

Now Madame Lefort's steely look of suspicion softened. She slipped the gun into the pocket of her dressing gown and put down the long metal torch, which was obviously very heavy for her. 'I was the last to see the poor dear alive, you know,' she said sadly. 'And it was me who found her.'

'Yes, I know,' Roberta said. 'I'm so sorry. It must have been terrible for you.'

'That's why I bought this gadget.' Madame Lefort patted her pocket. 'And this hearing aid.' She pointed at her ear. 'You can't be too careful nowadays, with all these filthy degenerates and maniacs on the loose everywhere. They should bring back the guillotine for them, I've said it for years and now look what's happened . . .'

'We didn't mean to disturb you,' Roberta went on apologetically in French. 'We only came to pay our respects. This is my friend, Monsieur Hope, and my name's Roberta, Roberta Ryder.'

'Ryder,' the old woman repeated the name, then chewed it over for a moment before asking, 'Then the Docteur Ryder, he must be your husband?'

Roberta blinked. 'I'm sorry?'

'The letter was addressed to Docteur Ryder in Canada,' the old woman said.

'That's me. I'm Dr Ryder,' Roberta explained, pointing at herself, much to Madame Lefort's astonishment, as if she'd never heard of such a thing as a woman with a professional title. 'But how did you know who the letter was addressed to?' Roberta asked her.

'Because I'm the one who sent it,' the old woman replied,

with a mixture of sadness and pride. 'The last time I saw Claudine alive, she asked me to go to the post office for her. One letter for Canada, the other for Sweden. Very important, she kept saying. That's all she'd tell me. Very important.'

Ben and Roberta exchanged glances. 'Sweden?' Roberta asked Madame Lefort. 'Are you sure?'

The old woman nodded earnestly. Absolutely sure.

'Madame Lefort,' Ben said gently. 'Did you post the Swedish letter by registered mail, like the Canadian one?'

Managing to recover from the shock of *two* French-speaking foreigners when one would have been incredible enough, Madame Lefort insisted that yes, she had.

'Then do you still have the customer receipt?' Ben asked. 'You see, we may need to contact Claudine's friend in Sweden, in case they don't know about what's happened . . .'

The old woman nodded eagerly, plainly distraught and only too glad to be of service. 'Attendez.' She disappeared into her brightly-lit, flower-filled apartment and they could hear her fussing about for a few moments before she returned clutching two small slips of paper, which she thrust at Ben. 'I never got the chance to give these to the poor, sweet child,' she said, on the verge of tears. 'After . . . *it* happened, I forgot I even had them.'

Ben thanked her graciously and examined the receipts. The post office teller had filled in the recipients' names and addresses by hand, one on each slip. The first one was addressed to Roberta in Ottawa. The second letter, mailed by registered international delivery at the same time and date, had been sent to a Herr Daniel Lund to an address near Jäkkwik, Sweden.

'So the big question is, who's Daniel Lund?' Roberta asked as they left the apartment building and headed back down the street towards the parked BMW.

'I don't think he's Claudine's pen pal,' Ben said.

'A boyfriend?'

'Someone she must have felt she could trust, at any rate.'

'You think she told him the things she told me?'

'It can't be a coincidence that she wrote to the two of you at the same time,' Ben said. 'From what she told the old woman, the letters were both equally important. So it's not impossible that they each contained much the same information.'

'Strange that she never mentioned this Daniel guy to me.'

'Seems like she never mentioned a lot of things.' Ben spoke his word command to unlock the Alpina, and got behind the wheel.

'What are we going to do?' Roberta asked as she climbed into the passenger seat. 'Phone him? His number might be listed in an international directory online.'

'First let's check out Fabien's place,' Ben said. 'Then we'll worry about Herr Lund.' He told the car to start, and the engine burst into life.

'I'll never get used to that thing,' Roberta said.

Chapter Seventeen

As the Alpina roared off down Rue des Trois Frères, one of the two occupants of the dark Peugeot 508 parked across the street reached for his phone and made a call. 'Target is on the move. The Priest's still with her.'

The person on the other end of the secure line had the luxury of not having to spend endless mind-numbing hours on surveillance detail inside a cramped car. Those days were long behind him now. Perched on an enormous chair at his desk in a comfortable office far, far away with a delicate china cup of cocoa at his elbow, the man most people called simply 'the Director' gazed through half-moon spectacles at the expanded high-definition onscreen image of the black-clad, blond-haired surveillance target they'd codenamed 'the Priest', photographed along with the Ryder woman on the park bench in Little Denton moments before the incident that had taken place there.

Since then, and in the light of that highly unexpected development, the image of 'the Priest' had been run through sophisticated facial recognition software and analysed against classified records to produce an identity match. The name that had emerged was Ben Hope.

The Director belonged to an organisation whose reach was extremely wide. Now they knew exactly who they were dealing with, down to the last detail. Details that explained a lot about why what should have been a simple clean-up operation in a sleepy corner of England had turned so messy and resulted in the loss of one of their valuable people. It had been an error of judgement, albeit one they couldn't entirely be blamed for making. Nonetheless, the Director was still suffering the fallout, and he wasn't about to let it happen to him a second time.

Two things he'd yet to figure out: first, how the person on his screen had become involved in this situation to begin with. It was hard to see how he could be in any way implicated. Second, the Director was still perplexed as to how exactly their two targets had managed to abscond into France undetected. If it hadn't been for the surveillance on Pommier's apartment building, they wouldn't have picked them up at all. Clever, this Priest.

But then, you'd expect someone with such a background to be very clever indeed. Resourceful, capable and hard to kill, however many years might have gone by since the peak of his operational training. These men didn't lose their edge. This one, this Hope, least of all.

The Director admired those kinds of men. Once upon a time, in what often seemed like another life, he'd been one of them himself. And when, as he so often did, he remembered the walking sticks leaning by his desk and looked down at his legs, withered, atrophied and virtually lost inside the brown corduroy trousers he was wearing, he envied them.

A pity to kill a man like that, the Director thought. Almost a pity. But there was simply no other way to play the game. So many had died before now, it didn't really matter any more.

Nor did it matter how hard such a man might be to eliminate. If there was one thing the Director knew intimately well, it was that *anyone* could be eliminated.

Anyone at all: it was just a question of expending sufficient resources, exercising enough power. The Director had exercised a good deal of it in his time. And he had access to all the resources necessary to crush or eliminate anyone at will, just by giving the order.

'Is the tracking device in place on their vehicle?' he inquired matter-of-factly.

'All taken care of,' was the reply.

'Stand by for further instructions,' the Director said, and put the phone down. His legs were hurting him. Damn them. The bullets that had permanently crippled his knees had come from the gun of a Spetsnaz colonel called Oleg Orlov, forty-four years ago. Since then the walking sticks had been his constant companions. One was ivory, the other ebony, custom made for him and intricately hand-carved with solid silver ferrules. If you had to have walking aids, they might as well be nice ones.

The Director leaned back, planted his bony elbows on the arms of the chair, knitted his fingers together and closed his eyes in meditation. Soon it would be confirmed to them where the targets were heading next. When the moment was right, he'd issue the order for them to be neutralised, but not if it meant half of Paris getting shot up in the process. Low profile operations were his speciality, and he'd been a master of them for over fifty years.

Chapter Eighteen

Ben didn't say much during the night drive to the GPS location on the map, and Roberta lapsed into her own thoughts. She spent a while musing over the numbers from Claudine's letter, then put the crumpled sheet away and gazed pensively out of the window. Traffic thinned out to almost nothing as they left Paris behind, following the Alpina's satnav system towards the ancestral home of Fabien De Bourg. They passed through the outskirts of a village with a sleepy railway station, then soon afterwards turned off the main road and found themselves meandering down a country lane skirting a high stone wall that seemed to go on and on.

Finally, they arrived at a set of enormous iron gates, black, spiked and forbidding. '*Vous êtes arrivés à vôtre destination*', the satnav announced in an incongruously cheery tone. Ben pulled up outside the gates and killed the engine. He wondered whether their unannounced late-night visit would find anyone at home.

If Fabien was in, he wasn't expecting anyone. 'Not again,' Roberta groaned when she saw the heavily-padlocked chain hanging from the iron bars. 'That's the second time today this has happened to us.'

Ben flung open his door and got out, grabbing his bag with the gun inside.

'You going to blow the lock?' she asked, pointing.

He shook his head. 'It takes more than a nine-mil to hurt a big old iron padlock like that. Besides, if this Fabien character turns out to be home, we don't want to draw attention to ourselves by making a load of noise.' He gazed up at the wall. The stonework was smooth and wouldn't be easy to scale, but the gate itself offered plenty of footholds as long as the long spikes on top didn't get them. He slung his bag strap over his shoulder, grabbed the cool iron bars in his fists and began to climb. Roberta sighed, muttered, 'Here we go' and did likewise.

A few moments later they dropped silently down on the other side, unpunctured by the spikes, and started making their way through the grounds. Ben used his torch to light the way down the curving private road. Clumps of weeds had sprouted up everywhere through the gravel and the lawns and shrubs either side were badly overgrown. It didn't take much to see that this once-magnificent property was sadly neglected by its present owner.

The private road wound through the trees until the house finally came into view. The silhouette of the eighteenth-century château, all spires and turrets and chimneys, stood out against the night sky. By daylight, Ben guessed, the place would probably look as uncared for as the grounds. The façade of the house had at least sixty windows, but none of them was lit. Either their boy was tucked up in bed with a bottle or a dolly bird, or he was away on one of his many socialite expeditions.

'Let's not waste too much time here,' Ben said. He swept the torch beam over the front and sides of the large house, looking for a discreet way in. 'We need to get inside and start searching for whatever the hell it is we're here to find.'

'Shine it over that way a minute,' Roberta said, pointing into the darkness away from the house. Ben did. The thin, bright beam cast a bobbing spotlight across the grounds: the dismal gardens filled with uncontrolled shrubs and a rampaging topiary, a walled courtyard with a disused old fountain at its centre, a range of stables with a clock tower that had been converted into garages, some parkland and woodland beyond a broken fence.

'Nothing, damn it,' she muttered.

'What are you looking for?' he asked.

'I was kind of hoping for a cemetery,' she replied, squinting through the darkness.

'A cemetery?'

She nodded. 'You know, little private family burial plot, fancy markers for the ancestors, spending eternity with the beloved, that kind of thing. Must have been quite a few generations of the De Bourg family that lived and died here over the centuries. These aristocrats would consider it way beneath them to be interred among the common folks.'

Ben scanned left and right with the torch and could see nothing but more walls and buildings and trees. 'Aside from the riveting insights into French social history,' he said, 'why are we looking for a graveyard?'

'Because I was doing some thinking on the way over here,' Roberta replied. 'Bear with me, okay? If I'm right, we don't have to go into the house. Give me the torch. Let's walk over that way, see what we find.'

Ben handed her the Maglite and followed, frustrated, as she led the way past the house, following a broad path that skirted round towards the gardens.

'Check this out,' she said, stopping suddenly. 'Look.'

Ben followed the line of the beam at the round building that had come into view behind the house, surrounded by a low wall and flanked by statues. 'It's a chapel,' he said as the torchlight flickered over its ornate stonework and the pointed conical steeple adorned with a tarnished bronze cross. 'But what—?' he began, but Roberta was already striding off towards it, leaving him behind. He trotted after her, more and more impatient that she wouldn't tell him what she was thinking. As he caught up with her, she'd already reached the chapel's arched doorway and was darting the torch here and there as if searching for something. 'It's locked,' she muttered. The beam landed on something and held still. 'Hello,' she said.

Roberta had found a small electronic keypad mounted on the wall. 'Bet your ass I'm right.'

'I can't wait to find out,' Ben said at her shoulder.

'Six-nine-eight-two.' She prodded each key in turn. Nothing happened for a second, then there was a muted beep and the lock opened with a click. Roberta grinned over her shoulder at Ben, pushed the door open and cast the light around the circular walls. There was a small altar, some benches, religious art and crosses everywhere, the usual fixtures of a small private place of worship.

'You want to say a prayer that my theory's right?' she asked. 'Someone up there might listen to you.' Her voice sounded echoey.

'I doubt that,' Ben replied, more concerned with knowing what she was up to as she avidly explored the inside of the chapel. 'You mind sharing this theory with me?' he asked as she let out a yelp of triumph.

'The two lines of numbers that we couldn't figure out from the letter,' she said excitedly. 'The second line, four digits – we just found out what that was, right? And as for the bottom line, those ten digits that didn't make any sense before?'

'What about them?'

'They're *dates*, Ben. Two lots of five digits, each consisting of day, month, and year. Just like the GPS coordinates, when you run them all together they look like nothing, but break them down into an ordered sequence and you get a pair of dates thirty-five years apart. Someone's birth and death. The only part that's missing is what century the dates refer to. It hit me while we were in the car.'

'Okay,' he said carefully, realising she was probably right.

'That's why I was looking for a cemetery,' Roberta said in a satisfied tone. 'And look what *I* just found.'

He strode over to where she was shining the light on a small archway recessed low down into the wall behind the altar. A well-worn flight of steps led down to a heavy iron door that was held fast by a massive bolt. 'Now, don't tell me that's a wine cellar down there,' Roberta said, pointing the torch.

'It's a tomb,' Ben said.

Chapter Nineteen

The bolt on the iron door was rusted almost solid and couldn't be waggled open by hand. 'I'm going to have to hit it with something,' Ben said after a few attempts.

'Try this,' Roberta said, and stepped across to pick up a hefty bronze candlestick.

'That should do it.' He was about to hammer the bolt knob with the candlestick's heavy base when he noticed something, and shone the torch closely to see. The rusty bolt knob was scuffed with fresh impact marks that had left fresh bare metal. 'Someone's been here before us, and not long ago,' he said. 'These marks will rust over quickly.'

Three smart blows from the candlestick, and the bolt was forced back. Ben pushed the massive door and it creaked open a few inches. The tomb was blacker than black inside. Cool, stale air wafted up from the entrance.

'Spooky,' Roberta murmured.

Ben shone the light on the stone steps that led down to the murky space below. Already he could see more signs that someone had been here recently. The thick curtain of cobwebs that hung inside the doorway had been disturbed. The fresh footprints in the dust on the steps hadn't been made by a man. They were as small and delicate as the shoes he'd come across in Claudine Pommier's wardrobe.

He made his way down to the bottom of the steps and shone the torch around inside. On a dusty marble pedestal was an ornamental crucifix, flanked either side by large vases filled with flowers, long since wilted to a husk. Whoever had been down here recently didn't appear to have come to pay their respects to the De Bourg family dead.

'I think you're right,' he said to Roberta, who was tentatively following him down the steps. 'Claudine was here.' Something in the atmosphere of the tomb made him lower his voice to a whisper. The chill in the air wasn't just a question of temperature. It felt like what it was, a place of death.

And it had been one for a long time, going back three hundred years to when the De Bourgs had buried their dead like kings of old, laying them to rest inside massive stone coffins housed in recesses in the walls. The more recently deceased were sealed in behind marble plaques, or in ornate crematorium urns inscribed with names and dates of birth and death.

The torch batteries were beginning to fade, and there didn't seem to be any electric light in the tomb. By the yellowing beam Ben traced the direction of the small footprints in the dust. They criss-crossed the flagstones on the floor, as if Claudine – if it had been her – had been hunting around for something. After a few passes to and fro they headed diagonally over to one of the old stone coffins. There were kneel marks beside it in the dust. Ben shone the dim light upwards and saw the scrape marks around the coffin's thick stone lid where someone had been prying at it with a sharp tool, like a crowbar.

Roberta was standing close to him, almost touching. 'Look at the dates on the casket,' she breathed. The carved inscription read:

Germain Christophe De Bourg
Né le 27 Janvier, 1756
Mort le 5 Decembre 1791

'Born January twenty-seventh, 1756, died December fifth, 1791,' Roberta translated. 'Put the dates into figures, take out the century and what've you got? Two-seven, one, five-six; five, twelve, nine-one. See? Didn't I tell you? This is where the letter was leading us.'

'The lid's been opened and slid shut again,' Ben said, noticing that it was slightly askew.

'Could Claudine have done that?'

'With a bit of effort, and a decent crowbar,' he replied. 'I'd say even a slightly built woman could have prised it open a few inches.'

'A crowbar like this one?' Roberta asked, stooping down and reaching into the shadows. There was a soft clang as she picked up an iron wrecking bar, three feet long, curved into a fork at one end and chisel-tipped at the other. 'Looks like she left it behind in a hurry.' She handed it to Ben.

'Now all we need to know is why Claudine might have needed to open a two-hundred-year-old coffin,' he said. 'Only one way to find out.'

'Great. We're grave robbers now.'

As they'd been talking, the torch had been fading more and more, and now it died completely. Ben reached into his pocket for his Zippo lighter. Its warm, flickering light made an orange halo. 'Hold this,' he said, passing it to Roberta. He dug the chisel tip of the wrecking bar between the coffin and its craggy stone lid, and heaved. Claudine must have used all her body weight to lever them apart. With a couple of hard shoves, the corner of the heavy lid lifted far enough to poke the end of the bar into the gap and force the lid sideways. Stone grated on stone. The gap opened, inch by inch, until the lid fell with a grinding crash.

'Sorry about that, Germain,' Ben muttered.

Roberta held the light over the exposed inside of the coffin. The soft flame shone on pale bones and tatters of decayed burial shroud. The skeletal remains of the coffin's occupant grinned up at them. 'Holy shit,' she said with a shudder.

'What's the matter, you've never opened up someone's coffin before?'

'It's not just that. His skull seems to be, uh, *separated* from the rest of him.'

'Guillotined,' Ben said. 'Those were dodgy times for French aristocrats. Germain De Bourg wasn't the only one who died young in the wake of the revolution.' He laid down the wrecking bar. 'Shine the light a little closer,' he told her, and peered down into the shadows of the coffin's interior. Then, leaning over its craggy stone edge, he thrust an arm inside to grope around and beneath the decapitated skeleton.

His searching hand brushed smooth bones and wispy cloth, and something else. Something that certainly hadn't been there since 1791. His fist closed on smooth, soft plastic.

He drew out the bag. It was opaque and had been carefully sealed with tape. Roberta watched as he broke the seal and opened it up.

'I don't think this belonged to the coffin's resident,' he said, showing her the detachable computer hard drive that was inside.

'Is there anything else?'

'Just this,' Ben said, and pulled it out of the plastic. The rectangular object was metallic, about eight inches in length, shaped at one end like a small hammer, a cluster of tiny switches and buttons and LEDs at the other. 'Some kind of tool, or gauge,' he said.

'Let me see,' Roberta said, looking at it intently.

The Zippo's steel case was growing uncomfortably hot in Ben's fingers and he wasn't sure how long its fuel reservoir would hold out. He handed her the strange object and held the flame to give her some light as she inspected it from all angles. 'What the hell is it?' he asked.

'I'm not an expert,' she said. 'But I think this is an update on the Tesla oscillator.'

'The machine you told me about? Where did she get it?'

'She could easily have built it herself. She was certainly smart enough, and she had the technical skills to create something like this. The original Tesla device was steam-powered, but this is electro-mechanical. Apart from that, I'm certain it's a replica of the very same machine.' She shook her head in confusion. 'Jesus, Ben. I just wish I'd been wrong about all this. But I wasn't.'

'Let's go over what we know,' Ben said. 'We're pretty certain that Claudine came out here, sometime within the last week or so, going by how fresh her footprints are. She obviously came alone, probably knowing that her ex was out of the way. He must have shown her all around the place when they were together. Now, believing that she's under threat, she decides to use the tomb as a hiding place, knowing that nobody would think to search in this particular spot. She goes to all this trouble to hide these items out here, then sends coded information about the location to at least two people she must have known she could trust: namely, you and this Daniel person in Sweden.'

'We have to get back and check it all out,' Roberta said. 'Whatever's there, Claudine wanted me to see it.'

'There's a computer in storage at the safehouse,' he told

her, slipping the hard drive into his bag. 'With any luck, we'll be able to access the files.'

Roberta was about to reply when a juddering crash shook the tomb and made them both whirl around, startled.

The massive iron door had been slammed shut from outside. And no gust of wind could have pushed something so heavy.

Someone had deliberately shut them in.

Clutching the flaming Zippo, Ben raced through the darkness towards the entrance and leaped up the steps to throw his body weight against the door.

Too late. Even as he reached the door he could hear the *clang, clang* of someone on the other side hammering the bolt shut. He pressed his ear to the cold iron and caught the sound of footsteps walking away through the chapel.

Ben pounded on the door, but he might as well have tried to punch his way out of an Abrams main battle tank. They were closed inside the tomb, and there was no way out.

'*Ben?*' Roberta's panicked voice cried out from the darkness.

'Stay calm,' he said, running back down the steps to join her. She latched onto his arm, gripping him tightly. 'Who's up there? Who closed us in?'

'Let's just say it's someone who doesn't want us to get out again,' Ben said grimly. 'But we'll find a way out of this.' He winced as the hot metal of the lighter singed his fingertips. The flame was beginning to gutter. Their only light source was soon going to run out.

'You smell that?' she said suddenly.

'Smell what?'

'Something's burning,' she said.

Now Ben could smell it too. And it wasn't the flesh of his fingers smouldering from the heat of the lighter. The sharp, dense odour of burning was coming from somewhere else.

'This isn't good,' he muttered under his breath. Breaking loose from Roberta, he ran back towards the steps and held the dying flame up high.

It was as he'd feared. Wisps of smoke were already beginning to trickle in, under and around the edges of the tomb door. The acrid stench was becoming stronger, and so was the growing crackle and roar he could hear from outside. He touched his hand to the iron door and felt the heat spreading through it.

Whoever had shut them in wasn't content with merely letting them starve to death among the corpses.

The chapel was ablaze above them.

Chapter Twenty

Whoever had set fire to the chapel, it wasn't kids messing around with matches. Ben had had enough experience of high-powered incendiary devices in his lifetime to know how fast a building could be reduced to a bone-melting inferno. If he and Roberta didn't succumb to smoke inhalation first, they'd soon cook in the heat. It was already getting uncomfortable standing close to the door. The smoke was pouring in more and more through the gaps. Every moment counted.

'What's happening?' Roberta asked as he leaped down the steps and started hunting around inside the tomb. She was still clutching the Tesla device.

'What's happening is, the whole bloody place is on fire,' he replied. He'd found what he was looking for. Grabbing the wrecking bar off the floor, he paused to reach back inside the coffin and rip a long piece of burial shroud from the skeleton inside. Loose ribs clattered to the floor as he jerked the cloth away. 'Keep this over your nose and mouth,' he told Roberta, shoving it at her.

'This was wrapped around a goddamn corpse.'

'Do it now!' he yelled. He dashed back to the door. Stinging tears filled his eyes as he stabbed the chisel end of the bar into the door seam and started trying to lever it open. He knew the risk of causing a backdraft that would suck fire into the tomb and turn it instantly into a super-heated oven. At least it would be over quickly for them then.

He forced the bar in deeper and levered with all his strength. A piece of stonework broke away. He kept on working furiously, hardly able to keep his eyes open, racked with coughing from the smoke. Another piece of masonry broke away from the door arch. The first flames were beginning to lick hungrily around the edges of the door. The situation was worsening more rapidly than he could deal with.

He knew now that this was futile.

'Come away from the door, Ben!' Roberta screamed. He hesitated for a second, then stumbled dizzily back down the steps and beat his way through the smoke to where Roberta was crouching in the fiery glow at the far side of the tomb with the piece of burial shroud clamped over her face. She was no longer holding the device.

He wanted to smash the tomb walls down, tear them apart stone by stone with the steel bar in his hands. But they were impossibly thick, and buried under ten feet of earth. The door had been their only way out.

There *was* no way out. Not any more. They were going to burn.

Ben dropped to his knees next to Roberta and wrapped his arms tightly around her, intent on shielding her from the flames with his body when the moment came, probably just minutes away. By then, the smoke would most likely have got to them. He could feel her ribs convulsing as she fought to breathe.

He buried his face in her hair. *It won't be long now*, he wanted to say.

His own life didn't matter to him that much. He'd come

very close to losing it many times before now – it had always just been a question of how the end would come about, and how soon. You got used to living with the idea. But it wasn't right that Roberta should die like this, just because she'd wanted to find out what happened to her friend. Just because she was good, and loyal, and caring. She didn't deserve this.

But even as he prepared himself for the worst, Ben was becoming conscious of something happening. Something strange. At first he thought it was his own pounding heartbeat filling his senses. But no; it was coming from underneath him, as if from deep beneath the flagstones: a kind of pulsing, quivering sensation that doubled in intensity with each passing second. A deep rumble, seeming to emanate from everywhere at once, flooded his ears.

Roberta could feel it too. She pulled away from his embrace, looked up at him through streaming eyes and seemed to be trying to say something, but her spluttering words were drowned out by the steadily rising sound. She motioned weakly into the shadows of the tomb.

Ben squinted through the smoke to where she was pointing, and thought he glimpsed the blink of tiny lights. Was it some trick of the retina, caused by oxygen starvation of the brain? No; he saw it again.

'What's—?' he croaked inaudibly, but the question died on his lips. The whole tomb now seemed to be shaking violently. The thrumming noise seemed to penetrate everywhere and everything.

It's an earthquake, said a voice in Ben's mind. But it was wrong, it was impossible. They didn't *have* earthquakes in northern France. Not like this.

With an ear-splitting crack, a whole section of the interior wall suddenly came crashing down in a landslide of crumbling masonry. Tentacles of flame quickly came snaking in through the jagged hole, hunting for something to consume.

Roberta struggled to her feet, bent double with coughing, and grasped Ben's hands. Confused and disorientated, he sensed that she was trying to pull him towards the deep, dark recess where they'd opened the coffin. Over the roaring of the fire and the deafening rumble he heard her say something about 'take cover'.

The flames were past the tomb door and rolling greedily in through the gaping cavity in the wall. But the most frightening thing was the all-encompassing vibration that rocked the floor under their feet and made it hard to stay upright. Roberta let go of Ben's hands and frantically gripped the edge of Germain De Bourg's coffin, struggling with all her strength to drag it out of the recess.

Seeing what she was trying to do, Ben grasped the rough stone, braced his feet against the wall and pulled with all his remaining reserves of energy, until his back felt about to break.

The coffin lurched outwards with a grinding scrape of stone on stone. A few inches, then a few inches more, until its weight overbalanced it and it toppled out of the recess and crashed out onto the flagstones, splitting apart and spilling the skeletal remains of its occupant in pieces across the floor.

Roberta clambered over the shattered coffin and into the hole, reached a clawed hand out to him to follow her. He half-caught her choking scream of 'Get in!' just as another great rippling crack shuddered through the tomb and a shower of rock and stone and dust came thundering down all over the floor just yards from where he was trying to stay on his feet.

Another wave of the inferno from the blazing chapel

above came spreading and licking down through the hole. Ben felt its scorching breath sear his back as he threw himself into the recess with Roberta. The two of them wedged themselves in as deeply as they could against the hard stone.

Now all they could do was lie huddled there and wait for whatever was going to happen to them.

Chapter Twenty-One

The terrifying vibration seemed to threaten to tear everything apart. It felt as though they were aboard some vast rocket ship taking off. Ben's blurred vision could just about make out the chapel's blazing timbers through the gaping hole in the ceiling of the tomb.

Roberta clung tightly to him. He heard her frightened gasp in his ear as another incoming onslaught of searing heat and flame rolled across the narrow mouth of the recess.

This was it. They were about to be roasted alive.

In a deafening chaos of noise and fire, the chapel timbers came crashing inwards amid an avalanche of roof slates, bringing down the rest of the tomb ceiling. It felt like being caught in a direct hit from a bomb.

Then . . . nothing.

Ben opened his eyes. Something was different. The terrible vibration had stopped. He turned his face towards the opening of the recess and realised he could taste air, fresh air, on his dry lips.

He could breathe again.

Still coughing from the smoke, he struggled out of the hole, stood uncertainly and gazed around him. 'What the . . .' he muttered to himself, blinking as if he were seeing things.

The whole building had fallen in on itself, extinguishing the blaze. Where the chapel had stood, there was nothing left but a circle of ruined walls and heaps of rubble. The bronze cross that had earlier adorned the steeple now lay blackened and half-buried under a ton of smouldering timber. A hundred small fires were still burning all around, and a vast column of orange-lit smoke was towering upwards to blot out the stars.

Ben glanced sideways and saw that Roberta was standing at his shoulder. Her face was glowing by the firelight. One cheek was blackened and her hair was almost white with dust. She couldn't stop grinning shakily as she squeezed his arm. 'Hey, looks like we made it after all,' she said in a raspy chuckle.

'. . . What happened?' was all he could say. His own voice sounded hollow and deathly.

'I couldn't see the controls in the dark,' she explained, talking fast. 'Just by chance I must have pressed the right button, then I rammed it into a crevice in the wall there.' She pointed to a pile of smoking rubble.

'What are you talking about?'

'The device must've been set up to automatically attune to the natural frequency of the building, instead of the manual analogue system Tesla used,' she went on. 'I guess we'll never know now, even if we could dig out whatever's left of it. Least we know it worked, huh?'

Ben stared at her. 'Hold on. Surely even you wouldn't be trying to tell me that that thing – that little tin pot piece of crap machine – did *this*?'

Roberta's excited grin dropped and she returned his fierce stare. 'Why, you think it was a miracle or something? God heard your prayers and sent down an earthquake to rescue us in our moment of need? That what you'd rather believe, Ben?'

He couldn't reply. The alternative seemed wild, insane. But there was no other way to accept what he'd just witnessed.

'You know it's true,' she said. 'So much for pie in the sky, hmm?'

He surveyed the devastation and shook his head. 'Jesus Christ.'

'He had nothing to do with it.'

'I'm supposed to be the crazy one,' he muttered. 'You almost got us killed.'

'I got us out, didn't I?' Her grin returned. 'Then you do believe me.'

'Principle of resonance,' he grunted reluctantly.

'Principle of resonance. You got it, Hope. You ought to trust me a bit more by now, after all we've been through together.'

'You're going to tell me everything you know about this stuff,' he said.

'With pleasure. And once we get home, with any luck we'll both be able to learn exactly what Claudine was doing and what she knew, which you can be damn sure was a lot more than I do.'

Roberta tried to shake the worst of the dust out of her hair and cleaned up her sooty face as best she could while Ben searched for his bag. He found it among a pile of wreckage, rather more battered now than before and partly singed from the fire. Its contents were warm to the touch. He could only pray that the heat hadn't affected the remote hard drive inside. He took out the machine carbine, checked it over and kept it handy as they clambered over the rubble that covered the tomb steps and picked their way through the ruins of the chapel.

'You think they'd still be hanging around?' Roberta asked nervously, glancing at the trees.

'Better not be, for their sake,' Ben replied. 'I don't much appreciate some joker trying to stonebake us.'

But whoever it was, they were long gone. The grounds were deserted as Ben and Roberta walked towards the gates, both happily filling their raw lungs with the wonderfully fresh night air.

'Alive again,' she said.

'For now,' he replied.

'That's what I always loved about you,' she said. 'That cheery optimism just never goes away.'

Everything was as they'd left it. The gates were still locked, the Alpina still in the same spot. It was as if nobody else had been there that night.

They climbed the gate. Ben was the first to drop down to the other side. He walked up to within a few yards of the car and halted, eyeing it suspiciously. 'They knew we were here,' he said. 'Nobody followed us from Paris, but they were able to pinpoint us exactly in the middle of nowhere.'

'How could they do that?'

'There are a thousand ways,' he said. 'None of them very reassuring from our angle.'

Roberta considered. 'Maybe they were there, in Montmartre. Watching us as we checked out Claudine's apartment. Maybe they didn't want to make a move, draw attention to themselves in a public place. But they could have stuck some kind of tracking device on the car, couldn't they?'

'It's a possibility,' he conceded.

'Then if we could find it, we could just detach it and leave it here in the bushes to make whoever's monitoring our whereabouts from a distance think the car was still here, while we drive back to Paris. Or else we could stick it on the back of a truck heading for Germany or some-where. Throw the assholes right off our trail.'

Ben glanced back over the trees at the smoke rising into the sky, still visible for miles even now that the flames had died down. 'Someone's bound to have reported the fire. Emergency services and police will be here any time soon, and they're going to know this was an arson attack. If the car's still here when they arrive, they'll start asking questions and it'll be reported in the media, which you can be sure our friends will be watching.'

'So?'

'So if we leave the car where it is, as far as anyone's concerned there's a couple of fresh corpses buried in the remains of that tomb back there,' he said. 'Mission accom-plished. Which is what we need them to think, if we want to buy some time before they catch up with us again.'

'You think they will?' she asked anxiously.

'It's what I would do.'

Chapter Twenty-Two

Ben and Roberta were half a kilometre away from the gates of the château and walking quickly up the dark country road in the direction of the small town they'd passed earlier, when the wail of sirens became audible in the distance followed by a halo of flashing lights on the horizon.

'In here,' he said, quickly directing her off the road towards a dark, dense patch of forest to their right. By the time the emergency vehicles came screaming by in a glare of lights, they were well hidden among the trees.

Silence again. 'Who're you calling?' Roberta asked as Ben took out his phone.

He wasn't calling anybody. 'I can't use this any more,' he said, and tossed the phone on the ground. He picked up a nearby lump of rock and dashed the device to tiny pieces that he stamped and spread into the dirt. 'These people know who I am by now. The fewer ways they have of tracking us, the better.'

Roberta touched his hand in the darkness. 'Got you into a whole mess of trouble, didn't I?' she said sadly.

He found himself moving stiffly away from her touch. 'Come on, let's go and catch a train.'

The little railway station was deserted. Roberta went to get them some coffee from a machine while Ben checked timetables and saw that the last late-night train headed for Paris was due to come through in another forty minutes. He bought tickets from an automatic dispenser, then fed the last of his change into a payphone and called Jeff Dekker's mobile number.

'It's me. I can't talk long. I'm okay, everything's fine.'

Jeff had known Ben long enough to know that 'everything's fine' could mean just about anything. 'Right,' said his sleepy voice.

'Listen. The police are going to be round at Le Val pretty soon asking questions about the Alpina. Before that happens, you need to report it stolen. Do it now, tonight. Say it was taken in the last couple of days but you only just noticed it was gone. Got it?'

'What the fuck are you up to this time?' Jeff said, rapidly awakening.

'I'll be in touch. You haven't heard from me.' There was so much more he wanted to say. In the brief pause before his long-suffering friend could muster a reply, Ben very nearly asked him if he'd spoken to Brooke, if she was okay, and if he'd pass on the message that Ben loved her and would call her as soon as he had a chance. But his questions stayed clammed up inside him and he quickly put the phone down, painfully aware of how hard and terse he must have sounded.

He walked slowly back to where Roberta was sitting on a plastic bench on the station platform. She handed him a paper cup, saying 'Sorry, it tastes like boiled shit'. The two of them sat and sipped the dismal machine coffee in silence. Still feeling dazed, Ben reached for his Gauloises, found the pack badly crumpled from earlier on, then discovered that his Zippo was lost, still lying in the ashes of the De Bourg family chapel. He slumped wearily back against the bench.

'We look like a couple of hoboes,' Roberta said, breaking the silence, gazing at their dishevelled reflection in a window on the other side of the tracks.

'You smell like a Connemara Smokehouse mackerel,' he told her with a faint smile.

'Gee, thanks for that one. It's not just me, I assure you.'

When the train arrived, the two hoboes sat at the rear of a near-empty carriage with just a small gang of harmless drunks for company. As they rattled away from the station, one of the gang came reeling up the aisle with an unlit cigarette in his mouth, looking for a light. With a pang of regret, Ben told him he didn't have one. The drunk sniffed the air and peered curiously at their blackened faces and dirty clothes. 'What happened to you two?' he slurred.

'Got caught in an earthquake,' Ben told him, and the drunk shambled back to his friends looking puzzled.

Roberta gave a dry smile. 'So, are you still in denial, or what?'

'I can't explain what I saw,' he said. 'But I won't deny it either.'

'Okay. Time for the backstory. 1898, New York City. Nikola Tesla was in his Houston Street basement laboratory when—'

'I thought you said he was Serbian.'

'He was, but he emigrated to the States in 1884, went to work for Thomas Edison and later became a US citizen. It was in New York, well over a century ago, that he designed and built the prototype of the oscillator device you saw today. Once it was completed he had to test it, and Tesla being Tesla, he did that by tuning it to the resonant frequency of the building in whose basement the lab was housed. A crazy thing to do, but then he was a pretty crazy guy by all accounts. According to the story, as he cranked up the power he and his assistants heard first a hum, then a crack, then another, then the whole building began to tremble, along with neighbouring buildings with similar resonant frequencies. Mayhem in the street. The fire department and police reserves rushing to the scene, everyone convinced a megaquake was about to happen. And who knows what *would've* happened, if Tesla hadn't taken a hammer to his machine before it could run away with itself and do too much damage.'

Ben just shook his head and wished he had his cigarettes.

Roberta went on: 'Now, that wasn't enough for Tesla, so he built a second oscillator, this time about the size of an alarm clock. He took the machine to a construction site in the Wall Street district and clamped it to one of the support beams of a ten-storey building. Within minutes, he said the structure began to creak and weave, and all the steel workers came rushing down to ground level in a panic because they thought the building was going to fall apart. In the middle of the chaos, Tesla just slipped the machine back in his pocket and made his exit, knowing – and I'm quoting – "I could have laid the whole edifice flat in the street". Is all this sounding a little more plausible now?'

It was, but Ben was still having trouble digesting it. 'And this was the same kind of machine Claudine built.'

Roberta nodded. 'Hers was an update, that's all. It's essentially a very simple concept. The original oscillator used just five pounds of air pressure acting on a pneumatic piston. Tesla initially pretended to the New York authorities that his Houston Street experiment must have been an earthquake, but he later claimed that the same five pounds of pressure could have dropped the Brooklyn Bridge into the East River or brought down the Empire State Building. In fact, the larger the structure, the easier it is theoretically to destroy, because the resonant frequency gets lower as mass increases. Like I told you before, Ben, there's no limit to what it can do. Remember how I said that Tesla believed he could split the world in two? With a large enough machine, no problem.'

'How large is large?' Ben asked, looking at her in bewilderment.

'Not as large as you might imagine,' Roberta said. 'Claudine once told me that Tesla claimed a scaled-up version of his device weighing two hundred pounds and measuring three feet high would be capable of transmitting motive power anywhere through the earth, over any distance. Sounds about right to me.'

'This is some pretty wild story you're telling me.'

'But you don't need proof any more that it's not crazy, right? You've seen this working with your own eyes. That should be able to convince even you.'

Ben shrugged helplessly. 'All right. You've got me. But I have a question. Why the hell isn't this stuff more widely known about? I mean, unless I'm missing something, it would seem fairly important.'

'Because,' Roberta explained, 'in common with a lot of other very important discoveries, which would include things like the secret of potentially creating eternal life or transmuting base elements into gold, it's been so wrapped up in hokum and conspiracy theories that it became, as far as science was concerned, an untouchable subject. That's why hardly anyone remembers the name Tesla anymore. In mainstream academic research circles, just to mention it makes you out to be a total crank.' She pulled a dark smile. 'And believe me, I've spent enough of my science career dealing with untouchable subjects to know what I'm talking about. That's one way to see why so few people know about Tesla's work. The other way to see it is as a deliberate cover-up, engineered by certain people who didn't want the public to know about it, for their own reasons. In which case the whole nutty conspiracy element provides the perfect smokescreen, just like the whole Roswell thing in the 1940s was deliberately allowed to be sidetracked by disinformation about aliens and UFOs, to protect the truth that the US government were developing secret aircraft technology.'

'So now you're saying the US government were implicated in this.'

'Well, they did take an interest in him from early on,' Roberta said. 'He was paid millions by the War Department to develop all kinds of diabolical secret weapons, none of which ever went into production. In 1917 he patented a wireless engine that he claimed could wipe out an entire naval fleet from ten thousand miles away, just by pulling a lever. Then years later in the lead-up to World War II, he unveiled plans for a so-called particle "death beam" weapon that was supposed to be able to bring down whole squadrons of enemy aircraft at a stroke or cause a million-strong army to drop dead in its tracks like some Bolt of Thor that would protect any nation who possessed it from foreign invasion. As you can imagine, it never got past the theoretical stage. I guess Julius Oppenheimer's lovely atom bomb project was more in line with conventional wisdom and won over the government's hearts and money instead.'

'I'm glad that one didn't catch on,' Ben said. 'Sounds like I'd have been out of a job.'

Ignoring his stab at levity, Roberta went on, 'But the powers-that-be never lost interest in him, no matter how wacky his ideas became. It's pretty certain that immediately after Tesla's death in almost complete poverty at the age of eighty-six in January 1943, agents of the FBI, the Office of Alien Property and the War Department conspired to magic away, impound and safeguard a bunch of his secret weaponry papers, blueprints and design plans. The legend is that, with the tacit knowledge of J. Edgar Hoover and various military top brass, sometime that January they broke into the safe in Tesla's room in the New Yorker Hotel, where he'd spent the last years of his life, and stole vital information along with a key to another vault at the Governor Clinton Hotel.'

'Which contained pink dinosaur eggs and a set of Hitler's lost dentures,' Ben said.

'Not exactly,' she corrected him with a hard look. 'If you go along with the stories, and Claudine said there was good evidential reason to do so, it was where Tesla had stored a prototype working model of the death ray machine.'

The train was clattering fast along the tracks, shaking them softly in their seats. Paris was just a few minutes away. Ben had slumped down low with his feet on the seat opposite, and was gazing out of the window as he sat absorbing what she was saying. The story of the theft of the death ray machine didn't seem to have moved him in the least.

'What's the matter, don't you believe me?' she asked, seeing the doubtful look that was spreading over his face.

'After tonight's episode, I'll believe that Jesus Christ and the Apostles sold cheeseburgers on the Temple Mount,' he said. 'That's not the problem.'

'So what's the problem?'

'Seriously? You're making a case that secret government agents murdered Claudine over her research.'

Roberta looked at him earnestly. 'Wouldn't that make sense, Ben? It would've been so easy for them to pin it on some maniac serial killer, just by copying his M.O. They do this kind of thing all the time. I mean, look at what's happening to us here. Who could track me to some tiny village in the asshole of England? Who could find us again in Paris, and stick a homing device on our car? Who's got those kinds of resources?'

'I agree, it seems to make sense in a lot of ways,' Ben said. 'But here's the problem. All right, let's say for argument's sake that the conspiracy buffs are right on the money, and that this is all true and that back in 1943 the FBI and the other government spooks were all desperate to get their hands on some loony weapon that can shoot beams at the moon, turn entire nations to stone, or whatever. We're talking about things that were dreamed up decades and decades before you and I were born. Even if these devices worked exactly as Tesla claimed they could, do you have any idea how wildly obsolete they'd be in the modern age? We have ICBMs now; we have drone warfare, battlefield robotics and depleted uranium warheads and weaponized anthrax and a whole list of horrible things designed to kill and maim, that make Tesla's creations sound like something out of an old black and white Flash Gordon matinée movie.'

'Fine. What are you trying to say?'

'Simply, that I don't buy that a modern-day researcher poking their nose into this stuff could get into trouble over it. Not after all these years. There's got to be some other angle.'

Roberta shrugged. 'Okay, then. Maybe Claudine discovered something new, something nobody's ever come up with before. Maybe that's what they're after.'

'In which case, why would they just bury it under tons of rubble? Why not make any attempt to acquire it?'

They pondered the issue, throwing questions back and forth and getting nowhere, until the train finally lumbered into the Gare Saint-Lazare in Paris. By now it was well into the small hours of the morning and the place was as quiet as any of Paris' main stations could ever get, with just a few strings of late-night travellers hanging about the platforms. The drunks piled rowdily out of the train first, then Ben and Roberta quietly disembarked and made their way through the complex of old and modern architecture to leave the station via the east entrance on Rue Saint-Lazare. A smattering of traffic was zipping around the square in front. Ben looked about for a cab and spotted a single beige Mercedes cab was sitting parked at a taxi rank thirty yards away. The safehouse was only a couple of short miles across the city. They could be back there inside five minutes.

As they approached the taxi rank, Roberta noticed the man who was loitering alone at the foot of the ugly modern clock sculpture near the station's entrance. He was dressed in jeans and a casual hooded top, smoking and apparently watching them from a distance. He suddenly flicked away his cigarette and started walking towards them, his pace quickening with every step.

Before Ben and Roberta reached the taxi rank, another group of people appeared around the corner: three women accompanied by two men, all dressed in evening wear. From the noise they were making, they must have had a good time that night. They got to the Mercedes first and spilled into it. The doors slammed shut with a last peal of laughter and then the car took off down Rue Saint-Lazare.

'Looks like the subway for us,' Ben said.

Roberta was still anxiously glancing back over her shoulder at the man in the hoodie top. There was no mistaking that he was making right for them. His head was inclined downwards and his hands were bunched up in his pockets.

'Ben? That guy over there – I think he's following us.'

Chapter Twenty-Three

Ben had already noticed him. The guy's body language had set off his own alarm bells the moment they'd emerged from the station exit. 'Keep walking, don't look back,' he said, taking Roberta's arm, and guided her across the street towards the nearest Metro station at the corner of Rue Saint Lazare and Place du Havre. Out of the corner of his eye he was watching the man closely, more and more certain he didn't like what he was seeing. At any moment a weapon was liable to appear from one of those hoodie pockets. Ben's pulse began to quicken with apprehension and rage. How had these people picked up their trail again so fast?

And if he was one of them, chances were he wasn't working alone. More of them could appear at any moment.

Down the steps into the bright Metro station; the man still followed. There was hardly anyone else around. Ben and Roberta headed briskly into the winding tunnels.

The man saw his targets disappear around a corner and pressed on quickly to catch up. Inside his pocket, the fingers of his right hand clenched around the handle of the knife. He rounded the corner after them, then halted and glanced about, perplexed. Nobody. His targets had vanished.

Suddenly the breath was driven out of him by a hard

impact out of nowhere and he was slammed against the curved tiles of the tunnel wall.

Ben delivered two hard, fast strikes to force him quickly into submission. The man slumped down the wall. His right hand pulled feebly at his pocket. Ben saw the blade before it had moved three inches towards him. The man let out a screech that echoed up the tunnel as the weapon was twisted violently from his fingers. Before he knew what was happening, the edge of the blade was pressed hard up against his throat.

'Who are you?' Ben said in English. 'Talk.'

The man was powerless in Ben's grip. His eyes and mouth were distended with terror. 'Quoi?' he managed to blurt out.

'I asked you who you are,' Ben repeated in French. 'You've got three seconds to spill it. Don't think I won't cut your throat. I've done it to better men than you.'

Everything about Ben's tone and expression was enough to convince the man very quickly that he wasn't joking. 'My name's Jules! Jules Leclercq!'

'Who do you work for, Jules?'

'Nobody! I don't work for anyone, I swear! I don't even have a job!'

Ben kept him pinned down and pressed the knife edge harder against his neck. But even as he did it, he could see the signs. The blade was dull and cheap, mail-order trash. Jules smelled of sweat and stale alcohol and his clothes were grimy. He began to whimper pitifully. A wet patch appeared in the crotch of his jeans and a puddle of urine began to spread under him.

There were slick, efficient professional killers who posed as down-and-outs, and then there were poor stupid opportunist lowlifes who thought they could harvest the odd wallet at knifepoint in a lonely subway station. It wasn't hard to see which one Jules was. Ben slackened his grip. He turned round to where Roberta was hovering in the background, and shook his head.

'Don't kill me!' Jules sobbed. 'Please God don't kill me! I just needed some cash . . . I'll never do it again, I swear.'

'I'm not going to kill you,' Ben said. 'Which means today's your lucky day. Remember, the next person you try it on with might not be so kind to you. Now get out of here.' He dragged Jules roughly to his feet and shoved him back up the tunnel.

Jules Leclercq was gone in seconds.

Ben sighed. 'I'm getting jumpy,' he confessed to Roberta.

It was 2.30 a.m. by the time they got back to the safehouse and locked the armoured door securely behind them. Ben and Roberta both knew that at some point they were going to have to get some sleep, but they were each too keyed-up and anxious to investigate what they'd recovered from the tomb to even think about rest.

After they'd quickly cleaned themselves up, Ben brewed a pot of very strong black coffee, lit a Gauloise from the gas stove and then dug out the notebook computer that had been stored away unused for a long time. 'It isn't quite state-of-the-art, but it'll do us.'

As he set the notebook up on the bare desk and pulled up two chairs, Roberta retrieved the hard drive from his bag. 'All right, let's check out what's on this thing.'

'Assuming its innards didn't get frazzled in the fire,' he said, plugging the drive into the computer. Roberta sat down at the keyboard. 'Don't say that, Ben. It's *got* to work or we've got basically nothing. We'll be right back where we started.'

After a few moments' tense wait, the machine recognised the hardware and they were in.

'This is it,' Roberta said with relief. 'Claudine's Tesla research. I hope to hell it tells us something.'

One thing was for sure – they weren't short of material to trawl through. 'This is going to take the rest of the night,' Roberta said, running her eye down the endless list of data files that had filled the screen.

Ben sipped the scalding black coffee. 'I've nothing else planned, have you?'

'Let's get into it. Where to even start, though?' She peered closely at the screen. 'All right, looks like we've got a lot of technical stuff here in these PDF documents.' As she opened up one after another, they came across what appeared to be scans of original blueprints for a weird and wonderful array of technological devices from the early twentieth century. 'These are all Tesla designs, as far as I can see. Christ knows where Claudine even got this stuff.'

Dispensing with the blueprints, Roberta opened another file that contained the drawings for Claudine's updated electro-mechanical Tesla oscillator, together with her own reports and images documenting the stages of building and testing it.

'We're going to need more than technical drawings to make sense of this,' Ben said, using the tip of his dying cigarette to light another.

'Ben, it's disgusting to chain-smoke like that.'

'I lost my Zippo.'

Roberta rolled her eyes, closed the file and scrolled further down the list. 'There's so much stuff. Wait, this looks interesting.' She clicked open a document file labelled 'TUNGUSKA'.

'The Tunguska incident?' Ben said as the document came on screen. It appeared to be a page scanned from a science journal from some years ago. Grainy monochrome images showed a desolate landscape ravaged by destruction, a giant crater surrounded by countless fallen trees.

Roberta's gaze flicked rapidly down the page. 'Okay, I know a little bit about this, so I'll summarize. June 1908, Tunguska, Siberia. The largest meteorite or comet impact on or near Earth in recorded history. Conservative estimates equated the destructive power of the incident to around ten to fifteen megatons of TNT. That's a thousand times more powerful than the Hiroshima atom bomb. Two thousand square kilometres of forest and eighty million trees wiped out. No significant human casualties, due to the remoteness of the location.'

'Why would Claudine have stored information about a comet collision?' Ben said. 'These things hit us naturally every so often, don't they?'

'Except that this one didn't hit us at all,' Roberta replied. 'The weird thing about it was, even though it's classed as an impact event, no actual impact happened. There's no crater, no metcorite fragments, no physical evidence of a collision. To this day, the cause of the explosion is unknown. An official mystery. The best most scientists can suggest is that the object burst above the Earth's surface, and the destruction was caused by the shockwave.'

'I'm sure that's very fascinating, but what's it got to do with Tesla?'

'It might have a lot to do with him. Some people believe he caused it.'

'You're kidding me.'

'It's all here,' Roberta said, scrolling down. 'Yup, here we are. "It was speculated at the time that Tesla might have used the Wardenclyffe Tower to deliver a charge of energy big enough to bring about that kind of effect."'

'The Wardenclyffe Tower?'

'It was a specially-built laboratory,' she explained, 'housed inside a giant tower on Long Island, sixty-five miles from New York City, funded by J.P. Morgan, the founder of US Steel and one of Tesla's biggest private sponsors. It was built between 1901 and 1902, kind of like a giant steel mushroom hundreds of feet tall, and was meant to be a revolutionary new wireless telecommunications transmitter. Secretly, Tesla planned it as a precursor to his death ray machine. He called it his "Peace Ray", and allegedly claimed that it could project an electrical shield that would make America invincible to attack, while throwing out beams of incredible power right across the world.'

'Hmm. Right.'

'I know how it sounds, but it's as simple as bringing down a building using small vibrations,' Roberta explained. 'The difference between an electrical current that can be used to run a small household appliance and one that can be used as a weapon of mass destruction is just a question of timing. The same amount of energy it takes to run a 240-volt appliance for an hour, delivered in a millionth of a second, would blow it to bits. Now imagine a transmitter generating 100 million volts of pressure and currents of 100 billion watts, resonating at a radio frequency of 2 megahertz. That means the amount of energy released in one cycle of its oscillation would equate to 10 megatons' worth of destructive energy. In effect, you've got the power of a nuclear warhead delivered by radio signal, at the speed of light, allowing the sender to instantly vaporise any location in the world at the touch of a button.'

It sounded too horribly convincing for Ben to go on acting sceptical. 'Forget Hitler,' he said. 'This Tesla's got to be the most dangerous lunatic who ever lived.'

'Funny, that's what the Wardenclyffe financiers thought

too, when they found out what he was up to. Before he knew it, the cash got pulled out from under him and the tower was closed down. But there are some who say even that wasn't enough to kill the project, not if Tesla had anything to do with it. It's been claimed he was still secretly experimenting with it as late as 1908.'

Ben went on blazing through the text of the article. Most of the technical data meant nothing to him, but he caught the upshot: at the time of the Tunguska event, Tesla, in a state of desperation over losing the precious funding for his Wardenclyffe Tower, was reported to have been attempting to direct energy beams at the Arctic Circle in order to catch the attention of Admiral Robert Peary, the polar explorer and expedition leader who had set out in July 1908 to become the first man to reach the North Pole. Months earlier, Tesla had contacted the influential Peary to ask him to take note of any unusual phenomena he noticed on his expedition.

But if Tesla had been hoping to gain some publicity for his little toy, the experiment went badly awry when he overshot his target and the beam hit the Siberian tundra by mistake, laying waste to a gigantic tract of it. Thanks to the remoteness of the location, the turmoil of the 1917 Russian revolution and the civil war that followed it, the sheer extent of the damage had gone unreported until 1927.

'But surely there's no real evidence for any of this?' Ben said.

Roberta gave a dry smile. 'When is there ever?' She closed the file and immediately opened the one directly beneath it that had caught her eye, titled 'TUNGUSKA 2' followed by several question marks.

The file was a scan of a small news report from a recent edition of a science periodical. 'Wow, this is strange,' she said. 'Listen. "In March a team of archaeologists, led by Dr

Hermann Murke of Bonn University to search for lost ancient Hindu temples across the mountainous regions of Kazakhstan and Mongolia, stumbled on a wide and hitherto unreported area of extreme devastation that has left scientists baffled. The nature of the damage appears to resemble that caused by the still-unexplained Siberian Tunguska incident of 1908, but on an even greater scale. Early reports suggest that an asteroid-like object may have struck the remote location, although these findings are disputed by leading astronomers and other scholars".

'Can't blame Tesla for that one,' Ben said.

'I guess not. So what's it doing on here? Good question.' She heaved a sigh, closed the file and moved on down the list. 'There are a bunch of image files here below. Let's take a look.'

Roberta started clicking open one image after another.

'Now this is getting a little weird,' she said.

Chapter Twenty-Four

They were pictures of disaster zones. One after another: the same thing. Shattered buildings and collapsed bridges and streets filled with tangled wreckage. People wandering forlorn among the levelled ruins of their homes. Homeless children playing in the dust. Survivors being pulled out of the ground.

'Earthquakes,' Roberta muttered. 'But why? Claudine wasn't a seismologist, or a geologist, or anything like that.'

'She didn't just take these images off the web,' Ben said, thinking back to the immigration stamps he'd seen on the passport in Claudine's apartment. 'She travelled there in person and photographed these sites herself. But why? And what's the connection with her Tesla research?'

'That's another good question,' Roberta said, looking perplexed.

The image she had onscreen was a panoramic shot of a city that had been utterly devastated by an earthquake, once-grand buildings reduced to a barren field of rubble with a few miserable-looking people sifting about for anything they could retrieve from the destruction. 'It's terrible,' Roberta said, then paused, peering more closely. She pointed. 'Look at the architecture, or what's left of it. And the people. Looks like somewhere in Central or South America.'

'There was a South American visa stamp on her passport,' Ben said. 'Republic of Taráca.'

'Sounds familiar,' Roberta said, trying to remember. 'Yeah, that's right. There was a huge earthquake there some time back, wasn't there? It was all over the news for a few days.'

'But what was she doing there?'

'Beats me.'

'There's one last image file below,' Ben said. 'It might tell us more.'

Roberta opened it up and they both stared at it, hoping for illumination. None came. The photo was of a house, or what had once been a house, in some leafy countryside setting surrounded by sunlit oak trees. All but one of the house's stone walls had fallen in, and the roof was collapsed. 'Where's this?' Roberta said.

'France,' Ben said. 'Possibly Belgium.' He pointed out the remaining window. 'You can tell from the shutters. My old place in Normandy had ones just the same.'

'It can't be earthquake damage,' Roberta said. 'Look how all the trees are still standing. And when was there ever a bad quake in this part of Europe?'

'Never. Either the house fell down with age, or . . .'

'Or?'

'Or maybe, just maybe, someone was out playing with their Tesla toys.'

'Claudine?'

Ben shrugged. 'Who else?'

'I wish there was more,' Roberta said in frustration. 'All we can do is keep trawling through and hope we learn something.' She closed the picture file and clicked on the next one down. The document opened up to reveal a whole mass of technical data analysing the steady build-up in intensity and destructiveness of earthquakes during recent years; there were charts and graphs of Richter scale readings, maps and aerial photos. 'Christ, more seismology stuff,' she groaned. 'I just don't get it.'

They ploughed on, both exhausted but too mesmerised to tear themselves away. The more they read, the more bafflingly diverse the material seemed to be. 'Either it's just a load of random stuff she loaded onto the drive purely for somewhere to store it—' Ben began.

'Or something else links it all together,' Roberta finished for him. 'Believe me, Claudine wasn't the kind of person who did things randomly. There has to be a common factor. And that's what I'm scared of. This goes way further than I'd imagined it might.' She drew away from the screen and rubbed her eyes. 'I don't think I can take much more of this. My eyes are burning.'

'Keep going,' Ben urged her.

'It gets weirder,' she said. 'Look at this one. Studies in predictive animal behaviour?'

For no clear reason, Claudine had collated a variety of veterinary psychology studies focusing on the unexplained phenomenon of how animals, either wild or in captivity, seemed to be able to tell when a major storm or a natural disaster was impending: dogs barking, birds fleeing their nests, zoo animals becoming distressed. Claudine's own report on the findings was included in the document. '"Typically, studies have shown that the behaviour of animal subjects can help predict the event some two hours or more in advance",' Roberta read aloud. '"Analysis of the data shows how consistent this phenomenon is".' She snorted impatiently. 'That's just great, Claudine, but what the hell does it *mean?*'

'There's a video clip embedded there,' Ben said.

As the low-definition video began to run, Roberta expanded it to full screen view. The footage had been filmed somewhere rural, arid and hot. 'Spain?' she speculated.

'Maybe. Or it could be Latin America again.'

As they watched, an unsteady camcorder shot panned over a dusty-looking herd of equines milling nervously behind a makeshift barricade. 'Why was Claudine filming horses?' Roberta said.

'They're mules,' Ben said.

'Of course. That explains everything,' she muttered.

The video's background showed obvious signs of earthquake damage: a wooded hillside partially slipped away, crumbled limestone buildings shimmering in the heat haze, a truck half-buried under rubble, a gang of labourers gamely sweltering under the sun trying to clear up the mess. As Ben and Roberta went on watching, the camera wavered momentarily to one side and the figure of a woman came into view for just a second: slim, dark, early thirties, in a loose top and shorts. 'That's her,' Roberta said sadly. 'That's Claudine. I wonder who was working the camera?'

Next, a burly guy appeared and Claudine's voice introduced him off-camera in French-accented English as Señor Diego Sanchez, owner-operator of the Santa Catarina Mule Sanctuary six miles outside the city of San Vicente.

'I'm sure I've heard of that city before, but I can't remember what country it's in,' Roberta said. Ben didn't reply and went on watching as an interview began in which Claudine quizzed Sanchez in her halting English about the behaviour of the animals in the lead-up to the recent earthquake. Sanchez described how, when the area had been hit by a smaller quake back in 1996, the animals had warned them a good two hours in advance by their nervous agitation. This time around, there had been no warning.

'It took them as much by surprise as it did us,' Sanchez said with a sigh as he looked across at his wrecked buildings. 'It was like they lost their, you know, their sixth sense. They just didn't know it was coming.'

There the clip ended.

'So what was that all about?' Ben said.

They'd been staring hard at the computer screen for nearly two hours. 'God, I need to sleep,' Roberta said, leaning away from the screen and covering her eyes with her hands. 'I haven't stopped since I left Ottawa.'

'One more,' Ben said. He was determined to try to make more sense of the puzzle before he took a break.

'I can't, Ben. I can't think or see straight, and none of this is making sense to me.' She stood up wearily, walked to the armchair and slouched heavily in it.

Taking over the computer from her, Ben clicked on a final file and found that it was full of saved emails. There were several dozen of them, without exception between Claudine and someone calling themselves 'D' who was using the kind of webmail account favoured by people who wanted to remain anonymous. The correspondence had taken place within the last eight months.

'Think you might want to see this,' he said to Roberta.

Chapter Twenty-Five

Message received May 29, 23.57:
Claudine
I'm sorry we fought. Plse listen 2 me. 2 dangerous 4 U
2 go on with this work. Seriously advise you quit
NOW, before it's 2 late.
D

Message sent May 30, 08.03:
Hi,
I already told you I can't quit when we've already
uncovered so much. If you want to stop, fine. But not
me.
Claudine

Message received May 30, 10.48:
Claudine,
Begging you. Remember what happened 2 Guardini
and Shelton. Same will happen 2 all of us eventually, if
we're not careful. THEY KNOW who we are.
NOWHERE is safe.
D

Message sent May 30, 11.06:
Hi,
I don't like you talking that way. Come to Paris. We'll
find someplace safe, where they can't find us and we
can go on working together like before. We can beat
them. We can expose them forever. Just have to
keep trying.
Claudine

Message received May 31, 04.16:
Repeat. NOWHERE is safe. U cant beat them. They
have total power. But U can still get out. Quit now. Go
back 2 Ur old life and dont breathe a word 2 anyone of
what U know. Have 2 promise me. Last chance.
D

Message sent May 31, 07.02:
I told you when we first met that I could never stop
what I'm doing, and I meant what I said. This is too
big and important, I thought you knew that. People
need to hear the truth. And one day they will, and the
whole thing will be made to end. Don't you
understand? This IS my life now. Stop trying to talk me
out of it, it won't work.
Claudine

Message received June 1, 18.37:
Sorry 2 hear that. Wish i could change ur mind.
Cant talk now
B safe
D

'D,' Roberta said, returning to peer at the computer screen. She was wide awake again and had read through the entire correspondence bolt upright. 'You thinking what I'm thinking?'

'D for Daniel,' Ben said. 'The guy she posted the letter to. Sounds as if they were heavily involved in this together.' He jumped up, went over to where he'd dumped his leather jacket and took the paper from his pocket that he'd written the details on earlier that night. It was crumpled and dirty but the name 'Daniel Lund' and the address near Jäkkwik in Sweden were still legible.

'So now's when we have to try and get in contact with him,' she said. 'He clearly knows what it's all about.'

'And how do you propose to do that?'

'We have his email address, don't we?'

Ben shook his head. 'Read the guy's messages. He's either a paranoid nut or he's genuinely in the same kind of danger as Claudine was, which is a distinct possibility.'

'Or he's dead,' Roberta conceded.

'Which we also need to consider. Whichever it is, I don't think he's going to reply to us. Assuming he's still living and breathing at this point, the moment our message hits his inbox he'll bolt like a scared rabbit and we'll never find him again.'

'Then what do we do?'

Ben looked at his watch. Sunrise wasn't that far away, and his head was spinning with tiredness. 'We try and get a few hours' sleep. Then we get some more hot coffee and some food in us. Then we go to Sweden. If he's alive, we'll find him. If he's not, at least we'll know.'

She smiled. 'You make it sound so simple.'

'I'm a simple kind of guy,' he said, but didn't smile back.

*

The first time Ben had ever brought Roberta back to the hallowed privacy of his safehouse, in the brusque and unsympathetic manner that had marked the beginning of their acquaintance, he'd made her sleep on the living room floor while he took the sole bedroom. This time round, the bundle of blankets on the rug would be for him.

'Damn it,' she said, rooting around in her travel holdall. 'I was in such a rush leaving home, I forgot to pack my pyjamas.'

'There's some old shirts of mine in the cupboard in the hall,' he told her. 'Might be a bit baggy on you, but feel free to borrow one.'

'Thanks.' She watched him as he arranged his makeshift bed for the night. 'You know, Ben?'

'What?' he said, pausing and looking up.

'I hate to make you sleep on your own floor. It's your apartment, after all. And you need to rest as badly as I do.'

'I've kipped in a lot worse places than the floor,' he said.

'Spare me the gruesome details. We could always share, you know?'

He looked at her guardedly.

'You don't have to be coy. I didn't mean it that way,' she said. 'In any case, apparently we already got over that phase of our relationship a long time ago.'

'I suppose we did,' he said.

'We're friends, right? And friends can share a bed without it meaning anything, yes?'

'I suppose they could,' he said. 'As long as everyone was clear that it didn't mean anything. That it couldn't possibly . . .'

'Everyone is clear,' she said. 'Don't make a big deal out of it, okay?'

But neither was unaware of the awkwardness between

them as they settled down to grab a few hours' sleep, as widely spaced apart as the double mattress would allow, with their backs to one another.

'Goodnight, Ben,' came her soft voice in the darkness after they'd switched out the lights.

'Goodnight, Roberta.'

A long silence, then: 'Ben?'

'What?'

'I'm glad you're with me.'

He said nothing. After a time he heard her breathing fall into the slow, deep rhythm of sleep. He lay and stared into the darkness, grappling with his thoughts and listening to the hypnotic, never-ending background murmur of the Parisian traffic until, sometime after dawn, he slipped away into a restless slumber of his own.

Chapter Twenty-Six

Virginia
Thirty-two days earlier

In the middle of a warm, sultry night in May, in an attractive townhouse in a sleepy, moonlit, tree-lined street in Shepherdstown, Fairfax County, a cell phone had started ringing on the bedside table.

The man in the bed woke up, shot an arm out from under the sheet and grabbed the phone. He scowled as he clamped it to his ear. 'Who the hell's this? Do you know what time it is?'

'Am I speaking to Jack Quigley?' said the caller. Male, maybe forties, gravelly voice, audibly agitated.

'This is Quigley. Who're you?'

'Carlisle,' the caller said. 'Yeah, Steve Carlisle, that's right.'

'You don't sound too sure about that, Mr Carlisle.' Quigley also thought he sounded as if he'd been drinking. 'I don't really care. I don't know you, I don't know how you got this number. Call me again and I'll have the cops on you, understand?'

'Don't hang up,' the caller pleaded. 'I need your help. Can't say who gave me your number. They said you could be trusted.' A pause. 'I worked for the government, too. Please listen to me.'

'I don't know what you're talking about. I'm just a private citizen,' Quigley lied. 'You need help with something, I suggest you go to the cops.'

'I can't go to the cops. I can't go to the Feds. You're Company, right? You're who I need.'

'The Company' was what its employees and other United States Government officials called the CIA. Jack Quigley was a Special Investigator with the agency, but what he did for a living wasn't meant to be public knowledge. 'Whoever told you that is mistaken, and this conversation's over. Do not attempt to contact me again. That's a warning. Goodbye.'

Quigley was just about to end the call when he heard the caller say, 'Mitch Shelton.'

He instantly snatched the phone back to his ear. 'What did you say?'

'Mitch Shelton,' the caller repeated. A pause, then: 'I know how he died.'

The words were like a slap. Shelton and Quigley had joined the agency at the same time back in the early 2000s and gone through several recruit training programs together, forming a friendship. There was a framed photograph of the two of them on the wall in Quigley's office, taken five years or so earlier on a canoe trip in the Missouri Breaks. Quigley, then 39 and still looking as fit as in his Marine Corps days; Shelton, a year older, tanned and handsome with a mile-wide grin – the two of them were in brightly-coloured wetsuits and mock-sparring with their canoe paddles. In latter years, Mitch had been deployed in various roles overseas, not all of which he could talk openly about, and they'd only been able to catch up now and then over a beer or six.

Then four months ago, while on a scuba diving vacation off the Florida coast with his wife Janice, tragedy struck.

According to the coroner's report, the cause of Mitch's death had been accidental drowning, perhaps brought on by a cramp, nobody knew. Even more horrifically, his floating body had been caught up in the propellers of a boat sometime after death had occurred, causing such mutilation that he'd had to be identified from dental records.

'Everyone knows how Mitch died,' Quigley said, swallowing hard.

'No, they don't,' the caller said. 'But if you wanna go on believing a bunch of lies, that's up to you. Not just about Shelton. He's just for starters.'

'Your name isn't Carlisle,' Quigley snapped. 'Who the hell are you?'

'There's a phone booth two blocks south of your house. Be there in ten minutes and dial this number.' The caller read it out twice. 'You got that?'

'I have it. But why should I do it?'

'You want to know more, don't you?' the caller said, then hung up.

Quigley almost didn't bother taking the bait. He didn't waste time on cranks and he was upset by the reminder of what had happened to poor Mitch. More importantly, to respond to this guy was an admission of what he did. It could be a mistake.

Minutes ticked by. Quigley sat on the edge of the bed and fretted, unable to put the call out of his mind. Finally, as time was running out, his burning curiosity overwhelmed him. He did want to know more.

He pulled on his clothes and hurried downstairs. The dog had come out of his basket and was wagging his tail in the dark hallway, full of expectation. 'Hey, Red. You feel like a midnight run?' Quigley said, grabbing the leash from the stand and clipping it onto his collar. He and the big Labrador lived alone together in the townhouse. There was no Mrs Quigley, not yet. The CIA didn't leave a lot of time for a personal life, especially for someone as dedicated to their job as he was.

Quigley leapt down the steps from his front door and sprinted up the night street with the dog pounding happily along behind him, tongue lolling. Quigley reached the phone booth two blocks south and dialled the number he'd been given. He was out of breath and knew he needed to work on his fitness.

'I was beginning to think you wouldn't call,' said Carlisle's voice.

'All right, you got my attention. I don't like this anonymous crap, and I especially don't like being gotten out of bed in the middle of the night. You know who I am, so you know the kind of trouble I can bring on you if you mess with me.' Against his better judgement, Quigley was coming out in the open now, but he was hooked.

'Nobody's messing. You alone? Definitely nobody followed you?'

Quigley waved his arm exasperatedly at the empty street around him. 'Who's going to follow me through Shepherdstown at this time of the goddamn night?'

'If you only knew. You really have no idea, do you?'

'You'd better start talking to me, asshole,' Quigley said, ready to put the phone down.

There was a pause. 'Three words,' Carlisle said. 'The Nemesis Program.'

To Quigley, it sounded like something out of a bad spy movie. 'What the hell is that? I've never heard of it.'

'If I'd thought you had, I wouldn't even be speaking to you.'

'Quit talking in riddles. Tell me about Mitch Shelton instead.'

'That's exactly what I'm doing,' Carlisle explained. 'Shelton was involved with Nemesis. He was recruited to the program nearly two years ago.'

'He never told me anything about it.'

'Go figure,' Carlisle said. 'These guys don't do transparency. Nobody talks about Nemesis, nobody knows about it. Not CIA, not Homeland Security, not even the President.'

'But you do,' Quigley said sceptically. 'That makes you someone really special, right?'

'I was part of it,' Carlisle said. 'I know everything there is to know. Shit that'd bring down the whole administration if it got out. The most highly classified government program there is, and for a good reason. What they're into makes the Defense Advanced Research Projects Agency look like kids' stuff.'

'So you can tell me all about DARPA,' Quigley challenged him, probing.

'I could tell you plenty,' Carlisle said. 'Look, you gotta believe me. I was with the Nemesis Program for three years, until I quit two months ago. Got myself discharged on medical grounds – depression and alcohol and substance abuse problems. Truth is, I just couldn't live with myself anymore, knowing what they were doing. I just had to get out. Now I'm scared, I'm shit scared, but I *have* to do something.'

'Do something about what?' Quigley demanded.

There was a heavy pause. 'That's all I'm gonna say for now. You want to know the rest, we have to meet in person.'

'You're telling me you're a drunken addict with mental health issues. That doesn't inspire a whole lot of confidence.'

'Like I say, you want to go on swallowing their mother-fucking lies, that's your business. What I have to say could bust everything wide open. I figured you could help me, but maybe I should just take my chances with CNN. When it blows up you'll be real sorry you missed out.'

'Hold on. Why me? I'm just an investigator. I'm part of a machine, a small part. I don't have any real power.'

'This is hot, my friend. I go straight to the higher levels with it, I'll get fried. What I heard is, you're a real straight shooter and you don't fuck around. That true?'

'I do my job,' Quigley said. 'Whatever it takes to get it done. If that makes me a straight shooter, then I guess that's the way it is.'

'Then meet me tomorrow night in D.C. The American City Diner on Connecticut Avenue Northwest. Know it?'

Quigley could feel himself getting sucked in deeper. He paused a beat. 'I'll find it.'

'Seven-thirty. Be there. You won't know me but I'll know you.'

Click. And the phone went dead.

Chapter Twenty-Seven

Paris wouldn't have been Paris in the morning without the aroma of fresh-baked bread in the air, and it still lingered in the streets along with the ever-present traffic fumes as Ben ventured out early to get them some breakfast. He returned carrying a brown paper bag from the *boulangerie* down the road, and was making coffee when he heard Roberta get up. Moments later she made a tousle-haired appearance in the kitchen doorway, bare-legged below the hem of the old shirt of his she'd borrowed to sleep in.

'I got us some croissants,' he said, averting his eyes.

'Oh. Nice. Guess I'd better put some clothes on.'

They had breakfast in the kitchen, sitting across the table from one another dunking their croissants in their coffee in silence. 'You look thoughtful,' she commented.

'The wedding rehearsal would have been this afternoon. I keep thinking about it.'

'I know. I'm sorry.'

Ben shrugged. He knocked back the last of his coffee, patted his pockets for his cigarettes.

'What's the point?' she asked, watching him.

'What's the point of what?'

'Of working so hard to keep in shape if you're just going to harm your body with those damn things anyway.'

'Bodily harm is my middle name,' he said. 'What's it to you?'

'Apart from having to suck second-hand smoke? Nothing. Just that I heard you doing your exercises earlier, that's all. You put a lot into it.'

'Sorry if I woke you.'

'I wasn't asleep. How many do you do?'

'Press-ups? A hundred, hundred and fifty.'

'Every morning?'

'Twice a day, usually. And a run, if I get time. It keeps me sharp.'

'Not bad for an old dog,' she said with a smile. 'You don't drink like you used to. That's good. But you really need to quit those cigarettes, Ben.'

He shot her a foul look, took a Gauloise from the pack, then muttered 'Fuck it' under his breath and shoved it back in. 'Hurry up and finish your coffee. We have a busy morning ahead.'

The fat taxi driver, crammed so tightly behind the wheel of his grey Mercedes that he looked like a permanent fixture in there, dropped them outside the Banque National de Paris off Boulevard Jourdan, close to the Porte d'Orléans on the southern edge of the city. Ben told the driver to wait, which the guy seemed all too happy to do in order to rip open a fresh pack of Haribo snacks from a bulging supply on the front passenger seat. Walking into the crowded bank, Ben took Roberta's elbow and steered her away from the tellers. 'Not that way.'

'I thought you came to get money.'

'We won't be making a withdrawal from an account,' he said. He still had a personal bank account in France, but couldn't afford to take the risk of tapping into it. Depending on who was really after them, an open, recorded transaction could potentially flag up a chain of computer alerts that would pinpoint their exact location within seconds. 'There's a better way of doing it.'

'How else do you get money from a bank?' she asked.

In his days of working the kidnap and ransom scene across Europe, Ben had maintained several safe deposit boxes in different cities. Some people kept diamond tiaras locked away in theirs, some people kept gold bars. Ben's boxes were strictly for the utilitarian purpose of storing quantities of cash, the false IDs he'd sometimes needed to carry out his business, and other tools of the trade for which he could dip in and out whenever he liked. Just as he'd never fully got around to selling off the safehouse, he'd never quite taken the step of closing down his deposit boxes.

Some old habits just wouldn't die. It was as if they'd been sitting there waiting for him all this time. *Maybe it's true,* he reflected bitterly. *Maybe I always knew I'd come back to this sooner or later.*

Following a few discreet formalities and a short wait seated in a velvety little lounge area, Ben and Roberta were shown through to the private viewing room where his box had been brought up from the vault.

She gasped when she saw the stacks of banknotes inside, wrapped in transparent plastic. Ben lifted the cash out of the box. He didn't need to count it to know there was about fifteen thousand euros there.

'Just a little something for a rainy day, huh?' Roberta said.

'I think we're in for a spell. But I'm hoping this should cover our expenses until we figure a way through this situation.'

Roberta's eyebrows rose when she saw the semi-automatic handgun that had been nestling underneath the cash. Ben lifted it out along with its five loaded spare magazines. It was an old Browning Hi-Power, superseded now as a military arm, but the model of weapon he'd spent more hundreds of hours training with during his time than any other and which suited him like a well-worn shoe. Not to mention that for his purposes, the Hi-Power was a hell of a lot easier to conceal, ready for instant use, than a bulky machine carbine.

No, some old habits really wouldn't die. *Here I go again*, he thought. He stuck the pistol into his belt behind the right hip, where it was neatly covered by his jacket, and dropped the magazines into his pockets. He was now carrying seventy-eight rounds of 9mm Parabellum on his person, not counting the capacity of the submachine gun inside his bag, where he stuffed the thick pile of wrapped money, minus a wad that he folded inside his wallet.

The last item Ben took from the box was one of several false passports he'd had made back when he'd been active on the kidnap and ransom circuit. He hadn't used them for years; the duplicates he'd kept at Le Val were still gathering dust in his personal safe in the training facility's armoury room. He picked one out, a cover that had never been blown or compromised: John Freeman, a professional wine buyer born in Oxford a few months before Ben's real birthdate. He hadn't done any travelling in quite a while – maybe now he'd get the chance again.

'I think we're good to go,' he said. He strapped the items up inside his bag, closed the box and called the guards in to come and take it away.

The enormous screen filled almost an entire wall of the Director's tranquil personal office. He was watching it now as he sat at his desk, his fingers laced together, lips pursed and a customary frown of deep concentration on his wizened brow. He might have been staring fixedly at the high-definition image of the vast container ship gliding across his screen, which a few days ago had been the primary focus of his current plans, but now the core of his thoughts was elsewhere. He picked up a remote and jabbed it at the screen; the image of the ship disappeared to make way for the news report footage that had been troubling him from the moment it had broken earlier.

French Emergency Services had completed their search for survivors among the ruins of the gutted private chapel on the De Bourg family estate near Paris. Their official report, which the Director already had on another screen in front of him, stated in effect that the only bodies in the place were the ones already interred in the family tomb beneath the chapel.

The Director had been in this game a long, long time, and he was an extremely hard man to trick. And yet, tricked he had been. It was now painfully clear that this Ben Hope, this troublesome new player who'd appeared out of left field, had caught him out with a ploy intended to buy time for himself and the Ryder woman.

The facts were all there on the desk. The BMW Alpina left abandoned at the scene was a company car registered to Hope's former business in Normandy, reported stolen the night before. Which meant, the Director realised, that Hope must have figured out about the tracking device planted on the vehicle. In turn, that also meant something almost unprecedented in the Director's experience: that the target was successfully staying a step ahead, for now.

How Hope and Ryder had effected their seemingly impossible escape from the chapel was anyone's guess, as was their current location. They could be anywhere, and the Director didn't like uncertainties. It would seem, he thought grimly, that McGrath had made a mistake this time. That couldn't happen again.

It was time to alert everybody. Hope was dangerous and he had to be taken down as a matter of top-level priority before he did more damage.

The Director's thoughts were interrupted by the beep of his intercom. He pressed a button and heard the voice of his closest aide, an efficient if slightly nervy fifteen-year veteran of his team named Isaac Friedkin.

'Sir, there's been a development. We have security camera images of Hope and Ryder walking into the Boulevard Jourdan branch of the Banque Nationale in Paris twenty minutes ago. The facial recognition software confirms their identities beyond any doubt.'

'Where are they now?'

'They haven't come out yet,' Friedkin said. 'We presume they're still inside.'

'Put it on my screen,' the Director snapped. He flicked the remote again, and the news report vanished as the video playback covered his wall. His wrinkled eyes scanned the milling crowds of pedestrians in the street outside the Banque Nationale. He saw a grey Mercedes taxi pull up at the kerbside and its passengers get out and walk quickly across the pavement to the bank's entrance. The blond-haired man in the leather jacket and his female companion were definitely his targets.

'What about inside? Don't we have access to the bank's interior video system?'

'Working on it as we speak,' Friedkin's voice said from the speaker. 'Should be hooked up any time now.'

'Not good enough. Work faster. Where's McGrath?'

'Already mobilised and on his way, ETA four minutes.'

The Director nodded. 'I want every exit covered on the

ground and eyes in the air. Don't let them get away this time. Am I clear?'

The Director leaned back in the plush chair and shut his tired eyes. He wasn't happy with the way this was heading. The time for discretion in this matter might very well just have ended.

Chapter Twenty-Eight

By the time Ben and Roberta had left the bank and returned to the waiting Mercedes, the taxi driver had finished up his packet of snacks and was crumpling the empty wrapper into his map compartment with a hundred others. He gave a belch and asked laconically, 'Where to now, folks?'

Ben told him an address near the Gare d'Austerlitz railway station. The driver nodded, took the wheel in his chubby fists and pulled unhurriedly away into the traffic.

'Of all the speed-freak psychopathic taxi racers in Paris, we had to pick the Incredible Human Sloth,' Roberta said, loudly enough for the driver to have heard if he'd understood any English. 'So where are we going?' she asked Ben.

'You've been there before,' Ben replied. 'Fred's garage. He's a guy I go to if I need quick transport with no questions asked.'

'I remember. The place we bought that little Peugeot that time? The one that ended up shot full of holes in a field.'

'That wasn't my fault,' Ben said.

The driver chugged his way eastwards up Boulevard Kellerman and then took a left onto Avenue d'Italie, aiming for the river. Ben glanced at his watch, contained his impatience and gazed up at the blue sky over Paris.

'What is it?' Roberta asked when he'd been craning his neck at the window for almost a full minute.

'Maybe nothing,' he said. Was it his imagination playing tricks on him, or was that helicopter up there deliberately keeping pace with their taxi? He lost it for a few moments behind some tall buildings, then saw it again, hovering slowly a couple of hundred feet above the rooftops. Without binoculars, he could just about make out that it wasn't a police chopper. It was either black or very dark green, with no markings that he could see.

'Take a right here,' he ordered the driver.

'That's not the way.'

'Just do it, okay?'

The Mercedes turned off the main street, cutting down between tight rows of parked cars. 'Now take that left,' Ben said, pointing.

'That's a one-way street,' the driver complained.

'Twenty euros.'

'You got it, pal.' They made the illegal turn, frightening a cyclist.

'What's happening? Are we being followed?' Roberta asked anxiously.

'We'll know for sure one way or the other in a minute,' Ben said. He kept glancing up out of the windows and the sunroof as they cut through the maze of backstreets. With luck, he was just being paranoid; if he wasn't, grey Mercedes taxis were everywhere in Paris and it shouldn't be too hard to blend in.

But when they rejoined the main street a few minutes later, Ben saw that he'd been wrong on both counts. The chopper was still there, hovering lower over the rooftops, very obviously tracking them and showing no sign of losing them in the traffic.

'Change of plan,' Ben told the driver. 'We need to head southwest back towards the Boulevard Périphérique.'

The driver shrugged. What did he care? It was their ride. They could take him all over Paris if they wanted.

'And step on it a bit,' Ben said. 'I'll make it worth your while.'

'Why the ring road?' Roberta asked him.

'When you're being watched from the air, the thing to do is go underground,' he said. Paris' circular dual carriageway was dotted with road tunnels. Just a few minutes' drive and a quarter circuit to the west from their nearest access route, Porte de Gentilly, the boulevard passed through two that were each more than half a kilometre long. Stopping in the fast-moving flow of traffic wasn't exactly permitted, but Ben reckoned than an extra fifty euros might persuade the driver to fake a breakdown, giving his passengers time to slip away on foot and disappear through one of the service exits that led off from the inside of the tunnel. When the taxi reappeared in the chopper's sights, it would be an empty grey Mercedes that would be leading its pursuers on a merry dance around the city, its driver supplied with a fistful of cash and instructions to keep dawdling about in circles all day long.

Ben soon saw that it wasn't going to happen that way, though. As the taxi changed course, cutting southwards towards Porte de Gentilly, he realised with a sinking feeling that his plan was already thwarted before it had even begun. 'Shit,' he muttered.

Roberta looked at him with wide eyes. 'What now?'

'Behind us. Three cars back. The black Audi Q7. They must be in radio contact with the chopper.'

Roberta turned to look through the rear window. The Audi SUV was weaving quickly through the traffic to catch up. Its occupants were hidden behind tinted glass. 'How could they have picked us up?' she asked breathlessly. 'Are you sure?'

Ben could read the vehicle's body language like a person's. He was certain it was deliberately tailing them. There was one way to find out.

'Slow down,' he ordered the driver. 'Do it now. Right down to a crawl.'

The driver gave him an irritable look in the mirror, then reluctantly nudged the brakes and brought his speed down enough to elicit a chorus of enraged honking from the Parisian drivers behind them. Cars shot past on either side. A hand poked out of the window of a red Renault and gave them the finger as it sped by.

'This slow enough for you?' the driver said resentfully.

Ben looked back. The Audi had slowed down with them and was keeping pace, making no attempt to overtake. That was good enough for him. 'It's too slow,' he ordered the driver. 'Put your foot down.'

'Go slower, go faster,' the driver muttered under his breath, picking up speed again. 'Doesn't know what he wants, this fucking guy.'

As they began to catch up with the rest of the traffic, the Audi surged forward as if it wanted to draw level with them. 'Faster,' Ben said to the driver. The Mercedes edged ahead.

'Oh, shit, Ben, there's another behind us,' Roberta said. A second identical black car had appeared in their wake, gaining rapidly on them. 'What are they going to do?'

'They want to box us in,' Ben told her. Outwardly he seemed calm, but he was thinking furiously fast. 'Any minute now a third will appear and try to head us off, force us to stop. After that, it could go two ways. Kill or capture.'

'We need to do something, Ben,' she muttered anxiously,

eyes fixed on the two Audis. The second Q7 was now close up behind them. The thudding beat of the helicopter was clearly audible above the engine and traffic noise. They were being systematically hemmed in.

Ben slipped the Browning out of his belt. He dropped the mag, checked it, snicked it back into place. Eased back the slide far enough to verify the round in the chamber. It was the pre-battle check he'd done so many times that he did it without thinking. He kept the gun out of sight behind the seat backrest in front of him. 'Are your brakes sticking or something?' he said harshly to the driver.

The fat neck twisted back towards them. 'Hey, you want me to lose my license? I'm already doing over the limit, pal.'

'This meathead's going to get us both killed,' Roberta said.

A pedestrian crossing was coming up ahead. At the side of the road, waiting for the lights to change, was a young woman with a pushchair and an additional toddler in tow. 'Don't slow down,' Ben told the driver as he prepared to brake. 'Another twenty if you burn the red light.'

Thankfully, the driver was as greedy for cash as he was for sugary snacks. As the lights changed he took his foot off the brake and went straight on through. The young woman shot the Mercedes a hostile look and then stepped out into the road, yanking her elder child along behind her.

Ben looked back. The two Audis had come to a sharp halt behind the crossing and were waiting impatiently to get through. He saw his moment. 'Pull over. Quickly. Just there.'

The driver shrugged carelessly and swerved the Mercedes to the kerbside. Ben thrust his Browning back in his belt and got out. He marched up to the driver's door and wrenched it open. Grabbing the driver's beefy arm, he hauled his bulk roughly from the driver's seat before the fat man could utter a sound in astonished protest. The driver staggered unbalanced across the pavement, eyes popping with fury.

'Thanks for the ride,' Ben said. He jumped in behind the wheel and flicked three twenty-euro notes out of the window. 'Don't eat it all at once.'

Behind them, the woman with the pushchair had reached the far side and the lights were changing again. The Audis shot forward with a squeal of tyres.

'They're coming,' Roberta said anxiously.

'All right,' Ben said, watching them loom up fast in the rear-view mirror. 'They want to play, so let's play. Buckle up.' He floored the pedal and the Mercedes took off with a revving roar, leaving the irate driver standing there shaking his fist.

Roberta was pressed back in her seat as Ben accelerated up the road. Parked cars and buildings flashed past in a blur.

The Audis weren't about to be left behind. The chase was on for real now.

Chapter Twenty-Nine

'Get us the hell out of this, Ben!' Roberta yelled from the back seat.

Ben's foot was hard down on the floor and the Mercedes' revs were pushing the red line as he accelerated up the street with the two black Audi Q7s in pursuit. Lines of traffic swerved desperately out of their path. Horns honked furiously. Glass shattered and tyres screeched left and right.

Ben pressed on aggressively through the melee. Another set of traffic signals came flashing up, and this time neither the Mercedes nor the Audis slowed down for the red lights but went racing over the crossing, scattering pedestrians and flying across a busy intersection and straight out into the dense counter-flow of traffic.

A juddering impact almost snatched the wheel out of Ben's hands as a Fiat, its driver's mouth open in a soundless scream behind the windscreen, cannoned into the side of the taxi with a crunch. Ben felt the Mercedes go into a slide, controlled it and accelerated determinedly on through the chaotic ocean of swerving, skidding, honking cars. Out of the corner of his eye in the rear-view mirror he saw one of the Audis collide heavily with another vehicle, slamming it aside in an explosion of shattering plastic and glass.

A motorcyclist locked up his front wheel, and parted

company with his machine, both sliding across the tarmac. Ben had to swerve violently to avoid running over him; the Mercedes veered towards the kerb and almost ploughed into a line of parked cars. Ben steered to the right of them, just clipping the wing mirror of the nearest before mounting the high kerb with a sound that made him worry deeply about the front suspension. But so far, German engineering seemed to be holding up to the job. The Mercedes went racing through the narrow gap between the shop fronts and buildings and the row of trees that lined the pavement. Shoppers scattered like pigeons.

Ben saw an opening in the line of parked cars and sent the Mercedes hurtling back out onto the road, the squeal of his tyres drowned out by the blare of horns from motorists skidding out of his path.

Both Audis were still in chase. Ben threw the car round a right turn, pushing it to the limits of traction and almost going up on two wheels. The first Audi followed his line around the bend. The second went wide and hit the opposite kerb, heading straight for the terrace of a corner café.

The breakfast crowd fled in panic at the car's approach. Plastic chairs and tables and people's morning coffee and croissants sailed up over its bonnet and into the air. The Audi ground to a halt and was quickly surrounded by a screaming mob, all beating on its windows.

Ben lost sight of the stalled Audi as he flew around another bend. The Mercedes blasted down the street with the other still right behind. A direction sign for the Périphérique shot past. Ben brutally hammered his way through the lines of slow-moving cars and followed it. The Audi came roaring after them.

The chopper was still directly overhead.

Tearing through the streets at such high speed, it was only

a few moments before they were weaving through the flow of traffic on the Paris ring road heading west. The Mercedes was going as fast as Ben dared let it, overtaking everything in sight and swinging all over the road like a pendulum. The chasing Audi collided from behind with a small hatchback that got in its way, and sent it spinning mercilessly into the roadside verge as it powered on by.

Ben couldn't see any sign of the second Q7, until Roberta's hoarse cry of 'There he is!' alerted him that it was back, certainly guided via radio communication from the chopper, and rapidly regaining ground on them. Whoever these people were, they were determined, and they took advanced pursuit courses.

The entrance to one of the shorter tunnels came flashing up. Moments later they were speeding though the underpass, concrete pillars zipping past, swerving from side to side to get around the slower traffic. The Audis were back in formation now, hunting constantly for an opening to draw level with the taxi.

'Ben, look out!' Roberta yelled as one of them suddenly charged up and began to creep up alongside to their left. The dark-tinted glass on the passenger side wound down and Ben was able to steal a glance at the men inside. The hard-faced, heavily-built driver was in his thirties or forties but had the silvery-white hair of a much older man.

The face of the front seat passenger wasn't something Ben gave much thought to. He was much more concerned about the pistol in his hand that was about to be aimed at the Mercedes.

Ben instinctively twisted the steering wheel and slammed the taxi sideways into the Audi, forcing it to the left. The Audi's left flank scraped the concrete centre embankment in a storm of sparks. Another pillar was coming up fast and

Ben meant to keep his pursuers pinned against the side and guide them right into it. At the last possible moment, he swerved violently away to the right so as not to get caught up in the devastating impact he expected to happen half a second later – but the Audi's driver reacted just in time, expertly managing only to shear off his left wing mirror and wheel arches with a screech of rending steel. The heavy vehicle slewed into a weave and the second Audi had to brake hard to avoid ramming it from behind.

The Mercedes exited the tunnel and burst back out into the bright sunlight at over 120 kilometres per hour. The two Audis had fallen back a good distance and now Ben saw his first real chance of losing them.

He sliced past a dawdling Vauxhall Corsa and then swore under his breath as he saw the two big trucks that filled the lanes ahead, blocking his way and moving at about half his speed. There was no way round or between them.

In short seconds, he'd lost his advantage and the Audis were coming up fast again. The passenger appeared at the window of the lead vehicle and aimed his pistol. The shot was no more than a muted pop over the roar of the engines. The taxi's rear window shattered, showering Roberta with glass.

'Fuck it,' Ben said. He twisted the wheel hard to the left and sent the Mercedes bucking and crashing over the central reservation into the opposite two lanes.

Suddenly they were in a sea of oncoming traffic hurtling towards them at combined speeds of over two hundred kilometres an hour. Roberta's shout of '*Are you nuts?*' dissolved into a scream as an oncoming Range Rover swerved out of their path and they only very narrowly missed a head-on collision that would have fused the two cars into one and annihilated everyone inside.

Ben was far too busy weaving his way at high speed through the mayhem to answer her. He needed every ounce of his concentration, as focused as a fighter pilot as he fought to keep them alive. Blaring horns wailed past on both sides and his vision was filled with headlights flashing furiously at him from everywhere.

But if he was nuts, the Audi drivers were too, because they were now carving their way rapidly upstream on the wrong side of the road in the Mercedes' wake. It seemed like nothing short of suicide was going to shake these guys off.

Nor the chopper. Ben could no longer see it, but he could feel the deep thump of the rotors in his guts and knew it was directly over them, keeping pace and flying low. This wasn't getting any better.

Suddenly, it got worse. Warning signs shot past announcing that a construction zone was up ahead. Beyond the sweeping curve of the next two hundred metres Ben could see the cranes and road works for the new overpass near the Porte de Sèvres, and the long elevated section of the Périphérique carrying traffic over the exit routes to and from the city. In the distance, traffic was down to a single lane in each direction and moving slow.

Just as Ben thought his options were dramatically falling away, he saw them drop to zero when he spotted the third Audi up ahead on the overpass. It had come round to head them off in the opposite direction and was storming through the oncoming traffic a hundred and fifty yards away and closing fast.

Whatever these guys were planning, they were betting on getting it done quickly. The trap was closing in and the endgame was just seconds away. Ben could visualise the passengers of the three Audis cocking an arsenal of small arms in preparation of hosing the taxi full of bullets and then beating a rapid getaway before the police came roaring down on the scene.

The Mercedes sped up the slope onto the overpass. The side barriers streaked past like ribbons. Streets and rooftops twenty feet below. The chopper hovering right above, its swaying belly visible through the sunroof. The two Audis closing in from behind. The third looming larger in front of them every second. Eighty yards; sixty. A game of chicken, with nowhere to go.

But Ben wasn't going to stop, even though there was no sane alternative. He pressed harder on the pedal. 'Wrap the seatbelt tight around you and stay low!' he yelled at Roberta over his shoulder.

Fifty yards. Thirty.

No sane alternative.

But sometimes there was no room for sanity.

Ben twisted the wheel. One quarter turn, hard right. Before Roberta had time to cry out, the Mercedes veered crazily off course, hit the side and burst through with a massive rending crash of metal on metal, ripping a whole section of barrier from its mountings.

The car flew over the edge of the overpass and into empty space.

Chapter Thirty

For just a second or two, it was like floating. Ben experienced a strange sensation of weightlessness that was somehow liberating and not unpleasant. The howl of the soaring engine and Roberta's cry from the back seat seemed muffled and far away.

Then reality cut back in with terrifying speed as the Mercedes dropped like a missile towards the road below and the traffic lumbering in and out of the Porte de Sèvres. Ben caught a glimpse of a huge articulated truck coming the other way and he was utterly convinced they were going to plummet right into its path and be smashed and rolled and twisted into tiny pieces all across the tarmac.

But then the bone-jolting impact as the taxi's spinning wheels touched down on the truck's roof told him that death wasn't going to be quite so instant. The Mercedes tore across the top of the truck with a shearing crunch that felt as if it had ripped the whole underside away, bounced, twisted in mid-air and nose-dived sideways towards the construction works at the side of the road. An inch difference in its trajectory and the car and its occupants would have been mangled against a steel rubbish skip. The car overflew it and landed on its left side in a ten-ton pile of sand that exploded outwards as if a bomb had burst against it

The driver's airbag punched Ben in the face as he was hurled forwards to meet it. He was stunned, but only for a moment: his first thought as his mind snapped back into focus was of Roberta. He wrestled the collapsed airbag out of the way, twisted himself around to see into the back of the mangled, overturned taxi and called her name.

'I'm okay,' came a muffled gasp from inside the flattened space between the rear seats and the roof. 'I'm fine, I'm okay. What about you?'

'I'm fine,' he said. He was blind in his left eye for some reason, and he could taste blood – but that didn't matter to him. He struggled to free himself of the seatbelt, only very dimly aware of the carnage that was happening just a few yards away on the overpass.

As the Mercedes had gone flying off the edge, the three Audi Q7s had hammered on their brakes to avoid a three-way collision, skidding all over the road. The one that had been approaching from the opposite direction had lost control, rolled spectacularly and gone spinning through the yawning gap that the Mercedes had left in the barrier. It tumbled in mid-air as it dropped like a stone, and landed on its roof.

At the same time, the articulated truck whose cab roof had been half torn away by the flying Mercedes had gone into a violent skid, its trailer slewing around and broadsiding one of the tall steel power masts that flanked the overpass bridge.

The helicopter pilot had brought his aircraft about and was hovering, uncertain as to what to do next, close to the side of the overpass as the destruction unfolded all around. The crippled power mast began to topple, dragged down by the weight of the cables. Before the pilot could react, the collapsing thick steel wires became entangled in the tail rotor and instantly shattered the blades in an explosion of sparks.

The aircraft's rear plunged downwards and it spun out of control, smashed into the side of the overpass and exploded in a bright little supernova of combusting avgas that rained fiery fragments all over the road below, instantly setting fire to the fallen Audi before any of its occupants, if they were still conscious, were able to escape. The truck driver leaped from his ruptured cab and ran for his life as burning debris blasted in all directions. The wave of fire that washed across the overpass engulfed another of the black Audi Q7s before anyone had time to get out. Thick smoke billowed skywards.

In seconds, the scene had become a battlefield.

Fully alert now, Ben kicked through what was left of the wrecked Mercedes' windscreen and clambered through the sand that came pouring inside the cab. He could smell petrol and spilled fluids and hear the ticking of hot metal. Still unable to see out of his left eye, he staggered around the mangled underside of the car, managed to haul himself on top of its scarred flank and with all his strength hauled open the rear passenger door.

He reached a hand inside for Roberta. She grabbed it and climbed out, and they slid down off the wrecked Mercedes into the soft sand. 'Are you sure you're okay?' he asked insistently. 'You're not hurt?'

'No, no. Just a little banged up, that's all. But you're covered in blood.'

He touched his fingers to his left temple and they came away thickly coated in red. Only then did he realise that blood was streaming down his face, filling his eye. He wiped it with the back of his sleeve, blinked and could suddenly see again. 'It's nothing,' he said. 'Just a scalp wound.'

'Look,' Roberta said, standing up. Ben turned and looked back at the overpass. Flames leapt high from the burning Audi. The blazing wreck of the helicopter was still clinging by its mangled skids to the side of the overpass like some grotesque giant insect on fire. The enormous column of black smoke rising up from the carnage blotted out the sunlight. Meanwhile there was bedlam as panicking drivers who had managed to stop short of the devastation now tried to U-turn back the way they'd come, creating a massive snarl-up extending hundreds of yards back from either side of the scene. A cacophony of blaring horns filled the air.

As Ben and Roberta watched, a secondary blast tore the chopper completely apart. Its blazing shell fell away from the overpass and crashed down into the still-burning wreckage of the Audi that had plunged to the road.

A sudden breeze tore a hole in the pall of smoke and Ben saw that just one of the three Audis had escaped unscathed. It had skidded a full hundred and eighty degrees round on itself as it came to a halt: he could tell from the damage to its left side that it was the car he'd rammed into the side of the tunnel during the chase. Its four occupants had jumped out, the vehicle so hopelessly boxed in by the log-jam of stationary traffic that they had no option but to quickly conceal their weapons and beat their retreat on foot.

One of the men paused to stare from the overpass barrier. Even from a distance, his eyes seemed to meet Ben's. Ben recognised the hard, lean features and distinctive prematurely-silver hair of the driver. He was a big, powerful-looking man, six-two or three and broad across the shoulders. Their eye contact lasted only a moment before the man disappeared into the chaos and the smoke.

The chorus of horns was swelled by the wail of incoming sirens. Flashing lights appeared on the overpass. The thudding beat of a second helicopter, a police chopper, grew louder as the aircraft hovered as low as it could over the scene.

'We need to get away from here fast,' Roberta said.

Ben didn't disagree. Wiping more blood from his face, he reached inside the car wreck for his bag and slung it over his shoulder. He grasped Roberta's hand in his bloodstained fist and they began to run up the middle of the road towards the nearest houses a hundred yards away.

'Watch out!' Ben slithered to a halt and almost yanked Roberta off her feet as a car suddenly shot out of a side street and came dangerously close to running them down. Its brakes squealed as the driver did an emergency stop. The door flew open.

It was an ancient Citroën Dyane, brush-painted green with an all-over mural of psychedelic flowers. The battered hippy-mobile was a good dozen years older than the curly-haired, bearded guy who darted out in alarm from behind the wheel. He took in the scene of the devastated overpass and the crazy-looking couple in the middle of the road, and his mouth dropped open. 'Fuck me. You two okay?'

'Is this your car?' Ben said, letting go of Roberta's hand and striding up to him.

'Did you know you're bleeding, man? Your head's like, fucking cracked open or something.'

'I said, is this your car?'

The hippy nodded blankly. Ben took a step closer towards him. 'How does it go? Is there anything wrong with it? Tell me, I need to know.'

The wail of sirens was building rapidly in the background. Ambulances were arriving on the scene. A second police chopper came pulsing overhead.

'It's fine, man. Stops and starts like it should. Almost, anyway. What do you want to know for?'

'Because I'm buying it. How much?' Ben said quickly.

'I was thinking of selling it,' the hippy replied with a bemused shrug. 'Five hundred?'

There was no time to haggle over pennies. Ben counted off the notes and pressed them quickly into the guy's hand. 'Let me get my stuff,' the hippy said, grabbing a satchel and a few things from the back. He gazed in astonishment at the money in his hand while Ben and Roberta piled into what had, until just seconds ago, been his car.

Ben gunned the raspy twin-cylinder engine, pulled a tight turn in the road and the Dyane sped off in a cloud of blue smoke.

Chapter Thirty-One

'Let me see that cut,' Roberta said as Ben pushed the little car as fast as it would go through the backstreets, intent on putting as much distance between them and the scene of destruction as possible. She pulled a tissue from her pocket and tentatively mopped the blood away from the laceration just under his hairline. 'I think it looks worse than it is,' she said.

'I'll take care of it later,' Ben said. He threw the Dyane into a corner, making it lean perilously over on its flimsy suspension, then floored the pedal without mercy to milk as much power as possible out of the feeble engine. Nothing happened for a moment, then the Dyane coughed and whined in protest as the revs reluctantly climbed. To make this underpowered tin can progress at any speed, momentum was everything. Every few seconds he stole a glance at the rear-view mirror in case there might be more pursuers after them.

None appeared. They seemed to have got away – for now. After a couple of miles he relaxed and began to slow down a little, not wanting to draw more unwanted attention from the cops.

Roberta patted the dash. 'Well, you wanted to buy a car. You got your wish.'

'Not exactly what I had in mind,' he said, torturing the gearbox for another approaching bend.

'It's cute. Kind of reminds me of my old 2CV.'

'That's the problem.'

Nonetheless, the old banger managed to get them out of Paris, not perfectly inconspicuously with its garish paint-job, but unnoticed at least by the people they were trying to avoid; it also had the decency not to self-destruct as Ben thrashed it pitilessly north-westwards along the N13. The engine note settled into a steady howl that made conversation difficult. Roberta slumped deeper into her seat, and fell asleep with her head against the window.

After a couple of hours on the road, they stopped for fuel at a motorway service station, where Ben managed to clean himself up, wash most of the dried blood out of his hair and change his stained T-shirt for the last fresh one in his bag. They bought some pre-packed sandwiches and bottled water at a shop within the complex and ate a hurried lunch in the car. Then, not wanting to leave Roberta on her own too long in case someone somehow caught up with them again, Ben drove about hunting for a payphone so that he could make the necessary arrangements for the next leg of their journey. Public phones were getting hard to find these days, which wasn't so convenient for people on the run whose every movement could be tracked via their mobile.

'It's all part of the same global conspiracy,' Roberta said darkly. 'They want to know exactly what everyone's doing, all the time. Coin-operated phones are just about the last real freedom of telecommunication we have left. They won't be around much longer, rest assured.'

After two circuits of the services complex, they finally discovered the graffiti-covered kiosk hiding behind a recycling bank. Freedom was in a sorry-looking state, but the phone still had a dial tone. Ben fed in a handful of coins and dialled Ruth's mobile number.

His sister didn't sound too enamoured with him. 'What do you mean, you're calling from a motorway services near Lisieux? Where's my plane?'

'It's safe,' he replied, fervently praying that was true. 'Listen, that's what I'm calling about. I need clearance to land in Sweden later today.'

'Sweden!'

'I haven't got time to go into it, Ruth. We have to get to a place near somewhere called Jäkkwik.' He spelled it. 'If you can find me a small airfield not too far away . . .'

'You'll be grateful as long as you live,' she finished for him tersely. 'If you live that long, bro. Tell me: by "*we* need to get" do you mean to say you're still gallivanting around with that woman?'

'I told you she's just a friend. That's the truth. And we're not gallivanting.'

'Hmm. Yeah. A friend in need. Brooke needs you more. Thought about her lately?'

'I haven't stopped thinking about her,' Ben said, and meant it.

'Really. I spent the whole of yesterday with her. I've been on the phone to her for an hour this morning. She can't stop crying. She's devastated, Ben. You hear me? You broke her heart. You just fucking *crushed* her.'

Ben gripped the receiver tightly and fought the urge to smash it to pieces in grief and rage against the steel casing of the phone box. 'Thanks for taking care of her,' he said with heartfelt sincerity. 'If you talk to her again, tell her I love her, okay?'

'I'd say that's for you to tell her, not me.'

'I will, in person, as soon as I get back.'

'I don't know if she'll even want to see you,' Ruth said. 'To be honest, right now, neither do I much. If you weren't my brother, I swear I wouldn't be having much to do with you. I hope you realise the damage you've done.'

'I'll make it up to her,' Ben said, controlling his voice. 'But now I need you to do this for me. There isn't a lot of time.'

There was a long pause. Then Ruth sighed and said, 'All right, give me your number there. I'll see what I can do.'

'Well?' Roberta said as he put the phone down. She saw the look on his face. 'What's wrong?'

'We need to wait. You stay in the car.'

Ben paced up and down under a dark cloud as the next ten minutes stretched painfully into what felt like an hour. Eventually, the pay phone rang. He snatched it up quickly.

Ruth didn't waste time on ceremony. 'Are we talking about the same Jäkkwik that's right up in the wilds of Lapland, nearly five hundred miles north of Stockholm? I had to search for it on the map. It's in the middle of nowhere. Nothing but forests and mountains.'

'It's the only Jäkkwik I could find,' Ben confirmed.

'I won't even ask what you want to go there for. Anyway, I had to twist a couple of arms to get this done so fast, but you have your clearance. The nearest landing point I could locate was a tiny airfield twenty kilometres away at a place called . . . got a pen and paper?' Ruth spelled out the name and gave him the coordinates to get there. 'I don't think it gets a lot of traffic. The Swedish military use it from time to time for exercises, so there should be plenty of landing space for you, okay? Now, you're looking at over twelve hundred nautical miles distance, so by my reckoning you're going to need fuel soon after Copenhagen. There's a small airport called Thisted in northern Denmark where private flights can come and go unscheduled. You can refuel on the Steiner Industries tab there. Just give them this reference number. It'll basically allow you to top up on the company account anywhere in the world. That's not a license to globe-trot, though, okay? I'll give you the coordinates for Thisted airport too. Ready?'

Ben noted them down. 'Got it.'

'I don't know what the hell you're up to. Just don't make me regret that I trusted you with my plane.'

'Thanks, Ruth. I mean it.'

'I don't want your thanks. You're an asshole, Ben. Just know that I feel like a real shit for helping you.' And Ruth ended the call.

With his heart in his boots, Ben returned to the car and slumped behind the wheel. Roberta seemed to sense that he didn't feel like talking. The journey resumed. Ben channelled his pent-up rage by taking it out on the poor little Citroën, for which this was destined to be a last voyage. By the time they reached the airstrip near Carentan a little over ninety minutes later, the engine was making terminal-sounding noises, smoke was streaming out from under the bonnet and the temperature gauge was deep in the red.

'You're a wrecker, Ben Hope,' Roberta said, gazing sadly at the little car. 'If you don't smash them up, you'll grind them down.'

'It's true,' he replied bitterly. 'Destruction. It's the one thing I'm good at.'

'I'm sorry,' she said, realising how deeply her words had cut him. 'I guess saying the wrong thing is what *I* do best, huh?' But he didn't hear her as he walked up to the airstrip's mesh fence. To his relief, the Steiner ST-1 turboprop hadn't been stripped to a skeleton by local scrap thieves, and was sitting unmolested and gleaming in the sun exactly where he'd left it.

Roberta appeared at his side. 'So, to Sweden?' she said.

He nodded. 'To Sweden.'

Chapter Thirty-Two

Washington D.C.
Thirty-one days earlier

When Jack Quigley walked into the crowded diner just before half past seven, he understood right away why the mysterious contact calling himself Steve Carlisle had chosen this rendezvous spot. The heaving establishment, all decked out in a nightmare of chrome and neon and sporting gaudy murals of James Dean, Elvis, Monroe and other fifties' idols, was more public than Disneyland and the least likely place imaginable for a covert assassination plot.

He waded through the throng and managed to secure a table near the window. He sat down and looked around him, wondering if Carlisle was already here, but all he could see were families, groups of friends, couples. This was probably bullshit, some idiot's idea of a practical joke. After less than a minute he was already itching to leave, and he was about to get up when the waiter appeared at his table, thickset and gruff with a badge on his uniform that said 'No Whining'. Quigley glowered at him for a moment, then relented and ordered a quarter-pounder burger with fries that he didn't really want, together with a soda water. *Twenty minutes*, he told himself. *Twenty minutes and I'm out of here.*

The burger arrived within the first five, looking like a flattened turd in a bun. Quigley didn't touch it and just sipped the soda water. Ten more minutes passed before a fat man in a rumpled suit with greying hair and a file under his arm bustled in through the glass doors and glanced nervously around the crowded room. His darting gaze settled on Quigley and he squeezed his bulk through the tables to get to him.

'Mr Carlisle,' Quigley said, not getting up. 'And before you ask, no, I wasn't followed.'

Carlisle settled his large frame into the seat opposite. He laid his file on the table. 'Sure about that?' he said, glancing nervously out of the window at the people and cars passing in the street. 'It can be just about impossible to tell.'

Quigley caught a whiff of cheap booze off the man's breath. 'We're alone,' he assured him. 'You've got my word on it. I don't bullshit people. All I ask in return is that they don't bullshit me.'

'This is one hundred per cent on the level, I promise you. Everything I'm about to tell you, I can verify.'

Quigley nodded at the unopened file. 'That the proof in there?'

'Like I'd just walk around with it.'

'Okay. I've no desire to hang around this place any longer than I have to, so let's get into it. Basics first. Your real name would be a good start.'

Before Carlisle could answer, the forbidding waiter interrupted them with his notebook poised. Carlisle ordered corned beef hash and cabbage and a large Bud. Once they were alone again, he leaned his mass across the table and said in a confidential whisper, 'Herbie Blumenthal. That's my real name.' He shoved the file towards Quigley. 'My ID and credentials are all in here. Take a look. I'm kosher, honest to God.' He let out a belch. 'Shit. Sorry about that. It's not me.' He grabbed his beer and swilled a third of it down in a single swallow.

Quigley slipped on a pair of reading glasses that he hated wearing, and sifted quickly through the file's contents. Forty-eight years of age, Blumenthal was an engineer by profession, had earned his degree from Carnegie Mellon University in Pittsburgh and done postgrad work in System Design at MIT before being recruited to the Department of Defense's DARPA agency eleven years ago.

'There's no mention here of you working for anything called Nemesis,' Quigley said, scanning the text.

'I told you, it doesn't exist, not officially. Nobody at DARPA's even heard of it, not until the guys in black turned up at the agency headquarters in Arlington one day and we were told that a select group of us were being taken over to the Pentagon. Me and these eight other guys were loaded into the back of two SUVs and they whisked us away under armed escort. It was spooky, man. They took us through checkpoint after checkpoint until we reached this place behind doors like a friggin' bank vault.'

'Okay,' Quigley said, still deeply uncertain. 'Go on.'

'It was a four-hour briefing and we had two hours afterwards to decide whether to take the job. Either way, we couldn't breathe a word to anyone. It was some serious business. I mean, with DARPA you're already buried in a ton of non-disclosure agreements. But this was something else. They basically said, you talk about this, finito. Game over.'

'But you're talking to me.'

'Yeah. Don't make me regret it.'

'What made you take the job?'

'The pay was incredible. There's a river of cash flowing

into the program like you wouldn't believe. Billions, I mean billions, of invisible funding. Plus the technology we were shown – it was only a taste, but for a scientist, it was breathtaking. At the time, I was just bowled over. The shit they're working on—' Blumenthal was talking fast but clammed up abruptly as the waiter returned with his order.

Quigley replaced the sensitive documents in the file, out of sight, until the waiter was gone. He gazed calmly at Blumenthal over the top of a mountain of corned beef and steaming kraut. 'Let's cut to the chase. What is the program about?'

'It's a weapons project,' Blumenthal said in a hushed tone, barely audible over the buzz of chat in the diner. 'One like there's never been before. At DARPA I worked on the first HCV hypersonic cruise vehicle weapons system prototypes, part of the Falcon Project. But this just blows that into the weeds. I mean, they've had more engineers and physicists on the payroll over the years than NASA.' He swept a huge pile of corned beef into his mouth and started chewing noisily.

'What was Shelton doing for them? He wasn't a scientist.'

'Security management,' Blumenthal said with his mouth full. 'I only saw him a couple times. He wasn't always on base.'

'Where's base?'

'Wherever we happened to be,' Blumenthal said enigmatically, forking up more dripping kraut. He was eating like a starving dog.

'There wasn't a fixed location?'

'Yes and no.' Blumenthal glanced anxiously all about him. 'I'll come to that later, okay? There's so much to tell.' He grimaced. 'Christ, my guts are aching so bad right now.'

Quigley eyed the rapidly-disappearing mound of food

and couldn't refrain from commenting, 'Maybe if you didn't shovel it up like a hippo?'

'I eat fast when I'm uptight, okay? I can't help it.'

'I can see you've had a stressful few years,' Quigley said, running his gaze over the guy's large outline.

'It's no joke. I'm on so many pills for depression and anxiety, my innards are shot. They're mulch. Basically fucked.'

'You have my sympathies. Let's get back on track. Tell me more about the weapons project. Are we talking nuclear, biological, or what?'

'Nope. Nemesis is totally different. And it's bigger and more scary than anything you ever imagined before. It's like . . .' – Blumenthal searched for an appropriate comparison – 'like the fucking hand of God, ready to smite His wrath down on earth, you know? Except that now *we* tell God where to point His finger.'

'I think you need to elaborate a little more than that.'

'Disasters,' Blumenthal said in a hoarse whisper that Quigley had to strain to hear.

'What?'

'That's what I said. Earthquakes. Tsunamis. Hellfire and devastation.'

'I didn't come here to be sold a crock of bullshit,' Quigley said. Now he was ready to leave.

'Please. This is real. Listen to me. Its reach is global. Stick a pin in the map, Nemesis can wipe that place *off* the map. Forget soldiers. Forget conventional weapons. Forget drones and hunter-killer robots. Those are outdated already. Warfare has a new future. But here's the best part. It's undetectable. Nobody even knows when a strike's taken place, because there's no way even a scientist can distinguish it from the real thing. See what I'm saying? You begin to get how clandestine this is? Why I need someone like you to help me blow the whistle on these bastards?'

'Wait a minute,' Quigley said, shaking his head and completely unsure about how much of this wild talk to believe. 'Slow down.'

'Oh, Lord. I need to go to the bathroom.'

'Right now?'

'I got the shits,' Blumenthal said, levering himself out of his seat. 'It can't wait. When I come back I'm gonna tell you the rest. I know what those fuckers are planning, and it's not pretty. I hope you got the evening free, cause it's gonna take a while. I was thinking we should go someplace more private.'

'Oh, sure. Then what?'

'Then you and I have to start figuring out what we can do about this.'

Quigley watched in bewilderment as Blumenthal lumbered his way towards the bathroom. Had he heard right? Was this some kind of a joke?

He waited impatiently for the fat man to return.

In fact, Herbie Blumenthal had been telling the absolute truth, and was eager to tell more, as much as he knew. He waddled quickly into the men's toilets and wedged himself into a cubicle as the rumblings in his guts grew acutely urgent.

Blumenthal was very much occupied by the time the tall silver-haired man strolled casually into the diner bathroom. His face was long and lean and wore a completely blank expression that would have unnerved the other bathroom users if they'd paid him any attention. A light sports jacket was stretched tight over his muscular frame. He was carrying a small leather document case on a strap around his shoulder.

He joined the other two men at the urinal. One after the other, the two finished up and exited the bathroom.

Alone, the silver-haired man washed his hands at a sink. In the mirror he could see that all the cubicle doors were ajar except one, behind which he knew his target was sitting. When his hands were dry, he slipped a pair of latex surgical gloves from his document case and pulled them on, then took out a sign that said 'OUT OF ORDER' and a small rubber wedge.

The man's name was Lloyd McGrath. He was a professional assassin of seventeen years' experience who took great pride in the perfection of his tradecraft. He opened the door, peeked out and then hung the sign from the handle outside. He shut the door and jammed the wedge under the inside bottom edge with his foot. Walking back towards the cubicles, he reached into the case again and drew out a pistol.

The compact handgun was designed to shoot a dart, which it propelled very silently from a small CO2 canister inside the grip. Three darts were loaded in a rotating drum magazine, each hollow and filled with an extremely specialised, officially nonexistent form of poison. The dart would completely disintegrate on entering the flesh of its target, which it could easily do from a few paces away. The poison itself was designed to denature rapidly so as to be untraceable in an autopsy. All that was left was a tiny red dot marking the point of entry.

They didn't use ricin umbrella guns any more. Things had moved on since the old days.

McGrath entered the vacant cubicle to the left of the occupied one. He stepped up on the toilet seat and looked impassively down over the top of the partition at the unprepossessing figure of Herbie Blumenthal sitting there in the next cubicle with his trousers rumpled around his knees.

Blumenthal glared up at him in red-faced outrage. 'Whoa, what the fuck are you doing, asshole? You some kind of perv—'

He shut up as he saw the gun pointing down at him. He raised his hands in protest, eyes boggling, squirming on the toilet seat and completely vulnerable.

McGrath's face remained still and impassive as he fired. The dart entered Blumenthal's flesh just below the ear. There was a muted squawk and a brief thrashing around. McGrath didn't need to see the rest. He stepped down from the toilet seat and slipped the gun back inside his document case. He walked calmly towards the door, collected the rubber wedge, then removed his gloves and slipped quietly out of the bathroom. Seconds later he'd exited the diner and disappeared into the night.

Five more minutes went by, and Quigley was still waiting. Seven. Ten. People came and went. Laughter and conversation all around him. He sighed impatiently, then plucked his phone from his pocket and called Mandy's number.

Mandy was twenty-nine and warm and beautiful and worked as a dance teacher. He still couldn't believe his luck that someone like her would have looked at him twice. After nearly two years of dating, they'd been talking about her selling her apartment so they could live together at his townhouse. The notion of getting married, starting a family, seemed tantalisingly just around the corner.

Her warm voice answered after a couple of rings. 'Hi, honey,' Quigley said, smiling despite the troubling things Blumenthal had just told him and his mounting impatience to hear more. 'Listen, I had to work late and it looks like it might take longer than I thought. Could you stop by the house and let Red into the garden? He's been cooped up a while and I hate to stress him out.'

'Sure, no problem. I'll be right over in, say, five minutes. How late is late? Is it worth waiting for you?'

'I should be back by ten-thirty. Hmm, make that eleven.'

'I'll be there with a bottle of that Chianti you like.'

'What an angel. No wonder I love you so much.'

'Love you too. See you soon.'

After the call, Quigley waited a little longer, until he'd had enough. Jesus, what was keeping the guy? He got up from the table and strode across the busy diner to the bathroom.

The 'OUT OF ORDER' sign on the door threw him. That's odd, he thought. He pushed against the door and it swung open. He stepped inside and his nostrils twitched. Someone was in there, for sure. 'Hey, Blumenthal, you going to be in there all night, or what? Blumenthal?' He tapped on the cubicle door. No answer. 'Blumenthal? You okay?'

Still no reply. 'I don't believe I'm doing this,' Quigley muttered to himself. He crouched down, pressed his palms to the floor and lowered himself to peer under the cubicle door.

Blumenthal stared back at him, unblinking. His eyes were bulging almost out of their sockets. His face was purple. His tongue was protruding from his lips.

Heart attack. The fat sonofabitch had suffered a cardiac arrest right there on the toilet.

Quigley muttered a curse under his breath. There'd seemed to be so much more Blumenthal wanted to tell him.

He hesitated. Glanced over at the door. Nobody was coming. Quigley might not have been in the peak physical shape he once was, but he was still agile. In one swift movement he sprang up, levered himself over the top of the cubicle door and landed quietly inside next to the dead guy.

He had to breathe through his mouth as he quickly went through Blumenthal's pockets. The corpse had nothing on him except a ring of keys and a cheap wallet. Quigley riffled through it, finding a few bucks in cash, a few credit cards and driver's licence, and a single crisp business card. He examined it. On the front was printed in bold the name MANDRAKE HOLDINGS, NEW YORK, with an address below. On the back was scrawled in messy handwriting the word 'Triton'.

What could it mean? There wasn't time to try to figure it out now. Quigley pocketed the card, then let himself out of the cubicle and went running out of the bathroom to alert a manager.

Soon afterwards in the quiet street in historic Shepherdstown, Mandy Fiedel parked her car outside the house in which she hoped soon to be living with her boyfriend. She killed her headlights and engine, got out and trotted up the steps to the front door.

She could hear Red barking from inside, which was a little unusual for him. Jack often joked that the Labrador loved people so much, if a burglar broke into the place Red would lick him to death.

Mandy had the house door key on the same fob as her own apartment key. She unlocked the door and stepped inside the dim hallway. Red came up to greet her, all beating tail and panting breath. He seemed agitated about something.

'Hey, beautiful. You need to get out to pee, huh? Okay, okay, let's get you into the back yard.'

Mandy reached out to turn on the hallway light. The switch clicked.

And she didn't have time to formulate another thought before a massive explosion ripped through the townhouse, from the rear outwards, and engulfed her. The front door and hall windows, debris and a huge rolling fireball blew out into the street.

Car alarms shrieked. Flames crackled and smoke poured thickly out of the shattered house. In seconds, lights were coming on all up and down the street. A baby was crying somewhere. Neighbours began to emerge from their homes. Somebody screaming. Someone else yelling into their phone.

When the fire department came screeching onto the scene minutes later, all they found of Mandy Fiedel was a single smouldering shoe, flung into the middle of the street by the blast.

Chapter Thirty-Three

The evening was sparkling clear and bright as, after four and a half hours in the air plus a forty-five minute stopover to refuel at Thisted in Denmark, Ruth's coordinates guided the ST-1 precisely in to touch down on the edge of Sweden's Pieljekaise National Park. From above, the airfield was just a tiny dot lost in an endless sweeping vista of unspoilt forest. Even as Ben circled low on his landing approach, the place seemed dwarfed by the wilderness that surrounded it. A single winding thread of road was visible through the trees, leading to the nearest village half a kilometre or so away.

Ben's landing was smooth and even. The plane contacted the runway with a yelp, and he taxied off the main strip towards the hangars where a disparate collection of aircraft, including an old Swedish military transport plane that had been partially dismantled, stood around on the concrete. Powering down the engine, he stretched his stiff muscles and took off his radio headset.

'Made it in one piece,' Roberta said from the comfortable passenger lounge. 'I'm more and more impressed, Hope.'

'Now and then I even impress myself,' he replied.

They stepped down from the plane. The summer evening breeze had a bite of Nordic chill, and the air felt wonderfully fresh and clear. There was a prefabricated hut on the far side of the airstrip with a couple of vehicles parked outside, but unlike at Thisted where a dozen little guys in neatly-pressed overalls had come to greet the Steiner plane, nobody was in sight and nothing moved.

Ben gazed around him at the forests and the mountains beyond, and instantly felt at home in this serene, empty place. He could live here, lose himself out there in that landscape, far away from everything where no person, no troubles, could ever find him.

'It could be northern Canada,' Roberta said. 'So quiet. What do you suppose this Daniel Lund does? You think he's some kind of weird recluse, maybe? I wonder how Claudine knew him.'

'We're not going to find out standing around here,' Ben said, shouldering his bag. He pointed beyond the airfield gate, where the road disappeared into thick woods. 'There's a village a few minutes walk that way. We can get transport there.'

'I doubt you're going to find a Hertz rental place out here,' Roberta said.

Ben wasn't surprised to discover that she was right. Half-hidden among the trees, the village consisted of just two or three narrow streets lined with wooden houses, a tiny church, a general store, a filling station and little else except a small log-built inn that looked like an Alpine chalet. In winter, the community was most likely cut off for months on end and accessible only by snowmobile or reindeer-powered sled. From the stacks of freshly-cut firewood in every yard it was clear that much of the summer was spent busily preparing for the next snowy season.

A few faces turned to peer curiously around as Ben and Roberta walked into the inn, the downstairs of which obvi-ously doubled as a bar for the locals. The owner was an amiable chubby-faced guy named Kristian who spoke some English. Ben ordered a double shot of whisky for himself, which he'd been secretly craving all the way from France. Roberta only wanted coffee.

So what brought these good folks here, the smiling Kristian wanted to know as he served their drinks. Savouring his long first sip of whisky and the burn on his tongue, Ben explained that he and his wife – Roberta looked at him with a discreetly raised eyebrow at the mention of the word – had been hitch-hiking their way north from Stockholm, wanted to tour around the national parks of Lapland and were interested in hiring or buying a car locally. That generated intense debate among the clientèle, none of whom could ultimately suggest anything useful until Dolph introduced himself in faltering English. Dolph was a lorry driver with a load of fencing materials to transport north to Jäkkwik the following morning. His idea was that the pleasant foreign couple should be able to find something there, if they wanted to hitch a ride with him. Ben thanked him, and they arranged to meet outside the inn at eight.

The locals went back to their conversations, leaving the two of them alone at the bar. 'That's that,' Roberta sighed. 'Nothing to do now but wait around and pass the time. I can't say I'm sorry. I feel totally beat.'

Ben's head was hurting. He wanted a cigarette and could feel the tug of fatigue dragging him down too, but to add to his gloomy mood he was restless and frustrated that they couldn't press on sooner with finding Daniel Lund. He ordered another whisky. 'You need a nice room for the night?' Kristian asked with a grin. 'Dinner too? Hold on, I get menu for you. My wife is great cook.'

They ate in a secluded little room in which they were the only diners. The menu was basic, but Kristian had been telling the truth about his wife's cooking and the meat stew they chose was tasty, even though neither it nor the beers he washed it down with did much to restore Ben's spirits.

'So tell me about Jude,' Roberta said out of a silence. 'I have to say that surprised me, hearing you had a son.'

'You weren't the only one,' he said.

'You really had no idea?'

'None, until a few months ago.'

'Must have been quite a shock, I guess,' Roberta said. 'So how did . . . I mean, who was . . . ?'

'You want to dissect my ancient history now?' Ben snapped; then, regretting the sharp tone in his voice, he softened and added, 'Jude's mother's name was Michaela. I knew her at college. She died last year. So did Simeon, her husband.'

'I'm sorry.'

'Me too.' He paused, gazing at his plate. 'Sometimes it seems that most of the people I've cared about are dead, or gone.'

Roberta reached across the table and brushed his hand lightly with her fingertips. 'Anyway, Jude seems really nice. You must be proud of him.'

'As long as he doesn't take too much after his father,' Ben said, 'he'll be fine.'

'He could do a whole lot worse than take after you,' Roberta said, to which Ben didn't reply.

After dinner, Kristian's teen daughter Elin showed them up the creaky stairs to their room. The decor was old-fashioned and rustic, and everything was varnished wood: the walls, the ceiling, the frame of the large, soft-looking double bed.

'Well, *you* were the one who told the guy we were married,' Roberta said, sensing Ben's discomfort. 'What did you expect, twin beds?'

220

'What was I supposed to tell him?' Ben replied irritably. 'The truth might be a bit much for folks to take. I'm not sure if even I believe it. Anyway, it doesn't matter. I told you, I've slept on a thousand floors. Once more isn't going to kill me.' Stepping around the side of the bed he yanked open a cupboard and saw that the room was well stocked with spare blankets. He hauled out an armful of them and carried them over to the far corner to make up his own makeshift bedding for the night.

Roberta's lip curled into a half-smile. 'I'd invite you in with me again, but two nights in a row might look like I was trying something.'

He dumped the blankets on the floor, started spreading them out with his foot, and made no reply. Roberta walked to the window and shut the drapes. This far north at this time of year, the sun didn't set until midnight and darkness only lasted a couple of hours. 'I'm getting ready for bed. Mind if I use the bathroom before you?' She opened the door and peered inside the ensuite. 'Well, I'm pleased to say it's better than your one in Paris.'

'Great,' Ben muttered.

'Then again, I suppose you don't give a rat's ass either way. You're the big, tough military guy who'll rough it any old how.'

'Uh-huh. Whatever,' he said, only half-listening. A thought had come to him and he'd started rummaging in his bag. His fingers closed on the familiar object and he pulled it out.

His battered old steel whisky flask. It had been around the world with him, soothed his soul in many a tense situation and even deflected a bullet or two for him. He shook it. Empty. That was something that had to be remedied right away, feeling the way he was.

'Where are you going?' she asked as he stepped towards the door.

'Down to the bar for a refill. I'll be back in a little while.'

'I might be asleep by then.'

'I'll be quiet.'

The guys down in the bar were fairly well lubricated after their evening session, and were rocking with hilarity over some joke Dolph had just finished telling. With his flask freshly filled a few minutes later, Ben crept back upstairs to the room and carefully opened the door without a sound. Only the bedside lamp was still lit. Roberta was under the covers with her hair spread out over the pillow and one arm outflung. She was wearing the same old shirt of his that she'd worn the night before. She looked cosy and at ease under the patchwork quilt. Pausing for a moment to gaze at her lying there, he suddenly realised that his dark cloud of gloom had lifted a little at the sight.

'I thought you were sleeping,' he murmured as she turned to smile at him.

'Not really.'

'What's funny?' he asked, sitting on the edge of the bed.

She rolled over to face him, raising her head from the pillow and propping it up. 'I was just remembering how this happened to us before. You and me in a double room, having to act like we were a regular couple. Remember that little hotel in the Languedoc? How the only room they had was the honeymoon suite? And there was that strange old guy who brought us champagne?' She chuckled. 'I tried to teach you to dance that night, to a couple of those old Edith Piaf songs. You remember all that? It wasn't really so long ago.'

'I remember,' Ben said.

She gave a yawn. 'And here we are again, just the two of us,' she murmured. 'Funny how life repeats itself. Why'd you suppose that is? You think in some weird way it was meant to happen, or something?'

'Nothing is ever meant to happen,' he said. 'It just happens. You're talking like a crazy person. Why don't you put the light out and go to sleep?'

She nodded drowsily, reached out an arm and clicked off the sidelight. The room was still only in half-darkness, with the pale light of the late Nordic sunset glowing in through the drapes. He could see the outline of her face and the gleam of her eyes watching him. 'You going to bed too?' she asked.

'In a while,' he said. 'Thought I'd just sit in the chair for a bit.'

'And drink.' She'd noticed the flask in his hand. Her voice sounded suddenly less dopey.

'If I want to,' he replied.

'You're thinking about her, aren't you?'

Ben shrugged and didn't say anything.

'She'll be there for you when you get back, Ben. You know that, right?'

Ben still said nothing. He unscrewed the top of the flask and took a gulp.

'That is, if we make it out of this alive,' Roberta added, sounding wide awake now. 'Which is far from certain, I guess. I wouldn't bet on our chances. On that note, pass over the flask. I think I'll join you.'

Ben handed it to her. She took a sip, gave a splutter and thrust the flask back into his hands. 'Holy shit, is that for human consumption or cleaning carburettors with?'

'We could probably run the aircraft on it,' Ben said.

'Give me some more.'

Ben reclined against the bed's carved wooden headboard as they spent the next few minutes wordlessly passing the whisky back and forth. The sun's glow was very slowly declining, inching the room into shadow.

'It's been a hell of a couple of days, hasn't it?' she murmured at last.

'You could say that.'

'I wonder what tomorrow will bring.'

'Try not to think too much about it,' he said, closing his eyes. They felt too leaden to open again. He could sense his own voice getting slurry and his body relaxing into the soft bed as the deep, deep tiredness finally overcame him. Roberta went on talking softly, but he was beginning to drift and didn't catch her words. He murmured something incoherent in reply.

From somewhere on the fringe of his half-asleep senses, he felt a hand very tenderly caress his face. It felt nice, comforting, like being a child again. He felt an involuntary smile of contentment spread over his lips. The sensation continued on, and so did the voice, both nearby and faraway. The last thing he thought it said was, or might have been, something like: '*If you can't go back to her, Ben, you know you can always come back to me, anytime you wanted.*'

. . . Then he was gone.

Chapter Thirty-Four

The sun had been up a long time when Ben awoke to find himself still on the bed, fully clothed, with Roberta's hair tickling his face and her arm draped over his shoulder. Without waking her, he delicately lifted the arm off him and rose to peer out of the window. It was almost 7 a.m. and the village was coming to life.

An hour later, true to his word despite the heavy night's drinking, Dolph turned up outside in his delivery lorry and honked the horn. By then, Ben and Roberta were downstairs, revitalised with black coffee and waiting for him.

As they clambered into the cab, Dolph greeted them with a grin and a thumbs-up, and the lorry rumbled off. The road was long and meandering, and carried them northwards through beautiful birch woods and over misty mountain passes. Along the way, Ben showed Dolph the address that had been on Claudine's letter to Daniel, saying that this was an old friend he hadn't seen in a long time and to whom he was thinking of paying a visit.

'Your friend live in a hole in the ground, huh?' Dolph asked, amused. When Ben asked what he meant, the lorry driver explained that the words 'Hand om' on the second line meant 'care of' in Swedish. The address was in fact that of the local post office, while it appeared that Herr Lund had none of his own, or at least none that he wanted to reveal.

'No worry, I drop you right there,' Dolph said, saying that their route passed through the place on the way to his delivery drop. 'You find your friend, no problems.'

The hamlet lay deep in the forests of the Pieljekaise National Park and centred on a cobbled square overlooked by a store, a tiny café and the quaint wooden post office to which Claudine's letter had been sent. Dolph dropped them off in the square and waved cheerfully from his window as he rumbled off in a cloud of diesel smoke.

The post office was completely quiet except for the ticking of a large wooden clock on the wall, and smelled of beeswax and brass polish. Standing at the old-fashioned counter, a skinny middle-aged woman with glasses on a chain around her neck and her steely hair scraped back into a bun was efficiently sorting piles of mail and other documents. There was no computer in sight. On the wall behind her were rows of neatly alphabetised pigeon-holes, some of them with letters and small packages inside. She looked up as Ben and Roberta walked in.

'Best you handle this,' Roberta whispered to him. 'I have no idea what to say.'

After establishing that she could understand English, and in fact prided herself on her ability to speak it, Ben told her that he was trying to make contact with an old friend, Herr Daniel Lund, who lived in these parts but for whom he only had this address. The postmistress assessed the two of them with a sharp eye. Ben's face was open and earnest. Roberta leaned on the counter and smiled sweetly. Deciding the two foreigners could be trusted, the postmistress said, 'Herr Lund come here in person to collect his mail each week. Where he live, it is too difficult for the deliveries to reach.'

'Out in the sticks, eh? Dan always did like his privacy,' Ben said, putting on a hearty smile. 'Do you know how we might be able to find him?'

The postmistress shook her head. 'Jag vet inte. I do not know. But . . . one moment, please.' Something seemed to have occurred to her. She turned away from the counter and ran a finger along the rows of pigeon-holes to the inlaid brass letter L. There were a number of mailing envelopes inside. She drew them carefully out, checked them one by one and replaced them exactly as she'd found them. Then, looking thoughtful, she darted over to a half-open door, put her head through the gap and spoke a few words in Swedish. A man's voice rumbled a casual reply from inside. The postmistress returned to the counter, looking pleased with herself. 'You are in the luck,' she said to Ben. 'Herr Lund has post to collect and my husband thinks he comes here this afternoon.'

'That's great news,' Ben said cheerfully. 'It's been so long since I've seen him. We were at college together. Tell me, does he still have the long hair and the beard? Everyone used to tease him about it.'

The postmistress pointed to her chin. 'A beard he had? And long hairs? No, no.' She laughed. 'You will see he has much changed, then. He is . . . how do you say? Nothing left here.'

'Bald?'

'Yes, yes, very bald, like a stone.'

'Poor guy,' Ben said. 'I suppose time catches up with us all eventually. He must be forty, forty-two now.'

'So young?' the postmistress replied, looking shocked. 'To me he seem older. Fifty? Or more. But the winters here in Lapland, they have bad effect on people.'

After some more chatter, Ben and Roberta thanked her

for her help and left the post office. 'Nice work, Sherlock,' Roberta said as they stepped outside into the fresh breeze. 'What now?'

Ben pointed across the street at the little café. 'Now we sit tight and wait for a fifty-year-old bald guy to show up.'

The café was as quiet as the post office, and they had their pick of the tables. The one they took was near enough to the window overlooking the square to be able to watch the post office entrance without being too easily spotted from outside.

'Keep your eyes peeled,' Ben said. 'He'll be dressed roughly, like someone living in deep country, and driving something with off-road capability.'

Roberta raised an eyebrow. 'Round here, that should narrow it down to about eighty per cent of the population. Assuming the right guy shows up, what do we do, collar him in the post office and introduce ourselves?'

'And have him freak out, run off and never be seen again?' Ben shook his head. 'I think we should get him to take us back to his place. It sounds as if there'll be plenty of privacy there.'

'I'm sure he'll be amenable to that.'

'He won't have a lot of choice,' Ben said.

The waitress came with a steaming pot of coffee. Roberta sipped some of the thin, stewed brew and made a face. 'Yeech. I don't know if I can take drinking this for the next several hours.'

'You'll just have to man up and take what comes.'

'Don't tell me. You've staked out in much worse places.'

'You wouldn't want to know.'

'You're probably right about that.'

As they soldiered through their second pot of coffee, around eleven in the morning, they saw the postmistress exit the doorway across the street and walk briskly off into the distance carrying a shopping bag. 'That's good,' Ben said. 'Let's hope she doesn't come back for a while.'

'Why's that good?'

'Because with her out of the way, if Daniel shows up he won't be told anything about his dear old college friend who was looking for him. I was a little worried about that, but I'm making this up as I go.'

The coffee held out a little longer, then with midday upon them they ordered some lunch. Ben had a pot of simple broth with a kind of flatbread called Gàhkko, while Roberta finally decided on a dish of sautéed reindeer and instantly regretted her choice. 'I'm eating Rudolf,' she groaned, picking desultorily at the dark meat.

'Santa will soon find another friend,' Ben said.

'Oh boy, you're really all heart, aren't you?'

But before Roberta had the chance to decide whether to finish her food, a beaten-up Land Rover long-wheelbase pickup came growling up the road outside and parked in the narrow side street a few yards from the post office entrance. Its all-terrain wheels and sides were covered in dried dirt and it had ancillary lighting and wire mesh guards over the headlamps. The windows were filmed with dust, preventing them from getting a good look at the driver.

'You reckon it's our guy?' Roberta murmured. Ben was watching keenly. He said nothing.

The driver's door opened and a man climbed down from the cab, crossed the narrow pavement to the post office and disappeared inside. He was alone, wearing boots, khaki trousers and a lightweight hunter's jacket. Solid in build. Florid in complexion. Somewhere in his early fifties.

'And bald like a stone,' Roberta said.

Chapter Thirty-Five

Daniel Lund remained inside the post office for just under two minutes, long enough to exchange a very brief few words with the postmaster, grab his mail and go. He emerged from the doorway. Walked straight back to the Land Rover, climbed in behind the wheel, tore another bite out of the thick half-eaten sandwich from the paper bag on the dashboard, and drove smartly off.

He headed north out of the hamlet, made a few turns on the narrow roads and soon left the metalled surfaces for dirt tracks that were only just wide enough in places for the big, boxy vehicle to go lurching through, bouncing and jolting over ruts and boulders and making his tools and metal jerrycans rattle about in the back.

He continued on like that for thirty-five minutes, cutting deeper and deeper into the thick forest and leaving all trace of civilisation behind. Out here there were just the deer and moose, the golden eagles, the wolverines and the occasional brown bear. And him, living all alone in his wooden cabin, far away from people.

The last couple of miles would have been impossible for anything but a dedicated off-road vehicle with low-ratio gears and a differential lock to reach. Through an archway in the trees, the hidden log cabin came into view. The rutted path ended at the bare-earth yard outside its front door. Daniel pulled up and turned off the Land Rover's engine. He jumped down, slammed the door and started walking towards the cabin, clutching his bunch of mail in one hand and his half-finished sandwich in the other. He took a couple more bites out of it, then tossed it away into the dirt as he approached his front door and reached for a set of keys. He disappeared inside and the door closed behind him.

'You okay?' Ben whispered in the back of the Land Rover. He pushed back the tarpaulin that he'd pulled over them.

'Fine, but I'll have the edge of this toolbox imprinted in my flesh for life,' Roberta muttered, rubbing her shoulder. Her hair was all tousled and in her eyes.

Ben crawled out from where he'd been lying wedged behind the spare wheel lashed to the bulkhead. It had been an uncomfortable journey on the bare metal floor. He eased open the rear hatch. A tree partially blocked the view from the cabin window and would hide them from sight as they clambered out. 'Let's go,' he whispered.

Behind the cover of the tree, Ben quickly unstrapped his bag. 'I need you to cover the front of the house for me,' he said, pulling out the Beretta submachine gun and handing it to Roberta. 'I'll go round the back. My guess is he won't be too happy he has visitors, and he'll make a break for it.'

Roberta stared at the weapon. 'We came all this way, now you want me to point a gun at the guy?'

'It's only going to kill him if you pull the trigger,' Ben said.

'It's loaded?' she asked, gingerly taking it.

'Wouldn't be much use if it wasn't. But all you have to do is stop him if he tries to do a runner. Point it and look mean. I know you know how. Shoot him in the foot if you have to. Just try not to blow his head off.'

'Gee, I'll have to try and remember that,' Roberta muttered.

Ben set off at a trot, moving stealthily and silently from tree to tree. He skirted around the rear of the cabin with his eyes fixed on the back windows, listening intently for the slightest sound. The one thing he most hoped he wouldn't hear was a dog barking from inside – but there was only silence. Nothing moved. Nobody was watching his approach. At the back of the cabin was a little lean-to filled with cut firewood. A large petrol-powered log splitter sat on deflated tyres. Next to it was a tree stump serving as a chopping block, with an axe stuck in it.

The cabin was raised up on a wooden base that had a plank skirting all around its bottom. Three flimsy-looking steps led up to the back door. Ben cautiously rested his weight on the first step, then the second. The planks bore him without creaking. He tried the door. It was locked, but he'd been expecting that. With his free hand he took the wire pick from his pocket. Back in the old days, he'd been pretty proficient at letting himself into kidnap hideouts and other places he wasn't expected.

He inserted the pick into the lock, careful not to let it rattle in the keyhole. He felt his way around inside, gave the pick a couple of twists, and felt the mechanism give. The lock opened smoothly. The door wasn't bolted from inside.

Ben padded into the small back hallway. The cabin was pokey. The boards were bare and rough-sawn. There were shelves with tinned provisions lined up, together with a pair of battered paraffin lanterns. Some heavy outdoor clothes hung on a peg. Two spare propane gas cylinders stood by the wall. A little hatchet and a cardboard box filled with kindling sticks. All the things needed for life cut off from mains services. There were two internal doors, the one on the left slightly ajar and leading to a rudimentary kitchen with a pine table. The door in front of him was closed. Ben nudged it gently, stepped through and found himself in a narrow L-shaped passage with boarded walls that led to the main room.

The room was small, square and simple. A cast iron wood burner dominated one corner. A couple of chairs sat around a plain rug on the bare floorboards. The bald man was standing by a table, opening one of the envelopes. Ben watched him study the mail inside, mutter something under his breath, discard it and pick up another.

'Daniel Lund?' Ben said from the doorway.

The man dropped the letter he was holding. He whipped round and then froze, staring, open-mouthed.

'It's all right. I just want to talk,' Ben said, showing his open palms.

Lund stood there frozen for a second longer, then moved much faster than Ben had anticipated and kicked out at the door with a heavy boot. It slammed shut in Ben's face.

Cursing, Ben raced forward. Wrenched the door open and found himself staring into the barrel of the shotgun Lund must have had propped in a corner close to hand.

Ben spun away from the doorway a millisecond before the shotgun boomed deafeningly in the small cabin and ripped a ragged hole in the opposite wall. Splinters and dust exploded.

Lund racked the pump on his shotgun, ejecting the smoking shell casing and chambering another as he backed away towards the front entrance. He burst out of the door, bounded down the front steps and started running like a wild man towards the Land Rover.

Halfway there, his heels scraped to a halt in the dirt. Roberta had stepped out from behind the tree and was pointing the Beretta at his chest with a purposeful look in her eye that said 'don't even think about it'.

Lund did, very briefly, but another second afterwards the muzzle of Ben's 9mm was poking into his back.

'We won't be needing that any more, Mr Lund,' Ben said, taking the pump gun out of his hands. Defeated, Lund gave it up easily. It was a standard Mossberg twelve-gauge, five round tube magazine, plain black stock, plain black sling. Still pointing the Browning at him, Ben jacked out the shotgun's remaining shells. They were bird-shot cartridges, useful enough for a countryman taking pot-shots at crows but lacking in penetrative punch for defensive purposes on a determined human target unless you got right up close and personal. Evidently, Herr Daniel Lund was no combat expert. Ben dumped the shells into his pocket and slung the shotgun over his shoulder. Roberta slowly lowered the Beretta. Lund didn't look so dangerous.

'I presume you *are* Daniel Lund?' Ben asked.

The Swede was breathing hard, and his mottled complexion had turned to a pasty grey. His bare scalp was beaded with sweat. 'You're not going to shoot me?' he asked, speaking for the first time. His English sounded well practised, with an Americanised intonation coming through his native accent like a man who'd travelled around a lot.

'I told you, we didn't come here for that,' Ben said. 'Let's go inside, Daniel. We have a lot to talk about.'

The scent of cordite was sharp in the cabin. Lund reluctantly led the way into the main room. He seemed weak at the knees and about to collapse from shock and terror.

'Why don't you take a seat,' Ben said.

Daniel collapsed into the chair Ben was pointing at. 'Who the hell are you people, accosting me in my home like this?' he demanded, glaring up in shaky indignation.

'My name's Ben. This is Roberta. We're friends of a friend.'

'Claudine Pommier,' Roberta said.

Daniel's eyes opened wide at the name. 'Claudine? I . . . I don't understand. What's this about?'

'The letter she wrote us,' Roberta said. 'You and I each received copies of the same one from her, just days ago.'

Daniel stared at her. 'There must be some mistake. I received no . . .'

'Check your mail,' Ben told him. If Daniel only visited the post office once weekly, the letter from Paris could have been sitting there waiting for him all this time.

Daniel nodded uncertainly. He stood up and went over to where the mail was lying, hovered over the table for a few moments as he sifted through the envelopes and shook his head. Then, spotting the unopened envelope he'd dropped on the floor as Ben had surprised him before, he stooped to pick it up. 'It's her writing,' he said, gripped by a sudden anxiety that contorted his face.

'Open it,' Roberta said.

With shaky hands Daniel ripped open the envelope, took out the paper inside and began to read urgently. Roberta stepped closer to peer at the letter in his hands. One glance was all she needed. 'It's the same as the one she sent me.'

'This is what I warned her about,' Daniel said breathlessly. The paper fluttered in his hands. He looked up. 'Something's wrong, isn't it? Why are you here and not her? Something happened. Tell me.'

'You'd better sit down again,' Ben said. 'We haven't brought good news.'

Daniel settled in the chair, tightly gripping the crumpled letter.

'There's no easy way to say this, so I'll say it straight,'

Roberta told him grimly. 'Writing to us was just about the last thing Claudine did before she was murdered. It happened in Paris, at her flat, a few days ago.'

Daniel's mouth fell open. As the news sank in, he screwed his eyes tightly shut and slumped forward in his chair with his head in his hands. 'No. No. Oh, my god. Oh, sweet Jesus. It can't be true.' He went on muttering incoherently for a while; then, suddenly: 'I'm going to be sick.'

He staggered up to his feet and lurched out of the room. A door banged, followed by the sound of violent retching. After a few moments' silence, a toilet flushed. Soon afterwards, Daniel returned, looking ashen and weak. He slumped back in the chair.

Roberta touched his shoulder. 'You were close, weren't you? I'm so sorry. She was my friend, too.'

'Yes, we were close.' Daniel shook his head. 'I told her to be careful,' he gasped. 'I *told* her it was too dangerous to go on.'

'We saw the emails,' Ben said. 'We know that you warned her. And we know you know what this is all about.'

Daniel struggled for breath and was unable to speak for a few moments. 'I'm in shock,' he wheezed at last, looking imploringly at them. 'I need a drink. Please – there's some vodka in the kitchen. Would you get me some?'

'I think we could all use a little something,' Roberta said.

Ben stepped over the mess of splinters in the passage and went through to the kitchen. He returned a few moments later with the bottle of vodka and three mismatched glasses. Setting them on the table, he poured all three and handed the biggest to Daniel.

Vodka wasn't the only thing he'd found in the kitchen. He opened the matchbox that had been sitting by the stove, struck a match and lit up a Gauloise. It was the first one he'd had since leaving the safehouse in Paris, and it tasted good. He slipped the matchbox into his pocket.

Hunched on his chair, Daniel swallowed his vodka down like water. 'How did she . . . how did it . . . ?' he asked bleakly.

'It's probably better that you don't know the details,' Roberta told him. 'The police think it's the work of a serial killer. We happen to disagree.'

Daniel took several deep breaths. The empty glass was shaking in his hands. 'No, of course it wasn't a serial killer,' he said with a sudden flare of rage. 'Those fucking animals. This is what they do. Lies. All lies. Oh God. My poor Claudine.' He closed his eyes.

'I'm sorry we had to break it to you this way,' Ben said. 'And I apologise for breaking into your home and frightening you. I didn't think you'd speak to us otherwise.'

'I thought you were them, come to kill me.'

'Hence the shotgun,' Ben said.

Daniel gave a weary, desolate shrug. 'It was just in case. I don't really know how to use it, never fired it until today. I just wanted to make myself safe out here. I always thought one day they might track me down.'

'It's not out of the question,' Ben said. 'You're not that hard to find.'

'Who were you expecting to come for you, Daniel?' Roberta asked in a soft voice. 'You know who these people are, don't you?'

Daniel sighed and didn't say anything. Sweat ran down his brow.

'I know how upset you're feeling,' Roberta said. 'But we really need you to talk to us. It's the only way we're going to make this right. They're after us, too. Please help us understand. Who are they?'

Daniel fidgeted nervously in his chair, then heaved a reluctant sigh. 'It's a long story.'

'We came a long way to hear it,' Ben said.

'Then sit down and I'll tell you everything,' Daniel said.

Chapter Thirty-Six

'First, what do you know about Claudine's work?' Daniel asked, shooting a nervy glance at the door as if someone might be eavesdropping on them out here in the wilderness of Lapland.

'The number codes in her letter led us to where she'd hidden her research material,' Roberta said. As she spoke, Ben was unstrapping his bag and taking out the notebook computer along with the remote hard drive they'd retrieved from Germain De Bourg's tomb. He laid it on the table, connected the drive and powered up the machine. Daniel stood, grabbed a pair of glasses from his desk and approached the computer as Roberta went on.

'Until we found this,' she said, 'I'd expected to find her research on Tesla, nothing more. But there was all this other stuff in there, too. Seismology reports, images of disaster zones. I know it makes sense, somehow. I just can't put it together in my mind. What was she doing, Daniel?'

Daniel's grief-stricken face hardened as he accessed the files, clicking from one to the next in rapid succession. 'Claudine showed how all this was connected,' he said. 'The unexplained phenomenon discovered in Mongolia in March is just one example. This is another.' Opening up the image file that showed the devastated city, he pointed at the screen. 'You know where this is?'

'None of the image files are labelled,' Roberta said. 'We thought it looked like Latin America.'

Daniel nodded. 'Taráca, a tiny republic between Bolivia and Paraguay. This image is of San Vicente, its capital city, after the earthquake that devastated the country eighteen months ago.'

'I heard about it at the time,' Roberta said, remembering now where she'd come across the name San Vicente before. 'But I don't . . .'

Daniel stared at their puzzled faces and his mouth twisted into a humourless smile. 'You're still not getting what this is all about, are you? Tell me, what other hidden items of Claudine's did you find? Perhaps a small electronic device, metallic, oblong, about seven inches long?'

'Her Tesla oscillator?' Roberta said.

Daniel looked gravely at her. 'You found it, then. I knew Claudine would have hidden it. Do you have any idea what it's capable of?'

'We had an interesting taster,' Ben said.

'Which is why we don't have it any more,' Roberta said. 'It got buried under a thousand tons of rubble that we only just managed to get out of ourselves.'

'Then you understand what this is all about,' Daniel said. 'Or perhaps you still don't want to, because it's too terrible to imagine.'

'Start from the beginning,' Ben said. 'What's your involvement in all this? Are you a scientist like Claudine?'

Daniel shook his head. 'I was a freelance investigative journalist. For some time I lived in the States, then for the next several years my investigative work took me from place to place around Europe.'

'Investigating what?'

Daniel shrugged. 'Environmental concerns, ecology, green issues, things like that. I spent time with protest groups, demonstrated against motorway construction, hung out with alternative types, anarchists, people with way-out causes. I guess a lot of it rubbed off on me. In time I started getting deeper and deeper into conspiracy theories. I became convinced that the reality the citizens of the modern world are presented with is really no more than a carefully designed tissue of lies intended to hide the truth of what our global ruling elite are really doing, the future they're creating for all of us. I became involved in a whole network of people who devote themselves to studying and investigating the secret goings-on that most people never hear about. My main interest back then was the global warming controversy and the growing evidence that the entire thing was invented purely to generate massive revenues in so-called green taxes, hijack the ecological movements for purposes of gain and impose more controls on us all. Whatever money I could make I spent travelling around Europe to meet up with like-minded individuals. Unfortunately, that world draws a lot of cranks and crazies.'

'That's not such a big surprise,' Roberta said. Ben had met his fair share of those, too, but he was getting impatient with Daniel's account. 'Get to the point,' he said.

'I'm coming to it. It was at one of those meetings, an alternative science conference in London, that I met Claudine. I saw right away that she wasn't one of the crazy ones. She was different, and she was serious. Before long, we found what we had to say to one another more interesting than the conference. So we left. A drink turned into a meal. We talked and talked until the restaurant closed and we went to her hotel to talk some more. I was attracted to her, but that was only part of it. She had so much to tell about the research she'd been doing that I suddenly realised my global warming crusade was like nothing compared to what she was uncovering. I was hooked, even though some of it seemed impossible to believe. She described to me how she had built this machine based on Tesla's original. I was pretty incredulous at first, but she told me she could show me an actual demonstration. The very next morning I found myself going back to France with her. We stopped in Paris, then she drove me out into the countryside, to where she had come across an isolated, derelict farmhouse.'

Ben remembered the picture of the old house they'd seen on the computer hard drive. He could guess what was coming next.

'The walls were still standing, though nobody had lived there for years. I stood back and watched as Claudine attached her machine to an outer wall. I didn't know what to expect. Then she switched it on.'

'We've seen how this works,' Roberta said. 'The device auto-tuned to the resonant frequency of the building and started to shake it?'

'It was unbelievable,' Daniel said, with a look of awe. 'One wall fell in, then another. Then what was left of the roof, right before my eyes. If she hadn't turned the machine off in time, the whole thing would have been turned to rubble. That was when I became completely persuaded that what she had discovered was true, no matter how terrifying it seemed.'

He paused for another long gulp of vodka, swallowed it down and looked at them with a leaden expression. 'The most terrifying thing of all is what ruthless people could do with a technology like that. Here are the facts. Shortly after

Tesla's death on 7 January, 1943, two US Secret Service agents who may have been one Bloyce Fitzgerald and one Ralph Doty, removed key items from his safe at the New Yorker Hotel as well as safety deposit box 103 at the Governor Clinton Hotel, leaving phoney benign material behind in their place for the investigators of the subsequent Trump Inquiry to find, so that everyone could be satisfied that Tesla wasn't working on anything of potential military interest to enemy spies at the time of his death. The Trump Inquiry concluded that Tesla had been increasingly eccentric and possibly mentally ill during the last ten years of his life, producing nothing but useless gibberish that had no practical or scientific value.'

'While the genuine items were being whisked away to some secret government warehouse,' Roberta muttered.

'More than a warehouse, a laboratory,' Daniel replied. 'Claudine believed that this became the basis for a highly classified and massively funded research and development program to explore and expand the range of Tesla's discoveries. For over seventy years they've been secretly furthering his work, amplifying the powers he discovered, fine-tuning them, perfecting them.'

Daniel paused to drink more vodka, the glass trembling in his hand. '*Now* do you begin to see what this is about? The seismological data, the graphs, the images – Claudine had spent years compiling them, analysing them, searching through them until she was completely certain, beyond reasonable doubt—'

'Completely certain of what, Daniel?' Roberta asked, in a tone of dread that showed she already knew the answer.

Daniel's face turned a little paler. He wiped his mouth. 'That not all of the large-scale disasters of recent times, the mass destruction, the loss of countless human lives . . . were necessarily down to such natural causes as we have all been led to believe.'

'You mean—?'

'They were caused on purpose, yes,' Daniel said quietly.

Chapter Thirty-Seven

There was a silence in the room. Roberta turned to look at Ben, then at Daniel. The Swede nodded gravely. 'Triggered. Deliberately. Using a highly refined modern-day version of Tesla's exact same design principle.'

'Hah! It's what I *told* you, Ben,' Roberta said in grim triumph. 'The goddamn US government has been behind this all along.'

Ben said nothing.

Daniel waved his hand in a gesture of ambiguity. 'Well, that's a little simplistic, hmm? You need to understand that, basically, at this point in history, the concept of nations is nothing more than a public relations scam and a way to distract us all from what really goes on. Forget governments. The true rulers aren't the guys you see on TV. They're not the finger puppets we vote for. The New World Order. Call it what you will, it's a reality. Do you understand the terrible, terrible power that's involved here, the kind of people you're dealing with? They will stop at nothing. I mean nothing.'

Daniel turned back to the computer and pointed at the image of the wrecked cityscape that had been in the background as he'd been talking. 'Republic of Taráca, one of the smallest South American countries with a population of just 2.6 million people, but rich in copper and natural gas. For decades it's been a one-party state run by General Alberto Suarez, pretty much a military dictator who enjoyed support from Russia and Cuba, then more recently from the Chinese who were very keen to tap into Taráca's resources. There were increasing rumblings about the country slanting towards Socialism. Then the earthquake happened. Eight point five on the Richter Magnitude Scale, way more powerful than the one they had back in 1996. Much of the city was reduced to rubble, including the Presidential Palace. There was no warning. The quake struck so suddenly that General Suarez and his family had no time to get out. The palace collapsed right on their heads, killing everyone inside. In the crowded poorer districts, people had no chance at all. The final death toll was over thirty thousand.'

'I remember seeing it on television,' Roberta said. 'It was awful.'

'Oh yes, and of course our western rulers were quick to express the usual shock and sympathy for the victims. Almost before it happened, the United Nations were right there to help with the aftermath. A few quick backroom deals later and massive aid was being poured into the place, the Chinese were quietly ousted, five minutes afterwards a new democratic government popped up with just a little support from the CIA and other globalist agencies, and now Taráca's up on its feet again and guess who controls the copper and gas industries?'

Daniel's eyes flashed with anger as he went on, 'That's how it works. The old trick never fails. Knock them flat with one hand, then rush to their rescue with the other. And all the public sees of it are the sensational images of disaster and mayhem that the media keeps pumping into their numb brains, along with the message of what a cooperative and caring world we live in thanks to our benevolent leaders. Of course, every story needs a bad guy. Who better to lay the blame on than Mother Nature again? Meanwhile, behind the wall of lies, the deals are being made, their empire gets expanded, the balance of power shifts bit by bit in their favour and their grip on the whole world gets a little tighter.'

Daniel had been talking so furiously as the vodka loosened him that he now had to pause to gather his breath. 'Let me get this right,' Ben said, cutting into the gap. 'You'd have us believe that this Tesla technology, this earth-splitting resonance gimmick—'

'A little more than a gimmick, wouldn't you say?' Daniel shot back.

'—or whatever the hell it is, has been weaponised by secret agencies to the extent that they can use it to destabilise whole countries? Destroying a city is a little bit of a step up from shaking a building apart, it seems to me.'

'That's exactly what I'd have you believe,' Daniel replied emphatically. 'The bastards have had decades to develop it. This is a tool designed to subvert nations. A weapon of limitless political potential, giving whoever can direct its power dominion over the world. They can use it to bend any country to their will.' He grimaced. 'Subtler and cheaper than war, twenty times quicker and more effective than old-fashioned espionage and subversion, and it brings their final goal one big step closer.'

'Their goal?' Roberta said.

'To create a global state with themselves right at the top of the pyramid,' Daniel told her, knocking back the last of his vodka. He leaned across to grab the bottle off the table, sloshed more into his glass and slurped it down. 'That's what they've wanted from the beginning, and now it's theirs for the taking. The ultimate might gives them the ultimate right to do whatever they want, and they'll always get away with it.' He snorted bitterly. 'Nobody's going to complain, are they? Certainly not the good people of Taráca, not now that you can get a Big Mac on every other street corner of their rebuilt San Vicente. Fools. I saw it with my own eyes, when Claudine and I visited the place last year.'

As Ben wanted to doubt it, he couldn't deny that what Daniel was saying seemed to fit perfectly with everything that had happened to Claudine, to Roberta and himself. In a globalist political game where innocent lives could be expended by the thousand without a second thought as mere collateral damage, the elimination of the odd troublesome scientist or potential whistle-blower was neither here nor there. Those with the power and resources to undermine an entire country could all too easily track an individual target from country to country, follow their every move and marshal the small amount of manpower necessary to wipe them out at will.

It was a compelling, frightening scenario. Did he want to believe it?

'I hate to pour cold water on your theory,' he said. 'But earthquakes happen. They've been happening for millions of years before human beings walked the planet, and they'll go on happening long after we're gone. Even if the technology for this exists, there's no way you can't claim to know what's a genuine natural disaster and what's a deliberate attack.'

'Oh sure, shit happens,' Daniel countered angrily. 'And it does: that's the beauty of their scheme. The "forces of nature" bring a country to its knees economically, we go in to help them, and then they're right in our pocket where we want them. Japan getting too powerful? China? No problem, we'll zap them where it hurts, bring them down a peg, and nobody ever suspects a thing. How could a natural disaster be engineered? Anyone would think it was crazy. And they'll systematically marginalise and discredit anyone who claims it's possible, just like they've managed to turn Tesla into a joke now, to cover their own asses. But I'll tell you this,' he went on, glaring at Ben. 'Claudine wasn't some radical conspiracy nut who wanted to jump at any wild story going. She was a true scientist. She thought about every angle, looked everywhere for proof. Only a genius like her would have had the idea about the animals.'

'The mule sanctuary video,' Roberta said. 'That was you working the camera, wasn't it?'

Daniel nodded. 'Claudine realised that interpreting animal behaviour could be a way to tell the difference between a natural event and one that was man-made. It's been proven over and over that animals can tell when an earthquake's coming, because they're so tuned into every nuance of their environment. It's almost like a psychic power they have. But Claudine was certain that when it came to a totally artificial phenomenon, the animals wouldn't see it coming. And she was right. The same mules that seemed to have predicted the real quake of '96 were taken as much by surprise as the humans, even though this was a far more destructive event. You figure that one out. Pretty damned suspicious, no? Okay, it wasn't solid evidence. We still couldn't be absolutely sure. It wasn't until we met Zimm that we really knew we were on the right track.'

'Who the hell's Zimm?' Ben asked, frowning.

'An American called Barney Zimm. That's what he told us his name was, at least. He made contact with us after we'd been going round San Vicente asking questions for a week. When we met in a hotel room, he wouldn't allow us to film or record his statement and you could see he was rattled about talking to us. He told us he was a junior administrative employee with the US Embassy in Taráca, which was just a few streets from the Presidential Palace. According to his story, the day before the quake happened, he and his fellow workers had been visited by agents of FEMA – that's the US Federal Emergency Agency—'

'We know what FEMA is,' Roberta said.

'—instructing them to evacuate the buildings ahead of some emergency drill or other that was due to take place the following day. Their reasons sounded pretty vague, but they were extremely serious about the whole thing. According to Zimm, the agents gathered up all the key embassy staff, loaded them into these black vans and took them off to some undisclosed location outside the city. Next day, Zimm and the other lower-down staff took the advice they'd been given and didn't show up at work. As it turned out, they'd have been flattened in the rubble of the embassy building. Of course, no such warnings ever reached the ears of the ordinary citizens of San Vicente.'

'Jesus,' Roberta said, shaking her head. 'Those sonsofbitches.'

Ben wandered over to the window, smoked the last of his cigarette and gazed out at the peaceful forest as he tried to process all this mentally. A small flock of birds had flown down from the trees to peck at an object in the dirt a few steps from the parked Land Rover. At first he thought it was some dead animal, then realised it was the remains of the sandwich Daniel had discarded earlier.

Leaving the birds to their feast, Ben turned away from the window. He walked back to the computer. Stubbing out his cigarette, he closed the image of the ruined South American city. In its place he opened the document file on the unexplained devastation that had taken place in the Altai mountains of Mongolia.

'Explain something to me,' he said to Daniel, pointing at the screen. 'This location's so remote, they didn't even discover the incident until March. How does this fit your theory? Is undermining the thriving Mongolian tourist industry a part of the New World Order's agenda too?'

Daniel sighed. 'You still don't want to believe this.'

'I believe in what makes sense to me,' Ben said.

'Like religion, is that right?' Roberta challenged him. 'You need cast-iron evidence for faith in God too?'

Ben tightened his lips and ignored the jibe.

'Let me explain it another way,' Daniel said. He pointed at the pistol in Ben's belt. 'You seem to know what you're doing with that thing. Am I right?'

'I'm familiar with it,' Ben said.

'I'll bet you're really good with it. But how did you get so good?' Daniel asked him. 'I'm no expert, but I imagine it must take a great deal of drilling and repetition, when you want to get proficient with a weapon that must seem at first very unfamiliar. Just as this technology is still in its relative infancy, very new to its operators, a learning curve like any other.'

'You're saying Mongolia was just a practice exercise?' Ben said.

'Practice makes perfect, yes? Especially,' Daniel added with a significant look, 'Especially when you have ambitious plans. When you're working up to . . .' He paused. 'The big one.'

Chapter Thirty-Eight

'What do you mean, "the big one"?' Ben asked with narrowed eyes.

'In energy terms, the Mongolia event is estimated at over nine point five on the Richter Scale,' Daniel explained. 'That far eclipses what happened at Tunguska in 1908, close on the equivalent of three gigatons of TNT. The biggest thermonuclear device ever detonated tips the scale at only fifty megatons. By comparison to this Mongolia incident, the Taráca quake was just a ripple.'

Roberta was frowning. 'So what are you saying, that they're increasing the power as they go?'

Daniel nodded. 'Assuming that the devastation in the Altai Mountains was not a natural event, and it's too strange and coincidental to assume otherwise, then that would appear so, yes. They're cranking up the volume bit by bit, testing the capabilities of the technology. I believe that what we've seen up until now was just a dry run, if you will. A rehearsal.'

'A rehearsal for what?' Roberta asked, her frown deepening.

Daniel spread his hands. 'I don't know. Neither did Claudine. But I think that Mitch Shelton probably did.'

'Okay, and who's he?'

'According to our sources, Shelton was a CIA operative allegedly also employed by the classified agency that may or may not be directly behind this. Seems he found out a little too much of what was going on, became alarmed and confided some of what he'd discovered to an American journalist and conspiracy investigator called Chester Guardini. When Claudine and I met Guardini at a Free Earth symposium in Frankfurt last October, he seemed terrified. Kept looking over his shoulder. Wouldn't say much, except that something big was in the offing.'

'Something big?' Roberta said. 'Like what?'

'I don't know. He kept talking about something called Nemesis. Some kind of secret program. He wouldn't say more, just that he and Shelton were planning to blow the lid off real soon. Said it would be the biggest thing since . . . well, the biggest thing since *ever*. But it never happened. And it never will. Just days after we spoke to him, we heard that Guardini's car had been totalled by a truck back home in Chicago. With him in it, that is. Pronounced dead at the scene. Around the same time, Mitch Shelton drowned accidentally on a fishing trip near Miami. Believe *that* if you can. Coincidence? I don't think so.'

'So with all the potential witnesses gone, we basically have no idea what this Nemesis program is?' Ben said.

'Pretty much none,' Daniel replied. 'And they're serious about keeping it that way. After we heard about the deaths of Guardini and Shelton, I started getting scared. Claudine and I had been right there with him, talking in a public place. Who was to say we hadn't been watched, followed, caught on camera? I told her it was getting too dangerous, that we should back off. If we get in too deep, I said, we'll never get out again. But she wouldn't listen. We argued.'

'She was wilful that way,' Roberta said. 'Once she got an idea in her head, that was it.'

Ben looked at her and felt like saying 'Claudine wasn't the only one', but he kept his mouth shut. A movement from the window caught his eye and he glanced outside to see that more birds had flown down to join the little flock greedily crowding around the food in the dirt. A shred of ham went flying; a crumb was snapped up by a darting beak. At least somebody was having a good time.

Daniel's face cracked. He bowed his head and he started to weep pitifully. 'I should have done more to persuade her,' he sobbed, his shoulders quaking. 'I should have been more forceful. Now she's dead and it's my fault. And next,' he sniffed, wiping his tears, 'they'll come after me. I know it. What am I going to do? I found a safe place out here. I leave, they'll zoom in on me and I'm history.'

With a sympathetic expression Roberta went over to Daniel and put her hand on his shoulder. 'We can get you out of Sweden without them knowing, Daniel. Can't we?' she added, turning towards Ben. Daniel's face seemed to brighten a little. 'You can? But how?'

'By flying right under those sonsofbitches' radar,' she replied. 'That's how we got here unnoticed. We have a plane.'

'You have an aircraft? Where?'

'At an airstrip, a little way south of here,' she said. 'We could get there in just a few hours in your Land Rover.'

'I'm ready to leave any time,' Daniel said.

'Ben? What do you say?'

'Two questions,' Ben said. 'The first, where are we supposed to take him? The second, where are we going ourselves? It looks to me as if we've hit a dead end.'

Daniel paused for a moment, looking thoughtful, then said, 'Maybe not. I haven't told you everything I know.'

But Ben had suddenly lost interest in what Daniel knew. Another movement outside had distracted his attention. The flock of birds gathered to peck at Daniel's tossed sandwich had suddenly scattered, erupting like a small explosion and flying away in all directions for the safety of the trees. Ben jumped up and strode quickly to the window.

'What is it?' Roberta said, her eyes widening in alarm.

He stared intently at the trees. Nothing moved. The forest seemed perfectly still. It could have been anything. The approach of some predator, a fox, maybe. Even just a ripple of wind through the branches could have frightened the wary birds.

And yet . . .

Ben's senses were jangling. Something was wrong.

'Ben?' Roberta asked anxiously. 'What have you seen?'

'Somebody's out there,' Ben said.

Chapter Thirty-Nine

They knew who they were dealing with. A full ten-man complement had been deployed for the assault team who were now making the final approach towards the isolated cabin on foot. The team leader led the way, stalking carefully and quietly through the trees, an assault weapon with fitted grenade launcher hanging from his neck. He and the other nine were clad in black tactical entry vests and masks, and wearing radio earpieces. Their automatic rifles were loaded and ready.

Their objective was simple: take out the targets. Take no chances. Leave no trace.

The team leader was Lloyd McGrath. Under the black ski mask, his face was hard. He signalled the men to pause as the parked Land Rover and the cabin beyond it came into view through the foliage. For a few moments, he watched and listened intently. Fifty yards away, the cabin seemed still. In his mind's eye McGrath could see the two men and the woman inside. The attack would be swift. Ten men. Not even a former SAS guy stood a chance. He might be good; he might be every bit as good as the old man seemed to think he was. But McGrath hadn't seen a Special Forces superman yet who wasn't made of the same mortal flesh and blood as anyone else. And McGrath was an expert on flesh and blood: how to destroy the one; how to spill the other.

Ben Hope wasn't coming out of this alive, not this time. Not after the embarrassment of Paris.

At McGrath's further signal, four men broke off from the team. Two moved stealthily under cover of the foliage around the sides of the cabin, left and right, working their way around to rejoin at the back. The other pair trotted forward towards the parked Land Rover, keeping low to the ground. They reached the vehicle and crouched down, awaiting further orders from their carpieces.

The forest was completely silent except for the whisper of the breeze through the leaves.

McGrath unslung his AR-15. He slipped a grenade from the holder on his belt into the tube assembly mounted under the weapon's barrel, forward of the curved 30-round magazine. Resting the weapon in the crook of a tree, he took careful aim at the cabin through his illuminated optical sights. He braced his feet apart against the recoil, then tugged the grenade launcher's trigger.

The steel cylindrical projectile fired out of the tube with a loud hollow thud. It sailed in an arc towards the cabin and smashed with a tinkling of glass through the front window where McGrath had been aiming.

A moment later, there was a muffled *crump* as the stun munition detonated inside the cabin. The shockwave was to disorientate the targets. To soften them up, not to kill them. That would come next. The Director wanted neat, identifiable kills, not a mound of charred body parts.

That remit still gave McGrath plenty of scope to enjoy himself. The last time he'd got to do a woman had been the Claudine Pommier job. Now he was looking forward to the sight of the Ryder bitch with her pretty features all messed up by a bullet.

'Go,' he said into his throat mike, and watched as the two initial entry pairs stormed simultaneously up to the front and back doors, weapons levelled.

McGrath waited for the gunfire. He heard nothing.

Seconds later the report came back through his earpiece: the targets weren't in the cabin.

'Find them,' McGrath said.

There hadn't been time to make it to the vehicle or escape into the woods. But the little trap-door under the living room rug had allowed the three of them to slip out under the cabin floor, hidden from view by the wooden skirt that ran around its base.

Ben was lying on his back on the bare, cool earth with Daniel's shotgun at his side, looking up at the floorboards two feet above him. The sturdy planking had protected them from the stun munition blast. Ben knew that was only the opening gambit.

Roberta was sprawled close by him, clutching the Beretta submachine gun, eyes wide and turned upwards, nervously biting her lip. Ben was a lot more worried about Daniel. The Swede looked about to fall apart in a sweating, gibbering panic. Ben put his finger to his lips and gave him a warning look.

Heavy footsteps rang off the boards over them. Through the gaps in the planking Ben could see the dark figures of the intruders striding about. As far as he could tell, there were three in the living room and a fourth had just walked out of the front door, reporting on a radio. He wasn't Swedish. He was American.

None of the other three had yet noticed the rug pulled

unevenly to one side or the small trapdoor neatly inset into the floorboards, but they soon might. One was standing right over the trapdoor. If he spotted it now, the game was up.

Ben gripped the Mossberg. Its five-shot tube magazine was refilled and there was a sixth cartridge in the breech. He silently, gently, eased off the safety. He gave Roberta a look that told her what he was about to do. His expression said, 'Stick close by me. It'll be fine.' She stared mutely back at him, visibly fluttering with adrenaline.

Ben didn't believe in prayer at a time like this. He closed his eyes for a second. Visualised his targets. Saw them going down one after another with speed and precision. Readied himself mentally and felt his heart rate ease a notch. He took a deep breath, counted *one – two – three*.

And then crashed the trapdoor lid open with the barrel of the shotgun and burst up through the floor.

Chapter Forty

There was a split-second pause as the man standing over the trapdoor stared down at Ben, the eyes in the ski-mask slits boggling in surprise.

Ben jabbed the shotgun barrel up towards him and squeezed the trigger at closer than point blank range. That close up, even a round of bird-shot could kill just about anything.

The twelve-bore went off with a sound like a bomb in the cabin and recoiled heavily in Ben's hands. The force of the blast picked the man up off his feet and threw him halfway across the room. Before he'd hit the floor, Ben was already working the action and tracking the gun anticlockwise through thirty degrees to engage his second target. Another deafening explosion; another man in black went down as if a scythe had taken his legs out from under him. Ben shot him again.

The sudden noise and violence had thrown the intruders into a confusion. The third man in the room was racing for the cover of the passage doorway. Ben got off another shot, but it went wide as the man darted out of sight. He saw flecks of blood hit the wall around the ragged hole left by the shotgun blast.

Ben felt movement at his feet and looked down. Daniel

was scrabbling past Roberta in his haste to get out of the trapdoor. 'Give me a gun!' he piped, panic-stricken. 'I need a gun!'

Ben ignored him. He was more concerned about that grenade shooter outside. Now the element of surprise was spent, the guy wouldn't be slow to figure out where to deliver his next charge. A stun munition going off in the confined space under the cabin would lay them all out unconscious, and make easy pickings of them for the attackers. Seconds counted, and there wouldn't be many of them to spare.

'A gun!' Daniel was still babbling. 'You can't leave me defenceless!'

Ben impatiently ripped the Browning from his belt and thrust it into Daniel's hands. 'Take it and shut up,' he rasped. He reached down past Daniel, grabbed Roberta by the hand and yanked her up out of the square hole with the Beretta hanging about her neck. At that instant, he heard the flat *whoof* of the second grenade firing from the trees and the clattering thud as it bounced its way deep under the cabin.

'Shit,' he breathed. Not good. Time was a little pressing now.

Ben hauled Daniel from the trapdoor as if he'd been a sack of coal. The Swede let out a cry as the Browning snagged and he clumsily let it drop from his hand. There was no time to go back for it. Ben dumped him in a heap on the floor and kicked the trap shut just in time to block out the pressure wave of the stun blast as it burst violently under the floorboards, shaking the whole cabin. Daniel staggered upright, pressed his hands to his ears.

'Close one,' Roberta said.

Ben looked quickly around him. The living room was cleared, but it wouldn't be for many more seconds. One dead man was lying spread-eagled on the floor, the other was slumped against the wall. The blood trail from the third led out into the passage. A glance through the shattered front window: more black-clad figures outside. Maybe three, maybe four. Making fast for the cabin. Footsteps crashing on the front porch.

A figure appeared in the doorway. The flash of black gunmetal; Ben swung round with the shotgun at his hip and let off another round before the shooter could fire. The booming Mossberg took a semi-circular bite out of the doorframe and wall. The black figure fell back. More swarmed up behind him. Ben racked the Mossberg and fired twice more. Answering shots rang out. Ben felt the wind of a bullet pass his face. Splinters flew from the wall behind him. His last shot was gone and his pistol was lost under the cabin. Roberta had the only working weapon and she was determinedly bringing it to bear on the entrance when Ben grabbed her from behind and pulled her back towards the passage before she got shot. Daniel had already darted through the doorway ahead of them.

Bullets drilled through the walls as they ran. Three yards down the passage, and they were suddenly confronted by the hobbling figure of the shooter Ben had winged. The man raised his gun. Roberta aimed the Beretta. Before either of them could get off a shot, Ben hurled the heavy steel mass of the Mossberg at him like a spear. The tip of the muzzle hit him in the chest. Then Ben was into him, knocking him violently to the floor and stamping his head as he trampled over the top of him. 'Come on!' he yelled at the others. There wasn't even time to pick up the fallen man's weapon before their pursuers appeared behind them in the passage. Two more shots rang out. Roberta let out a cry and clapped a hand to her arm.

Hauling her along behind him, Ben burst into the

cluttered back hallway through which he'd come earlier. The rear exit was in front of him, the kitchen door to his right. Through the dirty glass of the back door he could see two more men rushing towards the porch.

Barely time to think. Nearby were the two spare propane gas cylinders. He nudged them with his knee, felt the weight of the liquid gas inside. He snatched up the little hatchet from the kindling box and used the blunt end of the blade like a hammer on the valves on the top of each bottle. In two wild blows they were bent crooked and gas was hissing out. He dropped the hatchet and swept his arm up to the shelf above, grabbed the wire handles of the two paraffin lamps and ripped them down as he leapt towards the kitchen doorway.

The men outside were thundering up the porch steps. The ones inside were racing up the passage. Ben crashed into the kitchen, hauling Roberta through with him. Daniel followed in a panic. Ben shouldered the door shut. There was a heavy iron bolt. He slid it quickly home, then dashed across to the pine kitchen table. With a violent heave he overturned it with the thick tabletop facing the door. He grasped Roberta's hand and pulled her down into a crouch behind the makeshift barrier. 'Let me see that.' He ripped urgently at her bloody sleeve and saw with relief that the bullet had only creased the top layer of skin.

'This isn't the time for first aid,' she said, but her words were drowned out by the flurry of gunfire that began hammering into the kitchen door. Before Ben could stop her, Roberta had darted out from behind the cover of the overturned table, switched the Beretta to full-auto and was hosing bullets at the door. The kitchen filled with deafening noise as she let off the entire contents of the magazine. Empty cases rained down on the floor. The splintering wood was rapidly disintegrating as a large ragged hole appeared in the middle of the door. By the time Ben grabbed her and spun her back behind the tabletop, the Beretta was empty.

Now they had no weapon. Any number of heavily-armed attackers were just the other side of the door; it was going to fall apart any second from the overwhelming amount of gunfire being sprayed into the kitchen. Bullets were hammering like crazy into the tabletop, chewing away the wood, and it wouldn't shield them much longer. Daniel was cringing in a ball with his hands over his head.

Ben took the box of matches from his pocket and grabbed the two paraffin lamps. He sniffed them and caught the sharp tang of fuel he'd been hoping to smell.

'What are you doing?' Roberta yelled.

'It's time to warm things up a little,' Ben said, and struck a match.

Chapter Forty-One

One paraffin lamp sputtered rapidly into life, then the other. Ben peered over the top of the table. The ragged hole in the door was almost large enough for a man to crawl through. He hurled a lamp. It shattered against the edge of the hole. There was a flash of igniting fuel, a scream as the passage filled with flames. Ben hurled the second lamp. It went cleanly through the hole. He ducked back behind the table and pressed Roberta down, shielding her with his body from what was about to happen.

The two propane cylinders exploded almost simultaneously in a blast of expanding flame and rupturing steel. The kitchen door was blown off its hinges, and with much of the wooden planking of the wall, cannoned into the kitchen and into the tabletop barricade. Daniel cried out in terror. Ben felt the heat sear his flesh and pressed Roberta down harder. Then the burning pain was gone as the fireball swallowed itself back into the blazing passage.

Ben looked up. Everything beyond the door was a raging inferno. There was no way to get back up the passage, but as he now saw, that didn't matter any longer as the explosion had ripped the whole back off the cabin and half the kitchen wall was gone. He clambered off Roberta, took her hands and helped her to her feet. 'You okay?'

'Great,' she coughed. Still tightly clutching her hand, Ben led her at a run through the curtain of smoke and out of the shattered room onto the back porch. With Daniel staggering after them they jumped down onto the patchy grass of the yard. Suddenly they were breathing air and could feel the cool breeze on their faces. Ben turned back to look at the blazing wreck of the cabin and saw what carnage the exploding gas had inflicted on the attackers inside. A legless trunk had been blown clear and was burning on the ground. A severed hand lay nearby, still clutching a gun.

'Are they all dead?' Roberta asked, wheezing.

Ben shook his head and gazed into the crackling flames. 'I don't know.'

Suddenly the question was answered as two figures came running at them out of the smoke. From the weapon he was clutching, Ben instantly recognised the larger and more muscular of the two as the grenade shooter. He must have been too far from the cabin to have been caught in the blast. A big man, broad and powerful. The black-clad attacker sprinting along behind him was shorter and leaner, but no less deadly.

'Run!' Ben yelled. They dashed away from the porch. The only shelter was the open-fronted shed of the log store. They ducked past the large steel frame of the motorized log splitter. Bullets rattled and howled off it. Then the two of them were rounding the log store. Ben glanced all around him for a weapon, any weapon.

That was when he realised Daniel was no longer behind them.

The Swede was running wildly for the bushes, obviously hoping that the cloud of black smoke blowing from the cabin would mask him. It didn't. As Ben watched, helpless, the masked grenade shooter unholstered a semiautomatic pistol and let off four, five, six rapid shots at the ungainly running figure. Daniel stumbled, but stayed on his feet. He crashed out of sight into the thicket.

The man reholstered his pistol and signalled to his companion. They began to circle the wood store. Ben and Roberta had nowhere to run. Ben's eyes lighted on a chainsaw, and he was about to snatch it up when he saw the long-handled axe buried in the chopping block. He grasped the shaft with both fists and tore it out just as the first shooter came around the corner. The man's gun was aimed at Ben's face. The weapon cracked. With a resonating clang, the bullet deflected off the axe blade. Ben knew it was the luckiest moment he'd ever had in combat, but he didn't take the time to celebrate. Before the man could fire again, he swung the axe violently. Felt the sickening impact of metal on meat as the blade chopped downwards at an angle through his opponent's collar bone and almost took his head clean off his shoulders. The gun fell out of the man's hands as he collapsed lifeless on the grass with a last look of surprise and horror in his eyes.

Ben dived for his fallen weapon, but he was half a second too slow to snatch it up before a sustained burst from the larger shooter's AR-15 drove him back behind the log store. Bullets raked the wood pile and sent shreds flying. Ben grabbed hold of Roberta and was steering her urgently away from the source of the gunfire when he realised the weapon had fallen suddenly silent. He looked back and saw that the shooter was extricating a stoppage from his chamber. Failure to fire. For a precious moment, the rifle was nothing but an inert lump of black steel and aluminium.

Ben ran at him.

The big man saw him coming. The unfired round was clear of the chamber. He let his magazine drop into the grass, rapidly plucked another from his tactical vest and was slamming it into the rifle's mag well when Ben's diving leap sent him crashing backwards.

It was like wrestling a bear. Ben had to use all his strength to twist the rifle out of the man's iron grip. Pinning the broad frame down with his knees he clubbed him across the face with the retracting butt until the blood was leaking through the black material of the mask. 'Who are you working for?' Ben rasped, and hit him again, then again. 'Answer me!'

The answer was a punch that came out of nowhere and hit Ben square on the chin with tremendous force, knocking him backwards. His senses spun. For a precarious moment he was on the brink of a precipice, unconsciousness threatening to pull him down into the black depths. He blinked and shook his head to revive himself, just in time for his instinct to kick back in to deflect a battery of heavy blows that his attacker was hurling at his face and upper body. Fighting desperately back, Ben managed to grasp hold of a fistful of his hair through the mask. The man jerked his head violently away and the mask came off in Ben's fingers, along with a tuft of short silvery-grey hair.

Even as they furiously traded blows on the ground Ben recognised the man he'd seen in Paris. The hard, cold face that had looked at him from the pursuing car in the tunnel, and again from the burning flyover.

Ben lashed out with the edge of his hand and felt the man's nose break. The man made no sound, as if he felt no pain. He just kept fighting. Ben deflected a savage punch aimed at his throat, and managed to flip himself up onto his feet. But he was too slow to avoid the straight kick that would have smashed his knee in if it had been two inches lower. The impact made him stagger back. Something solid behind him tripped him and he sprawled backwards over it. A crippling jet of pain shot through his lower spine.

The man was up on his feet now, the lower half of his face covered in blood as he came on again.

Roberta ran over to the fallen corpse that had the axe still buried in it. She planted her foot on the dead man's chest and twisted the blade out of the gory wound, hefted it and lunged at the silver-haired man with a yell. He saw it coming and ducked back out of the arc of the swing. The blade scored the material of his combat vest. Roberta had put all she had into the blow, and the momentum of the heavy blade carried the axe too far, twisting her body around and exposing her flank to him. The sole of his combat boot caught her hard in the hip and sent her stumbling against the edge of the wood store with such force that a corner piece of its timber frame hit her on the side of the head and almost knocked her out. She slumped down, dazed.

Through the pain, Ben realised he'd fallen across the log splitter machine. He tried to clamber upright, but the silver-haired man moved quickly and punched him hard, making him flop back. He could see stars and taste blood on his lips. His left hip was wedged hard up against the static vertical cutting blade so that he couldn't roll off the machine, and there was no purchase for his legs. Another punch made him see stars.

The man reached towards the machine and yanked hard on the starter cord. The petrol motor spluttered, then roared into life. The man wiped blood from his mouth and grinned redly. His hand went to the vertical lever on the top of the machine and pulled it. A steel rammer emerged from the motor housing. Ben came to his senses just in time. With a violent heave he managed to twist his body off the machine before the rammer caught his side and pressed him into the static blade. If he'd been a log, he'd have been effortlessly chopped in half at the waist. He flopped to the ground, still stunned.

The silver-haired man was laughing over the roar of the engine. He walked around the side of the machine towards Ben and stood over him. 'I always wanted to face up against one of you SAS guys. Frankly, I don't see what all the fuss is about. This the best you can do?'

'I know you,' Ben said, looking up at the towering figure.

'Sure you do. I'm Lloyd McGrath. You might call me the handyman.' McGrath spat a gout of blood on the ground and smiled. 'After I kill you, then I'm going to have some fun with your girlfriend over there. Thought you might like to know that.' He motioned towards the wood store. Then his smile contorted into a red leer and he raised his boot to stamp it down on Ben's face with a skull-crushing blow.

Ben had taken a moment or two to realise what the solid object he could feel under him was. At first he'd thought it was a stone hidden in the grass. But it was colder, flatter. And sharper.

As McGrath's boot came down with the full force and weight of his body behind it, the shaft end of the axe handle flew up. Solid hickory connected with the soft flesh between McGrath's legs.

The broken nose hadn't got a reaction out of him, but that did. McGrath staggered back with a howl of pain and rage, clutching his groin.

Ben stood up. 'You haven't got the balls for it,' he said. He flipped the axe over in his hands and jabbed the flat end of the blade twice into the man's face.

McGrath lost his balance and sprawled across the roaring log splitter.

'So you were going to have some fun with me, were you?'

said Roberta's voice. Ben looked and saw her stride up to the machine. There was a smear of blood on her temple and a look of cold anger in her eyes. Before McGrath could wriggle his muscular body out of the way, she gripped the vertical lever and pulled. The ram pushed out of the housing and punched into his ribs. He screamed as the motor drove him relentlessly against the wedge-shaped blade.

Ben had seen plenty of men come to nasty ends, but this time he looked away. The sound of McGrath's inhuman gargling shriek and his wild thrashing against the pitiless machine was enough to tell him what was going on. It didn't last more than two seconds. When the only noise left to be heard was the roar of the engine, the man's legs were twitching on the ground on one side of the blood-spattered machine and the upper half of his body had slumped down onto the grass on the other. His eyes were still open.

Ben stepped over and switched off the engine.

'That was for Claudine,' Roberta said in the silence.

Ben nodded. He gazed across at the blazing ruins of the cabin, then at the trees. 'We'd better go and find Daniel,' he said.

Chapter Forty-Two

'He went that way,' Roberta said, pointing towards a thick clump of trees. 'I don't think they got him, but I can't be sure. He might be hurt.'

'Wait.' Ben paused by the gruesome corpse of McGrath. There was no point even trying to frisk the bodies for any kind of ID or a clue about who had sent them. But the pistol was still in McGrath's belt holster and Ben wasn't about to venture into the woods unarmed in case of survivors. He knelt down by McGrath's severed lower half. Reaching past the trailing intestines, he unsnapped the restraining clip of the bloody holster and drew out the handgun. It was the kind of old-fashioned pistol Ben favoured and trusted. All metal, no polymers or synthetics. A Colt Combat Commander model chambered in .38 Super. He wiped it clean on the dead man's trouser leg and was about to stand up when he frowned and paused to examine the Commander more closely.

'What is it?' Roberta said, looking curiously at him.

'Nothing,' he said, standing up. He tucked the pistol into his pocket, walked over to where McGrath had dropped his assault rifle and picked that up too.

They moved cautiously through the trees, calling Daniel's name. There was plenty of broken foliage to indicate where the Swede had gone crashing through in a hurry, but no sign of blood.

'I hope he's all right,' Roberta said.

They found him in the hollow of an old dead tree a few hundred yards from the cabin. He started as he saw them appear through the leaves, then relaxed with a sigh when he saw their faces. He was shaking and pale and still out of breath from his sprint. 'I'm sorry,' he stammered. 'I'm sorry I ran. I just couldn't . . .'

'You did the right thing,' Roberta said, taking his arm and helping him out of the tree hollow. 'Sure you're not hurt?'

Daniel shook his head. 'No. I mean yes. I'm not hurt.' His eyes darted from Roberta to Ben and back again, taking in their bloodied appearance. 'What about . . . Is it . . . ?'

'It's over. They should have sent more guys,' Roberta said with a dark smile.

'And maybe they will,' Ben said, 'So we'd best get moving.'

As they walked back through the trees, Daniel caught sight of the smoke rising from the ruins of his home. 'My cabin,' he gasped.

'It wouldn't have been much use to you any more, anyway,' Ben said. 'It's time for you to relocate.'

'I thought we said I was coming with you?' Daniel asked anxiously.

'We hadn't got around to deciding that,' Ben said.

'I can help. I know more.'

'Then you'd better tell us all about it,' Ben said. 'But you can do it on the road. I'm driving.' He held his hand out flat. 'You'd better tell me the Land Rover keys are still in your pocket.'

Daniel nodded uncertainly, reached for the keys and dropped them into Ben's palm. Ben took them without a word, walked over to retrieve his bag where he'd left it near the vehicle. His movements automatic and second nature, he removed the magazine of the AR-15 he'd taken from McGrath's body, slid out the take-down pin and broke the weapon down into its separate components, then packed them inside the bag before slinging it into the back of the Land Rover.

'Where are we going?' Daniel asked as he clambered into the back seat.

'Out of Lapland, that's for sure.'

'But how can you travel, with guns?'

'Borders mean nothing to us,' Roberta said. 'We have our own private transport, remember?'

Ben fired up the engine and they left the scene of devastation behind them, bumping and rocking harshly along the rutted forest track. 'Now talk,' Ben said, making eye contact with Daniel in the rear-view mirror.

'I was telling you about what Guardini told us, before he died,' Daniel explained. 'How he'd told us they were planning something, something big? Well, there was more to it that I didn't mention before. He said that Shelton had described to him a secret base where the agency was doing all its research and development of the Tesla technology. Told us all about it.'

'Where?' Ben said.

'Indonesia.'

'*Indonesia?*' Roberta said, turning round with a quizzical expression.

Daniel nodded. 'One of the old CIA bases left over from the mid-sixties, when they were secretly involved in the purge of the PKI, the Indonesian Communist Party. Half a million people were killed or executed. Then the Yanks supposedly went home after the "New Order" was set up. But they kept a foothold in the place, needless to say.'

'What is this base, a laboratory?' Roberta asked.

'From the outside it just looks like a big industrial facility, all sealed off behind wire and teeming with armed personnel,' Daniel said. 'I can only imagine what's inside the place, to be so heavily guarded like that.'

'So you actually went there,' Ben said. 'All the way to Indonesia.'

Daniel nodded again. 'That's right. It was Claudine's idea. She was convinced it'd lead us to the next stage. Personally, I wasn't so sure, but she just wouldn't let it rest until I finally agreed. We took a flight to Jakarta last April. We knew the base was on one of the islands, but Guardini had only given us a few clues, passed on from Shelton.'

'What clues?' Roberta said.

'Claudine had them all written down. She was the one who was leading the way, like always. I was just there as her helper. Anyway, it took over a week of travelling from island to island and a lot of very careful asking around. We were losing hope of finding a damn thing and just about to give up, when we eventually found the place. You have to cross over from Java to Sumatra to get there. It's on the west coast of the island, near a place called Arta Beach.'

Ben said nothing, but just listened intently as he drove the Land Rover along the bouncy track through the forest.

'Do you think you could find it again, Daniel?' Roberta asked.

The Swede shrugged. 'It's remote, right out on its own. Nothing nearby but a few small towns and villages. But sure, I'm pretty certain I could find it, if you were willing to risk going there. Like I said, the bastards have got the place wrapped up tighter than a max-security prison. The two of us didn't stand a chance of getting inside. Before we'd got two hundred yards from the fence, the alarm was raised and a jeep full of guys with guns came speeding out to intercept us. We just ran like hell and managed to get back to our car in time. I'm certain they'd have shot us if they'd caught us. I've never been so scared witless in my life. Until today,' he added.

'So after you came back from Indonesia,' Ben said, 'That's when you told Claudine you wanted out?'

'What was I supposed to do? It was just too dangerous. I said I was going to come back to Sweden and find someplace to lie low and try to forget about all this. I said she should do the same. I did everything I could to persuade her to give the whole thing up. But she wouldn't have any of it. She insisted on going back to Paris and carrying on like before so she could expose what these people are doing. Pleaded with me to join her, but I was so damn scared. It turned into a big fight between us. She said I was a coward, I said she was a fool. I really tried, but in the end there was nothing I could do. She broke things off with me and went off on her own. I came back here. Every so often I'd drive to a town and email her, try to make her see sense. But it was no use. The thing I was most afraid of happened.' Daniel shook his head forlornly. 'Now they've found me too. I won't be safe anywhere, ever again.'

Ben watched him for a moment in the rear-view mirror, then slipped the Colt he'd taken from McGrath out of his belt and passed it back to him. 'Here, you can hang on to this if it makes you feel happier. You're not much use to me if you keep running away whenever we get into a spot.'

'Does that mean you'll take me with you?' Daniel hesitated, then reached out for the pistol and turned it over in his hands with fascination. 'Oh, my God. I've never operated one of these before.'

'There's nothing to it,' Ben said. 'You're cocked and locked. The safety catch is the little lever by your thumb. Flip it down and you're ready to fire. There are still a few rounds left in the mag, plus the one up the spout.'

Daniel held the weapon tightly in his fist and a glow of determination seemed to spread over his face. He nodded solemnly to himself. 'I want to make this right,' he said. 'We can do this. I know we can do this. With someone like you ... I mean, the way you took those men down. I never saw anything like it – never met anyone like you before. You must be a soldier, right? Only some kind of special training could ...'

'I'm just a guy who was studying to be a priest,' Ben said.

'It's a long story,' Roberta whispered to Daniel.

'Let me come with you,' Daniel said after a beat. 'Please. I'm asking you. I'm begging you. Take me to Indonesia on your plane and I'll guide you to where the base is. We'll find those bastards and put a stop to this thing once and for all. This time, I don't care if I die trying.'

Chapter Forty-Three

New York City

Jack Quigley caught sight of his reflection in a plate glass window as he walked along the western end of Fulton Street in Manhattan's financial district, and saw a thin, gaunt and barely recognisable figure looking back at him. He'd aged years in the month since Mandy's funeral.

For most of that time, on compassionate leave from his job, he'd been vegetating in a state of near-catatonic despair in a motel outside Shepherdstown, staring into a glass of Jim Beam that was never full no matter how often he topped it up from a long line of bottles. Not caring about his career, not caring about his ruined home, not about anything except the loss of the woman he'd loved and wanted to spend the rest of his days with – and the certain knowledge that she'd been killed in a blast meant for him.

It was the lowest point he'd ever reached in his life and three times he'd reached for his .45 Kimber, fully intending to blow out his brains but always pulling back from the brink just before the hammer dropped.

But after all the pain, in the last days a new energy had begun to flow through Quigley's system – just a trickle at first, gradually building up to a flood. He'd come through the darkness. The grief that had crippled him was now focused tight, like a laser, and he felt only rage. Burning, calculating rage. He didn't know how exactly these murdering bastards had managed to induce a heart attack in Herbie Blumenthal, but he wasn't a child. He knew these kinds of covert assassinations had been part of the toolkit of agencies like his from the first. And he was certain deep in his heart that the intruders who had rigged the gas explosion that had torn the townhouse apart had had a clear plan in mind: to eradicate the only witness to what the fat man might have been blabbing about at that diner table in D.C.

And Quigley wasn't going to rest until he'd found out every last detail Blumenthal hadn't had time to tell him. If what Blumenthal had said was right, the death of Mitch Shelton was somehow implicated too. No matter what or how long it took, he was going to hunt down and destroy the people behind it all. He had little else to live for now.

Yet the fear was clinging to him like a cold sweat. All the way from Virginia to New York City, Quigley had been watching his driver's mirror for someone following him; he kept glancing over his shoulder now as he headed on foot towards the address he'd found on the business card in Blumenthal's wallet. He was tense and strung-out, and not even the solid presence of the big Kimber automatic in its concealed-carry holster under his jacket made him feel any happier.

Emptying its magazine into the bastards who'd taken away his life: now *that* might make him feel happier. When he thought about it, it made his hands shake. *Get a handle on yourself*, he thought. *You were a Marine once. So act like one.*

This was the place. He stopped walking and gazed up at the glass tower that loomed thirty floors above the street. In mirror-shiny letters six feet high above the entrance was the name Mandrake Holdings, Inc.

Quigley took out the business card and examined it once again. He'd spent half of last night online researching everything he could about Mandrake Holdings. Their range of business investments was as diverse as it was extensive: residential and industrial real estate all across the globe, zinc, tin and diamond mining, international cargo shipping and air freight, construction, energy. Quigley turned the card over and wondered once again, as he'd wondered a hundred times before now, about the name scrawled on the back.

'Triton,' he murmured aloud. What the hell was Triton? He'd found no reference on Mandrake Holdings' website or any of the other sources he'd checked out. But the same feeling in his gut that had served him well throughout his years as a Special Investigator was telling him this had something to do with what Blumenthal had been trying to spill to him.

He put the card back in his pocket. Took a last glance up at the glass tower, mustered his resolve and pushed determinedly through the entrance.

The building's trillion-dollar lobby was as impressive as its exterior. Marble floor, marble pillars, modern art and sculptures dotting the walls, busy executives scooting by like ants and a general hive-like buzz of activity all around. Quigley walked up to the desk, where an impossibly gorgeous receptionist in a sharp suit and a headset smiled up at him like a long-lost lover.

'My name's Jack Quigley. I'd like to speak to someone in authority regarding Triton,' he said, hoping the name alone would mean something to her.

'I'm afraid you're going to have to be more specific,' the receptionist said politely. 'What is it regarding?'

'Just Triton. I'd rather speak to someone in management, please.'

She had him repeat it three more times. By now the perfect smile was gone without a trace and she was a completely different animal. She picked up a phone, punched an extension number with a long red nail, and without taking her eyes off him she relayed his message to whoever was on the other end. There was a long pause, then she put the phone down and coolly told Quigley to take a seat in the waiting area across the lobby. Someone would be down to speak to him presently.

Quigley sat, feeling restless and gripped every few moments by a desire to escape back out into the street. Maybe this whole thing, coming out all the way here to New York like this when he was still so raw, was a dumb mistake. Maybe he should know better. Maybe he was suffering from some kind of post-traumatic—

His self-doubts were interrupted by the arrival of two terse-looking men in suits. Forgettable faces, identical hair-styles. Not one man, he noticed, but two. His presence here must have made double the impression.

'Mr Quigley?' said one, while the other just watched and listened with folded arms. Quigley replied that he was, and showed them his Central Intelligence Agency ID card displaying his employee number, status and security clearance level. In the same impersonal tone the man asked him whether this concerned agency business. Quigley said no, this was a private matter.

'If you'd be so good as to follow us, sir.'

'That would be my pleasure,' he said, mustering up his confidence.

The two men led him away from the lobby, down a series of twisting corridors and deep into a part of the building that was far less glitzy. They came to a security door. Before passing through it, they had him step through a scanner. He'd been hoping that wouldn't happen.

The scanner beeped. The two men's eyes fixed on him unflinchingly as he was asked if was carrying a weapon.

Quigley had no carry permit for New York, and knew full well that working for the CIA did not entitle him to go armed unless on official business, which he'd already confirmed this wasn't. Moments later security personnel had arrived and he was relieved of his sidearm, which he gave up reluctantly.

Through the security doors now, which closed behind him with a resonant and ominous click. The building seemed to go on forever. 'This is some fortress you have here,' Quigley said. There was no reply. Finally, his taciturn hosts led him into a small neon-lit windowless square that contained only two plastic chairs and a plastic desk and looked more like an interrogation room than an office, and promptly vanished. Quigley was greeted by a third forgettable-faced man in a suit, burlier than the first two, who again asked to see his ID, spent a long time frowning over it as though he were about to declare it phoney, then asked him to state the nature of his business at Mandrake Holdings, Inc. Quigley reiterated the same painfully vague question he'd asked in the lobby about Triton.

The burly man's face remained perfectly blank. 'And what would that be?'

'I was hoping you could tell me,' Quigley replied.

The man shook his head. 'Sorry, I can't help you.'

All this way into the building just to be told that? Quigley didn't buy it. 'What about the Nemesis Program?' he asked, pushing deeper. 'Can you tell me anything about that?'

The man didn't reply. His phone rang. He answered it without a word, listened expressionlessly, ended the call and said to Quigley, 'Please wait here.'

The man left the office and shut the door. The lock clicked.

'Hey!' Quigley exclaimed, rising from his seat. 'You can't shut me in here.'

But that was exactly what they had done, and there was no option but to sit down again and wait.

Five minutes, ten. Quigley shifted about in the uncomfortable chair. He drummed his fingers on the desk. Glanced restlessly about him at the featureless room.

Then the lights went out. Quigley froze in the total darkness. A chill crept over him. He jumped to his feet, found his way back to the door and beat on it. 'Hey! Let me out! You hear me? Let me out of here right now!'

The door suddenly burst open in his face, making him stagger back a step. The corridor outside was as dark as the room. All he saw of the three men who came striding in through the door were the glowing LEDs on their infrared goggles. Stunned, he felt strong hands grasp his arms. He was propelled backwards into the room and pinned down on the desk, struggling and wriggling against their grip. He managed to get an arm free and lashed out with a fist. A jolt of agony shot up his forearm as his knuckles split open on one of the men's goggles.

'What's happening?' he yelled. 'Who are you people?' His arm was being pinned back down and he couldn't move. He felt the short, sharp jab of a needle stabbing into his arm and being quickly retracted. Jesus Christ, he'd been injected with something.

Quigley fought and yelled furiously, but a rising tide was quickly rushing up to smother him. After a few seconds his protests diminished, his voice became slurred and his muscles began to go limp. A few seconds after that, the men were able to let go of him and he lay helpless across the desk. He wasn't quite unconscious yet, and could dimly sense himself being bundled up off the desk and out of the room. By the time they were halfway to the waiting vehicle, Quigley could sense nothing at all.

Chapter Forty-Four

'It's not a license to globetrot,' Ruth had said. But as Ben drove back along the winding forest and mountain roads towards Jäkkwik, tracing possible routes across the world map inside his head, he was intensely aware of the scale of the journey that now lay before him, Roberta and their new travelling companion.

It was approaching mid-afternoon by the time they finally reached the sleepy little airfield where the Steiner ST-1 was sitting in the pale sunlight looking exactly as they'd left it. There had been no new arrivals. None of the motley collection of aircraft, even those that were in a fit state to fly, had moved an inch.

'This is your plane?' Daniel said, staring in amazement at the Steiner turboprop as he got out of the Land Rover.

'No, we came in that one over there,' Ben replied tersely, and pointed at the partially stripped Swedish military transport aircraft by the hangars. He was feeling battered and sore all over from his fight with McGrath, and a dark, brooding mood had settled over him on the long road. First to board the plane, he dumped their bags in the aisle, then walked down the narrow fuselage to the bathroom, where he splashed some water on his face to clean away the worst of the blood. Most of it wasn't his own.

When he came out of the bathroom, he found that Daniel had already ensconced himself in one of the plush faux-leather armchairs, looking like a somewhat tattered and eccentric business-class passenger waiting for a hostess to bring him a glass of chilled Chablis. Ben ignored him and stepped into the cockpit, where Roberta was sitting in the co-pilot's seat and poring thoughtfully over a computer terminal built into one of the instrument panels.

'We have quite some road ahead of us,' she said, looking up as he squeezed into the pilot's seat next to her. 'Your sister would kill you if she knew what we were planning to inflict on her little plane.'

'Tell me about it.'

'Any thoughts on our itinerary?'

'Some,' he said, nodding. He reached across the controls and tapped a digital readout with his finger. 'This tells us we still have just over eight hundred and seventy nautical miles' worth of fuel. That's about a thousand miles, enough to take us as far south as Berlin or thereabouts. We can be there by this evening, take on fuel and some more supplies, and stay the night before setting off again.'

Roberta nodded and poised her hands over the onboard computer's keyboard, ready to run an online search. 'We're lucky to get any wi-fi reception up here at all,' she muttered. 'What should I be looking for?'

'Small and out of the way places,' Ben said. 'We can't just drop in out of the sky at a large airport. Besides, the bigger places will have Jet A fuel for your 747, but they might not be able to supply the 100LL avgas we need. There are always dozens of small airfields near any city that aren't too crowded.'

'Got it,' Roberta said, and typed in the keywords 'airfields near Berlin'. She paused a moment as she scanned the results that flashed up an instant later. 'Okay. Here's a place that looks like it could work for us. The Flugakademie Freihof, fifty k's south of Berlin. It's mainly a flying school, but small charter airlines and private planes use it as an airfield.'

'That sounds possible,' Ben agreed. At the tap of a key, the ST-1's sophisticated flight computer automatically logged the latitude and longitude coordinates, altitude and runway length data, and pre-set the airfield's radio frequency into the system.

Together the two of them spent the next hour figuring out the best route, while Roberta rapidly covered a notepad with details of distances, fuel range calculations, time zones and mile to nautical miles conversions. Point to point they were looking at an overall distance of more than seven thousand miles, divided up into legs by the number of times they'd have to refuel. From Germany they plotted a route that would carry them sixteen hundred miles south-eastwards to the limit of their fuel capacity to Tbilisi in Georgia, threading a careful path across the troubled zones of the North Caucasus and those autonomous or semi-autonomous Muslim republics such as Dagestan, Ingushctia, North Ossetia-Alania and Karachaevo-Cherkessia, which were kept on a tight intelligence and military leash by Moscow and which Ben was hesitant about overflying.

But it was an unstable and ever-volatile world out there, and there was no route that could take them where they needed to go without touching danger. From Georgia the flight path took them south across the mountainous plains of Iran and onwards to the relative sanctuary of Muscat in Oman, where the authorities would be so used to expensive private aircraft flying in and out that Ben was willing to take his chances with the regulation-heavy Sultanate regime there.

Then it would be the long trek across the ocean to the southern tip of India and another minor airfield Ben and Roberta searched out online, situated a few miles from the city of Bangalore. In Ben's experience India was generally a pretty relaxed place, riddled with the kind of lazy corruption that tended to come in handy in situations like this; there was enough cash left to cross an official palm or two with silver if it helped them pass through unhindered.

From there, the fifth and final leg of the journey would take them across the Indian Ocean to Medan on the Indonesian island of Sumatra. 'Assuming we can find a safe place to leave the plane,' Ben said, 'we're going to have to hire a vehicle so our friend back there can guide us the rest of the way to this secret base.'

'So there we have it,' Roberta said, looking at the finished itinerary and shaking her head in wonder. 'Like I said, it's one hell of a way. Based on a cruise speed of around two hundred eighty-five knots and allowing for rest stops and refuelling, I calculate it's going to take us around forty-eight hours to get to Medan. I'm worried about you doing all that flying.'

'Don't worry about me,' Ben said. 'Just worry that this one lead we have is worth trekking halfway around the planet to check out. Because if doesn't get us anywhere, it's game over. This is our one shot.'

Chapter Forty-Five

Just over three hours after taking off from the airfield at Jäkkwik, the ST-1 was touching down at the Flugakademie Freihof near Berlin. Ben had radioed in some time before their arrival, and was expected by the ground crew who shepherded the taxiing aircraft towards the refuelling station. The reference number Ruth had given them was like a magic wand that breezed them through the formalities, allowed them to fill up on fuel with no questions asked and secured them their own private hangar space for the night. If the dishevelled and slightly battered appearance of the pilot made any impression on the airfield staff, they didn't show it – they must already be familiar with Steiner Industries' informal new ways, Ben supposed – and they even organised a car to take them to the nearest town, Luckenwalde.

Leaving Daniel to his own devices for a couple of hours, Ben and Roberta raided a local Edeka supermarket for fresh clothing, food and bottled water for the rest of the long journey ahead. It was in the car heading back to the airfield that Ben turned to her with his idea.

'I've been thinking,' he said. 'You can travel anywhere from here without anyone knowing where you are.'

'I don't understand,' she said. 'I'm coming with you to Indonesia.'

'We don't know what we're going into. I'd be a lot happier if you stayed behind. I can give you enough money to lie low for as long as you need.'

'Lie low. You mean hide.'

'Call it what you like. You'd be safe.'

She stared at him as if he'd lost his mind. Shook her head vehemently. 'Absolutely no way. It was me who got you into this, and a whole lot more besides. You think I'd bow out now and let you carry the can? Forget it, Ben. I'm seeing this through, no matter what.'

He shrugged his shoulders. 'I tried.'

Then it was back to the plane, to illegally spend the night on board. It was hot and airless inside the hangar, but Ben didn't let it bother him. He was intent on grabbing as much rest as he could, ahead of the sleep deprivation he was going to suffer over the coming forty-eight or so hours.

Shortly after dawn the following morning, the Steiner ST-1 was back in the air and rapidly leaving Germany behind as they headed eastwards towards the Polish border on the first five-hour leg of the journey. Poland; Ukraine: the landscape unrolled beneath them, green pasture-land and small towns and villages, hilltop churches, lakes and forests. Skirting the northern coastline of the Black Sea, the sunlight dappling the waters; into Georgia, the landscape harsher, rockier. Soon afterwards, the plane was buffeted by high winds and a violent rainstorm that lashed the windows and shook the plane like a toy. Roberta joined Ben in the cockpit and sat anxiously by him as he wrestled with the controls.

They arrived in Tbilisi, just after 11 a.m. local time and only minutes behind schedule despite the heavy weather. The clouds had vanished and the sun shone brightly as they completed their second refuel on the Steiner Industries tab. It felt a little parasitical, like a mosquito drawing blood from its unsuspecting host. Ben consoled his pang of guilt by thinking of the billions the corporation pulled in from its activities all over the world. It would take more than a few drops of aviation fuel to bring his sister's company down. 'Anyway,' he said to himself more than once as the high-pressure pumps filled his tanks, 'I'll pay her back.'

Just ninety minutes after touchdown, they were off again, this time setting their course southwards. Roberta stayed up front with Ben while Daniel slouched and slumbered in the back, never once offering to make himself useful.

Flying, flying. The constant hum of the engines and the hypnotic vibration through the floor and the seats would have lulled Ben to sleep if he hadn't been so on edge about this long leg of the journey. Something else was on his mind, too.

'What's wrong?' Roberta asked, seeing his expression as he stared fixedly ahead.

'It's not important.'

'Tell me. Something's bothering y—' She broke off, suddenly remembering what day it was. 'I get it. You and Brooke would've been getting married this afternoon.'

Ben said nothing.

'You can still fix it with her,' she said, affecting a cheery look. 'You know that, right? It's going to be okay. Really.'

Ben said nothing.

Armenia came and went; then it was into Iranian airspace where his personal concerns were overshadowed by the very real worry of crossing paths with trigger-happy military fighter jets. Just as troubling was the significant potential threat from the ground. It was a restless and perpetually inflamed situation down there, and with a thousand disparate militia groups going about armed to the nines and a good deal of illicit training of Syrian and other rebel forces going on in hidden camps across the country, it would only take a single sniper to object to their presence and a well-aimed .50-calibre anti-materiel round tearing through their flimsy unarmoured fuselage to bring them down.

But Ben's anxiety proved unfounded. The long hours passed and they weren't shot down or pursued, and he settled a little in the pilot's seat as the vastness of the rocky landscape skimmed endlessly by beneath them. Roberta gazed out and marvelled at the rugged splendour of the Alpine-Himalayan mountain system that fringed the vast Iranian central plateau. 'Wow, I've never seen anything like this before,' she breathed.

'It looks pretty from up here,' he said. 'But you wouldn't want to be down there. It's not the most hospitable of environments.'

'I guess you'd know all about that kind of thing. Don't crash the plane, huh?'

'I'll do my best.'

Just as the craggy landscape seemed as if it might go on forever, the terrain began to turn into a flattening desert as they headed further south. Flying, flying: the burning sun casting a perfect shadow of the plane on the ground below them; the monotone of the engines taking on something of eternity. Ben was feeling the fatigue hit him acutely now after so many hours in the air. He kept having to blink. Only his frequent checks of their fuel readout were keeping him awake.

'Talk to me,' he said at last. It seemed a long time since he'd heard the sound of his own voice. It came out as a dry croak.

Roberta looked almost as worn out as he felt. 'Okay,' she said numbly. 'What shall we talk about?'

'Anything you like except Tesla and physics,' he replied.

'You want to hear a joke?'

'You actually know any?'

'Don't sound so surprised. Check this one out. What does a dyslexic insomniac agnostic do in bed at night?'

'I have absolutely no idea.'

'Lie there worrying about whether or not there's a dog.'

A weak smile was all he could manage.

'One to entertain your future congregation with,' she said.

'I'll be sure to remember. Got any more?'

She thought for a moment. 'Okay. Another religious one for you. Why did the scientist take a Higgs Boson into church? Because you can't have Mass without it.'

Ben looked at her. 'I thought we said no physics.'

She shrugged. 'Those are all the jokes I know.'

'Remind me to say a prayer for your sense of humour.'

'Hey. That's the thanks I get for keeping you awake?'

'Speaking of barrels of laughs,' Ben said, 'what's His Nibs up to back there?'

Roberta craned her neck and peered through the Perspex window in the bulkhead that separated the cabin from the passenger section. Daniel was slouched deep in a window seat with his head lolling on his shoulder. On the seat next to him were an empty crisp packet, two crushed drinks cans and several crumpled sandwich containers. 'Well, it looks like he's eaten his way through most of our provisions and now he's asleep again.'

Ben shook his head and had a vision of Daniel freefalling from the plane, a tiny cartwheeling figure getting rapidly smaller.

'Never mind him,' Roberta said. 'Whereabouts are we, anyway?'

Ben pointed to the right. 'About a hundred miles thataway is Kuwait.' He pointed left. 'About five hundred miles thataway is Afghanistan.'

'All I can see is sand and more sand,' she replied.

Sand and more sand was all they did see for a long time. But eventually, the arid monotony came to an end and they were greeted by the welcome sight of the Persian Gulf. Just gazing across the clear, flat waters, as pure and blue as the unbroken sky, was enough to make them feel quenched and refreshed after the unremitting wilderness. As Ben hugged the coastline, they roared above little towns and ports of whitewashed stone that glittered like pearls against the blue. Yachts and fishing boats dotted the crystal-clear ocean. Onwards south: Qatar; Abu Dhabi; then over the Strait of Hormuz, through which giant supertankers carried more than a fifth of the world's petroleum. From the air the busy shipping route looked choked with traffic and military convoys. Soon afterwards the plane was skirting the Gulf of Oman, overflying ancient coastal forts and palm-fringed beaches.

Every mile that separated Ben further from what should have been his home and his new life added to the dull, leaden pain that wouldn't leave his heart. Today, of all days, Brooke had never felt so hopelessly out of reach.

Chapter Forty-Six

At 6.33 p.m. local time, a little more than twelve hours since they'd left Germany, Ben touched down at a small commercial air base a few miles inland of the port city of Muscat. The heat slammed into them like a breath of fire as they stepped down from the air-conditioned plane. Within minutes Ben could feel his shirt sticking to him. The sleek white fuselage of the ST-1 was caked with sand and looked as travel-weary as pilot and co-pilot did.

The only one who appeared fresh and rested was Daniel. 'How's it going?' Ben asked him. 'Hope the journey's not too tiring for you.'

'There's not a lot of sandwiches left.'

'Fancy that,' Ben said.

The air base was filled with activity, with a variety of aircraft from small propeller planes to big Lear jets constantly arriving and departing. In a corner near the refuelling dock, a low shady building offered a lounge where pilots, crew and passengers could get out of the still-blazing evening sun and cool themselves with iced coffee. It was an inviting prospect. The asphalt felt like it was burning holes in Ben's shoes as he saw to the refuelling, and he ached for the chance to relax and close his eyes for a couple of hours.

But as the last few gallons of 100LL avgas were being

pumped on board, he caught sight of a Royal Oman Police Jeep speeding through a gate in the distance. Perched up front with an imperious air, in dark glasses and peaked cap, was an officer, most likely a captain. There were four heavily-armed khaki-shirted goons riding in the back, and they looked like they meant business. Ben watched as they screeched up a hundred yards away and all piled out of the Jeep to collar the pilot of a private Cessna that had come in to land within the last twenty minutes, checking papers and acting tough while two of the goons went aboard clutching their rifles as if they expected to flush out a nest of terrorists.

The last thing Ben needed was a bunch of overzealous storm-troopers combing through the inside of the ST-1 and start barking unanswerable questions about the little cargo of weaponry he was carrying. 'I think we've outstayed our welcome here,' he said to Roberta.

After less than a hour on the ground, Ben was back in the pilot's seat and pointing the aircraft south-eastwards for the 1,250-nautical-mile journey across the Arabian Sea to India. The Oman coastline shrunk away, the last land they would see for some time as the aircraft roared over the water. The giant fireball of the sun gradually sank into the western horizon, scorching the darkening ocean with shimmering reds and golds.

Darkness fell, and the cockpit was dimly illuminated by the glow of the instruments and the navigation lights that twinkled with the moonlight on the waves. Now and then they overflew a ship. Time passed. They were too tired to say much to one another. Ben felt Roberta's hand on his shoulder, and realised with a start that his chin had been sinking to his chest. He ground his teeth and willed himself to stay alert. Another hour ticked by, then another. Nothing seemed to exist but the infinity of dark ocean stretching out ahead, a surreal impression as if all the world's land masses had sunk without a trace while they'd been in the air.

'I'm sorry, I'm not very good company,' Roberta murmured, turning towards him so he could see her smile in the glow of the instrument panels. 'I can hardly keep my eyes open either.'

'Go and get some sleep in the back,' he told her gently, but she shook her head and replied, 'I'd rather stay here with you. If you want me, that is.'

'I do want you,' he said, and took a hand off the controls to reach out and softly touch her arm.

It wasn't until a few minutes later, in the long silence that followed, that he suddenly realised how his words to her had sounded like a lover's – a thought that cut through the mist of fatigue and made him feel strangely unsettled.

He *had* loved her, once. It had taken him a long time to get over her, and now here she was again. The warmth of her presence brought back a lot of old memories. Perhaps too many.

Don't get confused, said a stern voice deep inside his head. Ben let out a long breath to clear his mind.

'What is it?' she asked in the darkness.

'Nothing,' he replied.

'You always say that.'

The first they saw of India was a glow on the flat, black horizon. At long last, the illuminated sprawl of Mumbai rose above the sea. They skirted the southern edge of the city and stayed on course until, sometime before 1 a.m., Ben's navigational instruments told him that they were approaching the city of Bangalore and their nearby destination, an airstrip near Ramanagaram. Tall trees all around the strip made for a sharp descent and a tricky landing. Ben was so exhausted that he could hardly see the runway lights, but managed to get the plane down safely on the second pass with Roberta gripping his arm.

At last, Ben could tear himself away from the controls and rest his weary muscles. He more or less ignored Daniel as he gulped down the last of their German sandwiches. Then, completely spent, he fell back into one of the reclining passenger seats, felt the tension ooze out of him and was tumbling into a dreamless void the moment he closed his eyes.

The first thing he saw when he opened them again was Roberta sitting next to him. The first light of dawn was creeping in through the plane's oval porthole windows.

She smiled. 'It's beautiful here. I was going to go for a walk. You want to stretch your legs a little?'

The stars were fading, chased off by the crimson glow of the rising sun. They filled their lungs with the fresh, crisp morning air as they walked through the trees. That strange, unsettling feeling that Ben had experienced the night before returned as it struck him that they might have been a romantic couple strolling peacefully along together.

The feeling became stronger still when she suddenly stopped and took his hand. Hers was warm and soft, like the sound of her voice. 'I like being here with you, Ben. Even with everything that's happened, everything that could still happen, I feel happy. Please don't be angry with me for telling you.'

'I don't know what to say,' he muttered.

'You don't have to say anything. But I do.' She paused, glancing down at her feet. 'You know, I lived a long time without you. It was really hard for me, never knowing how you were, never hearing a word from you.' She looked up again, directly into his eyes. 'I don't want to relive that time again.'

'I'm sorry I hurt you,' he said. 'All I can do is keep saying it.'

'If we make it through this, you'll stay in touch with me, won't you?' she asked earnestly. Her face looked pale in the dawn light and her eyes were shining.

'Don't talk like that,' Ben said. 'Of course we're going to make it through this.'

'You didn't answer my question.'

'You're a good friend, Roberta.'

'I know that's all I can ever be to you,' she said. 'But friends keep in contact. Don't they?'

He nodded. Sighed. 'It's not as if I didn't think about you,' he said. 'I did, a lot.'

'I wish you'd called. Even just one single time.'

'You don't know me. There are a lot of things I'm not good at. Keeping in touch with people is just one of them.'

'I know you better than you realise, Ben Hope.' She gave his hand a gentle squeeze. 'Tell me I don't have to lose you again. That's all I want to know.'

'We should be getting back to the plane,' he said after a long pause. He delicately let go of her hand and they started slowly retracing their steps through the trees glowing in the morning light.

Chapter Forty-Seven

It had been a blur of space and time. The sun was clear of the treetops and already burning hot as the plane took off, carrying on board every drop of fuel the little airfield had to offer. 'It'll be enough,' Ben told himself. 'More than enough.'

By mid-morning they'd left the southern shores of India behind them and were striking out across the Bay of Bengal and the vast waters of another sparkling blue-green ocean. Children waved and smiled up at the roaring aircraft from fishing boats on the white sandy beaches of Sri Lanka, the last land that Ben and Roberta would see until they raised the west coast of Sumatra hours later.

As the last leg of the journey unrolled, lulled by the unwavering rumble of the twin engines, the constant monitoring of their course, speed and altitude, the cloudless sky like a vast aquamarine dome up above and the presence of Roberta at his side, Ben caught himself more than once almost forgetting what they were heading towards. It felt strangely as if the two of them could stay up here forever, just flying aimlessly across clear, warm oceans that would never end. It wasn't happiness – his troubles were never far beneath the surface – but it was the nearest he'd come to it for what seemed like a long time.

It wasn't until soon after midday, as the first glimpse of Sumatra's tropical landscape appeared on the horizon, that Ben's easy state of mind was broken and reality bit.

There was no warning of the fighters' approach until they were right there with them. A pair of F16s, with Indonesian Air Force markings and bristling with armament: they drew level either side of the ST-1, throttled off and boxed it in, dwarfing the little white turboprop like a sparrow flanked by two dragons. From the cockpit window Ben could clearly see the masked face of the fighter pilot to starboard, and the strong heat haze from the jets. As a show of intimidating strength, it was highly effective.

'Ben!' Roberta turned to him in alarm. But he made no reply, as he was already attending to the radio. The harsh authoritarian voice in his headset changed to English after a few moments, but he'd already got the gist.

'What are they saying?' Roberta asked, wide-eyed.

'They've demanded that we verify our authority to enter Indonesian airspace. If we can't do that in the next minute or two, they're going to force us to land.'

'Land? Where?' Roberta peered anxiously at the approaching island coastline. Beyond the fringe of beaches lay a vast tangle of tropical forest. 'They can't do this,' she said, biting her lip. 'Can they?'

'They can do whatever they want, Roberta. Like blow us out of the sky if they decide we're hostile.' The tinny voice in Ben's ear was barking furiously: *If you do not comply with our instructions we will employ lethal force. Repeat. We will employ lethal force.* And Ben believed it implicitly. The briefest of touches on the trigger of a rotary machine cannon, and the ST-1 would be instantly diced into tiny fragments and plummet to a watery grave along with its three occupants.

'What are we going to do?' Roberta gasped.

'It's not as if we can outrun them,' he told her calmly. 'These things can shift at over Mach 2 and are just about the most nimble thing in the sky. And I wouldn't bet on outgunning them, either.' He sighed, pursed his lips and pressed the talk button on his radio. 'Copy. This is Sierra Indigo four-two-nine-oh. Happy to comply with instructions. Changing course. Please state rerouted destination. Over.'

You will follow this escort to air force command base at Pekanbaru,' came the order over the radio. *'Remain with escort. Do not deviate course. Repeat. Do not deviate or we will shoot.*'

'You made your point succinctly, boys,' Ben said. He pressed the talk button. 'Copy that. Lead the way.'

The Sumatra coast was streaking towards them, growing larger each moment. The fighters altered course a couple of degrees to port and Ben reluctantly followed suit. There was simply no other choice.

'What happens when we reach the base?' Roberta asked, frowning.

'That depends on the forbearance of our fellow man,' Ben said. 'They might let us go with an arse toasting. Or they might arrest us.'

'The weapons,' she said, turning pale.

He nodded. 'They won't take too kindly to those. If we hit some cloud, might be a sensible idea to dump them overboard while the fighter pilots aren't looking.' Ben scanned the horizon. As far as the eye could see the sky was perfectly clear. *Shit,* he said inwardly.

'Isn't there anything we can do to get away?'

'We could jump out mid-air,' Ben said.

Roberta turned another shade paler. 'This isn't good, is it?'

'It's not ideal,' Ben said.

Daniel appeared in the cabin doorway, his face mottled and his jaw hanging open. 'There are two military fighters outside,' he blurted.

'Wondered if that'd get your attention,' Ben said. But he had other things on his mind than Daniel right now. Glancing at the instruments, his mouth went dry. 'Roberta, look up Pekanbaru air base for me on the computer, will you?'

Roberta turned to the keyboard and started tapping. 'How'd you spell that? Hold on, got it.'

'Okay, now feed the coordinates through to the main system so I can set a fresh course.' Moments later, the gadgetry showed up the data on the panel in front of him.

'We may have a problem,' he said.

Roberta gulped. 'Uh, I thought we already had a problem.'

'That was the old problem of what would happen when we reached the air command base,' he said. 'This is the new problem of what's going to happen *before* we get there.'

'Before?' she said, puzzled.

'We left India with just enough fuel to get to Medan,' Ben said. 'But Pekanbaru is two hundred miles further inland. We can't go that far.'

She blinked. 'What happens then?'

'The plane can't stay up without fuel,' he said, looking at her.

'You mean . . . we're going to *crash?*'

Ben clenched his jaw. 'Only if they don't shoot us down first.'

Chapter Forty-Eight

Minutes passed without anyone speaking, then more minutes. By now they had overflown the Sumatra coastline and were heading inland over the undulating green landscape. Here and there scattered buildings, small towns, industrial installations and swathes of decimated tropical forest passed under the shadow of the little ST-1 and its hulking escorts.

'You have to *do* something,' Daniel finally groaned in a shaky voice.

Ben activated the radio again. 'This is Sierra Indigo four-two-nine-oh. We're getting low on fuel here. Request to divert course to a nearer landing site. Come back. Over.'

Moments later the message came back. '*Negative, Sierra Indigo four-two-nine-oh. Proceed on course as instructed. Over.*'

'That might be a little easier said than done, boys,' Ben muttered, looking at the dwindling fuel gauge.

There was a tense silence in the cockpit that lasted a long time. Roberta was gripping the arm rests of the co-pilot seat so tightly that her fingers were white. Daniel was pacing nervously up and down the passenger aisle, chewing at his nails. Ben stared fixedly ahead in silence as his mind raced frantically. All the while, the F16s remained steadily either side, guiding them inexorably away from their original flight path. After thirty more fraught minutes, Medan passed by, far out of sight, several miles to the northeast.

And soon afterwards Ben's blood went a little colder as he saw that his fuel calculations had been all too accurate – his last chance of a margin of error was gone. The gauge was dropping lower and lower into the danger zone with every passing minute.

They weren't going to make it.

He tried the radio one more time. 'Unable to reach destination. I repeat, unable to reach destination. Require alternative landing within' – glancing at the constantly-diminishing fuel readout – 'within ten miles. Situation urgent. Over.'

Once again, the inflexible reply rasped in his earpiece. *'Sierra Indigo four-two-nine-oh, you have been warned. Any deviation off course will entail serious consequences. Over.'*

'Well?' Roberta asked breathlessly.

Ben shook his head. 'They won't play ball. They think we're pulling a trick on them, and they know we can touch down in places they can't. We make one false move, they're going to assume we're taking evasive action and they'll open fire.'

'Oh, Jesus. There has to be something we can do. What's that beeping?'

The amber warning light that had been flashing for some time on the instrument panel was now pulsing an angry red.

'Critical fuel alert,' Ben said. 'This is it. Daniel,' he yelled over his shoulder, 'for Christ's sake, stop pacing and buckle yourself into a seat back there.'

Roberta had tears of terror in her eyes. 'Ben—'

'We're going to be fine,' he said, keeping his own rising fear out of his voice. He glanced down out of the cockpit window. A solid green canopy of trees was racing by in a blur beneath them. All around were rolling hills and deep wooded valleys. He'd lost track of their position. All he knew was that there was nowhere to touch safely down. Nowhere at all . . .

That was when the port engine stuttered, coughed and then died. The left-side propeller was suddenly, horribly, static. The high-pitched beeping seemed to become more shrilly insistent. The red light flashed like a pulse of pain. Ben felt the shocking imbalance of the crippled aircraft through the controls and wrestled to stop the left wing from dipping downwards.

'Oh my God!' Roberta gasped. A cry of panic came from the rear as Daniel huddled in his seat.

'I can hold it,' Ben said through gritted teeth. But he knew he couldn't. The gauges were in a flurry. The aircraft was losing altitude and no force on earth could keep its nose from slanting downwards in a shallow dive. The alarm was piercing his ears. He smashed the red warning light with his fist, but the shrill beeping kept on.

Then the starboard engine cut out too. Ben turned to stare in grim dismay at the stalled propeller.

In the awful silence, the ST-1 began to fall out of the air.

Ben's radio earpieces were immediately buzzing with warning commands to stay on course. He tore the headset off and flung it away. His heart was icy cold. Every muscle in his body locked tight. They were going down and there was nothing he could do.

The stricken aircraft skimmed the treetops in a steepening dive, raking the upper branches with a violent crackling that sounded like the belly of the fuselage being ripped away. Then suddenly, just as it seemed they were about to plunge into the thick of the trees and be dashed to pieces in a fireball of exploding aviation fuel, the green canopy that was rushing up to meet them disappeared. In its place a vast, panoramic stretch of water came into view up ahead, twinkling in the sunlight and dotted with small islands.

Now Ben realised where he was. Lake Toba. A hundred kilometres long and thirty wide. The largest volcanic lake in the world, site of an enormous eruption seventy thousand years ago. He'd read about it once. Just never thought he'd have to ditch an aircraft into it.

This was it. Their one chance of survival. How slender a chance, they were about to find out.

'Brace yourselves!' he yelled.

Seeing their captive break off course, the F16s took instant action. With lightning agility and a deafening sonic boom from their jets they peeled off and looped upwards, barrelling over, then came arcing back at terrifying speed towards the stricken turboprop. Inside their cockpits, the pilots were arming their weapons, ready to blast their target to pieces.

Ben barely even registered the jets streaking into attack position. All he could see were the sun-dappled waters of the lake hurtling towards him. He fought to keep the nose of the falling aircraft at a shallow angle to lessen the impact.

Getting closer . . . closer. Racing across the water, almost touching.

Roberta screamed.

And then they hit.

Chapter Forty-Nine

The force of the crash landing hurled them harshly against their seatbelts as the aircraft's nose cleaved the lake like a bullet and the cockpit windows were plunged underwater. For a fraction of an instant Ben thought he'd touched down at too steep an angle, and that they were going to flip over and break apart.

But no, the plane's nose surged up and they managed to stay level, their wings ploughing the surface in a storm of white spray. The roar of the water bursting against their sides was enormous and it seemed impossible for the juddering aircraft to hold together. Out of the cockpit window, Ben caught a glimpse of one of the lake's volcanic islands looming horrifyingly close towards them as they skimmed across the water, and braced himself for the crunch against the rocks.

It never came. The crashed plane quickly slowed to a halt a few metres from the island and the churned-up surface of the lake settled around it, immediately beginning to suck it down. Still half-stunned, Ben looked down and saw the water pouring into the cockpit, rising fast.

He hammered his seatbelt release button with his fist and twisted round towards Roberta, who was hanging limp against her belt, her eyes half shut. The warm, foaming water was up to the instrument panel now, the electricals sparking and popping as they shorted out. Ben released Roberta from her belt and shook her by the shoulders. Her eyes opened and looked at him.

'Are you all right?' he yelled, but his words were drowned out by a deafening screeching roar as the F16s swooped down low over the lake and passed right overhead, holding their fire. In an instant they were gone, two black specks streaking into the distance.

Roberta nodded. 'I'm okay,' she murmured.

Now that they hadn't been pummelled to pieces by rotary cannon munitions, Ben focused on getting himself and Roberta safely out of the sinking aircraft. And Daniel, too. He was struggling in a panic to release his seatbelt clasp as the water level gained. Ben opened it for him and hauled him roughly out of his seat. 'Move,' he grunted. Spotting his old green bag, he grabbed it and slung it over his shoulder. He and that bag had travelled a long way together and he wasn't about to be parted from it, even if it hadn't contained the best part of fifteen thousand euros.

The front of the plane was going down first. Already the cockpit was almost completely submerged, and the mid-section of the slanting fuselage was thigh-deep as they waded towards the hatchway. Ben yanked the emergency lever and shouldered the door open against the weight of the water. Torrents cascaded in through the open hatch. Ben grabbed Daniel and the Swede was forced out first with a squawk and a splash. Then, keeping a tight grip around Roberta's waist, he jumped with her into the tepid water.

Foot by foot, the ST-1 slipped underwater behind them as they struggled the short distance to the island. Ben pulled Roberta clear of the water and went back for Daniel, who was floundering a few yards away, gasping and choking. As he dragged him bodily up onto the black lava rock, Ben glanced back to see the tail of the ST-1 disappear with a final gurgle and a surge of bubbles.

The three of them sat on the rocks, dripping. Above them, the volcanic island loomed a hundred feet up, patchy vegetation and trees shading them from the sun.

'There goes Ruth's plane,' Roberta said wistfully, gazing at the spot where the aircraft had sunk.

'Yup,' Ben said.

'It was worth a lot of money, wasn't it?'

'Yup,' he said again.

'Don't suppose there's any chance of getting it out of there, is there?'

'Nope.'

'I guess we're stranded here now,' she said glumly. 'Who knows when anyone might come to pick us up.'

Ben scanned the sky. 'I don't think we'll be waiting long. Those pilots will have radioed in to report that we went down. The military won't waste time coming to scoop us up.'

Daniel had gone very quiet, sitting with his arms clasped around his knees.

'What do we do? Make a break for it?' Roberta pointed across the lake. 'It wouldn't be a problem, if I could swim.'

'Not much point in trying,' Ben said. 'Even if we could all make it across to the other side, we wouldn't get far before they caught up with us.' He felt in his sodden pockets, took out his cigarettes and tossed the saturated mess away with a sigh. Turning instead to his bag, he undid the straps and took out the components of the AR-15 rifle. The plastic-wrapped stacks of banknotes at the bottom of the bag were still dry.

'You're going to make your stand here?' Daniel said, like

a line from a movie, looking up with a frown as Ben got to his feet holding the dismantled weapon.

Ben smiled coldly. 'I'm not expecting a whole regiment of crack troops,' he said. 'But even so, I don't think we'd come out of it so well, do you? The last time we were in a fight, you ran away.' He stepped up onto a large, flat rock that overhung the shore and hurled the rifle's curved black magazine as far as he could into the lake. It hit with a splash, followed by two more splashes as the weapon's lower and upper action segments went the same way. 'Now your pistol,' he said to Daniel, extending his hand for the Colt Commander.

'I lost it in the crash,' Daniel said.

Ben nodded. 'Fine. Then all we can do now is wait.'

They didn't have to wait long. Less than half an hour went by before the silence of Lake Toba was broken by the thump of an approaching helicopter. Ben shielded his eyes and looked up to watch it coming: an obsolete French Aérospatiale SA 330 Puma troop transport in Indonesian Air Force markings. Like most of the tin-pot military forces of the world, the Indonesians cobbled their armament together out of whatever old iron other nations cast off.

The helicopter descended into a low hover fifty yards from the island, creating a broad circle of choppy water. An outboard dinghy splashed down from its open hatch and four soldiers were lowered on board toting their Pindad assault rifles. The dinghy sped towards the island.

'For better or worse, here we go,' Ben said, standing up.

The soldiers piled out onto the shore, weapons shouldered. Ben, Roberta and Daniel were forced at gunpoint into the dinghy. The outboard rasped them back to the hovering chopper, where a rope ladder dangled for them to clamber up.

'It's going to be okay,' Ben said in Roberta's ear over the

noise of the rotor blast. She smiled uncertainly, then brushed her wind-tousled hair away from her face and unexpectedly leaned forward and kissed him before grabbing hold of the swaying ladder.

Ben felt helpless and anxious as he watched her climb up towards the waiting hands of the soldiers who pulled her on board the Puma. Daniel was next, Ben last, prodded in the back by a rifle barrel. One of the soldiers snatched up his green bag. The ladder was retracted, the dinghy winched up; then the helicopter climbed, turned and flew away towards the command base at Pekanbaru.

Chapter Fifty

After forty minutes in the air, the military Puma came whirring down to rest on a helipad within the razor-wire perimeter of the air force base. The soldiers had been laughing and joking among themselves for most of the way and paying little attention to their three captives. Ben was more and more certain that they'd be released after little more than a routine questioning, made to fork out for an emergency visa and maybe a fine or two, and given some dire warnings about ever flying without permission within Indonesian airspace again.

That was something Ben could certainly promise them, now that Ruth's plane was lying at the bottom of Lake Toba. He still had no idea what he was going to say to her. Under the circumstances, 'I'll pay you back' would sound pretty lame.

On landing, the soldiers ushered the three of them from the helicopter and marched them in relaxed fashion across the hot asphalt to one of the many generic military buildings that circled the compound. After being made to wait in a stifling ante-room they were hustled into an office to be greeted from behind a desk by an unsmiling NCO. The officer was holding the John Freeman passport his men had found inside Ben's bag, and studied it with a look of extreme dubiousness before launching into a barking, staccato barrage of questions at them in broken English: where had they come from? Which of them was the pilot? Who did the aircraft belong to? Why had they travelled to this country? Lastly, with a glimmer of deep suspicion in his eye, he wanted to know what such a large sum of cash was doing in their possession.

As patiently as he could, Ben explained that they were wealthy tourists and had been en route to Kuala Lumpur before their aircraft had got into difficulties: sadly, their Malaysian visas and most of their passports had been lost in the lake along with the rest of their things. The NCO listened to the story with an enigmatic half-smile and then informed them that his senior officer would attend to them shortly. Until then, they could wait in comfort inside a special hospitality lounge within the base.

To Ben's extreme disquiet, the hospitality lounge turned out to be a narrow, dingy corridor containing a row of steel cell doors. 'This isn't necessary,' he protested. 'We've done nothing wrong.' But he knew it was pointless to resist as the soldiers separated them and led Roberta and the sullen Daniel to their respective cells. Roberta shot Ben a reassuring smile; then her door was clanged shut and Ben was being ushered inside his.

Time passed. Ben paced restlessly up and down the length of the cell. The dank, airless, windowless room measured exactly six paces by five across, with a filthy toilet in one corner, a sink with a rusty tap that spurted brownish water and a metal bunk attached to the wall. The temperature was easily over forty degrees. The cockroaches liked it best. Now and then, one would scuttle out from behind the toilet and race across the floor.

What the hell was taking so long? He hated being

separated from Roberta. After an hour had gone by, his frustration had reached boiling point and he beat his fist on the door and yelled for a guard. Nobody came. Ben went on thumping against the door and shouting until he finally gave up and sat simmering on the edge of the bunk.

It wasn't until half an hour later that his cell door clanged abruptly open. Not just one or two guards, but five fully-armed soldiers whose faces he recognised from earlier on burst into the cell with their assault rifles trained right at his head, safeties off and fingers on triggers.

Something had changed. The soldiers' demeanour was completely different. Before, they'd been relaxed and nonchalant around their prisoners. Now, they were acting as though Ben was a serious threat and could take five men down unarmed with a flick of his finger if they took their eyes off him for so much as a second.

In reality, it would have taken more than a flick of a finger. But if it hadn't been for Roberta's involvement in this situation, he might have gone for it anyway.

Instead, he rose slowly from the bunk and stood very still as the soldiers circled him, rifle muzzles inches from his head. Those Pindads were an ungainly-looking mash-up of AR-15 and Kalashnikov designs and Ben wouldn't have trusted his life to one in a fight. But they were useful enough at this range to blow his brains all over the cell wall.

The little NCO walked into the crowded cell. He was as jumpy looking as his troopers. Regarding Ben with an expression of fear and loathing, as if five military rifles weren't enough, he pulled out a 9mm pistol and poked it at Ben's face.

Ben looked down the barrel of the pistol. It was wavering slightly in the officer's fist. 'If this is about those overdue library books,' he said, 'I can explain.'

On a command from the NCO, the soldiers jostled him roughly through the doorway and marched him down the corridor past the other cells. As he passed Roberta's door he called her name and received a sharp jab in the back from a rifle barrel.

'*Ben?*' Her voice was muffled behind the steel door. But at least she was all right.

Ben gritted his teeth and let himself be marched on down the corridor. He'd get them out of this.

Though maybe not quite yet.

The bare-block room they took him to was empty apart from a single wooden chair planted in the middle of the concrete floor where the light filtered through the bars of a dirty window.

'You people really know how to make a guy feel welcome,' Ben said. The NCO sneered at him and snapped another command at the soldiers. They hauled Ben by the arms to the chair and forced him to sit. A rifle muzzle hovered close to his temple as his hands were yanked roughly behind the back-rest of the chair. He felt the cold steel of cuffs around his wrist, and their bite into his flesh as they were tightly closed.

And then it began.

If he'd been caught smuggling drugs, if they'd suspected him of some heinous terrorist plot, if he'd been arrested for espionage, then the brutality would have been interspersed with a lot of questions. But there were none. This wasn't an interrogation. They didn't even ask his name.

It was the burliest, broadest of the soldiers who'd been allocated the muscle job. With a smile the guy handed his weapon to one of the others, shed his uniform jacket, stood by the chair with his feet braced apart and got to work. His arms were thick and heavily veined. Judging by the scars on his knuckles, he'd done this before.

Ben had been here before, too. The name the SAS gave to the bruising sessions it inflicted on fresh recruits was 'RTI: Resistance To Interrogation'. The punishment they dished out didn't feel like training – it felt genuine, and it was fully intended to push the subject past the limits of normal human endurance, probing to see where their breaking point was and to give them a taste of the unpleasant treatment they could expect if they were ever taken prisoner by a real enemy, in a real military conflict. Ben hadn't enjoyed it much, but one thing he'd learned about himself: if you wanted to break him, you'd have to kill him. He'd worn out three interrogators before they'd finally released him to the military hospital to be patched up.

Ben's guess had been right – the burly Indonesian had done this before. He enjoyed it, too. After the fifth hard punch to the face, Ben could taste blood in his mouth. He spat a bright red gout of it in the soldier's face. 'Is that all you've got to give? Old Winnie could hit harder than you.'

The soldier didn't understand English, but he got the drift of Ben's defiant tone and put his back into the next one. The punch caught Ben in the solar plexus and drove the wind out of him. Maybe it wasn't such a good idea to goad the guy, he thought as he strained against his bonds, gasping for breath.

The beating went on a good while longer. Ben sensed the blows but not the pain. He'd become detached, letting his mind wander through a series of disconnected random thoughts and memories. He was only faintly aware that his tormentor was beginning to tire, delivering his punches with far less enthusiasm. By the time they undid Ben's cuffs and dragged him from the chair, the burly soldier was puffing hard and shining with sweat, and had retreated into a corner of the room to nurse hands that looked like lumps of raw meat.

As they half-marched, half-carried him back to his cell, Ben's only concern was Roberta. It didn't matter what they did to him. He most likely had it coming anyway.

He tried to call her name again as they shoved him staggering past her cell door, but he was too winded to make a sound. They unlocked his door and threw him sprawling to the floor.

He lay curled up for a long time, his mind drifting, blood pooling where his face was pressed against the concrete. Slowly, slowly, his senses returned. With them came the pain, and with the pain came the rage. The boiling fury made him focus. He raised his head from the floor, blinked and tried to control his breathing to soften the agony that made his skull feel about to explode. With effort he managed to prop himself up on one elbow, then up onto his knees. He reached for the edge of the grimy sink, clasped it tightly and with a low groan pulled himself shakily, inch by inch, to his feet. He creaked open the tap, cupped his hands under the spurting brown water and splashed the brackish liquid over himself. When he'd washed the dried blood out of his eyes and could see again, he turned away from the sink. Dropped down to the floor and forced his aching, screaming body to pump out five press-ups. Then five more. Then five more. *Focus. Survive. Fight. Win.*

He was asleep when the cell door crashed open for the second time and the soldiers marched in to take him away again.

Chapter Fifty-One

At first, Ben thought they were going to drag him back to the room with the chair for another beating. He walked calmly, straight, not wanting to show pain or fear or even the slightest hint of weakness. His eye was fixed on the butt of the NCO's pistol as it protruded from its holster just a grab away. In his mind he played out in slow-motion detail exactly how he'd go about using it to kill all five of the soldiers before drilling a neat round satisfying little 9mm hole through the middle of the NCO's forehead. Right here. Right now. It was sorely tempting.

The cell keys were dangling from a ring on the officer's belt. Maybe, Ben mused, *just maybe* there was a way . . . His heartbeat began to quicken. His fingers began to twitch.

But his reckless, dangerous stream of thinking was interrupted when he realised he wasn't being taken for another dose of punishment. Rather, they were leading him back to the room where they'd first been processed on arrival at the command base.

The NCO strode ahead and pushed open the door. The first thing Ben saw inside the room was Roberta's face, breaking into an expression of alarm and horror as she turned to see him come in.

'What have they done to you?' she cried out. 'Jesus, your face . . .'

'I stood on a rake,' he said. 'Don't worry about it.' It hurt to speak. He looked around the room. Roberta was being guarded by half a dozen more soldiers he didn't recognise. But someone was missing.

'Where's Daniel?' he said.

'I haven't seen him since we were locked up,' she replied.

They were ordered to be quiet and pressed against the wall at gunpoint. There was a tense atmosphere, as if the NCO and his men were waiting for something.

Or waiting for *someone*.

Another door opened, and in walked a short, trim Indonesian officer in his fifties, wearing the insignia of a colonel. The NCO snapped a salute. The soldiers stood rigidly to attention, as much as they could without taking their eyes and gunsights off Ben.

But it wasn't the Indonesian Army colonel Ben was looking at. It was the man who'd entered the room with him. He wasn't wearing military uniform, just a plain khaki shirt and trousers, but the soldiers all seemed to defer to him just as much as they did to an officer of high rank.

'I don't believe this,' Roberta whispered, staring. 'How can it be?'

Daniel Lund looked like a different person. The hapless, nervy aura he'd exuded before was gone. He stood straighter, even walked differently, and his ruddy features wore an expression of calm superiority that they hadn't seen before.

In fact, he *was* a different person. The role play was over. They were seeing the real Daniel now.

The Swede ran his calm gaze around the room and smiled at the sight of Ben's bruised face. 'So, our friends roughed you up a little, did they?' He shook his head in mock sympathy. 'Only got yourself to blame, though. The more you struggle, the more it hurts.'

Even his accent had changed. He sounded completely American.

'You asshole!' Roberta hissed at him. She slapped away a rifle muzzle with a sharp 'Get that thing out of my face' to the soldier holding it, and stepped towards Daniel, eyes flashing in rage. The soldiers bristled and closed in around her, looking to their commandant for the order to shoot the woman. Daniel intervened, nodding to the colonel, who immediately gave a curt order to stand down.

The soldiers backed off instantly. It was clear who commanded the highest authority in the room.

Daniel turned to Roberta with an even smile. 'I'm afraid you've been misinformed, Miss Ryder.'

Roberta glowered at him. 'You mean you lied about the secret installation at Arta Beach. You lied about everything, you piece of shit. You were one of them, all along.'

Daniel shrugged, his smile broadening. 'I didn't quite lie about everything,' he said. 'The installation exists, all right. As a matter of fact, that's the reason I had you and Major Hope here released from custody. We're taking a little trip there right now.'

The same Aérospatiale Puma was waiting for them on the helipad when they left the building and stepped out into the blazing sun. Ben and Roberta were prodded and shoved into the back of the chopper and made to sit on the bare metal floor with half a dozen guns pointing at them. Daniel coolly took a seat up front with the officer. He seemed completely at ease and seldom threw a glance in their direction, but Ben never took his eyes off him as the helicopter lifted off and climbed high above the command base.

By Ben's reckoning, the Puma was taking them south-west. Teeming jungles, rivers and dizzy canyons passed below. Conversation was impossible over the loud roar of the turbine and the rush of warm air coming through the open hatch. Sitting close up against him, Roberta slipped her fingers through his and held his hand tightly while resting her head against his shoulder. Ben sat perfectly still and his breathing was calm, but inside a storm was raging. He'd have done anything to take her out of this situation, make sure she was safe. As for himself, if she hadn't been here he'd gladly have risked everything to bring the chopper down, whatever it entailed.

Thirty-five minutes in the air, and after flying over the snaking, crowded Trans-Sumatra Highway and a number of towns, the western coastline of the island came into view on the horizon. Ben watched as Daniel looked keenly down at the ground below. Soon afterwards, the helicopter began to descend.

The mysterious installation that Daniel had brought them halfway around the world to see was a far cry from the heavily-guarded hive of sinister activity he'd described to them back in Sweden. Standing a quarter of a mile or so from the nearest coastal town on the tip of a forested penin-sula not much above sea level, the squat grey building looked like a deserted factory or some kind of massive bunker. Behind it, the flat blue-green ocean stretched out with just the scattered land masses of the Mentawai Archipelago dimly visible on the horizon. The calm strait between the mainland and the small islands was dotted white here and there with faraway yachts and ships, a strangely serene sight.

As the helicopter came down to land by the huge building, the obvious signs of neglect and abandonment came into view. The security fence surrounding the perimeter had long since fallen into disrepair, sections of wire missing where they'd collapsed into the long, yellowed grass or been pillaged by locals. Weeds grew tall through the cracks in the concrete around the building. There wasn't a vehicle or a living soul in sight, let alone hordes of armed guards patrolling the place in Jeeps.

Roberta's anxious look asked the same question that was in Ben's mind: *why are we being brought here?*

The Puma touched down on the concrete near a dilapidated entrance that seemed to be the only way in or out of the building. At an order from their officer, the soldiers made Ben and Roberta climb down from the hatch and marched them across the weed-strewn ground. Daniel confidently led the way, striding along with a little half-smile on his face. The NCO deferentially walked a step behind him.

Roberta was glaring at Daniel with a mixture of contempt and hatred. 'We should have known,' she muttered. 'We should never have trusted him.'

Ben said nothing. It was only then that he noticed that one of the soldiers was carrying his old green bag. He hadn't reckoned on ever seeing it again. He began wondering why they'd brought it here.

Daniel reached the entrance, a tall double doorway of rusted, riveted steel closed off with a heavy padlock and chain. He produced a key, undid the lock and the chain fell loose. It took three soldiers to heave the steel doors open. Daniel passed through the entrance into the shadows of the building.

The rest followed. It looked as much like an old factory on the inside as it did on the outside, except that whatever industrial machinery it had once housed had all been stripped away, leaving only a cavernous, echoey shell containing only a row of brick columns that towered up to the roof girders forty feet overhead. The sound of the soldiers' heavy boots rang off the bare walls. The floor was thick with dust, the droppings of birds nesting high up in the roof space and sand blown in from the beach. The only windows were on the ocean side of the building, little more than slots high up in the wall, their cracked panes opaque with the cobwebs of a hundred generations of spiders.

'Not exactly what he led us to expect,' Roberta said acidly. 'This place has been abandoned for years.'

Daniel stopped and spoke a few quiet words to the NCO, who in turn gave an order to his men. The soldier carrying Ben's bag handed it to Daniel and then trotted over to join his troop as the NCO led them back towards the entrance and the waiting chopper, leaving the three westerners together.

Chapter Fifty-Two

'And here we are again,' Daniel said with a wide grin. 'Just the three of us. I told you I'd bring you here, didn't I? We made it in the end. Problem is for you, it really *is* the end.' He chuckled at his own joke.

'You're being very trusting, Daniel,' Ben said. 'Sending your guard dogs away like that. Don't you feel a bit unprotected?'

'Not that unprotected,' Daniel replied. 'I do have this, remember.' He reached into his trouser pocket and brought out a familiar-looking Colt Commander. He pointed the weapon at them with relish.

'And you told me you'd lost it in the crash-landing,' Ben said, looking at the gun. 'But then, we know not to believe too much of what you tell us, don't we?'

'Damn right we do,' Roberta growled.

In the background, the helicopter was powering up to take off.

Daniel motioned with the pistol. 'Maybe you wouldn't mind standing a little closer together, so I can keep both of you in my sights at once? That's better.' He gripped the weapon in both hands, holding it steady.

'Firearms expert now,' Ben said.

'Who needs to be an expert? Cocked and locked, isn't

that what you told me?' Daniel replied. 'There's nothing to it, huh?' His eyes were bright with pleasure. 'Believe it or not, guys, I'm sorry I had to deceive the two of you. We've spent so much time together I've almost gotten to like you.'

'Don't apologize,' Ben said. 'After all, it's your job to deceive people, isn't that right?'

'Hey, someone has to do it,' Daniel replied with a nonchalant shrug. 'Happens I'm pretty good at it.'

The helicopter was thudding in the air somewhere over the building now, its sound rapidly diminishing. Keeping the gun steadily trained on them, Daniel glanced at his watch as if he was waiting for something.

'If you didn't bring us all this way to kill us,' Ben said, 'I'm guessing we're here to meet someone. You have a little rendezvous set up for us?'

'You guessed right, Major Hope. It was the point of this whole journey. There's someone who wants to meet you.'

'I don't like to be called Major,' Ben said.

'Such modesty,' Daniel chuckled. 'From a man of such formidable skills. I'm very well acquainted with your impressive history. My employers sent your classified files out to every one of our agents before you even turned up looking for me in Sweden. You caused quite a red alert when you got yourself mixed up in this, believe me. That's the kind of interference they really don't want. And that, I'm afraid, is why I was ordered to bring you both here, for reasons that you'll soon find out.'

'I take it it's your employers we're about to meet?' Ben asked.

Daniel nodded. 'Correct again.'

'Who the hell are you, Mister Lund, if that's your real name?' Roberta snapped. 'NSA? CIA?'

'You'd never even have heard of us,' Daniel said. 'Nobody

has, not even most people inside the US government. I'll let the boss fill you in when he gets here. Shouldn't be long, just a few minutes. Gives us just enough time to say goodbye.'

'Why, we going somewhere?' Roberta said sardonically.

'I am,' Daniel replied with a smirk. 'You're . . . well, let's just say there are plans for you. A little entertainment lined up, you might say. I wouldn't want to spoil the surprise.'

Ben pointed at his old bag, which was lying in a rumpled heap of green canvas at Daniel's feet. 'If this entertainment of yours involves Roberta and me not leaving this place alive, I'm guessing the bag was brought here for plausibility's sake? What are backpackers without a backpack?'

'You don't miss much, do you?' Daniel smiled. 'Right on the money. We wouldn't want anyone thinking you'd been brought here against your will. Oh, and speaking of money, your stash is still there, just the way you left it. That'll give the cops something to speculate about when they find your bodies. They'll be thinking drugs. Typical story. The half-kilo of uncut heroin that's in there should help them arrive at the right conclusion.'

'Just in case anyone would connect the dots, huh?' Roberta said. 'You devious sonofabitch.'

'Attention to detail is a big part of my work,' Daniel said. 'You can call it devious. I call it good planning. Nobody will ask questions about a couple of dead drug dealers.' He sighed. 'It's a shame it had to end that way for you. But then, you did have to go meddling in things that didn't concern you.'

'Like the death of Claudine,' Roberta said. 'Something you know all about, right? You're one of the bastards who murdered her.'

Daniel's contented smile faltered. 'I didn't murder anyone. That's not what I do.'

'Bullshit,' Roberta said.

'I think he's telling the truth for once,' Ben told her. 'He's no killer.'

'That's right,' Daniel said, waving the gun insistently at them. 'I'm just a risk assessor. A brain guy, not a brawn guy. My job's strictly information gathering.'

'A mole,' Ben said.

'That's one word for it,' Daniel replied. 'I go deep under cover, moving about all over the world, to infiltrate conspiracy theory groups. To pose as one of them, gain their trust. From there I can figure out who are just the harmless nuts and which ones could potentially pose a real threat.'

'I get it,' Roberta said. 'And Claudine was a threat.'

'That was what I was supposed to find out,' Daniel said. 'I wish it had been different. But the more time I spent with her, the more she showed me of what she knew, the more damned impossible it became to tick her name off on my list as just some other conspiracy crank. She wouldn't be diverted, couldn't be bought. And she was right on track to blow the lid off all the secrets that I and hundreds of others have worked for decades to protect. Yes, goddamn it, she was a threat,' he went on, his voice rising as he became more agitated. 'And I did everything – I mean *everything* – I could to get her to lay off this crusade she was on. I liked her. I mean, I really did, far more than I should have. I had feelings for her, and I think she did for me. I went way out on a limb, did all I could to save her from herself. But she just wouldn't listen.'

'Oh, I'll bet you tried really hard.'

'I gave it my best shot, but there was only so much I could do. If she'd been a whacko like most of the ones I deal with, that'd have been a whole different ball game. The whackos are what we call Type B. They're an asset to us. We encourage them, even fund some of the craziest ones so they'll spread the disinformation we want them to spread far and wide and keep the whole conspiracy theory community at the level of a joke. It's the perfect cover for us.'

'Right, so you and your buddies can go on murdering and maiming thousands of innocent people,' Roberta said with a look of disgust.

Daniel gave a frown, ignored her and went on. 'But Claudine wasn't one of those types. She was what we call the Type A profile. Ticked all the wrong boxes, wrong for her that is. Incredibly knowledgeable. Highly intelligent. Totally dedicated and determined to keep pushing deeper with her research, no matter how risky it was, no matter how frightening it became for her. She was an idealist, and a great communicator, the kind of person that could be taken seriously and had the credentials to back it up.'

'Naturally, someone like that couldn't be allowed to live,' Roberta said.

'That part of it had nothing to do with me,' Daniel protested. 'I don't make the final decision, and I never hurt a fly. I just did what I get paid to do, pass the information down the appropriate channels. Then . . . the appropriate action was taken, like always.' For a moment he looked down at his feet, flushing as if a little pang of shame had touched him from inside.

'That's where the handyman came in,' Roberta said. 'Your colleague McGrath, the one I shredded.'

'I told you,' Daniel insisted angrily. 'I had nothing to do with that. It was totally out of my hands.'

'Someone else's department,' Ben said. 'Everyone has their role to play, isn't that right? Just doing their job, like the men who came after Roberta when they realised Claudine had passed information to her.'

Daniel scowled. 'You people don't understand. This is a war. Individuals don't count. I don't. You don't. It's a numbers game, pure and simple. You know something? When I heard Claudine was dead, I cried. I really did. I fell right down on my knees and cried like a baby. That woman meant something to me. But this is the real world we live in. I'm realistic about that. That's the whole problem with people like you. You're not realistic. Now you have to pay the price for that, like the rest. It's not my responsibility.'

Roberta looked as if she wanted to throw up. 'I thought I knew what a stinking low-life dirtbag was. Then you came along. I don't even have words to describe what you are.'

'Call me what you like,' Daniel said. 'I'm proud of what I do, and I'm the best there is.'

'You're a gifted agent, all right, Daniel,' Ben said. 'I bet you can speak what, four, five languages?'

'Six,' Daniel said.

'Your employers must value you highly,' Ben said. 'Someone who can think on their feet and improvise the way you can. That was a great show you put on for us in Sweden, after you called in the troops while you pretended to be sick, and had to wait for them to arrive. Giving us your whole spiel. Mixing up your lies with just enough truth to make it sound real. Then the way you managed to stay out of the fight – very slick. You certainly had me fooled.'

Daniel chuckled at the flattery. 'There was no acting there. I'll admit it, I was damn near crapping my pants. I knew who you were, what you were capable of. And when I activated the alert I had a pretty good idea what was going to happen next. If it hadn't been for those lousy birds getting spooked, I'd have found a way to make myself scarce before the team moved in. Then when I saw how the attack went to shit, I made my second call. That's when they told me to bring you here to Indonesia.' He laughed. 'And you swallowed the whole story. Dear me, you must be slipping, Major Hope. Too many years out of the regiment, maybe? Training getting a little stale?'

Ben nodded. 'You're right. I was slow on the uptake. I didn't figure it out completely until just a little later. That was when you made your big mistake.'

Chapter Fifty-Three

Daniel's grin dropped away and he flushed. 'You're wrong. I don't *do* mistakes.'

'Sorry to disappoint you there, Daniel,' Ben said. 'Attention to detail, remember? You see, I saw Claudine Pommier's passport at her apartment in Paris. There was no Indonesian visa on it. You never brought her here. I made you repeat it, just to be sure. And you walked right into the trap. That's when I knew you were lying to us.'

Roberta looked at Ben in consternation. 'You knew? That long ago?'

'I'm sorry I didn't tell you,' Ben said to her. 'I couldn't afford for our friend here to suspect anything.'

'That's why you wanted me to stay in Germany, isn't it?' she asked.

Ben nodded. 'I didn't like you being anywhere near this treacherous maggot.' He turned back to Daniel. 'See, you're not the only one who can play-act. It was all I could do to restrain myself from throwing you into the deepest part of the Arabian Sea to amuse the tiger sharks.'

Some of the colour had drained from Daniel's face, but he still managed to pull an uncomfortable smirk. 'So you knew all along, huh? Guess you think that makes you pretty smart.'

'Not as smart as your bosses,' Ben said. 'They think of everything, don't they? Like bringing a blank firing pistol to a gunfight to protect the identity of a valuable agent like you. Now *that's* clever.'

Daniel's face paled for real at Ben's words, his composure slipping visibly away. 'What are you talking about?' he stammered. His eyes darted nervously as his brain was set racing. The awful connections began to form in his mind. He glanced down at the pistol in his hand.

'I'm surprised it took you this long to cotton on,' Ben said. 'It was McGrath's pistol I gave you. The one I took from his body. The one he fired at you as you were running towards the woods. You probably don't remember. You were too busy trying to save your skin.'

'I . . . I . . .'

'It was their contingency plan,' Ben went on. 'Just in case the attack went wrong and either I or Roberta got away. They needed to make it look like you were one of their targets and make sure we got a good look at them shooting at you, to save your cover from being blown. Of course, you couldn't know about it. You had to look believably shit scared. And you did. Just like you do now, Daniel.'

'Bull. You're just trying to rattle me.'

'It's the truth,' Ben said. 'Just like you were telling the truth when you said you didn't know much about weapons. One of the only honest things you've said. And bad news for you. They should have given you a better training.'

Daniel's brow twitched. 'No way. Fuck you, if you think you can fool me so easily.' He took a step back and raised the gun higher in a white-knuckle grip, aiming it first at Ben's head, then at Roberta's, then back at Ben.

'You could check for yourself,' Ben said, pointing calmly at the weapon, 'If you knew how. It's loaded with 38-calibre blanks. Standard primer. Normal powder load. But the cartridge case mouth is just crimped shut where the bullet ought to be. The gun needs a special modification to be able to cycle the rounds, so it can't even handle regular ammunition. It's noisy enough, but nothing comes out of the barrel except burning gas.'

'You're lying!'

Ben took a step towards him. 'Come on, Daniel. Do you really think I'd have given you a live firearm to tote about with you, knowing you were lying, knowing you were one of them? But don't take my word for it. Go ahead and squeeze the trigger. Maybe I'll be wrong.'

Daniel backed away another two paces across the dusty floor. His Adam's apple heaved as he gave a swallow. The gun was shaking in his hand.

'Go for it, Daniel,' Ben said. 'Don't you want to kill us? Or are you waiting for us to starve to death?'

'I . . . don't want to kill you. The boss said . . .'

'Look around you,' Ben said. 'No boss anywhere to be seen. He must be running late, which means you're on your own. It's time to stand up and defend yourself, and right now pulling that trigger is the best chance you've got. Because if you don't kill me, I'm going to kill you, and soon.'

Daniel's face contorted into a wild look of loathing and terror. He thrust the gun out, took aim at Ben and squeezed the trigger.

A halo of yellow-white flame spat from the muzzle. The sharp report of the shot resonated all around the empty building.

Roberta started at the sound.

Ben didn't even flinch.

Daniel fired again. Another spit of flame from the barrel.

Another ear-splitting *boom* that reverberated off the walls and echoed up to the roof.

'Oh, God,' he moaned when he saw what had happened.

Because nothing had happened. There was no blood. No injured opponent rolling on the floor screaming in agony. Ben was still standing. Not just standing. Walking slowly, purposefully towards him. Daniel gaped at the weapon in horror.

'Kind of changes things, doesn't it?' Roberta said.

'I know what you're thinking,' Ben said to Daniel. 'Maybe he's lying about the blanks and I just missed, because I'm such a crappy shot. Or maybe it's true, but by some miracle the next round in the magazine will be live. Well, there's only one way to find out.'

Daniel fired again. The look of desperation on his face was turning to panic. Roberta wasn't flinching at the sound any more, but looked on with her hands over her ears and a fierce light in her eyes.

'Keep going,' Ben said to Daniel, nodding at the smoking pistol. 'Empty it. The worst you're going to do is give us tinnitus for a day or two.' He kept on walking towards him. For every step he advanced, Daniel was backing a step away.

'Wait,' Daniel said. 'I can explain everything.'

'Didn't you just do that?' Roberta said.

'Please! Listen, I told you, I'm just an assessor. I had no choice but to let Claudine go. If I'd told her who I really was—'

'Then you'd have put yourself in danger too,' Ben said. 'Maybe the handyman would've paid you a little social call. And we couldn't have that, could we?'

As though suddenly repulsed by its touch, Daniel flung the gun away. 'All right. Look! I'm not armed, okay? I surrender.'

Ben shook his head. 'I'm sorry, Daniel. We're past that stage. You're in too deep.'

'W-what are you going to do to me?' Daniel quavered.

'What I said,' Ben replied quietly. 'I never really liked you anyway, right from the start. Now I like you a lot less. So I'm going to break your neck.'

Daniel had retreated all the way to the far wall and couldn't back away any further. Ben was almost on him.

Daniel fell to his knees. 'I'm begging you!' he wailed, his cheeks suddenly wet. 'Listen, I have over four hundred thousand dollars in a checking account. It's supposed to be my expenses money. Let me go and it's yours, every cent of it, I promise. We'll get out of here together before the others arrive. I know where we can hide. We'll get the cash transferred to you within a day – hell, within the hour. Just let me . . . aggh!'

Ben had grabbed hold of him and hauled him roughly to his feet. 'It's just like you said,' Ben told him. 'The more you struggle, the more this will hurt.'

Daniel fought and thrashed and kicked and tried to bite as Ben held him in a clinch. He grasped Daniel by the jaw. Pushed, twisted, pulled, pushed again. There was a muted crunch and Daniel's scream was cut short. Ben held him a moment longer, then let the lifeless body slip to the floor.

Roberta stared wide-eyed at the corpse.

'I'm sorry you had to witness that,' Ben said to her, mistaking her look for one of shock.

'He had it coming,' she replied. 'Actually, I thought you went too easy on the rat.'

'He won't get any deader than this, Roberta.'

'I can see that. But it was over a little quicker than what I had in mind for him.'

'You can tell me all about it later,' Ben said. 'For now, I think we should get out of here before his friends arrive.'

But even as he finished saying it, the rapidly approaching throb of a helicopter told him they were too late.

Chapter Fifty-Four

There was still a tiny, rapidly dwindling chance they could escape the building before the helicopter touched down. Ben snatched up his bag and hurried after Roberta as she sprinted towards the entrance.

Just two strides behind her, he caught a glimpse of the descending chopper and the man in the tactical vest leaning out of the hatchway. He saw the compact black object in the man's gloved hands.

As if in slow motion, he watched Roberta run into the sunlight. He yelled 'Stop! Wait!' But she was moving too fast. Her momentum carried her out into the open.

And then the machine gunner on board the aircraft opened fire.

Bullets punched into the concrete, sent chips of masonry bursting from the wall around the doorway. Ben skidded to a halt. Roberta had sprawled to the ground right in front of him and he couldn't tell if she'd been hit. He reached out and grabbed her arm and yanked her violently back towards the doorway as the black Jet Ranger hovered closer with its nose raking the ground, its tail angled upwards and the shooter still firing from its open side hatch.

Ben dragged Roberta inside the building, his heart at a dead stop not just from the suddenness of the attack but from his own paralysing terror that she'd been shot. It began to beat again when she twisted to her feet and pressed against him in the shelter of the doorway.

'Jesus,' she gasped. 'Another close one.'

'Don't ever do that again,' he warned her, relief flooding through him.

There was little time for ceremony, though. The dust was billowing up from the floor as the chopper came in to land just a few metres from the building. Its skids were barely in contact with the ground before the shooter jumped from the hatch, effecting a rapid reload of his MP7 submachine gun as he dashed across the cracked concrete.

Ben ducked out of sight from the doorway and looked around him for a weapon. Any kind of weapon, anything that would give him an edge. Through the dust storm whipped up by the rotors he could see the fallen pistol lying a little way from Daniel's inert body. He made a flying leap for it: snatched it up, rolled in the dust and sprang back to his feet with the weapon brought to aim as the gunman burst into the building.

'Drop it!' Ben yelled over the din of the helicopter turbine. The modified pistol was as good to him as a child's toy and he was up against someone who clearly knew their business. He was all too aware that only the conviction in his voice and in his eyes could pull the bluff off.

And as the man took his finger off the trigger and lowered his weapon, for a short moment Ben thought his trick had worked. Another moment later, he realised the shooter had stood down for another reason entirely.

A man walked into the building. He was short, no more than five and a half feet tall, and from his thin white hair and heavily lined, yellowed face he looked at least seventy-five years old. A finely-cut suit that might once have been tailored to fit him hung oversized from his shrivelled form. He walked with a pronounced limp and leaned heavily on two walking sticks, one white, the other black, for support. He barely seemed to acknowledge the man clutching the submachine gun, as though the presence of armed body-guards was something he'd been so thoroughly used to for so many years that it no longer made any impression on him. Behind him came the rest of his retinue. Six men. The two thirty-somethings in plain dark suits and dark glasses had the aura of FBI agents, though Ben was pretty sure they were anything but. The other four looked like ex-Special Forces, expert guns for hire: hard faces, hard eyes, shorn hair, all wearing the same combat armour as the guy with the submachine gun and all carrying black AR-15 rifles like the one Ben didn't have any more.

Ben sighed and tossed away the useless pistol. Roberta slowly stepped closer to him, keeping a wary eye on the old man and his following.

The scrape and tap of the old man's sticks on the concrete floor echoed through the building as he limped up to them. He passed Daniel Lund's body without the slightest glance. Five feet away from Ben and Roberta, he stopped and peered at them. Much more striking than the wizened parchment skin of his face was the stone deadness in his eyes. They were the eyes of someone who'd seen things more terrible than most people could ever imagine. Someone utterly inured to the evils of this world.

'Benedict Hope and Roberta Ryder,' he said. His voice was as dry as sand. 'In your separate ways, your reputations precede you. My name is Victor Craine. The few people who know me at all, know me simply as the Director. You've led me a merry dance the last few days. It's a pleasure to make your acquaintance at last.'

'The pleasure's all yours, Craine,' Ben said. 'We didn't particularly want to be here.'

The Director gazed up at Ben's face with a strange kind of detached curiosity. For all their lifelessness, his hooded eyes were intensely penetrating. 'I see our Indonesian friends handled you a little roughly. Be assured, that order didn't come from me. If they felt the need to subdue you, it was only because they were afraid of you.'

'They have an interesting way of showing fear,' Ben said.

'They were briefed on who you are shortly after you were apprehended,' the Director said. 'Little wonder that your real identity terrified them so much. Your background is as impressive as your skill in evading us this far. You've cost the project a great deal of resources and robbed me of several of my most capable agents. Men not easily killed. Yet you dealt with them with almost embarrassing ease.' His lips wrinkled into a smile.

'You mean McGrath?' Ben said. 'I'm afraid he went all to pieces.'

'So it would seem. And now it appears you've disposed of Mr Lund just as efficiently, albeit without as much mess.' The old man shook his head. 'I don't know how I'll replace him. It's so hard to find personnel of calibre these days.'

'Have you tried Scumbags R Us?' Ben said. 'I'm sure you'll find what you're looking for.'

'It could have been you, you know. We pay handsome rewards to men with the right attributes.'

'I have other plans, thanks.'

'I'm afraid whatever plans you have are now cancelled, Major Hope. Your little chase is over now. You really only have yourselves to blame for this outcome.'

'I guess we should be flattered that you came all the way out here to tell us that,' Roberta said.

The Director turned to gaze at her. 'You and Major Hope weren't the principal reason for my coming to Indonesia, my dear.' For an instant he looked almost benign, grand-fatherly, before the dead coldness returned to his eyes. 'My main purpose is to oversee the exercise that is about to begin in . . . how long do we have, Friedkin?' he asked calmly, without looking back.

The taller of the two plainclothes agents who were standing behind the Director looked at the chunky military watch under the sleeve of his suit and replied, 'Twenty-seven minutes, forty-two seconds and counting, sir.' The aide didn't share his boss's calmness. Even the impassive mask of a highly-trained and obedient robot couldn't quite hide the quaver of anxiety in his voice, and he wasn't the only one. Ben could see the armed goons all shifting their weight edgily from one foot to the other and the frowns of nervy anticipation on their faces. They couldn't wait to get back to the helicopter. Whatever was about to happen, this was the last place they wanted to be just under half an hour from now.

'An exercise,' Roberta said. 'That's a nice euphemism for what you people do. So your little toy's about to get another outing, am I right? One last test, a little fine tuning before . . . before what? The big one? Lund wasn't lying about that, was he? He knew what was being planned.'

Craine smiled. 'Curious to the last, Dr Ryder. I applaud your selfless devotion to science. You needn't concern your-self with the technicalities of our operation, however, as very regrettably you won't be around long enough to see it reach fruition. Now, I think we must conclude this little chat and attend to business.' He turned to his men, who looked unanimously relieved that the old man was finally about to move things on. 'Bring him in.'

At the command, two of the armed heavies hurried back to the entrance, disappeared outside and returned a moment later with another man whom they frogmarched in long strides into the building. Their captive was taller than either of them, but bent over as if in pain. His wrists were bound with tape and there was a black cloth hood over his face. The front of his shirt was heavily marked with bloodstains. Ben could guess where those had come from.

Roberta glanced at Ben, questions in her eyes as she wondered what he was wondering: *who was this man?*

'Release him,' the Director ordered, and one of the goons reached up and whipped the hood off the prisoner's head while another slipped a military knife between his bound wrists and sliced away the plastic tie.

Ben peered at the man. He was in his early forties, a white westerner, thick dark hair, solidly built and in good shape but much the worse for wear after what, judging by the colour of the livid weals and bruises all over his face, had obviously been a sustained beating going back at least a couple of days. The man's eyes were swollen almost shut but he tried to take in his surroundings, glancing stiffly this way and that. His agonised gaze landed on Ben and Roberta, and it was clear he was thinking the same as they were: *who the hell are you?*

'A little company for you while you wait,' the Director said. 'You have just under twenty-two minutes to become better acquainted, before the show begins.' He nodded curtly to his men, who were all glancing with increasing agitation at their watches and throwing doubtful looks at Craine. 'Let's go. Seal the building. Make sure they can't escape.' He shuffled around on his sticks to face the entrance.

'No restraints, no handcuffs?' Ben said. 'I'm surprised.'

'You won't be, when you see what we have planned for

you,' Craine replied. 'You're about to take a ring-side seat at an event that should prove quite spectacular. Consider yourselves soon to become part of history. Adieu, Dr Ryder. Major Hope, it was a sincere pleasure.'

'*Au revoir*, Mr Craine,' Ben said.

'Don't be so sure about that. Every man meets his end. You've had a good run. Accept yours now.'

Apparently satisfied that he'd had the last word, Craine began limping as quickly as he could towards the doorway. The plainclothes suits followed in jittery haste. The soldiers hurried out last, keeping their weapons trained on Ben, Roberta and the nameless prisoner until the last moment. Then they heaved the tall steel doors shut with a clang and chained them shut from the outside.

Moments later, the helicopter took off. Once again, the three inside were left alone.

Chapter Fifty-Five

It was the bruised stranger who spoke first, flinching at the pain from his split lips. 'I'm Jack Quigley, CIA. Who the hell are you two?'

'That's funny. The CIA are the good guys now?' Roberta said.

Ben looked at his watch. He said, 'This is Roberta. I'm Ben. We can leave proper intros for another time, Quigley. There are more pressing matters right now, like getting out of here within the next nineteen minutes.'

Quigley motioned at the dead body on the floor. 'Your friend there have a name? Looks like his neck's broken.'

'I wouldn't have done it to a friend,' Ben said. 'His name was Daniel Lund. He was one of them.'

'I figured maybe you were one of them as well,' Quigley said. 'And that I was next on your list after this Daniel guy.'

'Relax, I'm not going to hurt you,' Ben said. 'We're all in the same boat here. What do they want with you?'

'I got in their way,' Quigley said, tight-lipped. 'I guess I need rubbing out, like everyone else who does.' The fury he was holding in suddenly boiled over, and with a passion that reopened the cuts on his face and mouth and started them bleeding again, he burst out, 'The bastards killed my girlfriend, Mandy. They even killed my *dog*. And they killed Mitch too. I know that now.'

Ben caught the name and remembered hearing it before. He instantly made the connection. 'Mitch Shelton, the CIA agent who drowned? Lund told us about him. Did you and Shelton work together?'

Quigley replied, 'He was my friend. I had no idea he'd got mixed up with these people. I still can't believe it.'

'He got involved, but he wanted out,' Roberta said. 'At the time of his death, he'd hooked up with a journalist, and they were going to blow the whistle on the whole thing.'

'So they murdered him and fixed it up to look like an accident,' Quigley muttered bitterly. He shook his head in barely contained rage. 'That's what I figured. Motherfuckers.'

'The journalist's not around to tell the tale either,' Roberta said. 'He had a little car smash.'

'Yeah, right. Just like my house had a little gas leak. Totally destroyed, with Mandy inside. And it was my fault, because I asked her to go let the dog out while I was working late. That was the night I was with Blumenthal and he told me about the Nemesis Program, before they got to him, too. That was no heart attack.'

'You know about Nemesis?'

'Just what Herbie Blumenthal told me.'

'Who was he?'

'Science guy in D.C. Ex-DARPA. He worked for them, too. Told me he'd quit and wanted to go public with the dirt he'd uncovered, said he needed my help. I didn't believe him at first. I didn't *want* to believe him. It was Blumenthal who put me on to Mandrake Holdings and Triton. Triton, you have any idea what that is?'

'None,' Roberta said, glancing quizzically at Ben.

'Blumenthal talked about some kind of . . . of a machine,'

Quigley went on. 'Some technology they've been working on for years. A weapon, but like no other weapon that's been used before. The new warfare, he said. Claimed they can cause things to happen. Disasters. It sounded crazy.'

'Trust me, it's not crazy,' Roberta said. 'It's real and we've seen it in action.'

Quigley stared at them incredulously from between his swollen, bruised eyelids. 'You're not kidding, are you? But it's impossible. Technology like that doesn't exist.'

Roberta smiled darkly. 'You have no idea. Nobody does, that's the whole point. But stick around, I get the feeling you're going to see for yourself.'

'How did they catch you, Quigley?' Ben asked.

'Mandrake Holdings,' Quigley replied. It's a corporation with offices in New York. They're involved in this somehow. I wasn't thinking straight, walked right into it. Next thing I knew I was taken to some cellar someplace and these two guys were beating up on me. Wanted to know everything I knew about the Nemesis Program. Then they stuck me on a plane and, well, here I am. What's your story?'

'You lost a friend,' Roberta said. 'So did I. Yours wanted to blow the whistle on them from the inside, she was trying to expose them from the outside. She called me for help. When I got there, it was already too late.'

As Roberta and Quigley went on talking, Ben broke away from them and started pacing the floor. Time was slipping away fast and they had to find a way out of this place.

He hurried over to one wall and examined it. The plasterwork was old and crumbly in places where the salt air had permeated it, but the stone behind it was thick and solid. He craned his neck upward to peer at the high windows. Above the massive cobwebbed latticework of rusty steel girders, the roof itself was heavy-duty tin plate. Long

347

ago in the building's history there had been a first floor up there and the roof space had been used as a storage area of some kind. Ben spotted a dusty coil of rope looped around one of the beams, some forty feet out of reach. It didn't look promising.

He ran back across the dusty floor to the entrance and leaned his weight a few times against the steel door. It barely moved half an inch before the chain outside became taut. Had some miracle provided him with a pair of heavy-duty bolt croppers capable of shearing the galvanised steel links, the gap in the door would have been too narrow to jam them through. The door hinges were massive affairs and set deep into the stone of the wall. Ten men with sledgehammers couldn't have budged them in an hour. And Ben didn't have an hour.

'We have just over sixteen minutes, people,' he said to Roberta and Quigley, glancing again at his watch. 'I don't know what's going to happen. I do know that we don't want to be trapped in here when it does. So I suggest we start thinking hard.'

'This is where Claudine's oscillator would have come in handy again,' Roberta murmured, looking around her at the walls of their prison.

'Be careful what you wish for,' Ben said. 'We barely got out of it last time.'

'What do you think's going to happen, Ben?' she asked him anxiously.

He shrugged. 'Craine could have had us shot. Quigley too. But they've gone to some lengths to bring us all here as a neat way of disposing of us that won't raise too many questions. Whatever they're planning, we're not intended to survive it and Craine must be pretty confident we can't. We can only assume he knows what he's talking about.'

Roberta nodded grimly. 'That's how I see it too. And if my guess is right, we won't be the only ones. Just three more victims.'

'Victims of what?' Quigley said.

'Something you don't even want to think about,' Roberta told him. 'Just pray I'm wrong.'

Quigley stared at her through his swollen eyelids. 'What are the chances you're wrong?'

'Slim to zero,' she said. 'Ben, we've got to get out of here, and fast.'

Ben checked his watch once more. Fifteen minutes, thirty seconds. The countdown was racing faster than seemed real. Pressure roared inside his head. *Thinkthink thinkthink . . .*

At the distant far end of the vast empty space, half-hidden and barely noticeable among the shadows, was a row of doors. A long shot, but worth trying. He raced across the concrete, wrenched open the first door and found himself inside what must originally have been an office, maybe an accounts room or an administrator's office. Now it was just a shell, bare and desolate. What might once have been an emergency exit or fire escape leading off from inside had long since been bricked up, along with the window next to it. He kicked the wall so hard it hurt his toe. No way out there, not even if he'd been able to find something large and solid to batter against it.

He left that room and tried the next door. It was larger, just as empty, just as inescapable. So far, the long shot was proving too long. He slammed the mouldy door, wrenched open the last and stepped through.

Nobody would have called it a bathroom in any true sense. The place was little more than a communal latrine that had presumably once served the needs of the factory workforce. The rows of toilets were still in place, dry and grimy, home to generations of rodents.

But it was enough to set off a spark in Ben's mind. A building of this size must have had some kind of sewer system larger than a domestic waste pipe. Somewhere in here had to be the head of a manhole leading downwards. He began kicking up clouds of dirt and dust and soon found what he was looking for. He crouched down over the heavily rusted iron cover plate. Wiped the dirt away and tried to get his fingertips into the tight gap between the metal edges and the rough concrete into which it was set. It wouldn't budge. If he could just prise it free . . . He needed something solid to lever it up with. Something metal. But there was nothing to hand, no handy wrecking bar left behind this time.

Thirteen minutes to go. Time was being sucked away into a vortex.

He leapt to his feet and ran back through the building. 'What are you doing?' Roberta asked him.

Daniel's blank firing Colt Commander was lying in the dust where Ben had thrown it down earlier. He scooped it up. 'Might have found something,' he said as he turned to run back to the latrine room.

By the time Roberta and Quigley had joined him, he was already down on his knees and trying to use some part of the dummy firearm to prise up a corner of the iron drain cover. 'If I can get this up, there might be a way out of here,' he explained. But even though it was made of proper metal instead of plastic, the gun was a hopelessly inadequate tool for his purposes. He tried the thin, hardened steel of the magazine feed lips. The front sight blade, the beavertail grip safety. None of the weapon's metal protuberances could gain enough purchase to lever up the cover.

'What's under there, a tunnel?' Roberta said, watching intently.

'That's assuming you have no objection to crawling through a little dirt to get out of here,' Ben grunted as he worked.

'I'd have married Daniel Lund to get out of here,' she said.

'If I had that big old Colt I'd try blasting away some of the concrete around the edge,' Quigley said, pointing at what Ben was doing.

'If you had this big old Colt, you'd know why that wouldn't work,' Ben replied. He paused for breath. This was no good.

'Pull the slide off and try the inside of the rails,' Quigley suggested.

Ben nodded. It wasn't a bad idea. He worked the slide release and the weapon slid apart in his hands. 'I see they teach you your weapons in the CIA.'

'Not the way the USMC do,' Quigley said.

'You were in the Corps?'

Quigley nodded.

'Okay, Marine,' Ben said, jamming the gun's slide under the edge of the plate and feeling it start to give, 'see if you can get your fingers under here and help me lift this thing. On three. One – two – three . . .'

They heaved, grunting with the effort. With a rending crack the rusted edges broke loose and the plate came up. They let it drop to the floor.

And recoiled at what was inside the manhole. The stench of the filthy water reaching almost up to its mouth was as foul as the decaying bodies of the two drowned rats floating on the surface. The sewer pipe had backed up or collapsed with age.

'If I've got to die,' Roberta said, 'I'm not dying in there. Forget it. No way.'

She was right.

Just under ten minutes to go.

Chapter Fifty-Six

Ben let the drain cover down with a clang that echoed all through the building. He thrust the disassembled gun into Roberta's hands, got to his feet and headed quickly towards the door. 'All right. Stay cool, we still have time to figure something out,' he said, working harder to convince himself than the other two. He stared up at the roof. 'If we can't go under the building, maybe we can go over it. We just need to get to those windows.'

'And break our legs jumping down to the concrete outside,' Roberta said sceptically.

Ben pointed. 'There's a coil of rope looped round and round one of those girders. See it? It might be long enough to reach the ground.'

'If it's not all rotted away to hell,' Quigley said doubtfully.

'He's right, Ben, what if it breaks?'

Ben shrugged. 'Then I'll fall and you'll know I was wrong. But at least I'll know I tried.'

She looked at him. 'You're a persistent fucker, aren't you?'

'I get like that when I'm about to die,' Ben said.

'How are you even going to get up there?'

Ben thought for a moment. 'Give me the pistol,' he said.

She handed the pieces to him and watched, puzzled, as

he quickly slotted the frame and slide back together. 'So now it's a useless gun again,' she said.

'Or a useful hammer.' Ben gripped it by the barrel end and used its butt against the plaster, reaching up as high up as he could. Three solid whacks did nothing but scrape the gun's frame.

'What are you doing, trying to break the wall down?' Roberta asked him, staring as though he was crazy.

'Wrong place,' he muttered and tried again a few inches to the right. This time a chunk of plaster broke away, leaving a hole just about deep enough to get his fingers in.

Seven minutes to go. But seven minutes was a long time if you could stay cool and keep your wits about you. Ben crouched and started whacking the wall at waist level. In a few seconds he'd penetrated through to the stonework. He raised his left foot and stuck it in the lower hole, then gripped the upper hole with his left fingertips and heaved himself upward. The plaster bore his weight as he started chipping another handhold further up.

'You'll never make it,' Roberta said.

'I don't see any other way, do you?' he grunted as he raised himself upwards, clinging tightly to the wall and ignoring the pain in his fingertips. He transferred the scuffed pistol to his left hand and kept working as quickly as he could. In two minutes, hammering like a madman and hanging precariously by his aching fingers and toes, he'd managed to climb halfway to the level of the windows. Roberta and Quigley watched him anxiously as he clawed his way upwards.

'If I can get up there,' he called down to them, 'I can throw down that rope and pull each of you up in turn.'

'Ben, we only have just under five minutes!' Roberta yelled.

This was taking too long. Fighting panic, he redoubled his hammering. Bits of plaster rained from the wall and shattered on the concrete below. Sweat was pouring off him. His hands were tingling badly from all the pounding; his toes were becoming numb and he had to will himself to hang on. He was far enough above the floor to fracture both his legs, and probably his spine, if he lost his grip.

You're not going to fall, he told himself, and kept on hammering and kept on climbing until at last, the gun gritty between his teeth, he was able to tear his left hand from its crumbling finger-hold and grasp the window ledge. Moments later, gasping and blinded with sweat, he hauled himself onto the ledge.

It was only then that he realised how far he'd climbed in such a short time. Roberta and Quigley were small figures forty feet or more beneath him. Ben warily straightened himself up on the crumbly ledge. The tin-plate ceiling wasn't far above his head, and the section of roof support around which the rope was coiled was just about within his reach. He strained outwards, fingers clawing as he leaned as far into space as he dared – and then a little further. His finger-tips brushed the rusted iron girder; then suddenly the coarse rope was in his grasp.

Here we go, he thought.

'Ben! No!' came Roberta's frightened cry from below as he swung away from the window ledge, dangling perilously from the loop of rope. If it had snapped or uncoiled itself from the girder, there would have been nothing to break his rapid descent to the concrete below.

'Ben, there's less than three minutes to go!' Roberta yelled.

Time was streaming away like sand through his fingers. But he still had to try. Dangling from the rope, he kicked his legs up, wrapped them around the rust-encrusted

H-section contour of the girder and managed to clamber up until he was perched astride its flat top, gripping its sides between his knees, calves and ankles. The rope was knotted tightly to the iron beam. He worked frantically to loosen it, and in a few seconds it was coming undone. He unravelled the coil off the girder, made one end fast and started lowering the other, praying it would reach the floor. He was pretty sure he could haul the lightweight Roberta up. Quigley's heavier frame might be another matter, but he'd worry about that when it was happening. Once all three of them were up here, they could use the rope to swing back across one at a time to the window ledge, drop the rope out and clamber down.

At least, that was the idea. Seconds were ticking away like gunshots inside Ben's head.

The rope reached the floor with two feet to spare. 'Loop it around your waist and hang on tight!' Ben yelled to Roberta. She quickly did what he said, then let it take her weight, testing that it would hold her.

Ben wiped his sweaty palms on his shirt. 'All right, now I'm going to pull you up.' Wedging his body against the girder, he took a strong grip on the rope and started to haul the rope in towards him.

Roberta was dangling six feet in the air when something started to happen. At first Ben thought it was his own heart hammering so hard that it seemed to make his whole body shake – but then he realised it was the girder shaking under him. A deep thrumming, a quivering barely noticeable at first but rapidly building in intensity. Not just coming from the girder – the entire building was filled with it, even the air seemed to vibrate. The sensation was unsettlingly familiar. It was exactly what Ben had felt inside the De Bourg family tomb, back on the other side of the world.

This was it. Ben didn't need to check his watch to know what was happening. Right on time, the event Victor Craine had promised was starting. *The bastards are really doing it,* he thought. It was true. Rage and disbelief and terror mingled with the adrenaline rushing through Ben's veins as he hauled harder on the rope.

Within moments, he could hear it as well as feel it. A growing rumble, like constant thunder. Rust began to vibrate off the beam, falling down in red powdery flakes. The tin plates were rattling overhead. Down below, Quigley was having difficulty staying on his feet and had to support himself against a wall.

'Keep pulling me up!' Roberta yelled. She was twenty feet above the concrete now, swinging in a circle. Ben had stopped as the sickening realisation hit him that this was too dangerous. 'What are you doing?' she shouted as he lowered her back down to the floor.

'Get down on the ground and protect your heads,' he shouted down at her and Quigley. The American was staggering like a drunk as the concrete underfoot began to heave up and down. He fell into a crouch and curled up with his hands over his head. Roberta yanked the rope away from her middle and did the same. Up on his girder, Ben thrust one arm through the single loop of rope attached to the steel and clung on tight.

The walls were moving, shifting, grinding in their foundations. Cracks appeared and spread everywhere like black snakes across the plasterwork. Chunks broke away and smashed on the concrete below. One of the intact window panes shattered and shards of glass rained down and burst across the floor, narrowly missing Roberta.

Ben held on tighter as the shaking became more intense, but he knew he couldn't hold on much longer as the vibrating girder gnawed savagely at his gripping legs and arms. The rumbling had grown into a constant roar. At its heart he could sense a deep source of power that, if fully unleashed, would make the small Tesla oscillator's effects on the De Bourg chapel seem tiny and pathetic by comparison. He could visualise the building's walls breaking apart and collapsing inwards, taking the centre columns with them; could almost feel himself falling as the roof girders came tumbling down together with a crash followed by hundreds of tin sheets, burying him, Roberta and Jack Quigley in a heap of rubble from which they'd never emerge alive. This was the end. The perfect execution, not just of Craine's plan but of the three people trapped inside what was about to become their grave.

But just as the terrible quaking seemed set to amplify itself yet further, it was suddenly diminishing as quickly as it had begun. Ben dared to slacken his death-grip on the girder and looked down at the cringing forms of Roberta and Quigley. In moments, the vibrations dropped to nothing – and the building was still standing. They were still alive. Nobody was even hurt.

'It's over!' Roberta yelled, clambering to her feet with a look of jubilation spreading across her face. Quigley stood up too, and the two of them gave each other a high-five and began to laugh like lunatics. Ben wanted to laugh, too. 'Is that the best you can do, Craine?' he wanted to shout aloud. The experiment had failed. The artificial quake had burned itself out before it could even do any real damage.

For two or three minutes they were all too weak with relief to do anything. Ben's muscles were trembling as the tension left him. He rested on the girder and breathed deeply, letting his heartbeat slowly return to normal. The pressure was off them, but only for a short while. It wouldn't be long before Craine and his men realised the failure of their exercise and returned to finish the job in the traditional way, with a bullet to the head.

'Roberta!' he called down to her. 'Fasten the rope around your middle like before. We're getting out of here.'

Still laughing, she nodded and stooped down to pick up the end of the rope. As she began to loop it around her waist, a movement out to sea caught Ben's eye and he glanced out of the now glassless windowpane a few feet away from him. 'What the—?' He did a double-take and stared.

The sky was filled with seabirds. Thousands upon thousands of them, a mass formation all flapping at maximum speed towards the shore, as if desperately trying to escape inland from something that was chasing them. Over their distant cawing and screeching came a new sound, a deep growling rumble rising fast like a storm gathering momentum.

Except it was no storm.

Ben's eyes opened wide as he saw what the seabirds were all fleeing from. A chill tingled up and down his back and into every extremity of his body.

'Oh, God,' he muttered.

Chapter Fifty-Seven

Ben blinked. No, he wasn't imagining things, though he wished he were. What he was seeing was real – and becoming more horrifyingly real by the split second.

In the distance, all across the horizon as far as he could crane his neck to see, the ocean was rising. Rising in a towering blue-green wall, eighty or a hundred feet high crested by raging white foam. It was a wave like nothing he'd ever seen or imagined, and it was growing larger and closer with incredible speed. The hazy far-off islands across the Mentawai Strait were no longer there. They'd simply been engulfed by what Ben realised was a giant tsunami now bearing down on the Sumatra coastline. The tiny white specks he could see being devoured in its path were ships, powerless to escape becoming entangled and crushed by the unstoppable force of water.

'Ben!' Roberta's voice below. She'd finished tying the rope around herself and was tugging it to distract him. 'What's the matter? Hey, Ben?'

He couldn't find the words to answer her. Could barely tear his eyes from the approaching wave. How far? Ten miles away? How long? Not long. Not long at all before it hit them. And there was no possibility, none whatsoever, that it would miss. Nothing could escape it. The tree line of their little peninsula would be helpless in the face of the wave. The trees would snap like cocktail sticks under the force. The exposed south-west wall of the empty building would be next.

And then the whole coastline. Hundreds of ports, beaches, towns and villages. Tens of thousands of people, already thrown into panic by the tremors but completely unprepared for the devastation that was coming for them next.

In just the few seconds that Ben had been staring helplessly at it, the wall of water had raced miles towards the shoreline and it was building fast, as tall as the masthead of the small sailing yacht Ben could see desperately trying to get out of its path. As he watched, the boat was snatched up and flung down like a toy before the monstrous wave swallowed it up and came rolling onwards. The distance to the shore was shrinking fast. It would be here in a short matter of minutes.

He tore his gaze away from the surreal spectacle and looked down. Roberta was tugging at the rope, smiling up at him. Both she and Quigley were still in a state of jubilant relief that the earthquake was over, completely unaware for the moment that what they'd all felt was just the residual tremors of a far bigger quake miles out to sea. A quake that Ben knew had been purposely aimed with deadly precision. Craine's show wasn't over. It had barely even begun yet.

'Climb!' Ben roared down at them, gesticulating at the window. 'Roberta! Climb!'

She stared up at him, not understanding. He began hauling on the rope. His voice was too choked with heart-racing panic to yell in more than monosyllables. 'Wave! Wave!'

Roberta's face fell as the realisation hit her. She grasped the rope and began to climb as Ben pulled upwards with all his energy. His mind was racing with calculations. Would there be time to get both Roberta and Quigley up here to the relative safety of the roof space before the wave hit the shoreline? And even then, would they be perched up high enough to avoid the direct impact of the water? The wave would break on the shore. There was no way it could reach any distance inland and still remain so high. But what if it could? And what if the building couldn't withstand the shock? He feverishly tried to imagine the kind of forces involved. Forces that could crumple the old factory like a doll's house, collapsing the roof and bringing them all down into the torrent under a ton of wreckage.

Roberta was struggling determinedly up the rope, her frantic movements making it sway wildly from side to side and even harder for Ben to keep his grip as he fought to reel her upwards, one hand over the other while trying to keep himself from toppling off the beam.

The roar of the impending wave was growing louder and louder. 'Faster!' Ben yelled. Snatching another glance through the window, he saw it was too late. The wall of water was nearly on them. It had to be tearing towards the coastline at five hundred miles an hour. Roberta wasn't going to make it.

Then the wave hit the shore in a simultaneous explosion the whole length of the miles of coast Ben could see from the window. The violence of the impact made the earth shake as the gigantic force of tens of millions of tons of rushing water swallowed up the shore and ripped unstoppably through the forest of the little peninsula. Instantly, the crushing momentum of the tsunami turned into a battering ram of unimaginable power as it became dense with the mass of a thousand disembodied and uprooted trees.

Ben could do nothing but keep hauling on the rope. Roberta was nearly there . . . nearly there . . .

In just a few pounding heartbeats, the mountain of water reached the building. Ben was very nearly jolted from his seating by an impact five times greater than the tremors that had shaken the building minutes before. He didn't even have time to shout to Roberta to hang on. The cracks in the ocean-facing wall widened into splits and suddenly a whole section of stonework gave way and came bursting inwards in an explosion of foaming water and rubble. The floor below was almost instantly engulfed. Desperately clutching the rope, Ben saw Quigley go down in the surging foam and vanish. He resurfaced for an instant and then was gone again as a gigantic uprooted tree trunk came crashing through the broken wall and seemed to roll right over him.

Roberta swung wildly on the end of the rope, her eyes and mouth wide open in horror. She was just a few feet short of the girder now, but the foaming water was cascading in relentlessly and rising faster than Ben could have imagined. Its roar all but drowned out Roberta's cry as the churning surface engulfed her legs, then surged up to her waist.

'I can't swim!' she screamed up at Ben. 'Don't let me—' But before she could get the words out, her shoulders and head disappeared under the surface and all Ben could see was the rope stretched taut between him and the rising water. He was suddenly grappling with a far greater weight as the enormous force of the current threatened to carry her away. He cried out as the rope slipped through his hands, stripping the skin off his palms. He didn't know how he was able to hang on, only that he couldn't – mustn't – let go.

He gritted his teeth and kept pulling. After shooting up twenty-five feet in a matter of moments, the water level had stabilised and was rising only imperceptibly. But the entire ocean seemed to be pouring into the building, bringing with it an endless mass of tree wreckage. More sections of wall were beginning to cave in.

Roberta's head and shoulders broke through the boiling foam. Her hair was slicked across her face and she was coughing and spluttering, but clutching the rope with an iron will. Ben quickly secured his end to the girder, then gripped on with his leg and flipped himself over to hang upside down so he could reach out and take her hand.

His fist closed around her wrist. 'I've got you! You're okay!' he shouted over the deafening thunder of the water. With a heave, he hauled her free of the swirling current and she was able to clamber up his dangling body to the girder. She clung there dripping, speechless from shock, trembling with cold. Ben righted himself and held her tight as the wreckage-laden flood surged just a few feet below them.

He'd given up on Jack Quigley minutes ago. It was with amazement that he saw the American suddenly surface, spewing water and hanging doggedly to the branches of the huge trunk that Ben had been certain must have driven him under and crushed him to a pulp. Quigley's tree was spinning round on itself in the current. A powerful eddy was drawing it towards the middle of the roof support section on which Ben and Roberta were perched. It was coming in fast. Too fast, Ben thought as he realised it was going to ram right into the central pillar supporting the beams.

It hit with a crash and an explosion of spray, smashing the pillar to pieces. With its underneath support gone, Ben and Roberta's girder gave a lurch and, with a screech of buckling metal, sagged towards the water. For an instant,

Ben was convinced they were going under – but the iron structure was still attached at one end to the last section of seaward wall still standing and held together, dangling low above the racing surface.

'Quigley!' Ben yelled. The American was thrashing blindly in the water, trying to disentangle himself from the branches of the tree. Any moment, the current was going to roll the trunk back over him, driving him underwater again. Nobody could be so lucky twice. 'Come on! You can make it!' Ben reached out to him and gripped his arm.

The battered, soaked Quigley scrambled up to join them on the girder. His face was white under the bruises, his hands were shaking violently and he was too aghast to utter a word.

The torrent had inched its way almost to the level of the windows. Ben knew that if the remnants of the wall gave way, the whole building was going to collapse beneath the surface and take them with it. He jabbed a pointing finger at the windows and shouted, 'We have to get to the roof! Keep moving higher!'

But the words were barely out of his mouth before the thing he'd been most dreading began to happen.

Chapter Fifty-Eight

As if in slow-motion, the section of wall holding up the end of their girder buckled inwards and collapsed. Torn from its anchorage, the roof support to which Ben, Roberta and Quigley were clinging like shipwrecked mariners began to fall.

Through the surge of foam rushing up to meet them, Ben caught a glimpse of something huge and white surging fast with the current. The realisation flashed through him: it hadn't been just the pressure of the water that had brought down the wall. It was the dismasted hull of the sailing yacht he'd witnessed being engulfed by the wave miles out to sea. The boat's wooden prow, smashed flat where it had rammed through the wall, cleaved the water just inches below the falling girder.

Gripping Roberta's hand, Ben leapt for the deck as it flashed by. The two of them splashed down on the slippery, waterlogged timbers and were immediately sliding out of control towards the stern as the boat raced onwards. Ben's shoulder struck the corner of the wheelhouse. He lashed out his free arm and grabbed hold of a deck rail, arresting their slide. A third splash nearby told him that Quigley had had the same idea.

If the collapsing girder had hit the boat it would have

broken the vessel in two and carried them all down to a watery grave – but it missed the stern by an inch and sent up a curtain of spray behind them as the half-wrecked, half-submerged yacht ploughed on with the current, only its forward momentum keeping it afloat. Tree wreckage battered and scraped the sides of the hull from all directions, knocking it violently left and right. Momentarily blinded by the sting of the salt water in his eyes, Ben hung tightly to the rail with one hand and to Roberta with the other. Something nudged his leg: Quigley, braced against a deck fixture and clinging on for dear life.

Ben blinked the water out of his eyes and saw they were heading straight towards the remnants of the opposite wall of the building. He cringed, waiting for the impact that might crush the hull like a concertina.

It was Quigley's tree that saved them by crashing into the wall first, ramming a huge V-shaped hole through the stonework. A second later, the hull of the yacht was juddering and scraping over the jagged remnants, bits of loose masonry striking and bouncing off the deck; then it was through, carried onwards inland by the force of the monster tide. There was a grating bump as the yacht ploughed down what was left standing of the perimeter fence. Ahead there seemed to be nothing but the endless racing water and the few trees dotted around the factory building that were still upright. They were being tossed about like a shell, knocked this way and that by the near-solid mass of wreckage all around them.

The force of the flood was incredible. It was as if they were plummeting out of control down a giant waterfall, only horizontally instead of vertically, the laws of physics having been laid on their side in the grip of some insane power. Blinded by the spray, Ben had a death grip on Roberta's hand. It seemed almost impossible that they could have survived the crushing might of the tsunami this long. Every second that went by, Ben fully expected them all to be killed. Every second that went by, another miracle happened to spare them until the next.

There was no telling how deep the water was as they were carried relentlessly inland, crashing violently through branches and vegetation, slamming off rocks, spinning round and round, the prow sometimes high in the air, sometimes buried in boiling foam with water churning right over the top of the wheelhouse.

How far had they come from the building? Ben managed to twist himself around for a backwards glance and could see nothing but unbroken sea where the peninsula had been. It was impossible to know how far inland the momentum of the tsunami could take them. All he knew was that they had to hang on tight and pray the wrecked hull of the yacht didn't get driven completely underwater and become swamped with wreckage.

A shuddering impact from the side rocked the water-logged hull and almost tore the rail from Ben's grip. The deck tipped up and he saw through the blinding spray that a giant tree stump had ploughed into them. Its massive roots had become entangled with the side of the hull, and now the motion of the current was dragging it down and threatening to capsize them.

Ben knew something had to be done before they were all tipped into the water and dragged under by the slipstream. Clipped to the outer bulkhead of the wheelhouse just a few feet away was an axe. If he could just make it the short distance across the wildly sloping deck and grab it, he might be able to hack away the roots and free them . . . but he didn't dare let go of Roberta.

'I'm all right!' she screamed over the roar. 'I'm holding on!'

Ben let go of her hand, then the rail, and felt himself sliding. All that stopped him from going overboard was the opposite deck rail. His feet hit against it with painful force. Suddenly the deck was righting itself as the tree was heaved up by the current. It might be seconds before it was driven back down again and might flip the whole hull over. Ben saw his chance. Sliding from side to side with the violent rocking of the deck, he scrambled towards the wheelhouse. A surge of water slammed him bodily against the bulkhead. Gasping for breath, too numb to feel the pain, he stretched out his arm to grab the axe shaft.

At the moment he felt it tear away from its retaining clips, a flat, angular shape he could barely make out came hurtling straight towards him out of the torrent of water. He flattened himself to the deck, his head and shoulders going underwater. A massive crash as the tin roofing sheet torn from the factory building passed overhead and sliced edge-on like a blade into the wheelhouse. It guillotined through flimsy wood, carrying away everything in its path. If he'd reacted half a second later, it would have cut him in two.

But now the boat was capsizing for real as the entangled tree was pressed deep underwater by the current. Ben managed to grab hold of the shattered framework of the wheelhouse and hung dangling as the hull tipped up to a near-vertical angle. He heard Roberta cry out but couldn't see her.

The boat overturned completely and Ben was plunged beneath the water. The powerful eddies tried to suck him downwards as he swam for the surface. Through the gurgling roar that filled his ears, he was dimly aware of a grinding crash from above. Something hit him hard across the back, driving an explosion of bubbles out of his lungs and pushing him deeper into the water.

For an instant his body was limp, motionless. Sinking, sinking. It was tranquil down here. He didn't want to fight it any more. He could just go to sleep . . .

Then his eyes opened and he started thrashing his way towards the surface. He could see the shapes of the wreckage drifting around him. The submerged, overturned stern end of the boat, too. Pale light sparkled down its side where its keel protruded from the water.

As consciousness came back, Ben realised that the boat wasn't moving any more, and that the current seemed to have slowed. He peered through the dense murk and floating filth and debris, and was able to make out the crushed nose of the hull wedged between two trees. That they were still standing meant that the momentum of the disaster was finally spent.

Ben burst gasping up to the surface, blinked the water out of his eyes and looked around him. Where were Roberta and Quigley? He yelled for them. No reply, no sign.

The capsized yacht had grounded on a high wooded ridge on the rising slope of the terrain inland. The uprooted trunk that had tipped the vessel over must have been torn away under the impact, and had taken half the hull with it. What was left of the boat was stuck fast between the two trees and its prow buried in a mud bank.

'Roberta!' he yelled again. 'Quigley!'

He swam for the bank, reached out for an exposed tree root and dragged himself up the slippery mud onto solid ground, where he clambered to his feet on aching, trembling legs and looked back in the direction of the ocean.

He'd never seen such unbelievable devastation, not even in war. From his vantage point he could see all along the coastline that stretched away to the east – except that it wasn't there any more. Only the tops of a few trees and buildings that had withstood the force of the tsunami protruded from the water. Further inland, the flood was still surging onwards over the lower ground. From a distance the wreckage-strewn tide seemed to move like lava. As he watched, a distant village was swamped. A truck, carried sideways on the current, smashed through the front of a wooden house. Tiny figures of running villagers were engulfed and disappeared.

Nothing could be done to save those poor souls. Ben looked away. 'Roberta!' he bellowed once more at the top of his voice. Still no reply. A feeling of chill dread began to grip him. He blamed himself for losing her. *Why, why did you let go of her hand?*

From the ridge where the boat had grounded, the forested terrain rose steadily upwards. Maybe she'd been flung clear of the water. He staggered through the bushes, searching left and right.

It was then that he heard a hoarse shout. Quigley's voice, coming from the far side of the overturned boat. Ben turned and scrambled back down the bank towards the sound, clambered over the upside-down hull and saw him lying in the mud near the water's edge.

Quigley's face was bloody from a fresh gash on his forehead. 'Help me!' he gasped in pain, pointing at his left leg. 'I can't move.' Ben saw why: his left leg was pinned underneath the boat wreck.

Ben hesitated for a moment, torn between the need to help the man and the overwhelming desire to find Roberta, but he couldn't leave the American lying there trapped. He slid the rest of the way down the bank, hunted around in the mud for something to dig with and found a large flat stone that could act as an improvised shovel. He crouched next to Quigley and began to scoop the wet earth out from under his leg.

'Where's Roberta?' the American gasped.

'I don't know,' Ben said grimly and kept digging. In a couple of minutes Quigley's leg was free. 'It's not broken,' Ben said, looking at the ugly swelling on his ankle. 'Just a sprain. Can you stand?'

'I think so.' Quigley gripped the hand that Ben offered him, scrambled wincing to his feet and limped up the bank to lean against a tree on the more solid ground. 'Holy shit,' Quigley breathed, gazing across the scene of absolute destruction.

'Stay there,' Ben said.

'Where are you going?'

'I have to find her,' Ben replied over his shoulder as he scrambled back down towards the water. Without hesitation he plunged in and began to swim out past the boat, fighting against the drifting debris, searching everywhere, yelling her name. With every passing moment the awful certainty increased: she couldn't swim. Even if she'd managed to escape being crushed under the overturning boat, the currents had overwhelmed her. He wasn't going to see her again.

He gasped in a lungful of air and dived deeper into the murk, propelling himself downwards with powerful strokes. Where the tree roots had torn part of the yacht's hull away he found the ragged hole eight feet down and swam inside the dark space. Hoping for a trapped air pocket. Visualising Roberta clinging on inside, still alive.

But there was nothing inside the wreck but dirty water. He swam back out through the hole and thrust his way back to the surface.

'There's no use,' came Quigley's call from the bank. 'Give it up; she's gone, man.'

Ben ignored him. He couldn't give it up. He battled his

way around the half-submerged stern end of the hull to where more of the western side of the ridge came into view, and swam hard towards it. Treading water, he paused to run his eye along the waterline, up the sloping banks to the trees. The edge of the flood was a seething, bobbing mass of debris. Above the waterline, he could see nothing but thick foliage. The voice of despair inside him was telling him that Quigley was right. It was hopeless.

Until that moment, Ben hadn't realised fully how much he cared for Roberta. He turned away, defeated, suddenly as weary as he could remember having ever been in his life. He could barely muster up the energy to keep himself afloat. The water was beginning to recede now, as if the ocean was calling it back. He could feel the current dragging him, and had to fight it. All along the edge of the ridge, the level was dropping visibly by the foot, so that the ground appeared to rise up from the surface, surrounded by the gigantic mass of wreckage washed up in the mud.

And that was when, out of the corner of his eye, Ben saw the bedraggled shape half-hidden behind a rooted-up tree grounded on the bank twenty yards to his right. His heart jumped. He turned and began splashing towards the bank.

'Roberta!'

It was her. She was lying limply in the mud. Her hair was slicked almost black over her face.

The relief that flooded through him as he swam towards her quickly dwindled to a sense of renewed terror as he saw the blood on her. 'Roberta!'

He reached her.

She wasn't moving.

Chapter Fifty-Nine

Ben wrenched away the foliage and branches that half-covered her limp body, took her in his arms and pulled her further up the bank. Her clothes were ripped and the exposed skin was striped by dozens of cuts made by the raking branches of the tree wreckage, but most of the blood had come from the deep gash on her forehead, just below the hairline. Where her face wasn't streaked with blood it was pallid, almost white. Her lips had a bluish hue. Her eyes were closed. She felt as cold as a corpse.

Clear of the water, he knelt beside her and urgently turned her on her side. Water gushed from her mouth. 'Don't be dead don't be dead,' he kept mumbling as he felt for a pulse. His own was hammering.

No pulse.

Ben instantly began CPU. Her lips felt icy and lifeless against his. He blew hard into her mouth, then straightened up to compress her chest and force her lungs to start working again.

Nothing. He tried again.

Again. Again.

A tiny gasp burst from her mouth. Her closed eyelids gave a flutter. She coughed.

Ben felt her pulse. It was back. It was there. But it was

terribly weak, and so irregular it might stall again at any moment.

'Quigley!' he shouted with a force that tore his throat. 'I found her! Over here!'

Quigley's replying shout returned a moment later. 'I'm coming!'

Roberta's eyelids gave another flutter, and slowly opened. She seemed not to be able to see him at first, then her gaze focused and she gave a tiny smile. 'Ben?' she murmured, almost inaudibly.

'I'm here. I'm with you. You're going to be fine,' he said, his heart hammering with intermingled joy and terror. He held her. 'I thought I'd lost you,' he whispered into her wet hair. 'I'm so sorry I let you go.'

'Ben—' she began, then passed out again. He quickly felt for her pulse. Still there, but still barely perceptible.

'Quigley!' Ben roared. 'Get over here!'

The American appeared moments later and came sliding down the muddy bank towards them. 'My God, is she okay? Is she alive?'

'She's had a bad blow to the head,' Ben said, hearing the ragged edge in his own voice. 'Looks to me like an acute concussion. She needs to get to a hospital. Help me move her.'

'We'll never make it up there,' Quigley said, eyeing the steepness of the thickly-wooded slope above them.

'Then we'll go that way,' Ben said, pointing east beyond the trees. 'The ground's lower. There's got to be a road somewhere.'

'The high ground's the only place that's not underwater,' Quigley replied. But as they spoke, the flood was receding faster and faster.

It was a long, hard struggle across the ridge, supporting

Roberta's unconscious weight between them as they clambered through mud and impenetrable thicket. The sun was dropping lower in the sky. In a few more hours, night would fall. But as they marched on, often having to stop while the limping Quigley rubbed his sore ankle, Ben saw that his hunch about the lie of the terrain had been right. The ground began to slope downwards and the forest gradually thinned out.

Breaking clear of the trees they caught their first view of the scale of the utter devastation, strangely sepia-lit in the glow of the descending sun. The flood waters had completely receded now, just a few gigantic pools here and there to show for the tsunami's passing. The drenched landscape was as flattened and ruined as if a nuclear blast had levelled it.

'Oh, Jesus,' Quigley muttered as they took in the surreal spectacle. 'How could they have done this?'

'They did it,' Ben said grimly. 'And they'll keep doing it.'

A little way further down, the trees gave way to what had been grassland but was now one vast field of mud and debris. The minor twisting road running through it was smothered almost completely. They walked, just three small figures picking a path through an apocalyptic wilderness of destruction. Somewhere, there had to be people. There had to be something left.

Ben carried Roberta in his arms. Her head lolled on his shoulder as he marched onwards. He could feel her breathing, slow and shallow, against his body. He kissed her brow. 'You're going to be all right,' he whispered in her ear, even though she couldn't hear him. 'I promise.'

'She will,' Quigley said, limping along beside him. 'Somewhere at the end of this road, there's gotta be a hospital. They'll fix her up. You have to have faith.'

'Faith,' Ben muttered.

An overturned truck blocked the road, half-covered in debris. The driver was still inside, drowned at the wheel. Ben and Quigley skirted around the vehicle through the mounds of debris and kept walking. Evening was beginning to fall and the temperature was dropping. The night could become very cold.

'You want me to take her a while?' the American offered after another half hour's weary trudge.

Ben's arms were aching, but he didn't want to let Roberta go. 'Thanks, Quigley,' he said, shaking his head.

'Jack.'

'Okay, Jack. I'll let you know when I can't carry her any further. Anyway, you can hardly walk.'

'Don't you worry about me,' the American said.

They lapsed into silence. Darkness was falling and Ben was getting more and more desperately anxious about Roberta, comatose in his arms. She needed treatment soon. Without it, Ben feared that she wouldn't last the night. He was deeply concerned, too, that Quigley was going to hold them back if his limp became any worse. The American was toughing it out but there was no hiding that he was in great pain from his ankle.

By now, they'd walked beyond the extent of the wreckage zone and the twisting little road seemed bizarrely normal, as if the disaster had never happened. Soon afterwards, it joined another, larger road and the extent of the disaster's human impact began to reveal itself as scores of trucks and cars, even motorcycles towing makeshift trailers, came past crammed with both the injured and the dead. One vehicle after another after another, in an endless procession of lights while the dark shapes of helicopters clattered through the evening sky towards the stricken zone.

The rescue operation had begun. It would be a long and

almost impossible task. Ben couldn't even begin to imagine the final death toll, not to mention the damage inflicted on the lives of countless survivors for whom nothing would ever be the same again.

An open-backed truck came rumbling past. Its tailgate was hanging open and in the fading light Ben saw that its flatbed was filled with people – but not so filled that there wasn't room for two or three more. He broke into a stumbling run, trying not to jolt Roberta too badly in his arms. 'Wait!' he shouted at the driver. 'Hold on! I have an injured woman here. Hospital – hospital!'

Just as the truck seemed about to press on regardless, it stopped and with thanks to the driver Ben carried Roberta to the tailgate where willing hands helped to load her delicately on board the flatbed. Ben helped Quigley climb up after her, then joined them and sat next to where Roberta lay on a blanket someone had offered.

The truck rumbled onwards. It was a rough road and every lurch brought cries of pain from the many injured people on board. One Indonesian man had a compound fracture of the femur and was drenched in sweat despite the cool night air, convulsing in agony. A young girl of eight or nine had a bandage around her head and blood all down one side. Many of the uninjured were too shocked to speak; others couldn't stop. There was a local woman called Mae who spoke good English and said she lived in one of the coastal villages with her family. It was no longer there. A white tourist in his late twenties who introduced himself as Franz from Alsace was eaten alive with worry having become separated from his wife Lisa after the wave had hit. He had a photo; had Ben seen her? Ben had to say no. In the hope that she'd made it onto one of the other trucks heading inland, Franz was trying very hard to convince himself he'd find her alive and well at the hospital in Padang Panjang, where most of the passengers concurred the convoy was taking them. Ben didn't know what to say to the poor guy.

The truck went on jolting and rattling for what seemed to Ben like hours as he sat over Roberta, tried to clean the blood from her face and kept waiting for her to wake up. An old woman held her hand and said prayers. Quigley leaned against the truck's side and closed his eyes, his head hanging to his chest. The injured went on crying out. The bereaved wept or sat numbly in silence. Franz talked on endlessly about finding Lisa. A long tail of headlights stretched out behind them from dozens of vehicles joining the rescue convoy. Now and then a faster-moving pickup truck or car would come shooting past, laden with more survivors.

The hospital grounds were heaving with a greater intensity of activity than Ben had ever before seen concentrated in one location. As the truck threaded its way into the gates and though a floodlit pandemonium of vehicles and jostling crowds to the emergency wards, it was immediately obvious that the medical staff were overwhelmed far past breaking point. They were every bit as confused and shocked as the hordes of limping, bloodied, bandaged, screaming, dying or near-dead, panic-stricken, terrorised humanity that kept pouring relentlessly into the place in makeshift ambulances, cars, trucks, on foot or even in wheelbarrows. TV crews were already on the scene to capture the mayhem on camera. Choppers rattled in and out every few seconds, their down-draught tearing at the sheets on the gurneys the paramedics were wheeling in in droves.

Inside the hospital, every inch of stifling space was filled with patients, while harried doctors and nurses ran to and fro to attend to as many as they could. Men, women and children huddled miserably in corners waiting to be seen. Broken bodies, not all of them alive, were wheeled about under bloody sheets. Doors were constantly banging open and shut with the traffic passing through. Pools and trails of blood on the floor went unmopped by orderlies too rushed to keep up. Those who'd lost someone in the confusion were hunting through the tightly packed throng for their missing loved ones, calling their names, showing pictures to anyone who would spare a moment to look before just shaking their heads. The corridors rang with screams and weeping and the calls of the doctors and nurses just a step away from losing control. Sights, sounds, smells. A swirling, dizzying cacophony of pain.

Through the middle of it, Ben carried Roberta in his arms. Eventually, he managed to find a nurse who had a few free seconds between attending to a dying man and a lost, howling child, and escorted them through teeming corridors to a ward where a bed had just been freed up by a patient being rushed into surgery.

Ben laid Roberta carefully down on the bed and covered her with the single sheet. The nurse hurried off with the promise of returning in five minutes; she vanished into the mayhem and it was twenty minutes before Ben saw her again, accompanied by a young Indonesian doctor wearing a name badge that said 'Dr Rahardjo' and who looked as if he hadn't slept in a week.

'Please,' Ben said. 'She's been unconscious a long time.'

The doctor examined Roberta's head injury, looked concerned at the deep gash in her scalp, peeled back one eyelid at a time and shone a light in her pupils, asked Ben a few questions about her symptoms and quickly diagnosed acute concussion. He spoke in rapid broken English and Ben caught alarming words like 'subdural hematoma' and 'subarachnoid bleeding'. How serious was it, he wanted to know. Dr Rahardjo wouldn't commit to a prognosis. It was potentially a good sign that for the few moments she'd been conscious, she'd recognised Ben and remembered his name. But they couldn't ignore the fact that the trauma was quite severe. He could say no more until they'd X-rayed and knew what they were dealing with.

Ben was reluctant to leave her side, but allowed himself to be shooed from the ward as the staff whipped a curtain around Roberta's bed and began the job of cutting off her clothes so they could bathe and treat her other wounds while preparing the X-ray. She was in good hands now, the nurse assured him.

Ben could barely stand up and was only now becoming aware of the pain from the scores of cuts and bruises that covered his arms, legs, back and chest. 'I'm fine,' he protested, but the nurse insisted on sitting him down to examine his injuries before jabbing a syringeful of antibiotics into him, followed by another of painkillers. Then she had to rush off as a fresh crisis demanded her attention, another in an endless line that would keep her rushing all night and into the dawn.

Ben found a corner in a hallway outside Roberta's ward and slumped, exhausted, on the floor with his back to the wall. All he could do now was rest, and wait, and hope, and trust in Dr Rahardjo and the nurses.

And pray. Bowing his head, he tried to mutter a few lines to appeal to God's mercy and ask for Roberta to come through this safely. But the words wouldn't come and it just made him feel awkward and stupid that he couldn't even muster up a prayer. Some future clergyman he was.

He closed his eyes and sat motionless for a long time, but

he wasn't asleep. Out of the worry and the pain and the confusion in his mind about his feelings whenever he thought about Brooke, or Roberta, came a new emotion. Cold and hard and searingly sharp, like a steel blade forged and tempered in ice and fire. It was pure murderous explosive rage that made his fists clench and the blood pump faster through his veins.

When he opened his eyes again, sensing a presence, Jack Quigley was standing over him. 'Hey,' the American said.

'Wasn't sure we'd see you again,' Ben said.

'I've nowhere much else to go. How is she?'

'I don't know yet.'

'Mind if I join you? They pumped me up with codeine but my ankle still hurts like a sonofabitch.'

'Be my guest,' Ben said, and Quigley slumped on the tiled floor next to him. 'I'd offer you a smoke, if I had any,' Quigley said.

'How about a shot of surgical spirit?' Ben said. 'I could do with one.'

'She'll be okay,' the American muttered after a silence. 'Don't worry.'

'Thanks, Quigley. I'm trying.'

'Jack.'

'Okay, Jack.'

'How long you two been together?'

The question took Ben by surprise. 'It's not – that is, we're not—' He sighed. 'She and I are friends, that's all.'

'I assumed . . . I mean, you seem pretty close.'

Ben said nothing.

Quigley's expression tightened and he gazed at the floor for a few moments, obviously deep in memories. 'Like Mandy and me,' he added in a whisper. 'We were going to get married.'

'I'm sorry,' Ben said.

'Yeah.' Quigley gave a grim smile and fell silent, staring into space for a while.

'I was getting married, too,' Ben said. 'It would have been two days ago.'

Quigley glanced at him. 'But I thought you said—'

'It's a hell of a long story,' Ben said.

'It's going to be a hell of a long night.'

'Some other time,' Ben said. 'Let's pick another subject.'

'Like what?'

'You said something about being a Marine.'

'Uh-huh. Semper Fi. Got the marks to show for it.' Quigley pulled up the sleeve of his grimy, bloodied shirt to show a tattoo on his upper arm. The faded blue ink depicted an American eagle perched atop the globe, with an anchor behind it and the letters USMC together with the Marine Corps motto *Semper Fidelis*. 'Eight years,' he said.

'Still got the chops?' Ben asked.

Quigley shrugged. 'Feels like a past life sometimes. But you don't forget. You?'

'British Army, 22 Special Air Service,' Ben said. 'I haven't forgotten everything either.'

'You trying to say something, aren't you?'

'Yes, I am.'

'I think I get the idea.'

'The minute she pulls through this and I get her somewhere safe.'

'And if she doesn't?' Quigley said, looking at Ben levelly.

'The same. Only worse. Either way, this ends.'

'I read you.'

'I can't do it alone,' Ben said.

'You won't be alone,' Quigley told him.

'We might not get out.'

'Like I give a shit. I only care about one thing now.'

Ben nodded. 'Then we understand each other. Tell me everything Herbie Blumenthal told you about Mandrake Holdings and Triton.'

Chapter Sixty

Quigley had been right: it was a hell of a long night. But while the American finally passed out from fatigue, Ben had to suffer every minute of it wide awake. The first time he tried to check on Roberta, he was sternly denied access by the doctor and backed off. The second time, he was told by an orderly that she'd been moved. Dr Rahardjo would know where to – except Dr Rahardjo was nowhere to be seen either.

Ben was reduced to pacing up and down to keep himself from going insane with worry. But then, he wasn't the only one for whom sleep was impossible. As the hours went by, the influx of injured disaster survivors showed little sign of abating and the hospital staff were given no rest. Sometime after three in the morning Ben caught sight of the nurse who'd helped him earlier, weeping in a corner as the strain finally got to her. He went to fetch her a drink of water. As she sipped it gratefully and wiped her tears, he gently asked if she had any news of Roberta. She said she'd try and find out more.

It wasn't until four-thirty that the nurse returned, grey and worn out, and said in an expressionless voice, 'Please follow.'

She led Ben through the corridors, which if anything had

grown even more chaotic and depressing in the last few hours. As he followed, his mind was reeling from the knowledge that this could be bad news. Where was she taking him? To some office where he'd be shown her personal effects – watch, shoes, tattered clothing – and made to sign her off as dead?

The nurse opened a door and waved him through.

And gave an exhausted smile.

That smile sent shockwaves through Ben's whole body. It meant Roberta was all right. He suddenly wanted to hug the poor weary Indonesian woman. 'Thank you,' he said, squeezing her hand. 'I really thank you.'

The nurse led him through a dimly-lit ward filled with male patients and pointed out the bed at the end of the row, screened off behind a curtain. 'She very weak,' she whispered firmly. 'Must rest. You not wake her.'

'And the X-rays?'

'She be okay. Must rest. Plenty rest. I go now. You not disturb her, okay?'

Left alone, Ben self-consciously walked by the other patients in their beds, some sleeping, some peering at him in the semi-darkness of the ward. He stopped at the curtain. Drew back one edge and peered anxiously through.

She was sleeping. There was a thick dressing over the cut on her forehead and the bruises were livid in places, but some of the colour seemed to have returned to her cheeks and as he stood there, almost too afraid to breathe himself, he saw that her breathing was steady and calm. He stepped closer to the bed, let the curtain swish shut behind him, and kneeled at her side. 'I'm so sorry,' he said in a whisper. 'You're going to be all right. That's all that matters.'

He wanted to hold her. Kiss her. He was so confused. But happy, happier in that moment than he'd been in a long time. Victor Craine, the Nemesis Program: all that stuff seemed suddenly very far away.

'None of this should have happened to you,' he whispered as she slept. 'You'll be safe now. I'll get you taken where nobody can touch you.' In a surge of tenderness he reached out and delicately brushed away a dark red lock of hair that had fallen across her face.

Her eyelids parted slightly, then opened wide. 'Ben,' she murmured, trying to focus on him. 'Is that you?'

'I'm here,' he said.

She gripped his arm. Her hand felt warm, but she was feeble. 'Don't leave me.'

'I'm not going anywhere,' he whispered, breaking into a smile. He caressed her hair. 'I'm staying right here with you until you're better.'

'Promise?'

'Let them try and stop me.'

They did try, but he was true to his word. All of the next day, the next night and the day after that, he camped resolutely by her side, eating only when he had to, sleeping in fits in a chair brought to him by the nurse he'd befriended, only leaving the ward when the medical team needed to attend to her. The hospital and its routines became like its own little world. The sole contact with outside were the news reports that leaked into the ward from some of the more mobile inpatients who had been catching up with hourly TV bulletins. The word was that the tsunami had been the worst ever recorded. The death toll was in the tens of thousands and offers of aid were pouring in from all the member states of the United Nations. The disaster had rekindled media buzz about climate anomalies, global warming, solar flares.

Ben listened to the reports and felt sick.

All that time he watched Roberta become stronger. Dr Rahardjo visited her bedside now and again, and with each visit his concerns about possible effects of the concussion such as headaches, blurred vision, memory loss, nausea, became less pronounced. By the second evening, he took Ben aside and told him she could soon leave hospital; in any case, he admitted, they badly needed to free up the bed.

Another occasional visitor was Jack Quigley, who seemed genuinely pleased that Roberta was recovering so fast. While Ben had been at her bedside, Quigley had been busy. The third time he came to the ward he was accompanied by a grave young man who introduced himself as Joe Mulligan from the US Embassy in Jakarta, in charge of ensuring the return passage of all American citizens caught up in the disaster. Mulligan was intelligent and affable, and Ben trusted him. Roberta would be flown to Chicago, where her medical care would resume until she was fully recovered and she could go home to Canada.

Whether or not Quigley had been pulling strings, Ben would never know and preferred not to ask – but things moved quickly after that, and by the morning of the third day, the arrangements were in place and a jet was on standby at Jakarta airport. Joe Mulligan and a female assistant brought clothes for her to wear. The nurses helped her out of bed and Ben was herded away as she changed. She was getting stronger all the time, but still too weak to walk unaided, and Dr Rahardjo thought it best to restrict her to a wheelchair.

Then it was time to say goodbye.

It was Ben who wheeled her from the ward. The hospital was a different place now that the initial crisis of the disaster had been contained. Joe Mulligan and some of his colleagues in dark suits were waiting across the lobby.

'I don't want to leave,' Roberta said.

Ben crouched in front of her chair and clasped her hands. 'Joe's people will be with you all the way to the airport and there'll be someone there to hand you over to the officials at the other end. You'll be safe there. Nobody can touch you. Then you can go home to Ottawa and get on with your life.'

'I mean, I don't want to leave without you,' she said. 'Come with me.'

'It's the only way,' he said.

She looked at him imploringly. 'There are so many things I want to tell you.'

'Me too,' he said. 'That's why maybe this is for the best.'

'Does that mean I'll never hear from you again?' A tear ran down her face. She quickly brushed it away.

He smiled. 'Of course you will.'

'No, I won't,' she said. 'I know you, Ben Hope.' After a pause she said, 'You're going after them, aren't you?'

'This isn't over. Like you said, destruction's the one thing I'm good at.'

'They'll kill you.'

'They tried, remember? I'm still here. So are you.'

Mulligan and his people were looking impatient, glancing at their watches.

'You have to go now,' Ben said. He smiled again. Squeezed her hands one last time, then stood up.

'I wish it could have been different for us,' Roberta said.

Ben didn't reply. He bent down and kissed her cheek, then signalled to Joe Mulligan. One of his female colleagues walked over with a smile and introduced herself as Fay Greenbaum. 'It's a pleasure to meet you, Dr Ryder. I'll be flying with you to Chicago.'

Ben let her go. He watched as the officials wheeled her down the ramp and out to the waiting car.

As they opened the back door for her, Roberta turned to give him a last look and a wave.

But he was already walking away.

He didn't want her to see him so upset.

In a quiet part of the corridor, he composed himself. Then he went looking for Jack Quigley.

'You ready?'

'I'm ready.'

'Let's get started.'

Chapter Sixty-One

The next seventy-two hours were a busy time. CIA Special Agent Jack Quigley's newfound alliance with Joe Mulligan procured a helicopter ride from Padang Panjang all the way southeast across Sumatra to Jakarta on the western tip of Java, and a small but comfortable apartment in the city within a stone's throw of the US Embassy. The apartment had two phones, and in true American style the fridge was stocked with pizza and canned beers. Ben and Quigley spent two hours gorging themselves on food, another three catching up on lost sleep, and then it was time to get to work.

Ben's first call was to Le Val, and he spent an hour telling Jeff Dekker what he needed to know and what Ben needed in return, which was for one of the Le Val team to deliver him a package in person as fast as he could get on a plane. Jeff listened and didn't ask too many questions. He knew Ben too well for that.

'Well?' Quigley asked as Ben put the phone down.

'Says Raoul or Paul will be on their way to Paris within the hour.'

'I take it you trust these guys?' Quigley said, cracking open a beer.

'With my life,' Ben replied. 'I've known them a long time.'

The same was true of Boonzie McCulloch, the grizzled former sergeant who'd been Ben's instructor in 22 SAS, his mentor and later his friend. As usual, it was Boonzie's wife Mirella who answered when Ben called the number of the peaceful smallholding deep in the Apennine hill country near Campobasso. The tough, wiry Scotsman, once the merciless scourge and terror of raw recruits whom it was his personal mission to transform into hardened fighting men, now spent most of his days tending with infinite care to his beloved tomato crop.

'I go fetch him,' Mirella said breathlessly when she heard Ben's serious tone of voice. He heard her in the background calling 'Archibald!' Her husband's regimental nickname had never stuck with her.

A few moments later, the familiar gruff voice came on the line. 'Benedict ma boy! How's married life treatin ye?' Despite all these years of splendid rural isolation in the south of Italy, Boonzie might as well have left Clydebank just last week.

'Didn't quite work out,' Ben said.

'What? How many days huz it bin? If anyone could bollocks that up, it'd be you, eh? Ye big bawheid.' Boonzie had always been fairly direct in his manner.

'Never mind that for now. I need to know something. Is old Lambert still operating out of Marseille? Have you got his number?'

'What the hell d'ye want to call that mad basturt for?' Boonzie asked, taken aback. Those who could still remember him and knew what he did for a living nowadays didn't call the long-ago-retired SAS trooper Loony Lambert for nothing. His speciality was weaponry: everything from small arms of dubious origin to explosives or even military vehicles, no questions asked and shipped with ultimate discretion to the destination of the customer's choice. His only rule: no animals were to be harmed. Loony Lambert was a devout vegan.

'I heard it was his birthday,' Ben said. 'If you don't have the number, do you know who else might?'

'I ken one thing. Naebody calls that heidbanger unless they've got a big problem tae fix. You're up tae something, laddie.'

'Absolutely not,' Ben said.

'Aye, I'll believe that. Where are ye callin from?'

'Right now I'm in Java. Tomorrow I'll be somewhere else.'

'Fuckin' *Java*,' Boonzie exploded. 'Listen, I might be gettin' auld, but I'm no soft in the heid. Ye need help, don't ye? What did I tell ye aboot that?'

'You told me to call you anytime and you'd drop everything,' Ben said. 'And I appreciated it.'

'An' I fuckin' meant it, an' all,' Boonzie warned him. 'Now fill me in, an' fast. If ye need help ye're goin tae say so an' ye're fuckin' gettin' it whether ye want it or no. Dinnae even think aboot tryin' tae stop me or ye're in serious shite. Clear?'

Twenty hours later, the flight from Charles de Gaulle airport touched down at Jakarta. Ben and Quigley drove there to meet it in the black Chevrolet SUV that had been provided for them by Joe Mulligan and looked like a cast-off from the US Secret Service.

But instead of Raoul de la Vega or Paul Bonnard, it was Jeff Dekker who stepped off the plane. 'Jesus Christ, what happened to you?' he asked when he saw the healing bruises on Ben's face. 'You look like you spilled the wrong guy's pint.'

'Never mind me,' Ben said, stunned. 'What the hell are you doing here?'

Jeff pointed at Ben's face. 'It's obviously about time you had someone to watch your back, mate. Whatever it is, count me in.'

'Not you as well,' Ben groaned.

Jeff chuckled. 'As well as who? Let me guess. McCulloch being stubborn again?'

'Promised if I tried to stop him coming to help, he'd rip my arm off and beat me about the head with the soggy end.'

'And he wasn't kidding, I'll bet,' Jeff said.

'No chance. I've seen him do it.'

Quigley drove the Chevrolet to the apartment. In the back, Jeff opened up a holdall and handed Ben a brown envelope. 'Here's the stuff you asked for.'

Ben inspected the fake passport in the name of John Freeman that had been stored in the armoury room safe at Le Val, a duplicate of the one the Indonesian army officer had confiscated. Along with the passport was a functioning credit card in the same name, and a bundle of cash.

'All there?' Jeff said.

'That's all I needed from you, Jeff. This isn't going to be a walk in the park.'

'Don't say another word. What's the plan?'

'London tomorrow night. Boonzie's flying into Heathrow to meet us. Then onto New York. After that, I don't know yet.'

'Look, mate, I talked to Jude. Have you called Brooke?'

Ben shook his head. 'When it's over,' he said. 'Then I'll call her.'

Chapter Sixty-Two

New York City

Two days later, the sun was blazing over Manhattan as a gleaming Lincoln Town Car pulled up. Four men got out and walked briskly westwards down Fulton Street. Their manner was purposeful but discreet, so that none of the passersby and business types on lunch break who thronged the busy sidewalk would have guessed that a team of ex-SAS, SBS and Marine Corps veterans were heading armed into the heart of the financial district to execute a carefully-planned mission.

'This is it,' Jack Quigley said as they reached the glass tower with 'Mandrake Holdings Inc' in polished steel letters above the entrance.

'Let's go,' Ben said.

They pushed through the doors and strode four abreast across the lobby towards the reception desk. The pretty receptionist looked up as they approached. She'd redone her nails a different shade. Her well-practised smile dropped as she recognised Quigley.

'Hello, sweet face,' Quigley said, leaning on the desk and flashing his new CIA ID card. 'Remember me?' He pointed at the phone next to her. 'Better tell your boss I'm back, and I'd like to talk to him.'

The receptionist hesitantly picked up the phone, shooting nervous looks at the four as she stabbed the keypad with a glossy nail.

Quigley pointed across the lobby, past the modernist sculpture pieces and plastic foliage to the door his two escorts had taken him through last time. 'It's that way.'

'Wait,' the receptionist began as they headed towards it. 'You can't—'

But they were already through it. Quigley remembered the way perfectly, and led them along the twisting soft-carpeted corridors, Ben second, Boonzie and Jeff bringing up the rear.

'Any time now,' Quigley murmured. They were fully expecting to be intercepted, and it happened right on cue before they reached the scanner and coded security doors. A lift whooshed open and three men in dark suits marched out. 'Excuse me?' the burly one in the middle said in a strong voice, raising his hand. 'Hey. You. Hold it right there.'

'That's him,' Quigley said to Ben. 'The guy who locked me in the room.'

The man's eyes narrowed as he saw it really was Quigley. He nodded to his companions and they spread out to block the corridor, ready for trouble. The one in the middle was reaching for the butt of his concealed sidearm when Ben pinned him roughly against the wall, drew a black Steyr automatic from under his jacket and thrust it hard under the jowls of his chin.

'Trust me, you don't want to do that,' he said quietly.

Boonzie and Jeff had whipped out their pistols and had them trained on the other two men. 'Drop them,' Boonzie snarled through his droopy salt-and-pepper moustache. 'Nice an' easy does it.'

Pale as ghosts, the men delicately drew their sidearms between trembling fingertips and tossed them on the ground.

Quigley scooped the guns up and then turned to the burly guy. 'Let's finish that conversation,' he said in a genial tone. 'Somewhere nice and private where we won't be disturbed. Unless you want to call the cops and discuss this in the District Attorney's office instead. No?'

The man's eyes bulged. He was too choked to speak with Ben's gun muzzle pressing against his windpipe, but he managed a quick shake of the head.

'I didn't think so,' Jeff said. Boonzie surveyed the man with a look of disgust and spat on the carpet.

Disarmed and helpless, the three men were frogmarched into an empty office. The air conditioning was whirring softly. At one end of the room was a bank of computers and a row of tall filing cabinets and a bare whiteboard. At the other was a stack of chairs.

'This'll do nicely,' Ben said, covering all three with the Steyr. Quigley locked the door behind them and then walked over to the window and slanted the blinds to give them more privacy. Jeff grabbed three chairs from the stack and clattered them down in a row in the middle of the room. Boonzie unzipped the shoulder bag he was carrying and took out a length of rope and a Ka-Bar fighting knife. Unsheathing the menacing black blade, he grinned at the looks on the men's faces.

'Make yourselves comfortable,' Ben said. When the burly guy hesitated, he grabbed him by his tie and sent him sprawling into the middle of the three chairs. The other two obeyed instantly. Boonzie stepped around behind the chairs, used his knife to slice three lengths from his rope and made short work of trussing the men securely to their seats.

Quigley stood with his arms folded and addressed the one in the middle. 'Now, before we got interrupted last time, you were just about to tell me all about Triton.'

'I don't know what you're talking about,' the guy growled. 'And you people just fucked yourselves by coming in here like this. You have no idea what you're dealing with.'

'I think these fellas are a wee bit uptight,' Boonzie said.

'Looks like it to me,' Ben said. 'How about a drink to loosen things up?' He reached into his jacket pocket and took out a quart vodka bottle. Unscrewing the cap, he stepped up to the three men as if to offer it to them.

'You're fucking nuts,' said the burly guy, but his tone changed to a squeal of fear as Ben upended the bottle and poured a third of its contents over his head. He did the same for the other two, then tossed the empty bottle away. The men blinked and gasped and shook their heads furiously. The sharp tang of gasoline filled the office.

'I'm not one for barbaric tactics,' Quigley said. 'But my friend here,' – pointing at Ben – 'he's another matter. Once he gets started I really don't think I'll be able to call him off. And he always keeps his promises. I'd urge you to bear that in mind.'

'Still don't know what we're talking about?' Jeff said.

From his other pocket Ben drew out a fresh pack of Gauloises. It wasn't an easy brand to find in Jakarta, London or New York City. Without a word he peeled off the plastic wrapper, flicked it away, opened the pack, took one out, slipped it between his lips and then clanged open his shiny brand-new Zippo to light it with. The cigarette's tip glowed brightly as he sucked in smoke.

He wasn't here to waste time on words. He blew out the smoke and said to the men, 'I'm going to count to five. Then I'm going to burn you.'

Instant panic. The men kicked and struggled in their chairs, rocking from side to side.

'One,' Ben said.

'Here's where we're at,' Quigley told the three gibbering, gasoline-soaked men. 'We're not idiots, so we figure *Triton* is the name of one of Mandrake Holdings' shipping fleet. Except it doesn't appear on any register. That's where you guys come in.'

'Two,' Ben said.

'You're going to assist our inquiry by telling us all about that ship,' Quigley said. 'Registration number, tonnage, personnel, cargo, every last detail. You're going to show us all your secret computer records, files, the works. You're also going to oblige us by saying whether there's a certain gentleman by the name of Victor Craine on board. You might know him better as the Director.'

'Three,' Ben said.

'Additionally, you're going to tell us the *Triton*'s destination and its exact current position and radio frequency,' Quigley said. 'Then we want to know the precise nature of the relationship between this company and the Nemesis Program. Names. Details. Dates and numbers. If that's too much to ask, then too bad for you. Out of my hands.'

The three men couldn't take their terrified eyes off Ben. The air-conditioned office was pleasantly cool but the sweat was pouring off their faces.

'Four,' Ben said. He sucked on the cigarette, making it burn hard. Took it from his lips.

'Barbeque time,' Boonzie said with a sadistic grin.

All three of the men broke more or less at the same instant, as Ben stepped up to them with the cigarette and was just about to toss it. 'All right! All right!' the one in the middle bawled. 'Don't burn us! I can tell you what you want to know! Just for the love of God, don't burn us! Please!'

'Sounds like cooperation,' Jeff said. 'That's what we like, isn't it?'

'We like it a lot,' Ben said. He put the cigarette back in his mouth and stepped back.

'Pity,' Boonzie said. 'I was hopin' they wouldnae talk.'

Quigley took a small digital recorder from his pocket and switched it on. 'Gentlemen,' he said. 'The floor is yours. Let's have it.'

Twenty-six minutes later, the four left the Mandrake Holdings building and headed eastwards back down Fulton Street to where the black Lincoln Town Car was parked. Ben bleeped the locks and took the wheel, Quigley up front next to him, Boonzie and Jeff in the back. Ben gunned the engine and took off with a squeal into the traffic.

'Just one question. Would you really have burned those guys?' Quigley asked Ben.

Ben didn't take his eyes off the road. 'What do you think?'

They drove several blocks and stopped outside a bar. The four of them got out and walked calmly inside. Music was playing in the background. Quigley and Jeff ordered beer. Boonzie had a taste for wine these days. Ben got a whisky, double malt, no ice. They took a table in the corner and drank in silence.

'So now we know what's involved,' Ben said after a few minutes. 'Anyone who wants to walk away now, say so. No hard feelings.'

'Hell with that,' Quigley said. 'You know where I stand.'

'Same here,' Jeff muttered. 'All the way.'

Boonzie didn't need to say a word, as the look of quiet ferocity on his craggy face said it for him.

Ben nodded. He drained the last of his whisky and clapped the empty glass on the tabletop.

'Okay,' he said. 'Let's go and sink a ship.'

Chapter Sixty-Three

Nine days later

Dawn was still some time away as the VLCS-class container ship *Triton* ploughed through the dark, choppy waters of the Gulf of Finland, the easternmost stretch of the Baltic Sea that cut two hundred and fifty miles between the coasts of Finland to the north and Estonia to the south, as far as the Russian city and port of Saint Petersburg to the east.

Measuring over a thousand feet from prow to stern, the ship's immense deck and holds were heavily laden with cargo. The towering prow pushed through the water at a steady twenty-five knots. Behind, the massive diesel-powered screws churned up a long, curving wake against the dark water. Every now and then another large ship would pass by on its passage from one Baltic port to another. But even though the *Triton* might look just the same as any vessel of her class, she was carrying a cargo no other ship in the world could boast of.

Ostensibly, for the benefit of any coast guard or customs officials who might want to come aboard for inspection, the stacks of containers lining her vast deck and the gigantic warehouse that was her hold were filled with raw industrial materials, all fully documented and accounted for. The real cargo was in a sealed-off section deep in the bowels of the ship, heavily guarded by armed personnel, virtually none of whom had any idea of its true nature.

High above the darkened deck and the helipad on which stood his personal helicopter, Victor Craine supported himself on his two sticks and gazed eastwards from the bridge to where the sun would soon be rising on the horizon. The Director liked to come up and refresh his lungs with some sea air now and again, even though it was cold in these waters and the chill seemed to pierce through to his frail old bones. He spent most of his time down below in the ship's command centre, a suite of plush, electronics-crammed offices that nobody would have guessed could be found on board such an outwardly crusty old vessel. In fact Victor Craine's mobile base, the true beating heart of the Nemesis Program, was home to an array of computer technology that could easily rival his land base deep within the corridors of the Pentagon.

Sensing a presence, Craine turned to see his aide Isaac Friedkin approaching. He was carrying a fine china cup and saucer on a tray. 'Your cocoa, sir.'

The old man hooked his ebony walking stick over a rail, leaned more weight on the ivory stick and took the steaming cup without a word. Plenty of cream, a good sprinkling of cinnamon. At one time he'd enjoyed a dash of green Chartreuse in his chocolate, but his slowly failing liver forced him to forgo that little pleasure nowadays.

'We'll soon be commencing initial targeting sequence, sir,' Friedkin informed him.

'I'll be below directly,' Craine said. 'Leave me now.'

He took his time finishing his cocoa and watched the very first red glow of dawn begin to creep into the sky ahead. Then with a final glance at the sea, he gathered up his sticks and started making his scraping, limping way below. He might not have looked it, but he was excited. The next few hours would be as decisive a moment in his career as he could remember since those heady long-ago days when, as a CIA counterintelligence chief, he'd locked horns with his opposite number in the KGB in a deadly game of subterfuge and assassination.

The anonymity of Craine's work was second nature to him after fifty years, and there was no room in this business for ego; yet there were moments when he privately regretted that the crowning glory of his professional life, the ultra-classified development program that he'd nurtured and overseen all these years, had given the name 'Nemesis' and was now about to see fulfil its true purpose, was something he was unable openly to claim the credit for. The pivotal moment in world history that was soon to take place never would, never could, feature in his official list of achievements. Shame.

Because everything else up until now had just been an exploratory foray into Nemesis' outstanding capabilities, a destructive power that far outstripped even the wildest imaginings of its original pioneer Nikola Tesla and sometimes even frightened Victor Craine himself. This was indeed, as the now-departed Dr Roberta Ryder had put it, 'the big one'. When it was over, Craine knew, the program would have to be decommissioned for a while. It was a technology that for political reasons couldn't be overused, however strong the temptation. Not even the power of the world media – and few people knew better than Victor Craine how readily it could be manipulated – would be able to cover up the fact that too many hugely publicised disasters, one after the other, conveniently targeted to suit the secret political agenda, might appear more than coincidental and inflame the conspiracy pundits.

So, after this one, the Director was going to have to put his pride and joy aside and turn his attention to other matters – such as tracking down and properly eliminating the last few remnants of the opposition. Hope and Ryder were dead, along with the unfortunate Jack Quigley of CIA, the whistle-blowers Shelton and Blumenthal, the journalist Guardini and of course the Pommier woman in Paris. But there were still a few lesser players to be quietly pruned. His own agent Gunnar Frisk, aka Daniel Lund, would have been one of those deemed to know too much, and if the late Major Hope hadn't kindly done the work for him, he would have been on Victor Craine's own list of loose ends to tie up. Fabien De Bourg, the ex-boyfriend of the Pommier woman, was another potential threat. His elimination would be a simple matter of staging a drink-driving incident. And on it would go, in the nature of these things, until every conceivable tie to Craine's precious Nemesis Program had been snipped.

Politics was a wonderful thing, the old man mused to himself on his way below decks, his sticks clicking on metal floors and steps as he went.

Deep below, guards flanked the security doors leading through to the command centre. A few faces glanced up from computer terminals as the Director entered, but most of the personnel were too busy or too intimidated to take their eyes off their work. The place was a bustle of activity in the lead up to the climactic moment that had cost billions of dollars to orchestrate.

Craine walked through into the main control room, his personal domain into which only his closest aides were allowed to venture. Behind the many screens glistened the dark hardwood panelling that clad the walls. More computer equipment smothered the length of a large table. Glenn Gould played Bach in the background. The old man parked his sticks by the large reclining leather chair and writhed himself into it. His legs were aching badly today. Let them hurt all they wanted – he really didn't care.

The command centre was the brain of the Nemesis weapon. The device itself, now into its twenty-seventh generation of development since Craine had taken over the Program in 1982, was housed in a special section of the hold inside a purpose-built container to protect the ship's personnel from radiation and surrounded by the high-tensile cables that fed it with the enormous amount of power that it needed when operating at full thrust. The days of tiny steam pistons were long gone.

Nemesis wasn't the only Tesla-derived technology that the US government had been working on since 1943, but it was by far the most secret. Unlike the HAARP facility in Alaska that directed radio frequency radiation at the ionosphere for – as its developers claimed – the purposes of communications and anti-missile technology, the Nemesis device delivered a focused and steerable electromagnetic beam directly at a specific ground target. The core of the system was the DARPA-designed computer targeting software that interacted with satellite technology to direct its electromagnetic pulse to any set of geographical coordinates fed into the central processor.

In its earlier stages of development they'd experienced the same accuracy problems that Tesla had encountered when he'd mistakenly fired his energy beam at Siberia, accidentally causing the 1908 Tunguska incident while aiming towards the North Pole. Likewise, the first attempts to operate Nemesis had resulted in the destructive energies being directed as much as two hundred miles off course.

Even now, the technology to deliver the weapon's potential with pinpoint accuracy from one side of the world to the other simply wasn't there yet, but the technicians were confident that it would be within two years, maybe even sooner. Then the Program could operate from a fixed base. Craine hoped he'd live long enough to see Nemesis operating from the secret silo currently being built for it, deep in the Nevada Desert.

In the meantime, the system was capable of focusing on a target as small as a house from up to six hundred miles away. The short range limitations had posed a major dilemma, with the feasibility of the entire project in doubt until Craine himself had proposed the idea of creating a mobile base for the weapon aboard a suitably-modified cargo vessel able to transport it wherever they wanted.

So had been born the very special relationship between Craine's secretive little corner of the Pentagon and Mandrake Holdings, one of the Americas' largest shipping conglomerates. Half a billion dollars had been spent converting the *Triton* into the ocean-going battery of almost limitless power that it was today. Not a single artillery piece on board, yet Craine's brainchild was capable of destroying an entire fleet of battleships literally at the touch of a button, or unleashing terrible destruction on virtually any terrestrial target on the planet.

Decades of honing had produced an operating system that even the Director, with no patience or tolerance for newfangled electronics, could work. All that was required was to key in the target coordinates, even just an ordinary postal code in the country of choice, and hit enter. The brain instantly liaised with its own satellite and the target was pinpointed within seconds. Then the operator need simply arm the trigger, which was based on the same design as the firing mechanism for a nuclear missile. A special key, of which Victor Craine possessed two of only three made, opened the bulletproof glass housing to reveal the large red button that he insisted nobody could touch but him.

The red button initiated the final awe-inspiring sequence. The ship's lights would dim as the Nemesis device sucked in gigantic wattages of power from the generators. The vessel would begin to tremble and hum. After exactly two hundred and forty seconds, the vast energy was released in a single pulse towards the designated target. Faraway, all hell would break loose. By the time the geophysical effects manifested themselves, the Nemesis device would have fallen dormant again, its power surge spent. That meant it was technologically impossible to trace any electromagnetic link between the ship and the affected location anywhere within a six-hundred-mile range, covering a circle up to nearly two thousand square miles in area with Craine's anonymous vessel hidden away at its centre.

In other words, the concept was foolproof. Never before had a weapon system been so covert and yet so incredibly destructive. The feeling of power and achievement it gave Victor Craine was tremendous. From his chair in the luxurious main control room he could watch the spectacle unfold as the targeting satellite beamed down live images of the destruction. The Indonesia mission had been one of their most rewarding operations yet – the complex mathematics and physics of generating just the right frequency of tremor to set off the tsunami had kept his scientists working day and night for weeks to crack.

To say it had been worth it was an understatement. With the *Triton* anchored safely out of range, Craine had been as transfixed as anyone else in the command centre at the sight of the giant wave descending on the Sumatra coastline and engulfing everything in its path. Politically, it was of minor importance except that it kept the topic of climate change high on the agenda, where the economists liked it. Technologically, though, it had been a landmark moment, the first time they'd managed to overcome the difficulties of striking at the ocean bed with such successful results.

Today's designated target was a much simpler matter. Everything had been leading up to this moment, one for which Victor Craine had been personally waiting for decades. The ridiculous simplicity of being able to achieve it at the mere press of a red button almost made him want to laugh for sheer pleasure. Almost; the old man hadn't laughed out loud in thirty years. But maybe today he would.

He gazed around him at the multiple screens and monitors that filled the room. The largest was his operations map, displaying a flashing red circle over the target area. Others displayed technical readouts, targeting coordinates, the ship's GPS position, various satellite images, live camera feed of the *Triton*'s deck and the slowly lightening grey sea beyond.

'How are we doing, Friedkin?' he asked his aide, who was working at a terminal across the room.

'The target will be within range inside the hour,' Friedkin said.

The old man nodded with quiet satisfaction and went on gazing at the map screen, thinking about what was going to happen. Devastation on an unprecedented scale. Perhaps a million lives about to be snuffed out, at a conservative estimate. The military strike of the millennium, without a single soldier involved or a single shot fired. And nobody to blame it on.

'They have it coming,' he muttered to himself.

Chapter Sixty-Four

It was from the rocky Estonian shoreline, just before the break of dawn, that the high-performance rigid inflatable boat cut rapidly across the waters of the Gulf under cover of darkness. It had no lights, and the men aboard were dressed all in black. It was cold. Their faces were hard, their eyes fixed purposefully on the dark shape of the ship on the horizon.

As the RIB approached, the *Triton* grew larger and larger ahead, like a vast mountain looming out of the pre-dawn murk. The small craft steered a course slightly ahead of the ship's, then cut its motor and drifted silently on the swell, waiting for the towering prow of the cargo vessel to catch up. Closer, closer; the RIB bobbed precariously over the foam of the ship's prow wave and down the side of the hull, a dangerous operation if the men on board hadn't known just what they were doing.

As the rusted side of the *Triton* streamed by, close enough to reach out and touch, Ben clamped a short magnetic mooring cable to the hull. With a jerk, the dinghy was suddenly being towed along with the ship, attached like a tiny remora to some vast leviathan and tucked tightly into the concave curve of its flank so that it was invisible to anyone peering down from the edge of the deck.

Phase One had been accomplished.

Ben turned to Jeff, who grinned at him from behind his diving mask and gave the thumbs-up while Boonzie McCulloch helped him don his oxygen bottle. As the ex-Navy diver, Jeff was better qualified for the next job than anyone. This was Phase Two, essential to the success of the operation.

Crouching in the bottom of the boat, Ben unzipped a bag and lifted out a heavy metallic round object, the size of a dinner plate but several inches thick. Two carabiner clips secured it onto Jeff's harness together with the life-line that would allow him to keep up with the ship once he went under. A moment later, the former SBS commando slipped with practised ease into the water and disappeared.

Ben waited tensely, counting the seconds by the illuminated dial of his watch. Nobody spoke – hand signals only.

Jeff resurfaced less than a minute later, pulled himself back to the dinghy by the life-line and clambered aboard, quite a few kilograms lighter now that the high-explosive limpet mine had been successfully clamped to the underside of the *Triton*'s hull. When remotely detonated it would rip a fatal hole that would sink her in minutes.

But sending the cargo ship to the bottom of the Gulf of Finland was just part of the plan. Jeff quickly stripped off his diver's gear, mask and flippers and, shivering with the cold, pulled on his trousers, assault vest and boots. Ben tossed him a backpack like the one everyone else was wearing.

Now they were ready to move to Phase Three.

In the *Triton*'s command centre, a radar operator named Rick Yemm jumped up from his station to report to one of his superiors the anomaly he'd just noticed. The message quickly filtered up the line and reached Isaac Friedkin, who went anxiously to relay it to Victor Craine in the main control room.

The old man turned with an icy stare as Friedkin's presence interrupted his thoughts.

'I'm very sorry to disturb you, sir. But radar is picking up a signal nearby. We think it's a small vessel.'

'This is a busy lane, Friedkin. It's full of small vessels.'

'This is different, sir. Whatever it is, it came extremely close and then disappeared.'

'It can't have disappeared,' Craine snapped, then quickly thought again. 'Unless—'

Friedkin nodded. 'Yes, sir. Unless it's moored itself to us. It's the only way the radar could miss it.'

Craine's brow wrinkled. If they were being quietly boarded, then by whom? It wasn't unknown for Finnish customs officials to mount surprise raids on the off chance of intercepting drug shipments, but even that sounded unlikely. 'Send a team to investigate,' he said abruptly. 'Do it *now*, Friedkin.'

Friedkin nodded again and hurried off to alert the security personnel.

The grappling iron burst with a breathy *thud* out of the muzzle of the launcher and sailed up the ship's side, trailing on its cable the lightweight rope ladder that unwound rapidly from the coil at the bottom of the RIB. The iron's rubber-coated hooks cleared the railing, thumped softly to the deck and slid a few feet before gripping something solid.

Ben tested the ladder with his weight. It was secure. He signalled the okay to the others and began to scramble nimbly upwards. Quigley, Boonzie and Jeff watched him climb, a diminishing black figure swaying from side to side on the flimsy ladder, padding lightly with his feet when the ship's motion swung him against the hull. He reached the top and signalled down before disappearing over the rail. Boonzie was next, powering up the rope rungs with the energy of a man half his age.

One by one, the team assembled on the deck to merge invisibly with the shadows between container stacks. In silence, each man opened up his waterproof backpack and emptied out the equipment inside. The MP5s emerged first. Loaded magazines snapped into receivers. Silencers were screwed tightly onto muzzles, bolts were cocked, rounds chambered. Tactical lights and lasers were kept off for the moment. They checked and holstered their pistols, and clipped on their grenades.

The scarlet dawn was just beginning to break in the east. Phase Three had begun.

Minutes later, the five-strong patrol who'd been sent out to check for a possible boarding party combed the deck, each man carrying his regulation M4 carbine with thirty-round magazine. So far they'd detected nothing suspicious. The tallest of them tried leaning out over the rail as far as he dared, with another two clutching his belt. All he could see was the ship's side and the heaving slate-grey sea far below. He shook his head. Like the others, he didn't see how anyone could have boarded the vessel, but they had their strict orders to search every inch of her thoroughly.

As they patrolled the aisle between two towering container columns, four shapes came flitting out of the shadows behind them. The dawn sun glittered redly on the blade of a Fairbairn-Sykes commando dagger.

The guards were taken by surprise. It was all over with a

few stifled cries and grunts, followed quickly by five faint splashes as the bodies were dropped over the side, minus their weapons and ammunition.

Ben's team retreated behind cover and began stealthily weaving a path from one container stack to the next, heading for the towering superstructure. Ben led the way, followed by Quigley, then Boonzie, then Jeff. They knew exactly where they needed to go.

At fractionally over six hundred miles away, the *Triton* was now almost within range of its target and the buzz of anticipation in the command centre was reaching its peak. The targeting sequence was now complete, the coordinates entered and identified by the satellite. Victor Craine eyed the atomic clock on the wall. It was split-second synchronised with the digital countdown on the computer screen in front of him. In precisely twenty-three minutes, it would be time.

The Director trusted nobody. He climbed out of his chair, picked up his sticks and was hobbling over to the other computer to triple-check the coordinates when the control room door burst open and the red-faced, breathless and clearly agitated Friedkin hurried up to him.

'Well?' Craine demanded.

'We may have a problem, sir. The patrol I sent to check the outside—'

'They found something?'

'That's just it. I don't know if they did, or what.'

The Director balked at such a reply. Was the man drunk, to come back to him with such vague information?'

'I don't know, sir,' Friedkin repeated insistently, 'because they're no longer answering their radios.'

'What? Then send another team out after them.'

'I did. They've fallen out of contact as well.'

Craine opened his mouth to bark a furious reply, but the words were snatched out of his mouth by the loud explosion that rocked the ship and made him stagger.

Chapter Sixty-Five

'Jesus Christ!' Friedkin cried out. 'What the—?'

Victor Craine steadied himself against the computer console and stared slack-jawed at the screen on the wall that showed a section of the *Triton*'s deck erupt in a bright leaping flash of orange flame. Through the mushrooming fireball tumbled pieces of wreckage and shattered container. A huge plume of black smoke rolled upwards, blotting out the rising sun. Instantly, alarms were sounding all over the ship.

'We're under attack,' Craine said with calm certainty.

'B-but how?' Friedkin stammered, wide-eyed. 'From who? There's nobody there.'

'Don't just stand there, man. Issue weapons to every available man and get them out there to search this ship from top to bottom.'

'Even the scientists?'

'Anyone with the right number of fingers can pull a trigger,' Craine said. 'I want the situation contained and whoever's responsible brought to me alive. Alive, understood? Now get out there and organise it. Report back to me in two minutes. It had better be good news.'

Friedkin obeyed and ran out of the door, leaving Craine alone in the control room. On the screen, little figures of security personnel and ship's crew were swarming to the site of the explosion, where a fierce blaze was now raging among a section of destroyed containers. Emergency hoses blasted foam and water at the flames, beating them back.

Craine gripped the arm of his chair for support as a second blast suddenly erupted closer to the ship's bridge. He caught a glimpse onscreen of the orange fireball and flying wreckage before the camera was hit by some piece of shrapnel and the image went black.

'Whoever you are, I promise you that you won't get off this ship alive,' he said out loud.

The pressure wave from the second explosion shattered dozens of windows in the ship's superstructure, raining glass down on deck and scattering a group of security personnel in all directions. Just as the fire hoses were getting to grips with the first blaze, the new one began to spread fiercely, threatening the bridge.

'That should keep them busy for a minute or two, aye?' Boonzie said with a grin. Alarms were keening everywhere. The raid team's arrival on board the ship was now well and truly announced – but with the diversion in full swing, nobody who was still alive had seen them yet as they filtered their way from cover to cover towards the hatchway that the ship's plans showed led below. Rounding the side of the last container stack the hatch came into view, just a short run across the open deck.

Ben glanced left, right, left again and signalled 'Go'. They moved out from cover and slipped unseen through the hatchway, trotting fast and silently along a short passage. At the end of the passage were two more riveted steel hatches, one to the left and the other leading to a downward flight of steps. Ben pointed ahead.

But before they reached the companionway, they caught

the approach of running footsteps and the hatch to the left swung open. Through it burst a group of security guards with their M4 carbines at the ready. Six against four, but the team had the advantage of surprise. Before the guards could bring their weapons to the shoulder, Ben had time to aim centre-of-mass and put a suppressed double-tap into the nearest one, then into the one next to him. Boonzie took the two on the left, Jeff the two on the right – but he snatched the trigger on the last one and his shot went wide. The guard's rifle swung up. The loud report from the .223 would have given their position away to half the ship, but it never came. Quigley fired a three-shot burst and the man crumpled and twisted to the floor.

'Good one,' Jeff said, slapping Quigley on the shoulder.

'Keep moving.' Ben stepped over the bodies and led the way deeper into the ship.

'You're late, Friedkin. Update me,' the old man said acidly as his aide came running back into the control room, red-faced and out of breath.

'Sir, every available man is scouring the vessel. But there's no longer any question that our security has been breached by a boarding party. We have eleven men down that we know of, plus five more missing. No wounded.'

Craine nodded sagely. 'Professionals.'

'Sir, the situation is reaching crisis point. We may have to get you off the ship.'

'Evacuate?' Craine said. 'On the verge of the biggest moment in political history? Out of the question.' He eyed Friedkin's jacket. 'Are you armed?'

The aide flapped open his jacket to reveal the holstered Glock 17. To Craine's certain knowledge, he'd never once drawn it except on the practice range.

'Get yourself an M4 from the armoury and join the others,' Craine ordered him. 'If you can't contain this, don't bother coming back.'

The alarmed Friedkin rushed from the room without protest.

The command centre was strangely quiet now that every member of the personnel had been sent out to hunt the boarders. Craine looked up at the atomic clock. Six minutes, forty-one seconds and they'd be within range of the target. Everything was ready. The technical stuff was all out of the way and all that remained was for him to arm the trigger device and press the red button.

Six minutes, thirty-seven seconds. Craine felt in his trouser pocket for the arming key. It was there, solid and chunky and reassuring.

Nobody could stop what was going to happen.

Craine reclined in his chair, closed his eyes and pensively caressed the carved surfaces of the ivory and ebony sticks resting across his lap. He felt tired and very, very old, yet a feeling of serenity came over him. Down here in the depths of the ship, insulated from all the chaos happening above, it was almost peaceful.

'Victor Craine,' said a voice behind him.

Craine opened his eyes. Snatched up his sticks and struggled out of his chair to face the presence in the room.

Ben was standing in the doorway. His MP5 dangled loosely from his hand. 'So this is where we play with our toys,' he said, glancing about the room.

Craine wasn't particularly afraid. He'd lived too long and faced death too many times in the past for that. 'Major Hope. You surprise me. I confess I'd taken your demise somewhat for granted.'

'I told you it was *au revoir*,' Ben said. He stepped into the room, followed by the others.

'Nice place ye've got here,' Boonzie commented gruffly.

'Agent Quigley too,' Craine said as he recognised the American. 'My, my.'

Jeff stepped over to flip a wall-mounted switch. With a clunk and a whirr, an armoured steel shutter glided down to bar the doorway. Designed to isolate the main control room in time of crisis, it would resist a rocket-propelled grenade and take all day to breach with a thermal cutter.

'It looks as though you have me at a disadvantage, Major Hope,' Craine said, leaning wearily on his sticks. 'You're an incredibly persistent man.'

'I do have that irritating tendency,' Ben said. 'And don't call me Major. I'm retired.'

Craine shrugged. 'Be that as it may, a man of such admirable tenacity would have been an asset to me.'

'Sorry, Craine, but destroying the world, wiping out thousands of innocent people – it's not quite my style.'

'Your profile says you're a drinking man,' Craine said. 'There seem to have been some issues with that, towards the end of your military career.' He shuffled away from his chair and over towards a polished cabinet by the wall. 'If you still imbibe, perhaps I can tempt you with a glass of something very special.' Hooking the ebony stick over his arm, he opened the cabinet and lifted out a bottle. 'This cognac is almost as old as I am. My doctor has declared it off-limits, but under the circumstances . . .' He carefully poured some out into a crystal glass. 'Care to join me?'

'I don't tend to drink with mass murderers so much,' Ben said.

Craine took a sip and smacked his wrinkled lips. 'I realise the superficial view a man like you must take of a man like me. You're a soldier. Soldiers follow orders without thinking twice about the deeper strategies involved, strategies conceived by deeper and more knowing minds. You perceive only the obvious. There are so many things you don't understand. You see, we're not destroying, we're building. Sparing lives. Working to create a better place for us all.'

'We don't have time for this,' Quigley said. 'Let's take him and get out of here.'

'Sounds good tae me,' Boonzie grunted.

Ben said nothing. Until that moment he'd paid no notice to the screens on the wall, but he was staring at them now. He stepped closer and peered at the illuminated map with the target location flashing bright red at its centre. To its left, another screen displayed the target's GPS coordinates. To the right, another again showed what looked like a live satellite image of a city. A city with an extremely distinctive skyline, lit in reds and golds by the rising sun.

Ben could hardly believe what he was seeing. And yet there it was.

'Moscow,' he said. 'I should have seen it. This is your next target.'

Craine sighed, with the regretful look of a surgeon committed to performing an unpleasant, yet vitally necessary, operation. 'I'm afraid that's so. The most populous city in Europe, home to eleven million people, shortly scheduled to be hit by an earthquake measuring approximately nine point eight on the Richter Scale.'

'The big one,' Ben said, aghast, remembering what Lund had told them.

Craine gave a dry smile. 'Indeed. The largest disaster in recorded history, surpassing the 1960 Valdivia earthquake in Chile by some ten gigatons or more. But then, it takes a heavy hammer to crack a nut so tough. And believe me, it will be cracked. I only have to press that button, and our dear Moscow more or less ceases to exist. Even you would have to admit that's quite a feat. I'd forgotten how good this brandy was. Sure you wouldn't care for a . . . what is it the Scots call it? A wee dram?'

'You're insane,' Ben said to him.

'No, Major Hope. I'm simply someone very well informed, who happens to be aware of where the pieces stand on the chessboard. In this game of ours, the stakes are high and we're playing to win.' He paused. 'We're at the dawn of a new Cold War. You have no idea what it cost us to come through the old one. I know, I was there. Now Russia is rising, and she's a far greater force to reckon with in the modern age, let alone if she were to unite with China. I don't think we can win again. The western economies would never survive the drain on our resources.'

'I don't suppose it would do your global empire-building plans any good.'

'That's simply a long-term agenda. There are more pressing things to worry about in the meantime. Possible nuclear war is one of them. I'm sure you wouldn't want that, would you?'

'So you can pre-empt your worst-case scenario by wiping out a few hundred thousand innocent lives now,' Ben said.

'Aren't global stability and peace worth the sacrifice of a single city and a few of its citizens?'

'I don't think I like the way your game is played.'

'It's the same one we've played for centuries, Major,' Craine said. 'The rules don't change, only the technology does. If something like Nemesis had existed fifty years ago, don't you think we'd have used it? Why do you suppose my predecessors were so interested in acquiring Tesla's plans? We could see what Stalin was doing, even in 1943 while we were ostensibly allied against Nazi Germany. The moment the war ended, our real problems with the Soviets began.

Unfortunately, the scientists of the day simply weren't able to make the technology work. Now we can. The timing could not have been more opportune. Naturally, it's easy to regard what we do as evil. But if you could learn to see with different eyes, you'd come to appreciate what Nemesis truly is. The end of war. The end of conflict. Ultimately, a force for good.'

'And of course doing good has got no end,' Ben said. 'First Moscow, then what?'

Craine shrugged. 'Since you ask: for some time now, western intelligence agencies have been concerned over the tacit support that the Pakistani government and its intelligence service, the ISI, offer to Taliban terrorist leaders. It's one of the most significant obstacles to their plans for the Middle East. The city of Karachi, being Pakistan's most populous city and the country's financial centre, was selected as our next target.'

'Destabilise the government, move in, take over, threat neutralised. You make it sound so easy.'

'Child's play,' Craine said with a little smile. 'Thanks to the Program.'

'Sorry to tell you, Director. The Program is over. There's a high-explosive limpet mine attached deep under the water-line of this vessel. We're going to send your little experiment to the bottom of the sea.' Ben nodded to Quigley. 'Show him, Jack.'

Quigley took out the remote detonator. 'Now I'll get to find out what it feels like to press the button, huh?'

'I was wondering what the purpose of this visit was,' Craine said.

'But we saved the best for you,' Ben said. 'We could just have let you go down with the wreck, but instead we're going to spare your life. You'll come with us, stand trial for mass murder and spend your last days behind bars.'

The old man was suddenly looking less sure of himself. A gleam of sweat appeared on his bald scalp. 'I'd like to see you try. You can't prove a thing.'

'Wrong,' Quigley said. 'We have all the evidence we need, Craine, thanks to your friends in New York. By the time it all comes out, not even the Pentagon will stand by you. You'll be fed to the animals.'

Craine was turning paler, and his breathing suddenly seemed to be coming in gasps. The glass dropped from his hand and shattered on the floor. He clapped his hand to his chest and collapsed, his withered legs folding under him.

'Great. That's all we bloody need,' Jeff muttered.

'Let him lie there,' Boonzie said.

'We have to get him out of here alive,' Quigley said. He set the detonator on the table nearby and hurried over to help the fallen man.

Craine was writhing on the floor, clutching at his sticks. Quigley reached out to raise him up.

Ben couldn't have moved fast enough to prevent what came next.

Chapter Sixty-Six

With surprising speed, Craine activated a hidden thumb latch on the silver ferrule of his ebony stick. Its slim carved shaft sprang away from the curved handle to reveal a concealed sword blade, thirty inches of spring steel with double razor edges and tapered to a needle point.

Nobody saw it in time. Quigley was leaning over the old man with his arms outstretched when the point of the blade hissed towards his chest with the speed of a striking rattlesnake. No sooner had it penetrated deep into his flesh than it withdrew, ready to stab him again.

Too stunned to utter a sound, the American recoiled two staggering steps, tripped over his own feet, and fell heavily backwards.

Ben raised his MP5 and fired at Craine, but the old man had already whipped out of sight under the computer table and Ben's three-shot burst struck empty floor. Craine rolled with uncanny speed and emerged from under the other end of the table clutching his ivory stick. He pointed it at Jeff. A wizened thumb pressed a latch that released a folding trigger; Craine squeezed it and a concealed striker inside the stick snapped forwards to set off a slim high-velocity rifle cartridge that fired with an eardrum-rupturing bark and a spit of flame from the end of the shaft. It hit Jeff in the thigh, spattering blood over the wall behind him. Jeff tumbled over, clutching his leg.

Ben fired again. A computer screen burst into fragments. Craine dropped the ivory stick and scrambled with stunning agility to where Quigley had dropped his MP5. The Director was no less familiar with the weapon than anyone else in the room. Ben and Boonzie dived for cover as bullets sprayed the air. Blood sprayed up the wall behind Boonzie. The Scotsman sprawled over the floor, clutching the ragged wound in his left shoulder. Craine paused, took deliberate aim: the remote detonator sitting on the table where Quigley had left it blew apart into fragments of plastic casing and circuitry.

Ben tried to scramble to his feet to return fire, but another burst drove him back down to the floor. Craine was on his feet, moving remarkably fast towards the wall switch that activated the security shutter over the door. He was laughing, something nobody had heard in generations. 'So you thought I'd let you undo all my plans? I was working on this before you were born.'

Quigley was down and not moving; Jeff was clutching his leg; Boonzie's left arm was hanging limp as he crawled over to his fallen weapon. Ben got off another burst in Craine's direction, but the old man had ducked back down behind the cover of the table, still cackling wildly.

The armoured shutter glided upwards.

And behind it were armed security guards, alerted by the deafening blast of Craine's walking stick rifle.

Suddenly, they were swarming into the room. Gunfire erupted all over the place. Ben felt bullets ripping through the air past him. He flipped the MP5 to full-auto and emptied the magazine, saw three men go down before his weapon locked back empty; he dropped the spent mag, tore another from his pouch and rammed it in, released the bolt and kept firing. A column of hot empty 9mm cases flew into the air from his ejector port. Noise and smoke filled the room.

Craine scrambled over to the trigger. Pulling the key from his pocket he inserted it into place and twisted it a quarter turn. The arming light came on and the unbreakable glass cover whirred up on its hinges to expose the red firing button.

What nobody had noticed, while he'd been keeping them talking, was that the atomic clock and its corresponding digital countdown screen now read past zero time. The target was now comfortably within range. Craine held his finger over the button and felt the power course through him. He only had to press it, and in four minutes Moscow would cease to exist as the world knew it.

Craine's finger descended towards the button.

But it never got there.

Boonzie had reached his fallen gun and opened up at the swarm of guards trying to storm their way into the room. Two more went down, piling on top of the bodies half-blocking the doorway. For one precious moment, the firestorm slackened and Ben saw his chance. As the old man's bony finger was coming down on the button, he threw himself across the consoles and wrestled Craine away from the trigger device.

Craine might have looked frail, but he was hard and wiry and could move lizard-fast. Suddenly the ebony-handled sword stick was back in his hand. Ben ducked back as he saw the slash coming, felt the razor-keen blade slice the air an inch from his nose.

Ben retreated. There was no time to do anything except avoid the slashing blade. Craine came on, fire in his eyes and teeth bared like a madman.

The guards were back at the door. Jeff was lying in a pool of blood. His gun rattled. Boonzie was backing him up. His gun ran empty. He reloaded. Jeff did the same. Ammo was running thin.

Quigley wasn't moving.

The firing mechanism deactivated itself after five seconds and the glass cover whirred shut.

'You!' Craine rasped. 'You think you can walk into my world and undo the work of a lifetime?' *Whoosh*. The blade came whipping sideways at Ben. He was running out of space to retreat. The blade scored his combat vest and he felt a sear of pain as it opened up a gash across his chest.

'Yeah, I do,' he said. Drew the Steyr pistol from his holster and shot Victor Craine between the eyes. The gun flashed and boomed and kicked back against his palm.

The old man staggered to a halt. The sword cane fell loose from his fingers. He gazed at Ben in vague puzzlement for a brief moment and then fell on his face.

Ben directed the pistol at the doorway. He fired, fired again, and again, and saw two more guards fall back and the rest retreat further into the command centre. But there were still too many of them waiting to storm the control room and kill everyone inside.

Ben glanced at the shattered remains of the remote detonator. Goodbye, limpet mine. There was no longer any way to destroy this ship. And no longer any possibility of avoiding getting shot to pieces by an enemy of overwhelming numbers. If they'd fallen silent for a moment, it was only that they were regrouping for the next assault. This could be the last stand.

Unless . . .

A crazy idea had begun to form in his mind. It wouldn't be the first. Might just be the last, though.

'Jeff? Boonzie?' The room was so thick with gunsmoke, he could hardly see them any more.

'Still here,' came Jeff's voice, thick with pain.

'Havnae had this much fun in years,' Boonzie called out.

Ben clambered over Craine's dead body to where Quigley was lying sprawled on his back. The American was still alive, but there was a lot of blood leaking out from the stab wound in his chest. Two inches lower, and Craine's blade would have thrust through his heart.

Ben gripped his arm. 'Hold on, Jack. We're getting out of here.'

Quigley's unfocused eyes gazed up at him. 'The mine . . .' he gasped weakly.

'Change of plan,' Ben said. He dropped the mag from his Steyr and slammed in a spare in time to let off three rapid double-taps at the guard who'd been trying to aim an M4 through the gap in the doorway. The man dropped his weapon and fell dead.

The crazy idea was growing in Ben's mind. He ran over to the targeting computer. His eyes searched the screen, taking in the complex menu. He thought furiously. Began to punch at keys.

The guards had regrouped, reloaded and now they were back in force. Gunfire raked the room, shattering screens, splintering the wood panelling. Boonzie and Jeff returned fire from behind their makeshift cover. Suddenly Boonzie's gun ceased firing. He yelled, 'I'm out! Ben! What the fuck!'

'Down to half a mag,' Jeff called out.

'Hold on!' Ben yelled back. Another bullet passed by his head, so close he smelled its trail of cordite.

He'd finished entering the new coordinates. He twisted the arming key. The glass trigger cover whirred open.

Quigley had managed to prop himself up, clutching in agony at his chest. 'What are you doing?' he gasped.

'You know what I'm doing,' Ben said.

'You crazy sonofabitch.'

'So everyone keeps saying,' Ben said.

The guards burst into the room. The one in front brought his M4 up to the shoulder and aimed it directly at Ben.

Ben smiled at him and pressed the red button. *Kill me. It's too late.*

The guard hesitated. His weapon wavered in his hands. His eyes darted across the room to glance at one of the few screens that hadn't been shattered in the exchange of fire. It was the screen showing the ship's GPS position near the eastern extremity of the Gulf of Finland. Then his gaze shot across to the screen of the targeting computer and his eyes widened. Because the coordinates were the same on both.

The . . . same . . . on . . . both. Which meant—

Realisation lit the man's face up in horror. He lowered his rifle. Stared at Ben for an instant as if to say the same thing Quigley had just said. Then he stumbled back towards the doorway, shoving past his colleagues and tripping over dead bodies in his panic. 'Run! Out of here!' he screamed to the other guards who were amassed in the command centre.

'What the fuck have ye done, Ben?' Boonzie asked, turning pale.

'We have a little under four minutes to get off the ship,' Ben said.

Chapter Sixty-Seven

Four minutes. Two hundred seconds. A hundred and eighty. A hundred and sixty. Time became very compressed when every moment mattered this much.

Ben led the way with the bleeding, half-conscious dead weight of Jack Quigley draped across his shoulders. Behind him, Boonzie had Jeff's arm around his neck, half carrying him, half dragging him as they struggled through the ship's passageways, clattered up steps, stumbled through hatches in a race to reach the upper deck in time. Ahead they could hear the echoing steps of the personnel members running in panic to abandon the vessel any way they could now that the word had spread like wildfire that they were about to self-destruct.

A deep vibration seemed to come from the core of the ship. The lights flickered and dimmed, as if some gigantic power drain were sucking in all its energy.

Ben kept moving, hanging tightly onto Quigley with his teeth gritted in determination. He could suddenly see Brooke's face in his mind and held that image there, letting it spur him on to run faster. 'Come on!' he yelled behind him to the others. 'Keep going!'

Ninety seconds. The fresh air and bright light hit them as they burst out of the last hatchway into the morning sun.

The sea was calm, the sky an unbroken expanse of blue except for the smoke still rising from the smouldering fires on deck. Running figures raced ahead of them between the cargo containers. Some of the personnel were trying to lower lifeboats, others clambering over the rail and leaping wildly into the sea from a height that would almost certainly be fatal.

Seventy-five seconds. Ben blinked the sweat from his eyes. He thought of the rope ladder hanging from the ship's side down to the moored rigid inflatable below. They'd never make it down to the boat.

One minute. 'The helipad!' he yelled. It was a short sprint across the deck to the resting chopper. Could he get it up in the air in time? He didn't know, but it was the only chance they had.

He ran, legs straining from his burden. He could hear Jeff and Boonzie's grunts of pain as they laboured to keep up.

Fifty seconds. Crossing the helipad, he tore open the aircraft's side hatch. He roared with effort as he bundled Quigley into the back. Racing around to the pilot's seat, he hurled himself in behind the controls. Boonzie and Jeff were clambering aboard now. Boonzie's grating rasp in Ben's ear: 'Fly this thing, laddie!'

Forty seconds. Ben glanced around him at the unfamiliar cockpit layout. *Come on. Get it together.* He flipped switches. Powered up the turbine. The rotors began to turn. Slowly, maddeningly slowly, then a little faster. Then faster still, until the yellow blade tips became a solid halo above the cockpit and the engine revs were rising to a howl. *Go, go,* screamed the voice in his mind.

Ten seconds. Nine.

The chopper's skids shifted on the deck as the aircraft started to go light.

Eight. Seven.

'Fly it!' Boonzie yelled.

Ben hauled on the controls. The chopper rose into the air, hesitated, rose a few feet more.

Five seconds. Four.

The helicopter climbed steadily upwards. The *Triton*'s towering superstructure was like a skyscraper next to them. Up and up. They were going to make it.

Then the ship seemed to disappear in a soundless explosion. It was as if an invisible hurricane of unimaginable fury had suddenly struck out of nowhere. Every intact window burst apart. Railings and cables and containers and bits of walkway and masts were suddenly shearing away, toppling, tumbling through the air. The hull crumpled and was torn apart at the seams just as easily as if it had been a child's plastic model. The ship's prow reared up as its back broke, hurling thousands of tons of cargo loose and crashing about the deck. The sea exploded all around. Foam and spray leaping skywards. The air black with flying debris.

Ben never even saw the steel cable that fouled the rotor blades with a massive shrieking crunch and sent the chopper gyrating wildly off course just as it cleared the deck enough to accelerate upwards and away. He couldn't hold it. The aircraft began to spin and then plunge towards the mountainous swell.

The last thing Ben saw before he blacked out was the white water surging up to swallow them whole.

It was the cry of a seagull that woke him. The bird flapped down to land beside him, eyeing him curiously. The sky above was clear blue and the grey sea rose and fell gently, tugging his body back and forth on the swell. He blinked and looked around and realised he was clinging to a shattered rotor blade. What had happened? His fogged mind began to piece the memories together.

Where the ship had been, there was nothing but a circle of floating wreckage half a mile across. He was alone. Just him and the bird, and the silence and emptiness of the whispering sea.

As he bobbed there on the slow heave of the ocean, he thought about his life, his past, his future. Maybe he had none to look forward to; maybe he'd die out here. Maybe that wasn't such a terrible thing, he reflected, and not undeserved either.

But if he somehow ever got back to shore, what would his life be then? A future with Brooke? He didn't know. Didn't even know if he'd ever see her again.

He thought about his friends. He'd brought them into this and now they were gone. Gone, like all the plans he'd made. More regrets. He had so many.

He drifted numbly, getting colder in the water. The seagull lost interest in him and flapped away to investigate the wreckage elsewhere. 'Be like that,' he called after it.

Then he was alone.

Though not as alone as he'd thought he was.

'Ben!' came a cry from across the water. He knew that voice. Clutching at the buoyant piece of rotor blade, he began to paddle through the drifting debris.

When he saw them, he let out a yell of joy and paddled faster.

'Look what we found,' Jeff said. His face was pale from blood loss and pain, but he was grinning from ear to ear. He, Boonzie and the weakly conscious but smiling Jack Quigley were sitting in the rigid inflatable boat.

'You got room for one more?' Ben let the rotor blade drift away. He swam to the boat and clambered aboard.

'Outboard's buggered,' Boonzie said.

'Guess I'm the only one fit to row,' Ben said, unclipping the single oar.

'Then you'd best get started, laddie. It's a fair distance to shore.'

The sun rose and fell overhead as the hours passed. Nobody spoke. Quigley fell asleep. Jeff and Boonzie silently nursed their wounds. The only sound was the slap and gurgle of the paddle in the water as Ben rowed. Somewhere beyond the horizon was the coast of Estonia.

'My son loves the sea,' Ben said absently after about four hours' silence.

'You have a son?' Boonzie said, amazed despite his pain.

'That's a long story,' Ben said.

If you loved THE NEMESIS PROGRAM you can find out more about the Ben Hope series, and forthcoming new adventures by Scott Mariani, as well as signing up for the Scott Mariani newsletter by visiting www.scottmariani.com

And follow us on Twitter @CrimeFix